FATE TOUCHED

A TOUCH OF VAMPIRE

BECKY MOYNIHAN

BROKEN
BOOKS

Published by Broken Books
www.beckymoynihan.com

ISBN-13: 978-1-7327330-8-4

Cover design by Becky Moynihan
Cover model by Ravven
www.depositphotos.com

To the dreamers:

Unapologetically pursue what brings you joy.

PROLOGUE

LOCHLAN

Last night, I held perfection in my arms.

Her body. Her skin. Her taste.

Every inch of her was perfect.

She was my heart. My soul. My whole world.

She was everything. *Everything.*

And yet, I broke my promise to her.

Hours after the most perfect moment of my entire existence . . .

I left her.

Left her all alone. Locked her in my room so they couldn't take her.

Even as her fear-filled screams tore at my insides, I faced the humans invading my home without her. I could have easily defeated them, but they'd come prepared. After one dart. Two, three, four. The pain drove me to my knees.

I thought death would claim me then. A bitter end after the sweetest moment I'd just shared with my soulmate.

But the humans had other plans.

As they took me farther and farther away from McKenna, her screams continued to follow me. *Haunt* me. I fought to answer those screams. Fought the silver liquid spearing through my veins, rendering me unconscious again and again. Fought to ease her pain, unmindful of my own.

But the sedative—clearly meant to subdue, not kill me—was too strong.

"We should try again," I heard someone say above my head. "We can still acquire our target."

"Our window of opportunity is gone," came an immediate reply, the voice's familiarity sharpening my awareness. "We're no match for several Venturi in their own territory. Plan B is our best bet right now. I've seen how she acts around him. Our contact speaks the truth. She'll find a way to come after him. And when she does, we'll be waiting."

Panic shot through me. Panic and blind rage. I fought harder against my constraints, needing to get to her. To protect her.

If they dared touch my mate, there would be hell to pay. I would destroy them. Destroy them all. Destroy the *world* if I had to.

No one touched McKenna. No—

A sharp pinch greeted my efforts to escape. Followed by a fresh rush of debilitating silver.

Darkness swallowed me whole.

CHAPTER 1

KENNA

Following Everett D'angelo into the woods was possibly the dumbest thing I'd ever done.

He could easily kill me with the flick of his wrist. He no doubt wanted to.

But I was desperate. More desperate than I'd ever been in my entire life.

"I thought you said the bridge was the only way on and off this island," I called out to him, my breath clearly visible in the chill morning air. Good thing I'd changed into sturdy boots and a thick winter coat before leaving. My body was still susceptible to the frigid temperature, even in my temporary vampire state.

Everett's only response was a dismissive snort. He didn't even glance back at me.

I struggled to match his frenzied pace through the ankle-deep snow. The castle I'd been trapped in for the past few days now lay behind us, a fact I should be grateful for—if it wasn't for where we were headed.

A cliff. And a deadly drop into the churning ocean below.

Every instinct demanded that I stop and reevaluate my questionable life choices. Except that I didn't really have a choice. Everett needed me and I needed him. It didn't matter that I was his least favorite person, or that he was a chauvinistic, homicidal maniac.

All that mattered was finding Lochlan D'angelo.

The man I'd hopelessly fallen in love with.

My soulmate. My *home.*

Before something terrible happened and I lost him forever.

Now that my panic over him being taken had somewhat lessened, I could feel our bond again. Feel *him.* A warm presence beneath my sternum, like a steadfast flame. It filled me. Completed me. Made me feel infinitely whole.

He was still alive. Every fiber of my being knew that he was.

But for how long?

"Sneaky bastards," Everett muttered under his breath, my temporary vampire hearing picking up the words. To me, he said, "They must have rappelled down a window and taken to the water. Their scent heads toward the ocean."

Snow, pine, and briney salt from the sea filled my lungs as I inhaled, but something else did too. Something deliciously mouth-watering.

Human blood.

Strong enough that I assumed one or more of them must have been injured during their fight with Lochlan.

I recalled the swift snap of bone as he freed me from one of the SCA operatives. Right before he locked me in his bedroom, leaving me alone and utterly devastated.

My throat seized. Not from thirst, but from an overpowering need for my soulmate. On the third try, I was able to swallow and say, "They came here by boat?"

"That's the only explanation. They couldn't have snuck onto Sanctum Isle any other way. Question is, which way did they leave and where are they headed?"

Even though darkness still clung to the sky, I couldn't miss the *look* Everett threw at me, one that said I should know the answer.

2

That my usefulness was hinged on knowing. That his patience was already wearing thin.

A half hour had passed since he'd discovered me curled up in a ball on the floor of Lochlan's bedroom. A half hour since I found out my aunt had been the one to abduct him. A half hour since being told someone inside the castle had betrayed us. Had laced the king's, his sons', and Kade's drinks with silver.

A half hour since I'd learned just how deep my soul connection with Lochlan really went.

Halting in my tracks, I closed my eyes and focused on the presence warming my chest once again.

Lochlan? Can you hear me?

I waited several beats for an answer, feeling beyond stupid. People couldn't really communicate with each other through their minds. The idea was completely ridiculous. *As ridiculous as supernatural creatures and soulmate bonds?* my mind sarcastically replied.

Good point.

I doubled my efforts and called out to Lochlan once more. Again and again, until a headache bloomed behind my lids. Releasing a frustrated sigh, I blinked up at Everett and shook my head. "Still nothing. I can't even feel his emotions. It's almost like he's . . ."

"Unconscious," Everett finished for me, jerking an agitated hand through his closely cropped black hair. "Right. Then we take an educated guess until he wakes up. Come." He stalked toward the cliff's edge again, as if he had every intention of jumping off.

Yeah, um, a vampire would survive the fall. But me? Not so much.

I opened my mouth to remind him of my frail, extremely mortal body when he suddenly stiffened and jerked to a halt. Something about the way his head canted to the side sent goosebumps racing

3

across my skin. I remained where I was, straining to pick up on what had alerted him.

A moment later, he was by my side. I managed to suppress a surprised squeak as he grabbed my upper arm and hauled me forward at a fast clip.

"Hey!" I protested, trying and failing to break free.

"Quiet," he hissed, dragging me to the very edge of the cliff. Freaking fates, that was a longer drop than I'd thought. "Hold onto me."

I gawked at him. "What? No. Why would I—?"

"Suit yourself," he muttered before spinning me around to press my back against his chest.

I immediately lurched away, but he snaked an arm around my middle, locking me in place. "Everett, let—" He clamped a gloved hand over my mouth, right before he threw us over the edge.

My stomach immediately bottomed out as nothing but air surrounded us. Wind roared in my ears and we plummeted down, down, down. Too fast, too *fast*. I was going to die! Terrified, I screamed into his glove.

The landing jarred every last bone in my body. My teeth clacked together, biting into my tongue. My ribs ached where Everett's arm still held me against him. But I was somehow alive. Alive and on solid ground, not smashed against the jagged rocks poking out of the roiling sea.

The moment he straightened his legs and released me, I whirled and gave him my best death glare. Before I could unleash a torrent of angry words, his blood red eyes pinned me with a warning look. "Quiet. We're being followed."

He grabbed my arm again, and this time, I didn't protest as he pulled me along a crude path beside the cliff's base. Questions sprung to the tip of my sore tongue, but they'd have to wait. Whoever was following us would no doubt try to stop us from going after Lochlan.

But what if it was Kade?

Either way, Everett had made it clear that he didn't trust anyone at the moment. Not after somebody inside the castle had laced his drink with silver last night. All he cared about was getting his brother back. And since our interests were currently aligned, I wasn't about to thwart his plans.

I replayed the words he'd said to me half an hour ago, right before I'd hurriedly donned warm clothing and allowed him to lead me from the castle: *Then find him, Kenna. Save him. Because without him, there's no way in hell you'll be able to break the curse. He chose you, whether he meant to or not, and your bond is now the only hope our kingdom has.*

Shockingly, after finding out that his brother was mated to a witch, Everett hadn't tried to kill me. His words about our bond were even more shocking, considering how hard he'd tried to keep us apart. I was supposedly under his protection now, but for how long? Until he didn't need me any longer?

Before I could worry too much over my precarious position, Everett ducked inside a cave mouth. Ocean water sprayed over my boots as I followed, my temporary night vision allowing me to clearly see what lay inside.

"We're in luck. It's high tide. We should be able to quickly navigate the cave and steer clear of any rocks," Everett said in hushed tones. Still, his voice faintly echoed as he dropped my arm and approached a sleek-looking motorboat. It was propped up on blocks at the back of the cave where the water couldn't reach. As if the boat weighed nothing, he grabbed the front and hoisted it into the air.

I gulped at the open display of vampire strength. "How did you know the boat would be here?"

"This is my home. I know everything about the island," he grunted, dropping the vessel into the water. "Now get in before we have company."

I cautiously picked my way toward the boat. The boat that had seen better days, upon closer inspection. "How long has this thing been down here?"

Would it even *start*?

"Does it matter?" Annoyance coated his words. "We need to intercept the SCA operatives before they take Loch beyond our reach. This boat is our best bet."

I held up my hands. "Okay, okay, point taken. I'm getting in."

Despite my lifelong fear of the ocean, of being lost to the dark depths the way my parents had—or how I *thought* they had until Noah told me otherwise—I forced myself to climb into the boat. Finding my soulmate trumped any childhood nightmare I had. It trumped *everything*.

The second I settled onto the stern bench, Everett jumped on board and started the engine. Or tried to, at least. The engine gave a pathetic moan before sputtering out. Cursing under his breath, he kept at it, turning the key in the ignition over and over.

Just when I was about to suggest he check the gas level, the engine roared to life. Before I could breathe a sigh of relief, a dark form blurred into the cave. Then another.

"Get down!" Everett barked, and gunned the engine. I crouched low, scrambling for a handhold as we made a beeline for the cave entrance. Before we could clear it, one of the dark shapes vaulted into the boat, crashing into Everett. We jolted to a dead stop, inches away from the cave's mouth. "Grab the wheel, Kenna!"

I lurched out of my seat, only for something to snag my coat from behind and *yank*. I barely had time to scream as I tumbled backward into the water. Panicking when I fully submerged, I flailed my arms, already desperate for air.

As a face swam before me, barely a shadow in the blackened depths, I froze in terror. Glowing red eyes peered into mine. Then a slash of a smile, tipped in sharp fangs.

A *vampire* had me.

He pushed my body down, down, down, until I struck the rocks below.

I struggled to break free, but his strength surpassed mine. Fear consumed me. Ice-cold and debilitating. I was going to drown. Drown *alone* in this wretched watery grave. Far from Lochlan, unable to see him one last time.

A scream built in my chest. Of pain. Of anger. Of desperation for my soulmate. The pressure grew and grew, until I could no longer contain it.

The scream violently erupted. Not into the watery world, but inside my head. My mind. My very *soul*. Radiating throughout every inch of my being.

The sound was a gale storm. Whirling. Crashing. Forming one desperate word.

LOCHLAN!

The cry tore through me, shattering an invisible barrier. A barrier separating me from *him*. I could feel it. The moment my call reached him. Awoke him. It was an awareness, a knowing that I was no longer alone. His familiar presence filled my head, quickly followed by his worried voice.

McKenna?

I would have sobbed if I didn't so desperately need the air. It was him. It was really *him*. Like he was here beside me at this very moment.

I need you, I gasped into the space where he was. *I can't hold on much longer.*

McKenna, where are you? When I didn't answer, his bellow rang through my ears. *McKenna!*

The overpowering need for air forced me into silence. To conserve the last of my strength. The vampire continued to hold me down, rendering my struggles useless. At least I got to hear Lochlan's voice one last time. At least I wasn't alone in my final moments.

My throat painfully seized, and I knew my time was up. I could no longer deny my lungs what they desperately needed.

But as I involuntarily opened my mouth to suck in the salty sea water, a rush of energy shot through me.

Of inhuman *strength* unlike anything I'd ever felt before.

My eyes flew wide. The second I met the vampire's gloating gaze, I wrenched an arm free and grabbed his wrist. He grimaced. Then silently howled in pain as my special brand of magic began to suck his life away. A familiar red glow from where our skin touched dispelled the darkness, boosting my resolve. I pushed off the rocks and surged upward in a cloud of bubbles, still holding onto the vampire.

The moment my head breached the surface, his piercing screams drowned out everything else. Lochlan's presence drifted away, and I reluctantly let him go. Even as I gulped in air and immediately choked on salt water, I continued to doggedly suck the life from the flailing vampire like a freaking leech. He clawed at me, but my coat took the brunt of his attack.

Within seconds, he went limp. I dropped his arm and morbidly watched him slowly sink beneath the water. Only when I was certain he wouldn't be coming back up did I search for the boat.

It had drifted from the cave by several feet, enough that my poor swimming skills were put to the test. While I mostly doggy-paddled toward the vessel, I noticed Everett standing in its center, gripping his attacker by the throat.

"I'll ask one last time. Who is your leader?" Everett hissed, so deathly soft that I barely caught the words.

"P-please," the vampire wheezed, obviously no match for the eldest Venturi prince. "The sun is almost up."

"Then you better talk *fast*, traitor," Everett sneered, clearly not concerned. "Tell me who's running your group."

"I-I don't know. They keep their identity a secret. Only a select few actually know who—"

His words abruptly ended in an agonized shriek. I reached the boat just as the first golden rays of sun leaked over the horizon. The vampire immediately began to burn, starting with his exposed face. Smoke rose from his skin, skin that was transforming back to its human color. At least in theory. He was so red and blistered that I couldn't actually tell what color his skin was supposed to be.

"Help me!" he screamed, his pain and desperation drawing a small kernel of sympathy from me. But Everett didn't even bat an eyelash, watching impassively as the Feltore's skin finally caught on fire. Bile rose in my throat and I looked away as the screams grew deafening. Everett dropped him, and he hit the deck with an unceremonious thump. When I chanced a peek at him a few seconds later, he was already a smoking pile of ash.

A gloved hand suddenly blocked my vision and I jerked my head up to meet Everett's pale green gaze. He looked human now. A broader, harder version of Lochlan. But he wasn't anything like his brother. He was cold and cruel and utterly ruthless. And yet, here he was, offering me his hand.

With hardly a moment's hesitation, I reached for his outstretched fingers. Allowed him to pull me on board like a half-drowned puppy. Watched as he callously kicked the smoldering pile of ash and clothing aside to restart the engine.

I made a decision then. To accept our forced partnership, however temporarily.

Because I would do anything to get my soulmate back.

I would follow the devil himself into the fiery pits of hell if I had to.

CHAPTER 2

KENNA

Wind buffeted me from all sides. It snatched my breath away. Whipped chunks of damp chestnut hair across my face. There was no escape from the cold penetrating every pore of my body as Everett pushed the boat to full speed.

Still, I clearly heard him say, "Try again."

"Were they r-rogues?" I stammered instead of doing as he asked, glancing behind us for the dozenth time.

"Yes."

"A-are they w-working with the SCA?"

A lengthy pause. "I don't know."

"What if they f-follow—"

"Unlikely. Feltore can't be out during the daytime, as you can see." He kicked at the pile of clothing. Ash stirred into the air, caught up by the wind. "Now try again."

I pursed my lips, but did as instructed, calling out to Lochlan through our mind connection. "N-nothing," I stuttered after a moment. "I th-think he's unconscious again."

Everett whacked the boat's steering wheel and swore. "You should have asked him which direction they were headed."

I blinked up at his hard profile, feeling disapproval oozing off him. "You mean while I was s-seconds away from drowning? Or while you were t-too busy interrogating the rogue to help m-me?"

His entire body went rigid. Well, *rigider.*

"I would have intervened," he replied tightly. "You're my brother's mate. I said I'd protect you, and I will."

I snorted, muttering under my breath, "Well, you're doing a crap poor job of it."

He looked at me sharply and I nearly swallowed my tongue. Oops. His hearing was better than I'd thought. Oh well. I secretly wanted him to hear it anyway.

Expecting him to defend himself, I was startled when he said, "Remove your coat."

I sat ramrod straight in my seat and clutched at the sodden material. "W-what? No way. I'm already f-freezing as it is."

Although I could barely feel the cold, I knew my body wasn't handling the icy dip into the water very well. The boost of strength I'd experienced earlier had almost worn off, allowing fatigue to deaden my limbs.

"Exactly," Everett went on. "Those wet clothes are only making it worse. Take them off and put this on."

I bit back a yelp when a scratchy wool blanket smacked my face. It smelled strongly of age and mildew, but I forced my fingers into action anyway, knowing he was right. I was the weak link here, the witch who barely had a handle on her magic. Who might as well be human right now for all the good it did her. The least I could do was proactively take care of myself.

"The pants too," Everett said when I'd managed to peel my coat and sweater off. "I won't look," he added with exasperation when I noticeably stiffened. "I still have no interest in you, especially now that you've had sex with my brother. You're drenched in his scent. He claimed you thoroughly and that's an instant turnoff for me."

I nearly choked on my spit. What the—? He could still smell Lochlan on me after my dip in the ocean?

12

"What did you m-mean earlier when you said Lochlan chose me?" I asked, desperate to change the subject. When he shot me an assessing look, I pulled the scratchy blanket over my shoulders, still unwilling to let him see me half naked.

"A line from the prophecy that's tripped us up for quite some time says '*Drawn to her blood, the three must choose, as one follows another, but never two,*'" he replied, then once again faced forward. With his attention on the distant horizon, I got to work removing my boots. "We figured out that the curse only allows one Syphon to be alive at any given time. The moment she dies, another is born. But we've never *chosen* one. Hunted them down, yes. Stolen them from their homes. Even killed them. But chosen? We didn't even know what that meant. Until now."

I paused with my pants halfway down my legs to gape at the side of his head. "S-so you think Lochlan chose me to be his soulmate?"

Everett's knuckles whitened on the steering wheel. "No. I think he simply chose to place his hope in you. You can thank fate, or the bloody curse, for the mate bond."

I finished removing my pants in stunned silence, doing my best to ignore the bitter undertone to his words. Stripped down to my bra and underwear, I tucked my feet beneath me and covered nearly every inch of my exposed skin with the musty blanket. "So you think," I began haltingly, "th-that when Lochlan chose me, he f-fulfilled part of the prophecy?"

"Yes."

A jolt of excitement shivered through me. "And you think that our bond—?"

"Will break the curse."

My heart skipped several beats. ""H-how?"

"I don't know. The last part of the prophecy is vague. A sacrifice

13

must be made, as well as a choice given. It could mean many things. Now try again. We're nearing the mainland but could be heading in the wrong direction."

"Doesn't the SCA have a—a headquarters or something?"

Everett threw me a droll look. "They aren't the CIA, Kenna. Human governments aren't even aware of their organization, as far as I know."

Sighing in disappointment, I set aside my many burning questions and closed my eyes, concentrating on the soulmate bond again. Instead of calling out to Lochlan though, I felt for him. His presence. His emotions. Anything that would make me feel closer to him. When I focused on our connection, on the warmth that somehow felt dimmer, panic filled me.

"Weak," I choked out, unable to stop my chin from wobbling. "It feels . . . weak."

"Weak how, Kenna?" When I didn't immediately answer, Everett's voice sharpened. "*Kenna*. Weak how?"

"Like . . . like it's been drained. *He's* been drained. Like all his strength has been sapped away."

"Silver, most likely. It's the only way humans are able to control us. They must have given him a heavy dose."

Pain swelled in my chest and I pressed a hand to my sternum. "Does it h-hurt?"

"Like hell. Silver in liquid form is extremely potent. Which was why it took me so long to wake up this morning. Thankfully, I didn't finish the entire drink or I might still be unconscious."

My eyes began to burn. Lochlan was in pain. They were *hurting* him. Before I knew it, my canines had lengthened into fangs and claws gouged my chest. I struggled to breathe around the ball of anger rising within me. It swelled, hot and out of control.

They were hurting him. *Hurting* him.

Red filled my vision.

Rage boiled in my veins.

Desperate for release, I threw my head back and screamed. Screamed and screamed and screamed until my throat grew raw.

When the rage finally cooled, I opened my eyes to find Everett watching me. For a single moment, a look of understanding softened the unforgiving planes of his face. When I blinked, the softness was gone.

Facing forward once more, he said, "You'll need every ounce of that anger if we're going to get him back. I heavily doubt your fake aunt will let him go without a fight."

I frowned. "Why do you keep calling her that? Fake."

He glanced back with a raised brow, completely blindsiding me with a few simple words. "Because she's not your aunt."

I moved as if in a trance, my bare feet shuffling along the sidewalk. My bedraggled state drew attention, but the large hand on my back propelled me forward, discouraging me from stopping, from succumbing to shock. Not because of the cold, but from the earth-shattering revelation that every last memory of my past was a lie.

"Tess Walker has been an SCA field operative for twenty-five years. Her mission for the past fifteen has been to keep you out of vampire hands. Someone told her about you when your parents died, which is the only reason she found and took you away. Before then, she didn't even know you existed."

I didn't want to believe him. That I had been nothing but a job to the woman who'd raised me. That she'd created a story I'd so gullibly believed. But his words made sense. They lined up with Noah's story about my parents' murder. And in my heart, I knew they were true.

My Aunt Tess wasn't real.

She was an imposter. A *fake*. Who'd lied to me my entire life.

I was floundering under the weight of her betrayal. Drowning in memories of us. Memories that weren't real.

Her fiery red hair and porcelain skin. So different from mine. From my parents'. I'd always seen the differences but refused to consider what they could mean.

Until now.

"She needs clothes, boots, and a coat. Fetch everything and return immediately."

The words jarred me back to reality, to the realization that we were no longer on the boat.

"What—?" I blinked, startled to find that we were in a small boutique store. "When did we get here?"

"Finally," Everett muttered, a clear look of agitation on his face. "This isn't the time for a mental breakdown."

I noticed then that I still wore nothing but my underwear and an old blanket. I threw him an accusatory glare. "*Seriously?* You paraded me around town like this?"

"What else was I supposed to do?" Everett hissed back. "There's no way I'm leaving you alone, even for a second. You attract way too much trouble."

I spluttered nonsensically, knowing he was right yet again. "Well . . . *fine*. But you're not watching me dress." I lifted my chin up, along with the remains of my dignity, and stalked toward the changing rooms.

When I'd whipped back the stall's curtain and enclosed myself inside, I caught the tail end of his long-suffering sigh. Despite how wretched I currently felt, a perverse sense of satisfaction filled me. Maybe I needed to add a new goal to my already long list: get under Everett D'angelo's skin as often as possible. Call it payback for the many times he'd threatened my life and scared me senseless.

"Miss?" a salesclerk called from outside the partition, and I poked my head out. She gave me a strained smile, nervously glancing back at Everett before saying, "Your boyfriend told me to give you these and anything else you need. If they don't fit, just let me know."

I wrinkled my nose. "He's not my boyfriend, but thanks. I'll let you know." As she placed the clothing in my arms, I saw Everett roll his eyes and turn to take up a post near the building's entrance like a freaking bodyguard.

I suddenly had an idea. A desperately foolish one. But one I couldn't shake free.

Just the thought of it sent my heartrate into overdrive, and I quickly ducked behind the curtain to change. I finished in record time, barely bothering to check my reflection, let alone how the clothing fit. My hands shook with nerves as I peeled back the curtain an inch. Everett was still near the door. Within earshot, but his attention was on a group of people milling outside the shop.

I waited. Waited until the salesclerk meandered my direction. "Um, excuse me," I said to her, loud enough that I knew Everett could hear. "These boots pinch my feet. Could I get a size larger?"

"Oh, of course," she said, bustling over. Just like I'd hoped, Everett barely glanced our way. My heart beat even faster as the woman reached the stall and held out her hand expectantly.

"Actually," I said, lowering my voice to a faint whisper. "Do you have a phone I could borrow?" I made a show of glancing fearfully over her shoulder to where Everett waited. "Just for a second. Please."

Her eyes rounded dramatically, then brightened in

understanding. Without hesitation, she slid a phone from her pocket and into my hand. "Is he dangerous? Should I call the police?" she whispered just as quietly, starting to peek at him over her shoulder. "I had a bad feeling about him the moment he stepped inside the shop."

"No, the coat is fine," I said, raising my voice. "Just the boots in a bigger size, please." She gave me a deer-in-headlights look, then nodded vigorously before taking off. I could barely breathe as I secured the curtain with trembling fingers before turning on the phone. I only needed a minute. One minute to complete my next goal.

I quickly tapped the Maps app, noting our location, then fumbled to type in a phone number. Cursing internally when I botched the first attempt, I tried again, slowing my fingers as best I could. As the phone began to ring, tears of relief burned my eyes.

Pick up, pick up, pick up. Please, please, please.

My legs nearly gave out when the rings stopped and a voice answered, "Kenna? It better be you. I'm going to raise hell if it isn't."

My throat seized with joy that he was okay. But also with pain that he sounded so unhinged. "It's me, Kade."

"Oh, thank the mother," he said, his voice audibly cracking. "Where are you, little Kenna? What happened? Where's Loch and Everett?"

"Listen carefully because I don't have much time. Lochlan was taken by the SCA. Everett and I are going after him. I'll find him, Kade, I promise. But I need you. I need you to find *me*. We're currently in—"

With a loud metallic shriek, the curtain and metal rod were viciously yanked aside. I jumped, sucking in a startled gasp as a glowering Everett stormed inside the stall and grabbed the phone.

18

"Come looking for us and I'll make sure you suffer, drothen," Everett growled, then snapped the phone in two. His angry gaze fixed on me and I backpedaled, bumping into the wall. When he crowded in close, towering over me menacingly, I nearly peed myself. "That was incredibly stupid, witch."

Instead of cowering like instinct demanded, I jutted out my jaw, hissing, "Don't call me that."

"What, *witch?* That's what you are."

"Yeah, but you make it sound like a *disease.*"

"Witches *are* a disease."

I jerked my head back, like he'd struck me. "Look, I know witches have screwed up in the past, but not all of us are like Edith. I—"

"Loch *told* you about her?" Everett snarled in disbelief.

"Yes. He told me everything because he *trusts* me. Because he knows I'm nothing like her."

Everett scoffed. "*Trust?* I doubt that. If he trusted you, he would have told you about the telepathic link *before* completing the bond. And if he'd told you everything about the past, you wouldn't be standing here right now. That much I know."

My heart began to pound like a runaway horse. "What's *that* supposed to mean?"

"Nope. My lips are sealed. I don't trust you not to seek revenge. Which is probably why Loch didn't tell you either."

I felt a crack form, directly down the center of my heart. I struggled to breathe, to *think.* I shook my head, clenching my shaking fists. "I don't believe you."

He rolled his eyes. "Not surprised. You don't trust me and I don't trust you. It's the age-old story of our two species."

My eyes narrowed to slits. "Well, *Kade* can be trusted, which is why I called him. He's Lochlan's drothen. Practically his brother. I know he'd never betray him."

"You know nothing," Everett snapped. "Loch is *my* brother. *My* blood. *I* should be the one protecting him, not somebody who only does so out of sworn *duty*."

I gaped, struck speechless by his words. When I eventually found my voice again, it trembled with equal passion. "Well, Lochlan is my *soulmate*, whether you like it or not. And I say we need more help. I barely understand how this telepathic thing works, and I'm scared that it'll be too late by the time I do. That he'll *die* before I ever get a chance to tell him—"

To tell him that I *loved* him. So deeply that I couldn't breathe without him. Didn't want to.

I swallowed the words though, wrestling my emotions back under control. My voice was steady this time when I said, "Please, Everett. I need my friend. I need Kade."

His lips thinned as he studied me closely. Then, without a word, he whirled and stalked from the stall. At the startled feminine squeak, I bolted after him, stumbling to a halt when I saw the salesclerk in his grip.

"P-please," she whimpered. "I won't tell anyone. Don't hurt—"

"Forget everything you just heard and saw, including our faces," he murmured, in a silken tone I was beginning to associate with thrall. "We were never here."

She nodded woodenly, right before Everett dropped her. She sank to the floor, a blank look spreading across her face.

"Let's go," he said, turning toward the exit.

"But . . . but we didn't even pay," I stammered, feeling guiltier the longer I stared at the lost-looking woman. "Her phone . . ."

Without warning, a hand was suddenly on my arm, forcing me to move.

"Wait. Everett, *wait.*" I tried to break free of his grip, but he only tightened his hold, drawing a wince from me.

"If you value her life, you won't fight me," he curtly said, marching me toward the exit. "Test my patience and I'll show you just how angry I am right now."

I immediately stopped struggling, knowing exactly what he'd do if I refused to listen. I'd already witnessed one human's death by his hands. I didn't want to see another.

CHAPTER 3

KENNA

There were two things I knew with absolute certainty as the day wore on.

Finding Lochlan was going to be harder than I thought, and I desperately needed blood.

The longer I failed to telepathically connect with my soulmate, the angrier his older brother became. Problem was, so did I. At my ill-timed craving for blood. At Everett's controlling threats. At *Tess* for pretending to be my aunt and taking Lochlan away from me.

But I was mostly angry at myself for being so utterly useless.

"It's not working!" I abruptly shouted, loud enough that I startled a flock of birds out of a nearby pine tree. They flapped into the sky, their rustling feathers the only sound in the isolated park. Feeling beyond frustrated and helpless, I shoved at the metal bench I'd been sitting on for the past half hour. The whole thing tipped over backward with a resounding clang, and I hurriedly picked it up.

"Take a short break," Everett said from his post against a nearby tree. "They won't keep him sedated forever."

"But what if they do? What if I can't reach him?" I countered, pacing the park's ice-encrusted trail. "And why did they take him in the first place? Why him and not—"

I skidded to a halt.

Why him and not me? Unless . . .

"They took him to get to me."

I suddenly knew, without a shred of doubt, that it was true. But that would mean they knew about our relationship. Why else would they have targeted him specifically?

"My thoughts exactly," Everett said, which gave me pause.

Everett *agreed* with me? Well that wasn't strange or anything.

"Chances are, they were after you, but Loch got in the way," he went on, oblivious to my surprise. "If you can't reach him soon, we'll implement plan B."

"What's plan B?"

Before he could answer, a trim blonde woman jogged around the trail's bend, heading straight toward us. I stepped out of the way, only for her to slip on a patch of ice. As she went down, Everett blurred forward at vampire speed and caught her.

Looking shaken but unharmed, she stammered a thank you. When he didn't immediately let go, she glanced up at him. And smiled. Freaking *smiled.*

Ah crap, lady, do not *go there.*

But she totally did, batting her lashes flirtatiously at him. "How did you get to me so quickly? I didn't even see you."

"Oh, I smelled you a mile away," he replied with a wicked tilt to his lips.

My eyes widened. Uh oh.

Her brow wrinkled delicately, but she didn't pull away. Stupid, *stupid* woman. "Smelled?"

"I've been so preoccupied that I haven't had breakfast," he said by way of explanation, gently swiping her long blonde hair back to expose the side of her neck. "But I can spare a few minutes, especially for a pretty blonde with blood pumping hotly through her veins."

My stomach plummeted.

"Everett," I warned, taking a step toward them, but it was too

23

late.

"Don't scream," he ordered the woman, right before he bared his fangs and sank them deeply into her neck. Her mouth opened in a silent scream, but no sound came out. She struggled, though, beating her fists against his arms and chest. He only pulled her closer, cupping the back of her head to anchor her in place.

Nausea flushed hotly through my insides, followed closely by the most horrific feeling. *Desire.* Despite how repulsed I was at what Everett was doing to this poor woman, I wanted to join in. To experience what fresh warm blood directly from the source tasted like.

As a dribble of red slid down her neck, I made the mistake of inhaling. My fangs painfully burst from their hiding spot, and I whimpered.

Everett whipped his head up and fixed his dilated eyes on me. At the expression on my face, a warning growl rumbled in his throat. "I don't share food," he said in a guttural tone, clutching the woman possessively.

I looked away, uncertain if I was going to be sick or challenge him. He wasn't Lochlan though, I had to remind myself. I doubted a challenge with him would be a simple staring contest to prove who was more alpha.

Apparently satisfied that I wasn't going to steal his *prey* from him, Everett went back to feeding. I sank onto the bench, doing my best not to breathe in the woman's cloying scent. I waited. Fifteen seconds. Thirty. Too long. At the listless way she was leaning against him, I knew he was taking too much.

"Everett. Everett, stop. You'll kill her."

When he continued to ignore me, I shot off the bench, ready to pry him away. I didn't heed his warning growl this time, stalking toward the entwined pair without pause. The second I came within range though, Everett's gloved hand shot out and gripped my throat.

For a split second, I panicked. Fear bled through me, followed by memory after memory of the times he'd held me at his mercy. I was weak compared to him. Weak and—

No!

I wasn't weak. And I certainly wasn't helpless. I was a *Syphon*, for fate's sake.

Shoving my fear aside, I grabbed his exposed wrist and willed my claws to descend. When they pierced his flesh, he threw his head back and roared. The woman crumpled to the ground as he released her to face me.

"Let. Go," he growled, promises of pain and death swirling in his pale green irises. He tightened his hold on my neck, baring his bloody fangs.

"You let go first," I managed to wheeze, tightening my hold on him as well. I kept a firm lid on my Syphon magic, but was prepared to unleash it if he didn't cooperate.

His gaze flicked down to our joined skin. "So I was right. You know how to control your abilities."

"Only recently." I tried to swallow, but his hold wouldn't allow it. "I was incentivized to learn."

He snorted derisively. "I bet you were. All so you could crawl into my brother's bed and seduce him."

At the bald insult, I snapped. Rage cut through my control like a serrated knife and my palm began to warm. Hotter and hotter until red fire engulfed my fingers. Everett's reaction was instantaneous. With a pained hiss, he wrenched back his arm. As he released me, I followed suit, severing our connection.

He was suddenly a hair's breadth from my face, bellowing so

loudly that my ears rang, "Do that again and I'll end you, witch! Don't for one second think that I won't."

"Insult my mate bond with Lochlan again and I'll drain your life force, you sadistic waste of air!" I shouted back, not giving an inch.

He blinked, as if I'd startled him. Blinked again, then straightened to his full height. We stared at each other for a long moment, me shaking with rage while he stood still as stone. Then, he slowly lifted an eyebrow and said, "Sadistic waste of air?"

Now it was my turn to blink, noting the fight drain out of him and his shoulders relax. I heaved out a breath, muttering, "I'll think of something more creative next time."

An actual smile curled the corners of his mouth. "Next time?"

I shook my head as annoyance replaced my anger. "I'm getting the impression that fighting is the only way you know how to communicate, so, yes. Next time."

A low moan diverted our attention to the woman at our feet. My gaze latched onto the blood smeared across her neck, and like a switch flipping, I was suddenly thirsty again. Swallowing with difficulty, I forced my eyes away.

"You should thrall her to forget or whatever," I said rather hoarsely, backing up a step.

When Everett didn't move, I glanced up at him and immediately froze. Ah crap. He knew. Sure enough, he tipped his chin at the woman and said, "Feed."

I shook my head, feeling panic surge up. "No way."

His eyes narrowed. "Why not?"

"Because she's already lost too much blood. And . . . and because she's *human*."

"I'll heal her. And what does it matter if she's human?"

I threw my hands in the air. "Because *I* was human not too long ago. Or, at least, I thought I was. You might not get this, but being preyed upon like a freaking deer really messes with your head. I know you're an apex predator, but treating humans like animals is so not cool."

He stood in silence, watching as I crossed my arms and struggled with that very urge to go all apex predator on this hapless woman. When it became clear I wasn't going to give in, he wordlessly crouched beside her and began cleaning up his mess.

Only after the woman was long gone, when the sun was directly overhead, did we move to a new location. Still unable to contact Lochlan, I followed Everett like a useless lump, finding it harder and harder to wrestle my thirst and desperation to find Lochlan under control.

As we walked across town at a fast clip, Everett repeatedly checked his phone. Every time he did, he walked even faster, until I was forced into a light jog.

"Where are we going now?" I huffed out, already pathetically winded from my body's need for blood.

"To get a car," he replied shortly, jamming his phone into his pocket.

I was almost desperate enough to make a grab for it. Almost.

"And then what? Blindly drive around until Lochlan wakes up?"

"For now, yes."

"We could cover more ground if—"

"No."

"But—"

"*No*, Kenna, we're not splitting up. I've tracked him down before and I'll do it again."

"But it's *different* this time and you know it," I argued, clenching my fists. "We don't have years to find him. The curse becomes

27

permanent in less than two months. And if the SCA decides to . . . to kill him, then all hope is lost. You said so yourself."

"If they kill him, I couldn't care less if my true form is exposed and incites a war. I'll start it myself, for that matter," Everett growled, walking even faster.

I stopped dead in my tracks, horror-stricken by his words. My aunt—or rather, *Tess*—already wanted to destroy the vampire race for posing a threat to humans. If Everett went on another vengeful killing spree like he'd done with the witches after Lochlan had been taken by Edith . . .

"What?"

I jumped, startled to find Everett beside me. I nervously cleared my throat, knowing that my next words could get me killed. Still, I had to say them. At least this way, I'd know the truth instead of blindly following him like a bull being led around by the nose. "It's just . . . you sound like a rogue."

Yup. I'd said it.

Sure, he'd just killed one of them mere hours ago, but that could have been for my benefit. To lull me into a false sense of complacency. For all I knew, this whole thing could be his idea. The silver-laced drinks, his brother's abduction, distancing me from my friends.

He knew about the soulmate bond. Knew that I would do anything to get Lochlan back. This whole thing could be an elaborate scheme to get rid of me, once and for all.

I gulped. Maybe following the devil hadn't been such a good idea after all. Yes, he was Lochlan's brother, but I barely knew him. For all I knew . . .

"You could be the rogue's leader."

Freaking fates, why had I said that out loud? I was *so* dead.

Everett just stared. Long enough that I was two seconds away from peeing myself. When he finally spoke, his voice was low. Calculating. "Yes, I could be." Oh crap, oh crap, oh crap. Then he added, "But I'm not," and whirled around, leaving me to gape after him.

And hope that he was telling the truth.

When dusk fell and his vampire form emerged, Everett bristled with tension. His road rage had grown worse with each passing hour, and I cringed every time he took out his frustration on the innocent humans driving home from a long day of work.

He didn't stop once. Just drove from one seaside town to the next, scanning the roads for any sign of his brother. It seemed pointless to me, but I didn't say a word, too busy trying to reconnect with Lochlan.

And keeping my hunger under control.

Blood, blood, blood.

My heart beat in time to the word, making it hard to focus.

I hadn't eaten since early yesterday evening. If I didn't satiate my thirst soon, I was going to be even *more* useless.

"Are you even listening?"

Everett's irritated voice snapped me out of my hunger craze and I glanced sideways at him. "Huh? No. I was . . ." I rubbed my tired eyes, unwilling to confess that I was daydreaming about blood. If he decided to catch another human for dinner, I might not be able to stop myself from feeding this time.

"I told you to call your fake aunt. It's time for plan B."

My heart stopped when he thrust his phone at me. Too shell-shocked to move, I simply gawked at the device.

"Take it, Kenna, before I change my mind."

I forced my fingers to grasp the phone, not knowing what to say other than, "Why?"

A muscle jumped in his jaw. "You were right earlier. Things are different this time. A lot more than my brother's life is at stake now. We have to be smarter in our approach." The steering wheel creaked beneath his white-knuckled grip, as if it took everything in him to admit those words. "Make the call."

Instead of feeling vindicated, nerves beat at my empty stomach. I hadn't spoken to Tess since the day she left me at Thornecrest Academy, alone and confused. She hadn't listened to me then. Why would she listen now?

Still, I had to try. Nothing she said was going to keep me and Lochlan apart this time. Her opinion of him was moot at this point. I knew better now, and whether she agreed with me or not didn't matter. As long as she gave him back to me, I could live with her disappointment.

Inhaling a fortifying breath, I slowly typed in her number and pressed the phone to my ear.

"Calm down," Everett tightly said. "I can't hear anything over the blood rushing through your veins."

My mouth dried. Blood. He just *had* to mention blood.

Before my thirst could distract me again, the phone stopped ringing and a familiar voice answered. "Hello?"

I was suddenly tongue-tied, too angry to speak. All the lies she'd told came rushing forward to taunt me. When I let the silence stretch, Everett nudged my arm. The physical jolt was enough to make me blurt, "Tess. It's . . . it's me."

There was a rustling on the other end, then, "Kenna Joy, is that you? Oh, Kenna, I've been so—"

Everett abruptly snatched the phone away. "This is Everett D'angelo speaking. You took my brother and I want him back. I'd like to propose a deal. Bring him to me unharmed, and I'll relinquish McKenna Belmont to you. Fail to do so and I can't guarantee your ward's safety."

Dread shivered up my spine. Was this his plan B? Trade me for Lochlan? I shouldn't be surprised. I'd even suspected it would come to this. He'd spent *years* scouring the earth for his brother, leaving a trail of dead witches and warlocks in his wake. Saving Lochlan was his only priority. I knew that.

Then why was a lump forming in my throat? Why did I feel so betrayed?

I'd been stupid to think that being Lochlan's soulmate actually meant something to him. That we were beginning to understand each other.

But our partnership was coming to a swift end. I was nothing more to him than a bargaining chip.

"I accept your deal," I heard my—Tess—say, and my heart sank further. "Meet me at Kenna's childhood home, tomorrow at dawn."

"Why not sooner?"

"I'll need time to have him released from SCA custody. No need to worry though. They'll agree to the exchange. We only care about Kenna's safety."

"Fine. We'll be there."

When the call ended, I was too numb to speak. To tell Everett how utterly awful he was for handing me over like a piece of property. But he must have read something in my stiff posture.

"It's the only way we're getting him back," he said. Silence. "It won't be permanent. Just until Loch is safe. We still need you."

More silence.

The hard lines of Everett's face softened. "Kenna . . ."

"It's a good plan," I interrupted, hating that it was true. "But I don't trust my aunt—I mean, I don't trust *Tess* to willingly hand Lochlan over to you. She chose my house as the meetup location for a reason. It's warded against vampires. Who's to say she won't kill you both the moment I'm safely behind the wards?"

Everett's blood red eyes met mine as he veered off the highway onto the nearest exit ramp. "I think that's exactly what she has planned. Which is why," he said, passing his phone over to me once again, "I want you to call for help. Smarter, remember?"

My breath caught. Was he serious? Was he freaking *serious?*

"Are you going to call or not? Because—"

"I take back everything bad I've ever said or thought about you," I gushed, giddily accepting his phone with a stupid grin despite the circumstances.

Everett rolled his eyes, but I caught the amused twitch of his lips as he refocused on the road. "Oh, and Kenna? Tell Kade to bring weapons. We're going to need them."

CHAPTER 4

KENNA

I slid the Snickers bar, bag of Cheetos, and bottled water onto the counter, trying my best not to breathe in the gas station employee's scent.

You're not a vampire. You don't need to feed.

Argh, nope. The pep talk wasn't helping. Hopefully the food would though, because I refused to drink blood from a living human, no matter how much pain I was in.

The second the guy handed me my receipt, I snatched up my purchases and beelined for the exit. Everett was still in the dark blue Volvo he bought earlier today. *Bought*, because the filthy rich didn't rent, apparently. He had parked on the far side of the lot, not that he needed to worry about humans or cameras spotting his vampire form. The gas station was so dark and rundown, it was barely operational. And at this late hour, we were the only customers.

He'd almost refused to stop, reminding me that Kade was on his way and we were nearing Rosewood, but my bodily needs had won out. He might have a steel-lined bladder and disdain for most food, but I sure didn't.

As I came abreast of the sole-working gas pump while awkwardly trying to open the Cheetos bag, a black SUV rolled into the lot. I cringed when the headlights swung my way, temporarily blinding me.

"High beams, dude," I muttered, pausing to blink the bright spots from my vision. When the vehicle stopped just inside the lot instead of pulling in, I resumed walking toward the Volvo. The second I cleared the gas pump though, the SUV's engine revved loudly.

Startled at the unexpected noise, I dropped my bag of Cheetos. Argh! I watched in dismay as cheesy artificial goodness scattered across the cracked asphalt. Tires squealed before I could finish mourning the loss, and I glanced up to find the SUV bearing down on me. It shot forward so fast that, instead of diving out of the way, I stumbled backward.

Right into a pothole.

Time slowed to a crawl as my ankle twisted, throwing me off balance. The water bottle and Snickers bar flew from my hand and I gracelessly fell sideways. There was no stopping my descent. No stopping the vehicle barreling straight for me. It didn't matter that I was a witch with the potential for great power. Or the last Syphon who could save the world from war.

One stupid misstep and gravity was taking me down.

I fell, my demise inevitable. And then I was soaring. Tumbling. Crashing to the unforgiving ground. Rolling and rolling, my body semi-protected by a set of steel arms and a rock-hard chest.

The moment we stopped, I was dragged to my feet, so fast that I knew a vampire had me. Dazed from the impact, I wheezed in a breath, ready to scream for Everett. But when the arms let go and a broad back filled my vision, I realized it was him.

Everett had rescued me.

I set aside my astonishment as brakes squealed and car doors opened. When I moved to see who was exiting the SUV, Everett quietly growled, "Stay behind me, Kenna."

"Who is it?"

"Feltore. I'm guessing rogues. At least seven."

34

My heart stopped. How? How could they have followed us? We'd been on the move practically all day.

Everett swore under his breath as, sure enough, seven vampires with blood red eyes emerged from the vehicle. "We never should have stopped," he said in an accusing tone.

"Hey, I had to *pee*," I blathered like an idiot, not knowing what else to say while the rogues loosely fanned out in front of us. "It's not like I can pee in a bottle like a guy. Which is totally unfair, by the way. Life would be so much easier with a—"

"Quiet," he hissed, grabbing my arm to pull me close as two vampires slithered toward us from either side. Corralling us. *Trapping* us. Everett growled at them, barking, "As your prince and superior, I order you to stand down."

A tall, black-haired female dressed in a burgundy trench coat stepped forward with a devilish smirk. "We have no quarrel with you, Your Highness. Let us take the Syphon off your hands and we'll be on our way. We know how much you despise her."

Everett's grip tightened. "It doesn't matter how I feel about her. She's the only one who can break our curse and is therefore under my protection. Try to take her from me and you'll all suffer a violent end."

Her expression hardened. "That's unfortunate to hear. I was told you were the reasonable one. Regardless, we have a job to do, with or without your approval." She flicked a glance at the other vampires. "Bones. Knox. Get the witch. The rest of you, incapacitate the prince."

Everett's bellow blasted my eardrums as the horde charged. Five bum-rushed him like projectile missiles, while the two creeping up on either side of us set their sights on me. Everett crowded me against the gas pump, using his body as a shield, but they came in too hot, too fast.

Claws snatched at my arm, jerking me sideways. I cried out as they gouged holes through my jacket and raked across my skin. Everett lashed out and caught the vampire before he could take me. With one savage yank, he ripped both arms from the rogue's body. A bloodcurdling scream pierced the night, sending a cold shiver down my spine. Everett tossed the severed limbs aside and went after another.

Before I could be sick over the blood spurting from the vampire's armless stumps, a terrible metallic shriek came from the gas pump. In a flash, it was gone. Ripped up and tossed aside like a freaking toy. With my back now exposed and Everett taking on several rogues at once, my survival instincts kicked in.

Everett roared my name as I took off at vampire speed, dashing for the store's safety. Or rather, it *would* have been safe . . . if I weren't being chased by bloodthirsty supernatural creatures.

The moment I yanked open the glass door, I realized my mistake. The gas station employee was standing only a yard away, slack-jawed and bug-eyed as he took in the scene outside.

Crap.

"Run!" I screamed at him, whirling to slam the door shut and lock it. Mistake number two. One of the vampires launched himself at the door and crashed right through. I backpedaled into the shocked employee, latching onto his arm and dragging him with me when he wouldn't move. Precious seconds were wasted as the guy relearned how to use his legs. As he realized too late that his life was in danger.

I tore down the aisles, knowing that hiding wasn't an option. They would simply sniff me out, and probably drain this human. Drain *me* too. Before killing me. So I ran, using every ounce of my enhanced speed and strength, forcing the human along with me. Trying with all that I had to get him out of this nightmare in one piece.

Seconds away from reaching the back door, something big and heavy slammed into me. The powerful blow tore us apart, and I cried out as the bulky object flattened me to the floor. Despite the pain flaring up my back, I shoved it off me and struggled into a sitting position. A freaking sunglasses display stand now lay tipped over beside me.

Seriously? Someone threw a *display stand* at me?

I quickly found the fallen employee and crawled toward him, noting his injuries. A nasty gash on his forehead caught my attention, and I was suddenly unable to move. Completely frozen as I keenly watched a drop of his blood splash against the yellow linoleum.

No, no, *no*.

Every muscle in my body locked up as wave after wave of need pounded through me.

Just one taste, just one taste.

NO.

I gritted my teeth as my gums began to burn, but my fangs descended anyway. Panting, I forced one arm forward, then the other, tearing my eyes from the guy's blood. The seconds it took to reach him felt like hours. My entire body shook from the strain, but I managed to keep my gaze glued to his pale face as I said, "We need to go. Now."

He recoiled from my touch, scrambling back a few feet in horror. "Y-your teeth. What . . . what are you?"

Freaking *fates*, we didn't have time for this right now. If only I could thrall him.

Wait. That was it!

"Don't be afraid," I told him, infusing the words with all the calm persuasion I could muster. "Don't. Be. Afraid."

At first, I didn't think it worked. Cursing myself for wasting time we didn't have, I reached for his arm, prepared to pick him up if I had to. But then I noticed the stark fear bleed from his eyes. A second later, his face relaxed.

Holy crap, did I actually just thrall a human?

Shoving down my surprise, I hauled him to his feet, relieved when he came willingly. We were inches from the door. *Inches.* When a bone-chilling *hiss* halted us in our tracks.

"I can smell you, Syphon," a male voice hummed from near the entrance. "You and the human you're so pathetically trying to save. Continue to run and you'll make the chase that much more exciting."

At the vampire's dark laughter, I ducked behind an aisle, yanking the employee down when all he did was stare in confusion. Crap, maybe thralling away his fear hadn't been such a brilliant idea.

"Stay," I breathed, looking him hard in the eye. He nodded woodenly, which was good enough for me. Creeping to the end of the aisle, I listened before poking my head out. When all I found was the broken display case and nothing else, I quickly shoved up my sleeve and willed my claws to extend. The moment they did, I dragged one across my wrist. Wincing at the sharp bite of pain, I let my blood dribble to the linoleum.

Seconds later, a frenzied growl rattled the shelves. I leapt back, forcing my terror down as I heard the vampire approaching fast. Pressing myself against the shelves, I waited, willing my frantic heartbeats to slow. Just like I'd hoped, the vampire went straight for my spilled blood as if unable to stop himself. The moment he crouched to dip his fingers into it, I pounced.

Without hesitation, I went for the jugular, knowing that my life wasn't the only one in danger. My hands snaked around his neck and I dug my claws in. Red fire immediately engulfed our joined skin as I let my power burst forth. The rogue bellowed in agony, dragging me down with him as he dropped to his knees. I clung to him, wholly focused on draining his life force as quickly as possible.

Which was why I didn't see the blow coming.

I must have lost consciousness for a moment, because when my vision cleared, my arms were jacked up behind me and there were now two vampires. The new one held me tightly, keeping well away from my skin. My latest victim had recovered enough from my attack to once again stand. He was glowering down at me. The moment our eyes met, he whipped his claws out, catching my cheek.

The sharp sting drew a gasp from me. With a gloating smirk, he brought the black claws to his mouth and slowly licked them. Licked my blood, which was now sliding down my face. A rumble of pleasure sounded in his chest as he eyed my cheek greedily.

Moments later, his nose wrinkled, like he'd tasted something sour. "She's recently been claimed. I can taste his scent on her." He reached for my cheek anyway, even as his upper lip pulled back in a grimace.

"Careful, Bones," the one holding me warned. "Dani will have our heads if we rough her up too much."

"Dani is busy with the prince," Bones said, but dropped his arm. "She doesn't have to know that we decided to have a little fun. Besides, the witch tried to kill me."

My captor grunted. "What did you have in mind?"

At Bones' Cheshire cat grin, dread trickled through me. In a flash, he turned and grabbed the gas station employee.

I fought to get free, snapping, "Don't hurt him."

Bones crouched to my level, dragging the complacent human down with him. "Oh, I'm not going to hurt him. That wouldn't be nearly as fun—" his grin turned downright evil "—as watching *you* do it."

I recoiled, not understanding his meaning.

He slid into my personal space, pulling the employee with him. "A vampire can always spot the signs, you see. Dilated pupils. Distended neck tendons. Cold sweats. Fixation." His voice lowered an octave, to a croon I knew all too well. "You want to feed on him. You desperately crave his blood."

Every muscle in my body locked in horror. He was using thrall on me. I could feel his words sliding beneath my skin, urging me to listen. To *obey*.

"Take it," Bones purred, tugging the human's head back to expose his neck. "Take it *all*."

No!

I clamped my trembling lips shut, but I already knew. Knew that I didn't have the strength to resist. It had been too long. Too long since I'd last consumed Lochlan's blood. I had no defense against the thrall, no way to stop myself from leaning forward and placing my mouth on the human's vulnerable neck.

Yes, my instincts sighed, showing me exactly what they wanted by lengthening my fangs even more. I squeezed my eyes shut, tears sliding down my cheeks as I fought with myself. *You don't want this. You don't want this!*

I choked back a sob, shaking from head to toe as I felt my jaw tense. As the tips of my fangs puncture his skin.

NO! I inwardly railed at myself, all while knowing that the fight was hopeless. I was going to drink this human's blood. I was going to drink it, and I was going to like it. No, *love* it. And I wasn't going to stop.

The deeper my fangs sank, the more my resistance faded. Until all I could think about was my *need, need, need* for blood.

The fight was over. I was a slave to my cravings.

I opened my mouth wider and—

Glass violently exploded as something huge crashed through the store front. The sound ripped me from the bloodlust fogging my brain. I jerked back, bashing in the nose of my captor. As he howled in pain, I yanked my arms free and shot to my feet. Lunging at a startled Bones, I did the only thing I could think of.

I grabbed his head and twisted. Twisted *hard*. Cracking his neck. *Breaking* it.

Fates, that *sound*. The feel of his bones shifting beneath my hands and the light leaving his eyes.

My instincts screamed something new now.

Run. Run away before I could do any more damage. Run, before I could *kill* again.

Stumbling over Bones' lifeless body, I managed to snag the employee's shirt and yank him up. Somehow, I pulled us through the back door, navigating the length of a short alley before turning to face him.

"I-I'm sorry," I stammered, trying not to look at his neck. At the thin trail of blood there. Forcing my eyes to his, I used my newfound ability on him, hoping he recovered from this ordeal better than I would. "I want you to forget about everything that just happened. Don't come back here until the sun is out. Now run. Run until you find people. Lots of them. Only then will you be safe."

He immediately took off running, but I didn't have time to feel relieved. The back door of the gas station banged open and I propelled my feet forward again, making sure to head in a different direction than the employee. The asphalt soon gave way to sludgy snow as I veered into the woods behind the building at vampire speed.

I didn't for a second fool myself into believing I could outrun a full-fledged vampire, but I didn't know what else to do. Everett probably still had his hands full—if the rogues hadn't incapacitated him already—and I didn't want to hurt anyone else. But even if I did manage to evade my pursuers, I couldn't run forever. They would eventually catch up when my strength failed.

I desperately needed food and sleep. And blood, despite how utterly terrified I was of it right now. Of how it could make me do terrible things.

I made it maybe a mile into the woods when my sensitive ears picked up a sound other than my ragged breathing. Straining to hear it better, I didn't notice the tree in time. I veered sideways to avoid a head-on collision, smacking my shoulder against the trunk instead. Pain shot down my arm and I clenched my teeth to keep from crying out.

Before I could pick up the pace again, a familiar whooshing sound froze me in place. I pressed my back to the tree and stopped breathing, staring wide-eyed all around me. But even with my temporary night vision, I didn't see it coming in time.

There was a blur of movement, then crippling agony as my arm snapped in two.

CHAPTER 5

KENNA

My scream was deafening.

It tore from my throat, echoing through the trees as I curled forward to protect my broken arm.

I caught the whooshing noise over my keening howls, but I was once again too late to react. A forearm slammed into my throat, silencing my screams and knocking my head back against the tree.

As more pain ratcheted through me, threatening to steal my consciousness, a voice growled in my ear, "That was for Bones. Be glad you didn't permanently kill him or I would have broken more than your arm."

The pressure on my throat completely cut off my air and darkness quickly rushed in. I reached for him with my good arm, desperate to find his skin, but the pressure was too much. My limbs went numb and I felt myself falling. Falling into darkness where I couldn't escape.

He let me go and I fell hard, crumpling to the snow face first. The wetness jolted some sense into me and I dragged air into my starving lungs before I could pass out. Dazed and confused, I lifted my head in time to see my attacker pelted by several throwing knives. His body violently jerked and he stumbled back.

As he went down, a dark figure wielding what looked like a sword rushed toward him. In a flash, he slashed the blade through the vampire's neck. The severed head tumbled to the snow, quickly followed by the body.

A feminine screech of rage suddenly ricocheted off the trees. Before I could move an inch, the rogue female with the burgundy trench coat blurred toward me. I saw fangs and claws and flashing red eyes full of fury. She was inches away from reaching me, and I just stared like an idiot. Stared while her claw-tipped fingers came closer and closer. Close enough to grab me and whisk me away.

She was about to do just that when another dark figure jetted in from the side and knocked her clean off her feet. She flew through the air several yards, striking a tree with a sickening crunch. Everett crouched low in front of me, *protecting* me, hissing when the female vampire groaned and struggled to rise. Before she could, a third figure rushed in and pinned her to the tree.

"Don't kill her," Everett said, straightening to his full height. "She has information we need."

When the hulking figure with the sword approached me, Everett immediately blocked them with a warning growl.

My breath hitched as a sharp stab of anger suddenly pierced my chest.

"She's injured. Let me pass," a deep voice rumbled, and the hulking figure pushed toward me once more. At the sound of his voice, a ball of emotion lodged in my throat.

"Kade," I choked out, blindly reaching for him with my good arm as tears blurred my vision.

He was immediately there, enveloping me in his strong arms. I leaned into him, instantly comforted by his familiar scent. "I'm so sorry, little Kenna," he said, sucking air through his teeth when he saw my broken arm. Guilt tugged at me. The unexpected emotion made me gasp in surprise.

"Kade..."

More guilt.

"I should have gotten to you sooner. I should have stopped him from hurting you."

"Kade."

"I can make the pain go away, Kenna. I can—"

"*Kade.*"

He pulled back to look at me, clearly worried. "What's wrong? Did something else happen? What—?"

"I can feel you," I said. My chin wobbled when understanding slowly dawned on his face. "Your emotions. I can . . . I can feel them."

Shock coursed through him for several moments. Then he ducked his head and inhaled my scent. Straightening with a jerk, he blinked at me in stunned silence. "You completed the bond?"

I nodded, allowing my tears to fall as joy—*his* joy—swelled in my chest.

"He claimed you," Kade whispered, his voice cracking with emotion. He huffed a laugh. "He finally claimed you."

"He *what?*"

"Troy, watch it!" Everett barked, startling me. With a sharp *whoosh*, he zipped forward at lightning speed. Despite how quickly he burst into action, the escaped female rogue managed to evade his grasp. She took off, so fast that I blinked and she was gone.

Kade suddenly lunged to his feet. He drew me against him, his sword firmly in hand as Lochlan's younger brother stalked toward us.

"Stand down, Feltore," Troy hissed, looking angrier than I'd ever seen him. "She isn't yours."

"You're right," Kade replied, his voice lined with steel. "But I swore to protect her if Loch wasn't able to, so stay back."

When Troy bared his fangs, Kade angled his sword toward him

in preparation for a fight.

"*Enough*," Everett snapped, coming between the two. "Kenna is under *my* protection until we get Loch back. We still don't know who betrayed us last night."

From under his baseball cap, Troy's eyes glittered dangerously. But at his brother's words, he grunted and raised his hands in acquiescence. "Hey, don't look at me. I'm just along for the ride."

"A ride I distinctly remember not inviting you to," Everett said with narrowed eyes. "How did you find us here anyway?"

Troy shrugged, his anger from seconds ago nowhere to be seen. "Tracked your phone. I would have found you sooner but the *drothen* wouldn't stop tailing me. I finally managed to ditch him, yet here we are," he finished with an eye roll.

"Yes, here we are. No closer to finding out who the rogue leader is because you let the female *escape*," Everett growled.

Troy's mouth tightened. "I was caught off guard by the drothen's words. The rogue took advantage."

"But she was a *Feltore*," Everett hissed. "A wounded one at that. There's no excuse."

"And there's no excuse for you taking off without me," Troy hissed right back, getting in his brother's face. "What about 'brothers stick together' and all that bull?"

"I already told you. We have a traitor in the castle who laced our drinks. I'm assuming they also tipped off the SCA. Until we find out who that is . . ."

Their fighting became too much. I wanted to scream at them to stop. To focus on the here and now. My freaking arm was broken, not to mention I was still starving. The combination stole my breath away, leaving me weak and trembling. I bit my lip to keep from whimpering, from giving away just how miserable I was.

But there was no hiding my pain from Kade.

"Stop. Both of you *stop*," he commanded. "None of that matters right now. Kenna's arm is badly broken and needs to be fixed."

I gulped when both brothers stopped arguing to look at me, as if noticing my injury for the first time.

"Don't expect *me* to help her," Troy drawled. "Unless I'm allowed to thrall her, she won't be going anywhere near my skin, let alone my blood."

"What?" I squeaked, my mouth drying. "I'm not drinking anyone's blood."

"It's the fastest way to fix your broken arm," Kade said, gentling his tone when I threw him a panicked look. "Vampire blood has healing properties, remember?"

"But . . . but I can't. Just take me to a hospital."

"Too risky," Everett said, stepping toward me with purpose. "We can't expose ourselves to that many humans, and you're not entering a hospital alone. I wouldn't put it past the rogues to stake another ambush." Clenching his jaw, he yanked up his shirt sleeve. "Here. Take mine."

"*Ever!*" Troy bellowed, making a grab for his brother. When Everett dodged the attempt, Troy completely lost it. "Are you *insane?* She's already gotten under Loch's skin. I can smell his claim on her from here, that fool bastard. She obviously won't stop until we're all under her control. Don't give *in*, brother."

"This isn't about me," Everett said in clipped tones. "This is about saving our kingdom, no matter the cost. Kenna may be a witch, but she's also the key to unlocking our curse. It's time you accept that before it's too late."

Troy reared back as if he'd been struck. He stared at his brother, stared as if he were a stranger. Slowly, his expression hardened. "This isn't like you. There's something you're not telling me. But I'm going to find out. And when I do . . ." His eyes locked with mine. At the unspoken promise in their depths, I shivered. In the next instant, he was gone.

Shaking his head with a sigh, Everett turned back to me. "Promise not to use your magic on me and you can have my blood. Break my trust and I'll make sure you regret it."

Trust.

I gawked at him like he'd grown three heads. Never in a million years did I think he'd utter that word to me. Maybe I'd misjudged him after all. Still, I could tell by the lines bracketing his mouth that he didn't want to do this. He may be willing to help me for the sake of his people, but Everett D'angelo most *definitely* did not want me sucking on his arm.

Which was why I found myself blurting, "Thanks, but I'd rather have Kade's blood."

The second the words were out, I wanted to take them back. But it was too late. Kade was already turning toward me.

"You sure?" he said, studying me carefully—and probably feeling my mini panic attack.

"Y-yes," I stammered, avoiding eye contact. "If you are."

He placed his finger beneath my chin—his *bare* finger—and I quickly blocked my magic from hurting him. When he tipped my chin up the way Lochlan so often did, emotion tightened my throat. The moment our gazes met, he grinned crookedly and said, "It's only me, little Kenna. I won't bite."

I sputtered out a nervous laugh, flicking a pointed glance at the *fangs* peeking out from behind his lips.

His grin widened. "Not unless you want me to, that is."

A memory suddenly blindsided me, one of me kissing Lochlan's chest, of me sucking his nipple into my mouth. Of me *biting* him. And his reaction that followed. His unfettered desire and passion as he made love to me.

A muffled sob slipped past my control.

"Oh, Kenna," Kade miserably groaned. "Your pain is breaking my heart."

"I'm sorry," I whimpered, furiously blinking back tears. "I just miss him so badly. It hurts to breathe without him. And I'm just so—"

"Scared?" he finished for me. "So am I. We'll get him back though, I promise. But first, we need to get you better."

I inhaled a shuddering breath. Then another. Until I was able to nod and say, "Okay. So tell me how this is going to work." At his confused look, I blurted, "I won't bite you."

His expression cleared. "I would never ask that of you. I respect Loch too much. And you."

Everett shifted on his feet, reminding me of his presence. I cleared my throat, wishing we didn't have an audience. This was uncomfortable enough as it was.

But when Kade began to roll up his jacket sleeve, my focus locked solely on him. On the way his fangs sank into his forearm. My heart thundered as the unique smell of his blood saturated the air. A growl rumbled in my stomach, giving my hunger away.

"Drink your fill, Kenna," he said. "You won't hurt me."

Oh, Kade, if you only knew, I inwardly whispered, even as my eyes greedily tracked the blood trickling down his arm. If he only knew how badly I'd wanted to rip into that gas station employee. If he'd only seen how ruthlessly I'd drained a life and snapped a neck less than twenty-four hours ago.

I'd hurt people. I'd *killed*. To survive. To get closer to the one thing I desperately wanted more than anything.

My soulmate.

I'd kill again if I had to, I suddenly realized with perfect clarity. Yet here Kade was, placing his complete faith in me, like I could do no wrong. Like I was *innocent*.

"Please, Kenna," he urged, raising his arm to my lips. All but begging me to take his life force. "Do it for Loch."

For Loch.

My breath caught. I would do anything for him. Even this. But I couldn't do it on my own. Not when Kade was looking at me so trustingly.

I wanted to hide from that look. I didn't deserve it. Only good people who didn't have blood on their hands deserved a look like that.

I knew he must be feeling my guilt and shame. They were loud, drowning out my ability to move. To do anything other than helplessly stare at him. But, despite my inner turmoil, he gently grasped the nape of my neck and eased me forward. Placed my lips on his skin without an ounce of fear and coaxed me to drink.

I balked at first, refusing to open my mouth. But the second his blood touched my tongue, my reservations fell away. I gripped his arm tightly and sucked from the bite marks, sighing when his blood coated my raw throat. He stroked my hair, holding still as I slaked my thirst, letting me take what I needed.

His blood didn't sing in my veins like Lochlan's did. Nor make me crave him. But it satiated me, bringing me relief and slowly whisking the pain away.

When I was finished, Everett immediately stepped forward, saying, "Hold her still." As he reached for my broken arm, I cringed back with a hiss. He paused, pinning me with a hard stare. "The break is too severe. I need to set your arm before the bone heals wrong. With Kade's blood in your veins, you only have minutes."

"But . . . but there has to be another way," I pleaded, hiding my arm from view.

"The bone won't heal straight on its own. And you drank vampire blood. Thralling the pain away is no longer an option," he said, not bothering to sugarcoat it.

"That would have been nice to know *before* I drank Kade's blood," I grumbled under my breath. Not that I would ever willingly let either of them thrall me. I glanced up at Kade for help, but when his regret seared my chest, my hope crumbled.

"I'm sorry, Kenna," he said, drawing me into his arms. "It'll be over soon, I promise." When his hold tightened, panic flooded me. I struggled to break free, but his arms might as well be steel cables.

"I'm sorry," he repeated. Over and over as I begged him to let me go. As Everett grasped my broken arm and tugged sharply. I screamed into Kade's chest, the pain whipping through me like ropes of fire.

A presence suddenly surged up, eclipsing my pain and screams. He rose like a leviathan emerging from the ocean's depths, roaring to the surface in a gale of fury.

MCKENNA, my mate bellowed, thrashing inside my mind as if to reach me. To protect me. To free me from my pain.

Before I could cry out to him, before I could draw comfort from his warm presence, darkness dragged me into its cold embrace.

CHAPTER 6

LOCHLAN

When she slipped away from me in a haze of pain, helpless rage consumed every inch of my being.

The agony of not knowing what was happening to her—the pain she was going through and the forced separation—was too much. I couldn't bear it any longer. Couldn't bear not being able to do anything.

Unlike the last time I'd been abducted and subdued by silver, my pain meant nothing. It was insignificant in the face of McKenna's current agony. All I could think about was easing her pain, lending her what little strength I had so she wouldn't suffer. But our connection had broken once again. I'd lost my chance to aid her through our mate bond, and it was destroying me.

My helpless rage burned through my veins. Hotter and hotter until it practically *melted* the silver still pumping through me. All but disintegrating it.

When the muscles in my arms spasmed, obeying my commands for the first time in hours, hope surged through me. Hope that my boiling rage was actually freeing me of this bodily prison. With renewed vigor, I poured every ounce of concentration into regaining control of my limbs.

"He's waking!" someone shouted in alarm, which only made me fight harder. I had to break free before they could inject me again.

I had to get to her. Had to *protect* her. The need was visceral. A pounding chant inside my skull. An instinct more powerful than my need for blood.

Protect. Protect her. Protect my mate.

And with that chant thudding through my veins, my strength started to return. Roared through my blood until a bellow of fury rumbled up and out of my chest. My eyes shot open, right as a syringe loaded with liquid silver plunged toward my neck.

I clumsily knocked the syringe aside, my reflexes much slower than usual. Still, the human was slower, unable to evade my grip. When I yanked him toward me with a feral growl, the man's fear saturated the air. Along with the acrid stench of his urine.

"Containment breach. Deploy gas!" a female voice from nearby frantically yelled. As I whirled toward her with the man still in my grasp, she shrieked and quickly backpedaled toward a reinforced steel door. Reaching it, she pounded on the metal, shouting, "Let me out. Help me!"

I was behind her in an instant, wrapping an arm around her neck. The two humans fruitlessly struggled against me, no match even for my weakened state. I was about to speak when a *hiss* from above reached my ears.

The moment I looked up, pain seared my eyes. I squeezed them shut, only for a fine mist to rain down on my head. The droplets attacked every inch of my exposed skin, burning my shoulders, arms, and naked torso.

The pain drove me to my knees. Even as I roared in agony, I determinedly held onto the humans. The mist, no doubt infused with silver, continued to coat me, soaking through my pants until my entire body was a raging inferno.

The room filled with the stench of my scorched flesh. My skin sizzled, melting away, yet healing just as fast. The torture didn't let up for several long minutes, but neither did my grip on the humans. I shook from the strain, desperate not to pass out. Desperate to survive this fresh version of hell.

I had to survive at all costs. I had to survive for *her*.

No amount of pain was going to stop me from returning to her. No obstacle or living being was going to keep me from her.

I didn't care how monstrous I had to be. How evil or corrupt. Anything that stood in my way would know fear. Would cower at the sight of me. Without a shred of remorse, I pulled the woman close and growled in her ear, "Tell them to stop the gas or I'll drain you."

She violently shivered, choking out a sob when I allowed one of my fangs to nick her earlobe.

"*Do* it," I snarled, filling my voice with thrall as she hesitated.

When she continued to sob but didn't immediately obey my command, I bit out a curse. Of course she was protected from thrall. This was the SCA, after all. I should have known better. Changing tactics, I wrapped my fingers around the man's throat and squeezed. At the choking sound he made, the woman raised her hands in surrender. "Okay, okay! I'll make the call. Just don't hurt him."

I watched through hooded eyes, barely able to keep them open as she slowly removed a handheld radio from her jacket. Despite my best efforts, I was seconds away from losing consciousness. If the silver mist didn't let up soon, my desperate attempt at escape would end in failure.

My breathing grew labored, vision wavering as I heard her say into the radio, "Stop the gas." After another agonizing moment of nothing happening, I put pressure on the man's throat again. "For heaven's sake, stop the gas!" the woman shrieked into the device.

It worked. The mist switched off, followed by a loud voice over an intercom saying, "Release the operatives and step away from the door."

I barked a mirthless laugh. "Not happening. The only way these humans are getting out of here alive is if you open this door. And I'd suggest you do it soon before my patience runs out. One hostage is as effective as two."

The man whimpered, struggling to swallow around my grip. We waited in tense silence for several moments. Until, finally, a sharp buzz and click announced what I'd barely dared to hope for. I surged upward with the two humans in tow and grasped the door handle. With a hiss, I jerked my smoking hand back.

"Open it," I ordered the woman, who wisely scrambled to obey me this time.

The second we stepped outside the reinforced cell, a sea of masked operatives pointed their automatic weapons at us. I immediately released my shadows. They readily shot from me, billowing outward like a malevolent dark cloud. A few of the masked operatives flinched back at the show of powerful aggression, their weapons noticeably shaking.

"Here's what's going to happen," I said before any of them could attack. "I'm going to walk out of here and you're not going to stop me. Try and I'll kill anyone who stands in my way, starting with these two." The man I held whimpered again, trembling so badly that I had to support most of his weight.

No one moved. The tension thickened, until I was two seconds away from bursting into action. Before I could, a commanding voice said, "Everyone stand down."

I recognized that voice. One that made me bristle with fury.

Weapons lowered as a blond-haired, powerfully built man

shouldered his way past the masked operatives. The second his stormy blue eyes locked with mine, my lips peeled back in a silent snarl. He slowly raised his hands, showing that he was unarmed.

"I'm not here to shoot you," Sheriff Andrews said, the man who'd plugged a silver bullet into my heart—and who also happened to be Isla and Noah's father. "I'm here to make a deal."

That piqued my interest, a fact he seemed to realize. As a warlock, he would know that supernaturals often made deals to settle their disputes. I was surprised to see him here though. After our last encounter, I knew he worked with the mostly human-operated Supernatural Containment Agency, but I didn't know he was *in* the SCA. High in the ranks, too, by the looks of it.

"I'm listening," I said, warily eyeing his empty hands. Hands that could shoot deadly pulses of magic from them.

"You walk out of here free as a bird. None of our operatives will pursue you."

I squinted at him suspiciously. "And in return?"

"In return, you don't harm any of us. And," he said, lowering his hands to pin me with a probing look, "you tell me where my children are."

My suspicion grew. No mention of McKenna had been made. No deal to secure her under SCA custody once again. Still, I nodded and said, "I accept your deal." But I didn't release the humans in my grasp.

The sheriff's expression grew hopeful. "You know where they are?"

"I do," I offered, watching as his tough exterior disintegrated.

"Are they well? Are they—?"

"They're alive. And safe. But there have been . . . complications."

"What sort of complications?" Alarmed, he stepped toward me

and immediately halted when I growled a warning. He held up his hands again apologetically. "Whatever information you can give me, I'll gladly accept. It will have no ill bearing on our deal. I only care about the welfare of my son and daughter."

I flicked a glance at the masked operatives still loitering behind him. "What about them? Is that all they care about too? They went to great lengths to capture and contain me."

"The SCA's job is to contain supernatural threats, you know that," he replied, his stern sheriff persona sliding back into place. "But the problem has been taken care of. All we want now is the safe return of Isla and Noah Andrews."

An alarm rang through my skull. He was hiding something. Something that had to do with McKenna. The SCA had never dared infiltrate Sanctum Isle before. But that was before McKenna. Before they'd actively become involved in a Syphon's life.

Saving innocent people from the monsters of the world was the only thing they cared about. Breaking the vampire curse wasn't on their radar. I couldn't really blame them, though. Not when several Syphons over the past century had all died brutal deaths. Not when our violent behavior had driven them to form the SCA in the first place.

I knew they wanted McKenna back. And the fact that Sheriff Andrews hadn't mentioned her could only mean one thing.

They already had her.

"Where is she?" I bit out, the guttural words sounding anything but human.

The sheriff frowned. "Who?" he said, but I caught it. Among the dozens of other heartbeats, I caught the blip in his. The nearly imperceptible tell that told me all I needed to know.

"There will be no deal," I snarled, tightening my hold on the humans. "Not until you tell me where McKenna Belmont is."

Indecision clouded his expression as I gave him an impossible ultimatum—in his eyes, at least. I was asking him to choose her or his children. If he only knew. If he only knew that taking McKenna from me was the dumbest mistake imaginable. But he didn't know. Which was why he stupidly said, "I can't do that. I won't jeopardize Kenna's safety."

Internally, I howled. The pain of being separated from her—of not knowing where she was or who had her—was tearing me to shreds. But I masked my inner turmoil, reacting with a simple lip curl. "Then we're done here."

His nostrils flared. "You're making a huge mistake."

"The only one making a mistake here is you. You and anyone else who would dare take McKenna away from me." When I stepped forward, using my two hostages as a shield, a few operatives raised their weapons.

"Don't shoot," the sheriff ordered. "Not while he has Michael and Vivian."

As I inched forward, a path slowly cleared before me. Every muscle in my body was prepared to react if necessary, but no one fired. The building wasn't overly big or complicated. A few turns and hallways later, I found an elevator that brought us topside. No one stopped me. But I knew, as soon as I let my captives go, they wouldn't hesitate to shoot.

Sure enough, the second I exited the building and released the operatives, bullets and arrows and all manner of silver-tipped projectiles rained down on me from the rooftop above.

Not a single one touched me, though. I was already gone. A blur of shadows. Running faster than I'd ever run before in pursuit of my mate.

She was the only thing that could truly harm me. Losing her would more than kill my body. It would destroy my soul.

CHAPTER 7

KENNA

"McKenna," he whispered, stirring me awake. "Show me where you are."

I sighed, comforted by his voice, even if it was only in a dream.

"Open your eyes, solemae," he continued to whisper. "Show me what I need to see."

I did, briefly fluttering my eyes open. Then closed them, settling the image of what I saw behind my lids.

"I'm coming, love." The words started to fade, along with the dream. "I'm coming."

I awoke with a start to the scent of amber, sandalwood, and musk.

His scent.

Gasping, I jolted upright and frantically searched for him.

Across the room still draped in shadows, a dark form stirred. At the sight of blood red eyes, hope leapt inside my chest. Only to plummet a second later.

"Where is he?" I asked Kade, even as I knew, just *knew*, that I wouldn't like the answer. "I can smell him."

Kade's expression was unreadable as he approached the bed I'd been placed in sometime during the night. My gaze swept the large room, briefly taking in a black ornate loveseat and a wall of bookshelves.

"Where am I?" I said, panic tightening my throat. "Where is he,

Kade?"

When the mattress dipped under his weight, I forced my eyes to his again. Although his face was still unreadable, his emotions were coming through loud and clear. "They still have him, little Kenna. I'm sorry."

I shook my head in disbelief. "But I can *smell* him," I whispered, drawing my legs to my chest like a lost child. Both arms easily bent around my knees. The injured one was only slightly stiff and sore, the forearm wrapped in a makeshift cast.

"We're at the lake house in Rosewood," Kade explained, his voice heavy with apology. "This is Loch's room."

I glanced down at the silken sheets pooling at my feet. Sheets that smelled like him. Sheets that looked vaguely familiar. My heart sank.

He wasn't here.

And he wasn't coming for me.

Last night had only been a wishful dream.

As another smell teased my senses, I abruptly scrambled off the bed. "Why do I smell Lochlan's blood?"

"Uh . . ." Kade rose as well, avoiding my gaze as he rubbed the back of his neck. "I kind of performed heart surgery on him where you're currently standing not too long ago."

I jumped back with a stifled yelp. "Kade Carmichael, why didn't you *warn* me?" I hissed, only slightly relieved when I couldn't find a blood stain.

Before he could answer, the door slammed open and Everett's broad shoulders filled the frame. He thoroughly scanned every inch of the room, including me. Kade rolled his eyes, but Everett ignored him. Apparently satisfied with what he found, he leaned against the door and crossed his arms. "You're up. Good. Get dressed and eat something. It's almost dawn. We need to head out."

Troy poked his head through the door, but when no threat revealed itself, he left just as quickly. An improvement over last night, at least.

"Um, I don't exactly have a change of clothes," I said, realizing that my coat and boots were gone. At least my top and jeans were still on, albeit ripped and soiled.

Everett uncrossed his arms to twist the gold and ruby ring around his pinky finger. "We picked up a few things along the way last night. There's clothing for you on top of the dresser. When you're dressed, Kade will show you to the kitchen." With that, he backed out of the room, quietly closing the door behind him.

I blinked at the spot where he'd been, listening to the sound of his retreating footsteps before turning to Kade. His shocked expression mirrored my own.

"Did he sound almost . . ." I started.

"Friendly?" Kade finished.

We stared at each other for a moment, then simultaneously snorted. Everett and friendly in the same sentence didn't compute.

"Did I hit my head last night? That would explain the confusion."

Kade cracked a small smile. "Nah, I caught you when you passed out." A second later, his smile faded. "Does Everett know about the . . . ?"

The soulmate bond, I instinctively knew he wanted to say, but didn't. I nervously fiddled with the hem of my shirt before nodding.

Kade swore softly. "Well, that explains why he's protecting you instead of killing you. They're rare and extremely sacred among supernaturals—even if they're unconventional, like yours and Loch's. Everett has always been a traditionalist. His belief in the old ways should keep him in check."

"What about Troy and his father? Will he tell them?"

"Not if he thinks it'll do more harm than good. The D'angelo brothers made a pact to protect each other a long time ago. They don't often keep secrets from one another, but they'll keep things from Ambrose on occasion."

That didn't give me much comfort. If Everett was the rule-follower type, then keeping the soulmate bond a secret from his family probably didn't sit well with him.

As I turned toward the dresser to inspect the clothing left for me, Kade haltingly said, "Are we okay? After what happened last night?"

Instead of answering right away, I tugged my shirt off, careful of my cast. I heard him shuffle around to give me more privacy, which I was grateful for. "We're okay. My broken arm would have only slowed us down. You were right to fix it the way you did."

"And drinking my blood? You're still okay with that?" When I reached for a soft gray sweater exactly my size without replying, he sighed. "The bond goes both ways, Kenna. I know you're upset about something."

I paused, then hurriedly slipped on the sweater. "I'm fine. No need to worry."

"Kenna," he groaned, yet kept his distance while I finished changing. "If you're mad at me about something, please tell me. I can't stand not knowing—"

"I'm not mad," I rushed to say, willing my voice not to shake. "This isn't about you or your blood, I promise. I just . . . I don't want to talk about it right now, okay?"

His concern came through our fledgling bond loud and clear, but I did my best to ignore it. I wasn't ready to face the things I'd done, or the person I was becoming. And I definitely wasn't ready to feel Kade's disappointment when he knew the truth about who I was.

The second I finished buttoning a pair of ripped dark-washed jeans, I felt his warmth at my back. "Okay," he said, gently squeezing my shoulder. "But could I at least give you a hug? Because—"

I didn't let him finish, already whirling around to bury my face in his chest. Tears clogged my throat when he folded me into one of his signature bear hugs. He didn't press me further. He was simply there for me, like he was for Lochlan. Offering comfort without question.

"Thank you," I whispered, hoping he knew just how much I appreciated him.

He kissed the top of my head, replying with a simple, "Anytime." I relaxed against him. He knew.

Less than twenty minutes later, we were on our way to the meetup point, all four of us crammed into Everett's Volvo. They all carried various weapons hidden beneath their clothing. Kade had his sword strapped to his back like a freaking Samurai warrior.

"So do we have a plan or are we just winging it?" I said when the silence became unbearable. There'd *better* be a plan. I was so not cool with Tess calling all the shots.

"Troy and Kade will be our lookout from the woods," Everett replied from the driver's seat. "The second they spot Loch, they'll get him to safety."

The tension along my shoulders eased a bit. "And me? What should I do?"

"Be the good little hostage and keep your mouth shut," Troy drawled from the passenger's seat. Kade bristled beside me, but when I shook my head at him, he kept silent.

"You'll act as my hostage," Everett affirmed. "If we can draw out your fake aunt from the house's protective wards, then we'll have the upper hand. But if she refuses to come out, you might have to go in."

As my heart gave a nervous flutter, Kade dropped an arm over my shoulders to pull me close.

"I'm not completely helpless, you know," I said after a moment. "If the only option is to turn myself in so Lochlan can go free, I can fight my way out again."

Troy snorted. "Says the girl who got her arm broken and was nearly kidnapped by rogues."

"I was exhausted and outnumbered then," I snapped, suddenly done with his snarkiness. "I'm ready this time."

"And you think they aren't?" He drew his hat low over his eyes as if to take a nap. "It's the SCA we're dealing with now. They won't pass up a chance to take out the Demonic Trinity. Mark my words. The house will be crawling with operatives. We'll be lucky if Loch isn't already dead."

Those final words were like a bullet to the heart. They shattered the last of my calm and I lunged at him with a feral growl. Kade caught me mid-lunge, restraining my grasping fingers now tipped in claws. Struggling to break free, I roared, "He's not dead! Take that back!"

Troy turned in his seat to coolly assess me. "How do you know he's not dead?"

I silently cursed my outburst, uttering a lame, "I just do."

Suspicion darkened his hazel eyes before he faced forward again. "Crazy witch."

Everett slammed on the brakes, so hard that Troy's head struck the dash. Cursing, he tore off his hat as blood gushed from his forehead.

"What was *that* for?" he growled at his brother, wiping the blood on his sleeve. Within seconds, the gash was already halfway sealed.

"Time to get out," Everett smoothly said, even as his grip tightened on the steering wheel. Troy swore again, but exited the car without comment. Before he could slam the door shut, Everett called after him, "Follow the plan, Troy. The fate of our kingdom is at stake."

He nodded sharply and took off into the woods. Kade was slower to go, turning his hold on me into a hug. "No heroics, little Kenna. We'll get both you and Loch out of there one way or another."

I fiercely hugged him back, recalling the last time we'd attempted to rescue someone. How she'd ended up dead. How the grief of losing my best friend had torn me apart.

That couldn't happen again. I wouldn't survive it this time. Not if my soulmate was the one to die.

When Kade was gone, leaving only me and Everett in the car, I closed my eyes and focused on the presence warming my chest. As long as the flame burned steadily within me, I knew Lochlan was still alive. Wishing I could curl up inside the warmth, I inwardly reached for it. The flame responded to my attention. Growing stronger. More alert. As if suddenly aware of my presence.

Lochlan? I called into the void inside my mind.

The flame flared bright, making my heart flutter erratically.

When he responded back, breathing my name like a prayer, I combusted with joy.

. . . coming, he said, his voice oddly distant. Muted. *Stay where . . . are.*

I mentally frowned in confusion. *What?* Silence. *Lochlan, listen to me. We're coming for you. We made a deal with Tess and will be at the house in a few minutes. Just hold—*

No, he abruptly said, his voice coming through loud and clear. *McKenna, stop. Stop what you're doing right now. I'm not there, do you hear me? Whatever you're walking into, it's a trap. Get out of there. I'm already on my way to you. I should be there in about—*

"We're here," Everett said, jarring my eyes open when he lightly shook my shoulder.

No, no, *no!*

I slammed my eyes shut and desperately tried to reconnect with Lochlan, to confirm his words, but Everett spoke again and broke my concentration.

"Your fake aunt didn't come alone, just as we thought. I can detect several heartbeats fanned out across the property's perimeter. I can't tell how many are in the house though, or which heartbeat is Loch's."

We were parked at the end of the long, gravel driveway near the mailbox. The only other visible car was Tess's, parked in front of the rickety white house. Maybe she thought we wouldn't be able to detect the operatives hiding in the woods. Or maybe she didn't care. Either way, I was doubly glad that Kade and Troy were here. If everything went south, we still might have a fighting chance to escape.

"When we're out there, follow my lead. I'll only hand you over to her as a last resort," Everett said, tucking a black handgun into the waistband of his jeans. The sun barely brightened the sky, but I could still clearly see the seafoam green of his eyes as he turned to study me. "You ready for this?"

Before he could see more than I wanted him to, I replied, "Ready." Then I was out the door.

Everett quickly joined me, rounding the car to grasp my upper arm. I let him lead me down the gravel drive, taking a moment to stretch out my heightened senses. There were definitely several humans hidden in the trees. I couldn't see them, but my ears picked up the slight shifting of weapons. I could also smell them, their rich, warm blood a temptation I refused to acknowledge.

The closer we got to the house, the more my resolve hardened.

I marched forward with purpose, taking the lead in my haste to get this over with.

"There's at least one life form inside the house," Everett muttered under his breath. "Probably your fake aunt. I haven't detected Loch's presence yet."

I remained silent.

When we reached the porch, flashes of memory hit me. Watching Everett kill August. Dragging Isla up the stairs to safety. Seeing Lochlan afraid when Everett gripped my throat. But the strongest memory was of the woman who'd pretended to be my aunt. Of her rushing from the house in an attempt to stab my soulmate. Of her bashing me over the head, all so she could "protect" me.

Those memories fueled me. Drove me up the stairs and across the porch to stand in front of the door to my childhood home. I didn't wait for Everett to take the lead. I raised my hand and knocked.

The door immediately swung open, revealing a pale, brown-eyed, red-haired woman. The woman who'd taken me in after my parents' death. The woman who'd read me bedtime stories as a child. The woman who'd dashed my dreams every time she'd forced me to move and leave everything behind. The woman who'd *lied* to me my entire life. Who now posed a threat to everything I cared about. To everything I *loved*.

Quick as a snake, I grabbed the gun from Everett's waistband and shoved him back. In the next breath, I stepped over the door's threshold and pointed the gun at the woman, murmuring, "Hello, Aunt Tess."

CHAPTER 8

KENNA

I'd moved too swiftly. Too unexpectedly.

Neither of them were prepared.

Everett flung himself at the door, only for the magical wards to thrust him back. He staggered to the edge of the porch, but caught himself from tumbling down the stairs. Surging forward again, he halted a mere inch from the wards. "Kenna, get out of there *now*," he barked, a note of desperation in his voice.

I shook my head, tightening my grip on the gun. "No. This has to end."

"We don't even know where Loch is yet. He could be—"

"He's not here."

At my decisive words, I received twin looks of shock. Tess was the first to find her voice. "Kenna, put the gun down. You've been brainwashed with vampire thrall, but you're safe now. Those filthy creatures can't touch you in here."

"I'm not brainwashed," I countered, holding the gun steady. "The only one who's ever brainwashed me is you, into believing a lie."

Her surprised look quickly turned to one of disapproval, a look I knew all too well. "McKenna Joy Belmont," she snapped, straightening her short frame. "I'm your legal guardian. You will not speak to me that—"

"But you're not my aunt."

The words were barely a whisper, but I knew she heard them. "What did you say?" she sputtered, blinking rapidly. "Of *course* I'm your aunt. Why would you—?"

"Stop *lying*," I yelled. Her mouth snapped shut with an audible click. "You're an SCA operative, nothing more. You covered up the murder of my parents and pretended to be my family. You made me believe that you cared about my safety, but all you've done is use me as *bait* so you can kill off any supernatural being you deem a threat."

She'd never looked more stunned. When she didn't respond, some of my resolve wavered.

"Did you *ever* care about me?" I weakly asked, hating that I still cared, still hoped.

Her lips quivered. "Of course I did, Kenna. I still do. You're like a daughter to me. But . . ."

"But what? I'm less important than your *job?*" When she stepped toward me, I immediately leapt back, waving her away with the gun. "No! I need to say my piece for once. I was *devastated* when you ditched me at Thornecrest Academy. You didn't even call to speak to me on my birthday. Practically all the witches there either feared or hated me, and Headmistress Mayweather ended up being a freaking elder who wanted to make a deal with the vampire king."

She gasped at that last part, and I barked a mirthless laugh.

"Sucks to be kept in the dark, doesn't it? But you were the closest person I knew for *years*, Tess. The only family I had," I said, my voice cracking. "How could you throw me away like . . . like I was nothing?"

"I didn't throw you away, Kenna," she replied beseechingly. "I'd failed you as a guardian and thought you hated me for it. I was giving you space to become who you were meant to be."

"What, a *vampire* killer?" I spat, curling my lip to show her my distaste.

"For the sake of the entire human race, *yes*. Vampires need to be stopped, especially the Demonic Trinity. They've been terrorizing innocents for way too long. None of us are safe until those vile creatures are destroyed."

She was still defending her actions. Still painting every single vampire as a villain. And she wasn't going to stop, I realized. She wasn't going to see things differently unless she gave up her prejudice. Unless I somehow changed her perspective on good versus evil.

Without warning, I reversed my grip on the gun and held it out to her. "Then here. You can start by destroying me. I can turn into a wicked, vile creature after all." With that, I let my fangs descend and my claws lengthen to sharp, deadly points.

A strangled cry left her as she stared at my transformation in horror.

"Go ahead, Tess," I said, urging her to take the gun. "Go ahead before I drink all your blood and mutilate your body. I mean, that's what all vampires do, right? Even temporary ones. Oh, but make sure to kill Isla Andrews next. She'll probably want revenge after you kill her best friend. As a full-fledged vampire, she'll be overwhelmed with bloodlust and homicidal rage."

I carefully avoided looking at Everett as I said the words. I'd labeled him evil and cruel only a day ago. But he'd changed in that short time, proving that labels could be wrong.

Which was why I was here right now, risking everything when I didn't need to. When Lochlan wasn't even here.

Fate had given me a task, and I still had every intention of fulfilling it. But I couldn't save the vampires from their curse or stop the world from going to war if the woman before me kept trying to "protect" me.

So, for the sake of supernaturals and the entire human race, I told her everything. About the rogues and their plans to dominate humans. About the good I'd seen during my time with the vampires. That they weren't all mindless, bloodthirsty monsters. That most of them wanted to live quiet, peaceful lives.

She listened to every single word. Not once interrupting or shooting me down. I started to hope. Hope that maybe, just maybe, she was beginning to understand. That maybe—

"They killed your parents, you know," Tess said, destroying the impossible image I'd only just begun to build.

"Wh-who?" I stammered, letting the gun hang limply from my fingers.

She flicked a glance at Everett still outside the door. "Them. The princes."

My blood froze to ice. I stopped breathing, too busy envisioning the D'angelo brothers, envisioning *Lochlan* tearing apart my parents in my own front yard. Brutally killing them while a three-year-old me helplessly watched from the safety of the house.

No. He wouldn't do that. *Couldn't.* Maybe Everett and Troy, but Lochlan? Not my soulmate. My soulmate couldn't possibly do that to me.

Still, pain stabbed at my heart. The gun clattered to the floor as I rushed out the door.

"Kenna!" Tess shouted.

Ignoring her, I pushed past Everett and slumped over the porch railing. My meager breakfast threatened to reappear, but nothing came up.

"We didn't do it," I heard Everett say. His voice was distant, as if he stood on the other end of a long tunnel.

"Lies," Tess spat. "Sheriff Andrews' wife *saw* their mutilated bodies. When Bill returned to investigate not an hour later, the bodies were *gone*. We know it was you three. The Andrews saw you in the area before that day."

"I'm telling you, woman, it wasn't *us*," Everett snapped right back. I clutched the railing for dear life as another wave of nausea hit me. "Rogues discovered we were watching the house and ambushed the parents when we weren't looking. We never even saw their bodies. Only blood in the snow. We assumed Kenna had been killed too, only to discover years later that an SCA operative had taken her."

"Stop fighting," I groaned, but neither of them heard me. They continued to yell at each other, until I didn't know what to believe. All I knew was that I'd been lied to yet again. *Betrayed*. And it hurt like hell.

A deafening roar suddenly shuddered through me, the sound so raw and fierce that all the hair on my body stood on end. I knew that roar. Knew it with aching familiarity.

At first, I thought the sound was only in my head, his reaction to my pain through our bond. But then a powerful slew of emotions struck my chest. I staggered back with a gasp, wrenching my eyes open. Something at the end of the drive caught my attention. Something that nearly drove me to my knees.

A tall figure surrounded by billowing shadows.

There was no mistaking that form. No denying what my heart already knew.

Even from here, I could feel his gaze on me. Hot and blindingly intense.

My heart fluttered erratically in recognition, and the warmth inside my chest exploded. Until I wondered if my soul was visible to the world. Beaming like the brightest star as it beheld its mate. It strained to bridge the gap between us, like a hand urgently tugging at me from the inside.

Go. *Go!*

Unable, *unwilling* to deny my soul its greatest desire, I tripped down the stairs toward him. The second my feet hit the gravel drive at a dead run, he surged toward me in a swirl of shadows.

My eyes only saw him. My protector. My *home.*

Not the world around us, nor the people in it.

So when a shot fired, the sharp crack ripping through the air like a whip, I didn't react quickly enough. Lochlan, on the other hand, put on a burst of speed and slammed into me. The collision would have hurt had he not softened the blow by spinning us around, so fast that the breath was knocked out of me. Before I could recover, I was on the ground, bits of gravel digging into my palms.

Another furious roar shook the ground. Lochlan stood over me protectively, facing a row of approaching operatives. My heart stopped when I saw that their weapons were all trained on him.

"No," I whimpered, scrambling upright to throw myself at him. To create a shield between him and death.

"Hold your fire!" I heard Tess holler as I wrapped my arms around Lochlan's naked torso. He stiffened in shock. In *fear.* But only for a split second. Faster than I could blink, I was on the ground again, completely obscured by his shadows.

Panicking, I grabbed his leg and yanked, trying to knock him down. He didn't move an inch, so I did the only thing I could think of. Rolling away from him, I shot to my feet again and shouted, "Don't shoot!"

MCKENNA, his voice thundered in my mind, causing me to wince. He reached for me, but instead of sending me to the ground again, he pulled me against him. His claws dug into my hip bone, locking me in place.

"Let her go," Tess barked, and my eyes widened at the sound of a cocking gun. The gun I'd stupidly left for her to use.

Everett was suddenly there, knocking Tess's weapon aside as he arrived in a swirl of shadows. The weapon flew through the air and skidded across the gravel. Kade and Troy arrived just as quickly, streaking in from the woods.

The air filled with the sound of growls and clicking weapons as everyone prepared to attack.

Lochlan! I internally cried, desperate to stop this before it turned into a bloodbath.

But he couldn't hear me.

Protect my mate, his thoughts repeated over and over. He bared his fangs, ready to defend me. To unleash the Lochness Monster at the slightest threat. Kade, Everett, and Troy were equally focused, weapons at the ready.

But there were over two dozen combat-trained humans surrounding us, waiting for Tess's command to fire. And even though she looked torn, flicking her gaze from me to the vampires boxing me in, this stalemate wouldn't last much longer. Someone would make the first move and all hell would break loose, whether she gave the command or not.

So *I* made the first move, roaring as loudly as I could, "Everyone, STOP!"

My unexpected command worked better than I could have hoped. Every gaze shot to me. I gulped, but quickly plowed ahead before I lost my chance.

"We shouldn't be fighting each other," I said, loud enough for my voice to carry across the yard. "We should be fighting *together* against our common enemy, the rogues. Unless you're working with them." I shot Tess a probing look. "Unless they helped you infiltrate

Sanctum Isle."

Her eyes widened in genuine surprise. "Of course we're not working with them. I personally received an anonymous tip that led me to you. My only goal—*our* goal—was to extract you from danger by any means necessary. It's what we've always done to keep the supernatural world in check."

"Well, the rogues want nothing more than for the curse to become permanent. For all vampires to be exposed to the human population. But they don't plan on letting humans eradicate them. They plan on *defeating* them. On making vampires the rulers of this world and humans their subjugates. But I'm telling you now that the vampires with me today don't want that. They've been working to *stop* the rogues, even killing them when they've posed a threat to my life."

"And what's to stop them from killing *you?*" an operative said, jerking his chin at the four powerful vampires surrounding me.

I reached a hand up, pausing when Lochlan's gaze snapped to my fingers with preternatural focus. *I would never harm you*, I spoke to him in soothing tones, knowing the Lochness Monster was riding him hard. It might even see me as a threat. Still, he didn't move a muscle, didn't even flinch when I slowly placed my palm on his bare chest. On the rose tattoo directly over his heart.

"I could kill him right now," I said out loud, making sure everyone heard. "With one touch, I could bring him to his knees, destroying him from the inside out." Lochlan's eyes shifted to mine, continuing to silently watch me. "But I won't," I said, my voice slightly wavering. "Because he's not evil. Because I *love* him. And because . . . he's my soulmate."

Gasps and murmurs followed my confession, but I continued to hold Lochlan's stare. He still didn't utter a word, but the shadows whipping around us suddenly froze, as if stunned by what I'd said.

"Kenna?"

Reluctantly, I broke eye contact with Lochlan to acknowledge Tess, taking in her crestfallen expression.

"I know you didn't want this for me," I quietly said to her, a painful lump rising to my throat. "I know you were only trying to keep me safe the best you could. But I promise you he won't harm me." Her lips began to tremble. "I need you to know that this is *my* decision, not yours. I want to help the vampires break their curse. I want to stop humans and supernaturals from going to war. And I won't let you take my soulmate away from me again."

"Oh, Kenna," she whispered, so brokenly that a tear spilled down my cheek.

No one moved as she stared at me and I at her, both of us communicating what words couldn't. I'd never felt closer to her than I did in this moment, and my heart twisted in sorrow at all the lost opportunities. At what could have been, but probably never would.

"Let me go," I said to her. Now it was her tears that spilled. Tears she'd always kept locked away. Tears she'd never let me see. "*Please, Aunt Tess.*"

I knew this wouldn't be easy for her. Duty and her need to be my guardian were hardwired into her brain. I worried that she wouldn't be able to. That letting me walk away was beyond her capability. That we'd have no choice but to fight our way out, and casualties would be inevitable.

But she suddenly straightened. Suddenly wiped her tears away and said in a commanding voice, "Stand down. No one's in danger here."

For a terrible moment, the tension between both sides thickened. I stopped breathing, waiting for someone to disobey the order. To attack anyway. But when Kade slowly lowered his sword, several operatives followed suit, pointing their weapons at the ground.

I inhaled my first full breath since this all began and leaned against Lochlan, blowing out a relieved sigh.

"I'm taking McKenna somewhere safe," he abruptly announced to no one in particular.

Everett turned to thoroughly eye him up and down, as if searching for injury. After a long moment, he nodded. "Where?"

"Somewhere safe," was all he said. "No one is to follow us. Or look for us."

"Take the car," Kade said, nodding at Everett to give him the keys. "You know where to find us when you're done."

When I felt *amusement* coming from him, I threw Kade a questioning look. His knowing smirk was the last thing I saw before Lochlan swept me into his arms and whisked me away. I gasped as he picked up speed and practically flew to the car, tucking me inside and revving the engine in five seconds flat.

As the tires squealed and we shot down the road, I didn't interrupt the silence that settled between us. Instead, I focused on his emotions. They were a tangled mess, loud and intense. I soon became overwhelmed by them and tried to pull away. His hand shot toward me and captured mine. As if desperate to keep me close.

There were still things left unsaid between us. Important things. Scary things. But I wouldn't ruin this moment for the world. Wouldn't unravel the tentative control he had over his sanity. It was poised on the tip of a knife, and my only thought was to soothe him. Calm him. Bring him back to himself.

I slid my fingers between his and held on tight.

CHAPTER 9

LOCHLAN

I carried her inside the cabin, firmly closing and locking the door behind me.

She's safe. She's safe. She's safe, the rational part of my mind tried to reassure me.

The other part—the part that almost went wild with rage when someone had dared shoot a bullet in her direction—wasn't so easily convinced. She could have died. A slight miscalculation could have taken her from me forever. If that bullet had hit her, I would have unleashed the darkest parts of myself on those humans and damned the consequences.

Her mortality had never scared me more than in that moment. Even with our bond now complete, she was still vulnerable. Still little more than human. A soulmate bond couldn't change that. There were so many things that could hurt her, and my protective instincts were screaming at me to take her away from it all. To find someplace safe. So I did, putting everything else on hold. Putting the *world* on hold.

When she'd figured out where I was taking her, I heard her heart skip a beat. Felt the glow of her happiness warm my chest. My breath had caught. She was happy. Happy to be here with me. I still struggled to accept this impossible reality, to believe she *wanted* to be with me, even after all the hardships she'd endured. Was *still* enduring.

When she'd given herself to me two nights ago, mind, body, and soul, I'd never felt such peace. Such contentment. Knowing that she was undeniably, irrevocably mine. And I knew then that I'd give anything, do anything, *be* anything for her. She was the best part of me, the light that even now attempted to tame my darkness.

But I needed her *safe* first. Only then could I bask in her light and allow the beast to settle. Only then could I lower my guard and fully let her in.

As I stood in the entryway with her still in my arms, I could feel her poking around my scattered thoughts, trying to make sense of them. I continued to keep her at bay, only letting her hear what I wanted her to. Unwilling to lower my defenses until I was sure nothing could harm her.

I stood there for several minutes. Simply holding her. Convincing myself she was real. Listening for threats. Afraid the SCA had followed us.

And then she spoke.

Words meant to soothe. To calm. To comfort me.

"It's okay. I'm safe now. *We're* safe."

And just like that, I crumbled.

My back struck the door and I slid to the floor, still holding her tightly in my arms. Heaving breath after breath, I cradled her between my legs and fell apart.

CHAPTER 10

KENNA

He was groaning. Gasping. Coming undone completely.

And it thoroughly wrecked me.

I curled up against him and wept. Wept with relief and agony and joy. Because we were here. Together and safe. But he was broken. So utterly broken. I'd never seen him like this before and it crushed me.

What did they do to you? I whispered through our bond, too choked up to speak out loud.

Protect her. Safe. She's safe, were the only thoughts I could get from him. Everything else was muddled. Disjointed strings of consciousness with no beginning or end.

He dug his fingers into my hair and pressed my face to his chest. Held me there. Held me while I listened to his gasping breaths and the wild beating of his heart.

I didn't move or speak for several minutes, simply letting him hold me. Letting him slowly realize that we were both safe.

When his breaths and thundering pulse eventually evened out, he released my hair. Allowed me to lift my head and search his face. I nearly sobbed at the dry trail of tears staining both his cheeks.

Words failed me. I didn't think anything I said could fix this anyway.

So I touched him.

Slowly reached up and ran my thumb over his lips. Watching as they parted under the pressure.

Swallowing, I sent him an image. From my mind to his. Showing him what I desperately needed. What *he* desperately needed.

At first, I didn't think he received the message. That I'd misunderstood how our bond worked.

But his breath suddenly hitched and I found myself straddling his hips a second later. "McKenna," he softly groaned, dragging me closer. Closer. Until his forehead touched mine and I felt his hardness between my thighs.

I forgot how to breathe. Forgot everything as image after image burst into existence behind my lids. My face flushed scarlet as I realized what they were. Erotic images of us naked. *Doing* things to each other. Intimate acts. Some of which I didn't even have a name for.

Despite how foreign and shocking some of the images he sent me were, heat rushed to my core. I gasped, suddenly desperate to experience those things with him. Desperate to touch, to kiss, to feel every last inch of him. To have *all* of him.

"Please," I whimpered, my entire body trembling. When I punctuated the words by pressing my core into his erection, he took me.

Hot. Fast.

First my mouth, catching me completely unaware when he slid his tongue past my lips and kissed me like I'd never been kissed before. Greedily. Possessively. Desperately.

He kissed me as if afraid. Afraid that this moment—that *I*— could vanish in an instant. That now was all we had.

I whimpered again, tasting him as he tasted me. Clenching my fingers in his hair to keep from floating away. From letting my magic hurt him. I firmly reined it in. Tensing whenever it flared up. Shaking when I could barely remember my name, let alone how to control anything.

He took me soundly. As if the space between our bodies was an enemy trying to separate us and his only thought was on obliterating it. I matched whatever he gave, nipping at his lips. Licking them. Twining my tongue around his until he moaned my name. The sound sent fire curling up and down my body, peppering me with sweat. I let go of him to tear at my coat, promptly getting the zipper stuck.

When I hissed in frustration, he grabbed the material and ripped it apart. My sweater was next, shredded from me by his claws. I shivered, not from the cold but with excitement. With anticipation for what was to come.

His lips abruptly left mine as he cupped my backside and lifted me. My bare stomach slid up his, until my breasts were practically in his face. Apparently just where he wanted them, I realized, when he leaned forward and took my left nipple into his mouth. As his hot breath and wet tongue branded my skin, even through the thin fabric of my bra, I arched against him and groaned. He sucked and nipped at the sensitive nub until I was panting, begging him for more.

With a flick of his wrist, he undid my bra and tossed it aside. In the next instant, he closed his lips around my right nipple and bit down. *Hard.* I choked out a scream as pleasure-pain rocketed through me. As he left a trail of bite marks across both breasts, thoroughly claiming them. His teeth didn't break the skin, but I suddenly wanted them to, desperate for him to make me his again. To bury his scent beneath my skin and slake his thirst on my blood.

I sent him another image and a growl tore from his throat.

I don't know if I can be gentle, he spoke into my mind, his voice half feral.

"I don't want you to," I replied breathlessly, gripping his hair with both fists.

I just wanted *him*. Even if he was more predator than anything else right now. Even if he covered me in bite marks and bruises in his need to reassure himself that I was here. That I was his. That I wasn't going anywhere. I would gladly endure a little pain if it would make him feel safe again. If it would bring back the peace and contentment we'd both felt after completing the bond.

I bared my neck for him, full-body shivering when he trailed his nose over my breasts, then carved a path upward to the spot where he'd last bitten me. Sweeping my hair aside, he nuzzled my skin and deeply inhaled. When I felt the sharp points of his fangs, I stiffened, preparing myself for the pain.

He suddenly jerked back with a hiss. "I can't," he said, his voice low and gruff. "It's been too long since I last fed. I won't be able to stop."

"I'll stop you, Lochlan," I immediately reassured him, coaxing his head down again. "I promise you won't hurt me."

When he continued to hesitate, his arms noticeably trembling, I made my fingers loosen their deathgrip to gently massage his scalp.

You need this, I whispered through our bond. *So do I. Please, Lochlan. I'm safe with you.*

His breathing grew uneven as he struggled with indecision. But when I bared my neck to him even more without an ounce of fear or doubt, he blew out a curse and yanked me close. In the next second, his fangs were in my neck, sinking deep, deeper. As I shuddered against him, he gripped my hair and held me in place, rendering me immobile.

With any other vampire, fear would be coursing through me. But this was Lochlan. My soulmate. And what he was doing felt *right*. Natural. Like he and I were created for this very moment.

It didn't take long for his venom to spread through my body. I relaxed against him like the first time he'd bitten me, utterly overwhelmed by the euphoria pumping through my veins. But unlike last time, I wasn't going to let him pleasure only me. I knew he was about to, his hand on my backside slowly shifting me into a better position. But just as he reached between my legs, I sent him another image.

I felt his guttural groan to the tips of my toes.

He was suddenly standing, his fangs still buried in my neck as he set me on the entryway table. I was dimly aware of my back hitting the wall and a wall mirror crashing to the floor, but I couldn't concentrate on anything but his hands on my jeans. Unbuttoning them. Tugging on them. *Ripping* them.

As he tore the last of my clothing from my body, I was already swimming in a sea of ecstacy. Riding on the high of his venom. But when he spread my legs and swiftly thrust into me up to the hilt, I cried out, long and hard. I shook from the shock. From the pleasure-pain as he filled me completely.

When he began to move inside me, it wasn't slow and rhythmic like the first time. This was *nothing* like the first time. It was fast. And raw. Frantic. I tore at his back with my claws and gasped his name. He fed from my neck in greedy gulps, pounding into me without mercy.

I was all but hyperventilating, trembling like a leaf as we both sought release. As we openly shared our every thought and emotion, heightening each other's pleasure and deepening our bond even more. It felt like our very souls were entwined in a lover's embrace, joined together so perfectly that they became one entity. So complete that nothing could tear them apart.

It was only when I was on the edge, my pleasure almost impossible to bear, that he slowed. That he whispered through our bond, *Say it again, solemae. Say that you love me.* When all I did was pant, frantic for release, he slowly pulled out of me.

I clenched my thighs, desperate to keep him inside. "Please," I whimpered, completely at his mercy.

Say it, he persisted, circling his swollen tip around my slick entrance. *Say what I need to hear.*

"I love you," I breathlessly said, equally hating and loving those torturous circles. Again and again I said the words, giving him what he needed. Basking in the wonder and joy that sparked through our bond as I did.

He suddenly thrust into me, so hard and deep that I tipped my head back and screamed. Screamed as a powerful orgasm ripped through me, shredding me to pieces. He joined me seconds later, nearly crushing my rib cage as he withdrew his fangs from my neck and roared, shaking the very foundations of the earth.

The bubbles in the tub softly fizzed and popped, the only sound in the silence that had settled between us. After our frantic lovemaking, Lochlan had carried me upstairs and laid me in the bathtub, stepping in to pull me back against his chest.

The intimacy, the oneness we'd shared, seemed to have eased his fear. To allow him a semblance of peace, at last. His muscles had loosened, his mind no longer disjointed. His index finger was lazily playing with my hair, coiling and uncoiling the damp strands.

Content to simply lay in his arms and soak up his nearness, I once again checked that my magic was safely locked away. It was still an effort, a conscious thought I had to keep a firm hold of. I still worried about what would happen if I fell asleep while our skin was touching. But my desire not to hurt him was strong. It kept me vigilant. Alert to my every move. And his.

I watched as he carefully lifted my left arm from the water, touching the edge of my cast.

I almost stopped earlier when I saw this, he said through our bond, a simmer of concern disrupting our mutual contentment.

It doesn't hurt anymore, I quickly assured him, choosing to keep the silence between us by speaking mind-to-mind. Besides, I felt closer to him like this. Communicating with him in a way no one else could. When I started to pick at the cast, bent on removing it, Lochlan stilled my fingers. With the lightest touch imaginable, he slowly unwound the material. When it fell away, he brought my arm to his mouth and kissed it.

I shivered at the feel of his soft lips on my skin. *Kade helped heal the break,* I said, and he froze. After a moment, he tucked my arm close to my chest and pulled me more firmly against him.

Show me, he said, pressing his mouth to the spot where he'd bitten me. *Show me everything that happened while I was gone.*

I immediately balked at the thought of him seeing some of the terrible things that had happened to me. He'd only just calmed down. Witnessing the pain I went through was sure to rile up the Lochness Monster again.

Please, McKenna, he beseeched, his lips lightly grazing my neck. *I need to see. It's killing me not knowing what happened to you.*

You won't like it, I said, still loath to burst the peaceful bubble we were currently floating in.

I'll behave.

Surprised, I tipped back my head to glance at his face. *You mean the Lochness Monster will behave?*

The smallest of smiles curled the corners of his mouth. I openly stared, wholly captivated by the sight. *I promise he won't make an appearance*, Lochlan said. *Even if I have to add a few more people to my kill list.*

I blinked. *You have a kill list?*

His smile dimmed. *Yes. It's not as long as it used to be, but the rogue who first bit you is at the top.*

I grimaced, recalling the brutal way his fangs had torn into my flesh. *He didn't . . . leave his scent on me, did he?*

Lochlan's expression clouded even more. *He did. And he'll pay with his life for marking something that wasn't his.*

I didn't know whether to swoon at his possessiveness or laugh.

He must have felt my mixed emotions through our bond, because he narrowed his eyes at me suspiciously. *Do you find this amusing?*

I quickly sobered, biting my lip for good measure. *No. Maybe. I mean, I got super angry at the thought of you having a harem.* The blush returned. *So I get it. I might have wanted to hurt them too.*

When his cock suddenly hardened against my backside, my eyes flew wide. A chuckle rumbled in his chest, the vibration sending butterflies swooping through my stomach. "I like when you're jealous," he purred into my ear, finally breaking our silence.

"I can see that," I grumbled, wiggling my backside against his erection as payback. "Or feel it, more accurately."

He softly groaned and splayed his hand across my stomach, halting my movements. "Keep that up and I won't be able to stop myself from having my way with you."

At his words, my core throbbed, and I squeezed my aching thighs together. "Maybe I want you to," I teased, fighting back a grin when he growled. This open, easy banter was new for us. New and exciting. We'd rarely had a chance to be playful with each other in the past, and I never wanted it to end.

But his ability to avoid deflection defied all logic, because his next words were, "Oh, I will. I'll take you over and over until you can't walk straight. But I need you to show me first, McKenna. Show me everything you've been through."

My stomach swooped again, this time with nerves. I stared at the bubbles on the water's surface for a long moment, then slammed my eyes shut with a sigh.

I started at the very beginning, sending him an image of me on his bedroom floor at the castle. He shifted in the tub, tightening his grip on me, but his thoughts remained blank. When I showed him Everett leading me from the castle, several of his emotions flared through our bond. Alarm. Fear. Anger. Protectiveness. I laid my head on his shoulder, comforting him as best I could.

I spent the next several minutes replaying the last twenty-four hours in my mind, feeling each and every one of Lochlan's tumultuous reactions. True to his word though, he didn't hulk out once. Didn't even growl. I ran soothing circles up and down his arm when I showed him an image of me almost drowning. Nuzzled my cheek against his chest when he witnessed my arm break. When he saw me feed from Kade and had my bone reset by Everett. At the last second, I glossed over a few details from my short time inside the gas station, still unwilling to hash out those memories.

He didn't utter a sound the whole time, but I could practically hear his blood simmering. Seconds away from reaching boiling point. When I was finished, I waited in silence, letting him work through his emotions. They were loud, but his thoughts were quiet. Muted. Almost as if he was hiding them from me somehow.

Eventually, the tension ebbed from him and he said, "Thank you for showing me." Then, "Kade did the right thing by feeding you his blood." When I stiffened against him, he added more softly, "I felt your fear and guilt at showing me the memory. I'm not mad. I asked him to protect you and he did."

Panicking, I did what I did best and deflected the conversation. "Can you show me what you went through? I want to see."

When he paused, I cringed, expecting him to call me out again. Instead, he stood from the tub in one smooth motion, lifting me as well.

"There's not much to see," he said. "They kept me sedated the entire time. There was only pain and darkness. And an overwhelming desperation to get back to you. To protect you from whatever was hurting you."

My heart turned over for him, for the helplessness he must have felt. The powerlessness. No doubt a similar experience to his imprisonment at the hands of Edith. "I'm sorry," I whispered, shifting around to face him.

"Not as sorry as I am," he gruffly replied, gripping my waist to pull me close. When our bodies aligned in that perfect way, like two puzzle pieces made for each other, every inch of me tingled awake. Despite how recent we had sex, my libido was suddenly begging me for another round. The feeling crashed and burned a second later when Lochlan said, "Now, are you going to tell me what you're trying to hide?"

Feeling like a cornered rabbit, I sought my escape by reaching for a towel. He beat me to it, gently wrapping the fabric around my body, as if to torture the information out of me with tenderness.

"McKenna," he said, in that way of his that never failed to weaken my resolve.

I dropped my gaze, only to realize that he was still very much naked *and* sporting a massive erection. I swallowed with difficulty

90

and focused on the shower tiles instead, determined not to cave.

But when he slid his fingers beneath my chin and tipped my face up, I nearly came undone. I finally met his eyes, hopelessly drowning in their dark depths as his worry filled me. "What are you hiding from me, solemae?" he said in hushed tones, dipping his head toward mine.

My chin began to wobble and I finally gave in. I opened my mouth to tell him everything, but what came out was something else entirely. What came out shocked us both into stupefied silence.

"Who killed my parents?"

CHAPTER 11

KENNA

He was hiding his thoughts from me. I knew that for certain now.

I didn't know how he was doing it, but as I trailed him into the bedroom across the hall, I couldn't hear a single thought. His mind was white noise. Static. Not empty, but locked behind a door I couldn't walk through.

Now it was my turn to pursue *him*, openly watching the towel at his waist drop to the floor as he pulled a fresh pair of sweatpants from the dresser. I unapologetically ogled his perfect backside while he slipped on the sweats, possibly drooling a little at the sight.

Why did he have to look so freaking *sexy* all the time?

Focus, Kenna, I inwardly hissed at myself, realizing too late that Lochlan could hear. He didn't show any sign of hearing me though, too busy *hiding* from me.

Still wearing the towel he'd wrapped around me, I crossed my arms and said none-too-gently, "What is the point of our bond if you keep hiding things from me?"

Yeah, I was being a little bit two-faced right now, but I had every intention of telling him everything.

Eventually.

He didn't turn around, reaching up to rub the back of his neck. "McKenna," was all he said, then lapsed into silence again.

Hating that our peaceful bubble had popped, hating that *I* had done it, I took my anger out on him, snapping, "I thought you were done with secrets. I thought you *trusted* me."

"I *do*," he said, slamming his palms on the dresser to grip the edge. "I trust you more than anyone. Even Kade."

"Then *why?*" I cried, hurt that he was doing this. Afraid of the reason why. "Why are you hiding from me?"

He was suddenly in front of me, catching both my arms when I stumbled back in surprise. "Because fifteen years ago, I made a huge mistake," he said in a strained voice, shame coating each word.

As I stared at him, as I waited for him to continue, it became hard to breathe. Hard not to think the worst. And I must have thought those awful things. Must have projected them onto him. Because his face crumbled and he fell to his knees before me.

"No, love. No. I didn't kill your parents."

My vision blurred and I choked out a sob. I believed his words implicitly, but sorrow still clung to me. Because, for a split second, I'd dared to think that he'd killed them.

I joined him on the floor, hating that I still couldn't hear his thoughts. That the door was still firmly shut. "Then *what*, Lochlan?" I said, steeling myself for whatever he had to say. "What aren't you telling me?"

I waited, growing more anxious, more afraid with each passing second. What could he possibly be keeping a secret that was so awful? So terrible that guilt and shame were pouring off him in waves?

Then he said it.

Three little words.

Three words that had me staggering back in horror.

"I turned them."

Once again, he stopped me from tipping over backwards. When I shrugged off his touch, hurt filled his eyes. I immediately wanted to apologize, to make that hurt go away. But even more, I wanted to shout at him. To demand he explain himself.

Still avoiding his touch, I stammered, "I-I don't understand. You said you didn't kill them."

"I didn't. I found them at dawn the morning of your third birthday, completely bled dry. Probably by rogues. At first, I thought you'd been killed too. Or taken. But then I heard your little heartbeat, coming from inside the house's protective wards."

Overwhelmed with emotion, I wrapped my arms around myself, desperate to hold myself together. Desperate to hear more. To finally understand what had happened that day.

"I'd never found a Syphon so young before," he continued. "It was the first time in a century that I asked my brothers to wait. To let the child live with her parents a few more years. You were so innocent, and I couldn't bear the thought of you getting hurt. I'd never felt anything but numb detachment toward the other Syphons, but you . . . you were different. I was drawn to you in a way I couldn't explain, even then.

"Before I could secure your safety, a car pulled up. The sheriff's wife. I knew she'd been keeping an eye on you and thought she would take you then. But she left you inside the house, probably afraid vampires were still close by, waiting for you to emerge.

"I made a decision then to turn your parents. It was reckless. Impulsive. An instinct I couldn't ignore. But in doing so, I lost my chance to secure you. An SCA operative by the name of Tess Walker showed up shortly after and took you away. In the chaos that followed with my brothers' arrival, I lost sight of you.

"Ashamed of what I'd done, ashamed that I'd lost you, I lied to my brothers. They still don't know that I turned your parents, or that I knew you'd been taken by the SCA. Not even Kade knew right away. I spent fifteen years trying to find you again. Trying to fix my mistake."

He paused to swallow, his Adam's apple bobbing. I didn't utter a sound, in too much shock to speak. Even my thoughts were silent.

"So now you know my terrible secret," he said, barely able to look me in the eye. "I destroyed your childhood, and I've been too much of a coward to tell you. But I knew, once our bond was complete, that I couldn't hide from you any longer. My thoughts would betray me, which was why I didn't warn you about the telepathic link. I was selfishly hoping for more time before you realized what a despicable monster I was. Selfishly wanting your love when all I really deserved was your hate. And I can't forgive myself for it. For hurting you. And I don't expect you to forgive me either—"

"*Stop*," I cried, shaking my head in a vain attempt to clear it. "Please stop. I feel how much you loathe yourself for what you did, and I can't stand it. All I know is that my parents are *alive* because of you." Tears sprang to my eyes as the truth finally sank in. My parents were *alive*. "Where are they now? Can I see them?"

"That's just it. I don't know where they are. Not after I forbade them from looking for you. As their sire, they had little choice but to obey me."

I gaped at him. "But . . . but why?"

"Because the second they became vampires, they posed a threat to your safety. And I couldn't . . . I can't . . . The thought of them hurting you, even unintentionally . . ." He lowered his head, saying almost too softly for me to hear, "I'm sorry, McKenna. There's no excuse for what I did."

He lapsed into silence, but the door to his thoughts burst wide open.

She'll never forgive me. She shouldn't. I'm a monster. I wouldn't blame her if she ran away after this.

And I couldn't think. Couldn't separate my emotions from his. There was too much misery. Too much hatred. I didn't know if I felt that way, or if he did.

"I . . . I need a moment," I forced out, clutching the towel to my chest. "Please."

His expression shuttered, but I still felt his fear. I almost stopped him. Almost called him back as he slowly stood and made for the door. But I didn't, even when he paused to say over his shoulder, "I'll give you space to think. Take all the time you need."

When the door snicked shut, I let my tears fall. Except they wouldn't come. Neither did the anger I expected to feel.

I only felt hurt that he'd kept this from me. And sadness that he'd carried this burden for so long. That I'd lost all those years with my parents, even as vampires.

But as saddened as I was that he'd ordered them to stay away from me, I understood why he had. Two newly-turned vampires taking care of a Syphon child would have been a disaster. He also had the curse and his kingdom to think about. Allowing my parents to pursue me would have been dangerous for all of us.

It wasn't long before I stood and walked to the dresser. Pulling open a drawer, I removed one of his shirts and slipped it on with barely a thought. Like it was the most natural thing in the world to wear his clothes as if they were my own. Traces of his scent immediately soothed my nerves, and I was suddenly out the door in pursuit of him. I clambered down the stairs, sidestepping the mess in the entryway and barrelled past the living room.

I whipped around the corner and stopped dead in the kitchen doorway. Stopped and stared, my heart thudding like a jackhammer as I drank in my soulmate's slumped form at the breakfast table.

"You don't know me very well," I burst out, watching as he slowly raised his head, defeat etched across his beautiful face. I stepped into the room. "You don't know me if you believe that, even for a second, I'd think about running away from this."

Hope flickered through our bond, there and gone again in a blink, as if he'd willfully squashed it. His head lowered once more.

I marched forward, bare feet slapping the tiles as I crossed the room to stand in front of him. When he wouldn't look up, I grabbed his face and forced him to meet my eyes. "Minutes ago, I was an orphan. Now I know that, somewhere in the world, my parents are alive because of you. How could I possibly hate you for that? You *saved* them, Lochlan."

He searched my gaze for a moment, then gently grasped my wrists and pulled his face away. "Saved? More like cursed."

Frustration filled me. "Stop that. Stop punishing yourself. You made an impossible decision, and I can't fault you for wanting to protect me. I may have lost some time with them, but when the curse is broken, we can—" I gasped when he suddenly flipped his hand over and slashed open his right palm with an extended claw. "What are you *doing?*"

"Swearing an oath to you through a pactum. Promising to never keep you in the dark again," he quietly said, offering me his hand. "If you'll accept it."

I stared at his outstretched palm, at the blood pooling there. The scent of it reached me, reigniting my thirst. I swallowed with difficulty and shook my head. "You don't need to do that. I—"

"*Please*, McKenna. Let me do this for you."

I could tell how much this meant to him. How desperately he wanted to make this oath. Still, it was on the tip of my tongue to refuse him, to assure him that his word was good enough for me. But I hesitated, slowly realizing why he wanted to do this for me. So

I would know, without a shred of doubt, that there were no secrets between us. And I couldn't deny him that. Not when he was trying so hard to make things right.

So I nodded, murmuring, "How does a pactum work?"

His relief was instantaneous. He finally straightened in his seat, as if by agreeing, I'd sparked life back into him. "With all binding rituals, it's the intention that matters most, more than the actual words or mingling of blood. With a pactum, the cut symbolizes your dedication to the oath. It's also a reminder of the pain you'll endure if you fail to uphold it. Several people can enter a pactum, but only those who voice their intentions are bound to uphold the oath. They alone will face unpleasant consequences should they break it."

"What kind of unpleasant consequences?"

"A broken pactum will feed on your greatest fears. You will experience the pain as if those fears are realized."

I shivered, not liking the sound of that. But his gaze was resolute, so I begrudgingly flipped over my right palm to inspect the smooth skin. "So I just . . . cut it?"

"Yes. Only deep enough to draw blood."

I willed my claws to emerge, dragging one across my palm before I could further question the decision. I winced at the sharp bite of pain, but quickly held my hand out to him. "Okay. Now what?"

"Now, you let me do the rest." He engulfed my hand between both of his, cradling it gently as he pressed our bloodied palms together. His gaze was determined, unwavering as he firmly said, "With this oath, I swear to reveal everything hidden, to always be truthful, and to never keep secrets from my soulmate, the woman who holds my heart and my world in her hands, for as long as I shall live. May I endure the pain I'd feel from losing her if I dare break this oath."

The tears finally came, falling unchecked down my face. "Lochlan," I whispered, equally touched and horrified by his words.

"It's done," he said, once again slumping in his seat as if a great weight had been unburdened from him. "No more secrets. Ever again."

My heart broke for him, for the fear that had driven him to speak this oath. With my hand still firmly clasped between his, I sank onto his lap and straddled his thighs. *Lochlan,* I said again, this time through our bond. I waited for his dark gaze to lift before saying, *You won't lose me.*

He was silent for several moments, then heaved a sigh and looked away.

"You *won't,*" I persisted, lifting our joined hands. "I'm not going anywhere. I *forgive* you."

He stilled, so still that he stopped breathing. When several more moments passed, I turned over his bloodied palm and kissed it. Showing him my gratitude for his sacrifice the only way I knew how.

When I punctuated the kiss with another, "I forgive you," he stirred awake. Reaching both hands up, he cupped my face. Softly. Reverently.

A crease formed between his brows as he whispered, "I don't deserve it."

"Doesn't matter," I whispered back. "I forgive you anyway."

He shuddered beneath me, leaning forward to gently kiss my lips. He abruptly froze. As another shudder racked his body, I glanced at his mouth, noting the red blood smeared there. *Our* blood. When I met his eyes, the black of his irises were brightening to a wine red. Without breaking eye contact, I flicked my tongue out and licked his lips.

A soft growl rumbled in his chest, one that grew louder when my eyes fluttered shut and I quietly moaned. His hands left my face, feathering down my arms and waist to grasp my thighs. To pull me flush against him.

We both froze this time, eyes widening at what he found. Or *didn't* find, more accurately.

As his fingers slowly sought to confirm what he already knew, I didn't move a muscle. Didn't even breathe when they brushed my inner thigh, inches away from my apex.

"You're not wearing underwear," he said in the weighted silence, stating what we already knew.

"Nope," I needlessly confirmed, refusing to squirm. Refusing to be embarrassed. He was my soulmate, the only man I'd ever been intimate with. If I wanted to walk around without panties on, then—

He suddenly pressed his thumb against my center. I choked out a gasp, grabbing onto his shoulders for dear life as pleasure barrelled through me. My legs instinctively wrapped around him, getting stuck on the chair back instead. When his thumb began to rotate in firm circles, every inch of me started to tremble.

As my eyes drifted shut, I heard Lochlan's voice whisper in my mind, *Open your eyes, solemae. Let me see how my touch affects you.*

Freaking *fates*, he was trying to kill me.

Struggling to breathe, I forced my eyes to meet his. The second I did, he bore down on me even more, wringing a cry of ecstasy from me. He made a pleased sound, smiling softly as if my pleasure gave him joy. The sight made the last of my inhibitions fall away. Made me arch into his touch and silently ask for more.

He readily gave, like pleasuring me was his lifeline. Like making me feel good was his way of earning my forgiveness. Of easing my pain. And his.

And I wouldn't take that away from him for the world. Not when he needed this moment, this restitution so badly.

So when he slipped a finger inside me, then another, all while his thumb continued to thoroughly pleasure me, I gave him my all. I showed him *exactly* what his touch did to me, moaning and gasping without restraint. Until, shaking uncontrollably, I climaxed against his fingers. Letting him see through my eyes how incredibly perfect he made me feel.

CHAPTER 12

KENNA

I stared at the fully stocked drawer with emotion thick in my throat.

Lochlan came up behind me, so close that his bare chest brushed my spine.

"When did you do this?" I asked, gesturing at the clothing meant for me.

"Shortly after the last time we were here. A maid came in and added a few things. I hoped we'd be back someday."

I smiled, so wide that it hurt. I was beginning to think of this quaint little cabin as ours.

Me too, Lochlan said through our bond, making my heart swell to the point of bursting. He reached around me and plucked a burgundy cashmere sweater and stone-washed jeans from the pile. *If you insist on wearing clothing, then wear these.*

I pressed my lips together, fighting off a blush as I accepted the clothes. I was still in nothing but his shirt, a fact he seemed to be enjoying. But if I didn't put up a stronger barrier between us soon— even one as flimsy as clothing—then I was going to beg him to touch me again.

He chuckled darkly and I whirled around with an accusatory glare. "Did you just read my mind?"

"Yes," he replied unapologetically, reaching up to tug a lock of my hair. I batted his hand away, beyond mortified, but he only chuckled again. *You don't need to deny yourself, McKenna.* His voice slid through my mind like smooth molasses, practically caressing me from the inside. *I'm more than willing to pleasure you whenever you have a need.*

Fates!

I choked on my spit, nearly hacking up a lung before I was able to splutter, "R-really, I'm fine. I'm not usually this—"

"Horny?"

Gah! He just *had* to say it.

"It's the mate bond frenzy," he nonchalantly added, making my eyes nearly bug out of my head.

"Mate bond . . . *frenzy?* What, like when our bodies were pushing us to have sex so we'd complete the bond?"

"Like that, yes, but more intense. Our souls are now trying to cement the newly completed bond in place. Sealing any cracks, making it strong and impenetrable. Sex is the most efficient way to do that."

I froze with my mouth open, remembering Kade's parting words. And the *look* he gave me. "Kade was amused about something before we left. Did he know this would happen?"

When Lochlan slowly raised a brow, I cursed, not even needing a verbal reply. But that meant . . .

"My brothers know too. Which was why neither of them stopped us from leaving."

Gah! Shoot me now.

"How long does it last?"

"Days. Weeks. Months. Sometimes years. Every bonded pair is different."

I blinked. "So you're saying that a year from now, I could still want to jump your bones every hour or so?"

Both his brows climbed toward his hairline.

Crap. Why did I *say* that? I cursed again and reached down to pinch my thigh, beyond embarrassed.

Lochlan's fingers caught mine before I could, bringing them to his mouth. "I would love that very much," he purred, languidly kissing each of my fingers. With every press of his lips, his wicked amusement grew, until that sinfully delectable dimple of his winked at me. My knees wobbled under the force of his penetrating gaze, one filled with desire and promise.

Fates have mercy on my soul.

"Your soul is perfectly safe with me, solemae," he whispered against my knuckles. "I'll guard it with my life."

Warmth rushed through me, all the way to my toes. "And I'll guard yours," I whispered back, my voice catching.

His amusement slowly faded. "Not if it endangers your life."

I frowned, hugging the clothing tightly to my chest. "So you can protect me but I can't protect you?"

"You're mortal. There are a million things that can kill you."

"Yeah, but . . ." I floundered, searching for a comeback. "But that silver bullet in your heart could have killed you."

"True, but my weaknesses are few compared to yours. Only a couple hours ago, that idiot operative almost shot you. Just like that, you'd be gone. Lost to me forever."

A rebuttal was on the tip of my tongue, but as his fear flared through our bond, it fizzled out. His worry and desperation ate at me. My soul yearned to comfort her mate. To make everything right.

So it just slipped out. Words I wasn't expecting. Words I couldn't have foreseen or prepared for. "Then maybe I shouldn't be mortal."

The words shocked him even more. His pupils dilated and he stared at me like I'd lost my mind. "Get dressed," he brusquely said, then stormed from the room in a haze of twisting shadows.

I gawked at the spot where he'd been, completely baffled. Seconds later, I heard him banging around downstairs. The scrape of glass against wood reached my ears as he swept up the mess we'd made. But his movements were jerky. Agitated.

Angry.

Frowning, I quickly tugged on the clothing and went after him. I stopped at the base of the stairs, my eyes widening when he picked up the mirror's thick golden frame and snapped it in half.

"Lochlan," I quietly said as he jammed the two pieces into a trash bag and tied it shut. Without a word, he brushed past me on his way upstairs, noisily rummaging around in the bedroom. I pursed my lips and remained where I was, giving him the space he'd given me.

Less than a minute later, he was back, dressed in black jeans and a dark fitted Henley. He grabbed the trash bag and yanked on a pair of boots, then paused. "The fridge isn't stocked. I need to hunt," he said, his hand on the front door handle.

Frustration bubbled up, but I didn't reply.

His grip on the handle noticeably tightened. "I can't go without you. I won't leave you here alone."

I blinked. Oh. He wanted me to go with. *Want* might not be the right word, though. He obviously needed some alone time to sort out his thoughts, but his protective instincts wouldn't let him.

I moved toward the hall closet without comment, surprised to find it stocked with boots and coats for me as well. I grabbed a vibrant red peacoat, along with some white Ugg boots, then preceded him outside.

The snap of the trash can lid closing and the crunch of boots on snow were the only sounds as he led us around the cabin. We followed a thin trail through the woods, allowing a heavy silence to fall between us. His thoughts suddenly came through loud and clear, startling a gasp from me.

She will never be turned. I won't allow it.

At the sound of my gasp, he noticeably stiffened.

Clenching my jaw, I hurled a thought at him in return. *What if I want to be turned? How else am I supposed to remain ageless like you?*

He sent me a growl without uttering a sound. *There are other ways. I will gladly feed you my blood on a daily basis to prolong your mortality.*

I missed a step, nearly face planting in the snow.

He glanced back at me. *There you go again, projecting fear and shame at the thought of drinking blood. I thought you liked my blood.*

I-I do. Gah, even my *mind* stuttered when I was nervous. Time to steer this conversation back to where it belonged. *But drinking your blood won't truly make me immortal. My body will still be weak compared to yours.*

I'll lend you my strength whenever I can.

I blinked. *You can do that?*

Our bond doesn't allow me to share my immortality, but I can share other things with you, like strength. It's how you were able to defeat the rogue when he had you pinned beneath the water.

Oh. *Oh.* The rush of inhuman strength I'd felt after connecting with Lochlan that first time.

Realizing I'd slowed, I hurried to catch up with him. *That's great and all, but it won't stop me from getting hurt. I could still die a million different ways.*

He stopped so suddenly that I plowed into his back. Before I could fall, he whipped around and grabbed my shoulders. *But if you're turned, you* will *die,* he passionately said, giving my shoulders a shake. *Draining a mortal body of all its blood is the only way. And there's always the chance that the transition won't work. I can't take that chance. I won't.* He stared me down. *Hard.* Before whirling around to resume his trek."

Yeah, um. *NO.*

Using my vampire speed, I zipped past him to block his path. The second he ground to a halt, I lit into him. *Look, I get that you're afraid of losing me, but I won't have you making all my decisions for me. I got that enough with my aun—with Tess.* I gentled my tone, seeing the fear flash in his eyes again. *You're my soulmate. I don't want to die from old age or a frail body when you'll stay young and strong forever. All I ask is that you let me make the choice when the time comes.*

When his pupils dilated once more, I hurriedly added, *I'm not saying I want to be turned today or even tomorrow. I mean, I need to be a Syphon in order to break the curse, right? So we at least have a couple of months until a decision is made.*

His jaw hardened to granite. *And then you'll choose to kill yourself?*

No, I said, blinking back frustrated tears. *I would choose to live forever. With you.*

He lapsed into silence, his stony face and emotions an impenetrable wall between us. I worried he'd stay that way forever, stiff and unreachable. But the wall suddenly crumbled and he tugged me into his arms.

For several minutes, he simply held me, breathing in my scent as if he couldn't get enough. I buried my face in his chest and soaked up the closeness, wishing I could ease his worries somehow.

"So brave," he finally whispered, pressing his lips to my forehead. "Far braver than I'll ever be."

I opened my mouth to correct him, to tell him how wrong he was. At the last second, I shied away from sharing the secret I was holding onto. Proving to myself what a coward I was.

"You're still keeping something from me," he said, continuing to feather his lips across my skin.

"Yes," I admitted, even as I cringed, hoping he wouldn't probe further. No such luck.

"Tell me," he said, the silken quality of his voice like invisible fingers stroking my mind.

I shivered at the feeling, knowing that I was going to give in. I blurted the words in a rush, not giving myself time to retreat again. "I'm scared of what I'm capable of. I've done some terrible things lately in order to survive. I've killed. I've *wanted* to kill. I've wanted to drain a human dry. I almost did."

Now that I'd started, I couldn't stop. No matter how ugly the words were, I needed to speak them all. I needed Lochlan to see, to *know* how wretchedly messed up I was.

"I never thought of myself as violent, but lately, I've wanted to hurt people. When you were taken from me, I knew that I'd do anything to get you back. I'd lie, I'd steal, I'd threaten, I'd kill. And I did. I took a human's free will away with thrall. I snapped someone's neck. I've sucked the life force from *two* vampires now. I pulled a gun on my guardian with the intent to shoot her. You continue to look at me like I'm this innocent thing, but I'm not. I'm something else now. Something I don't recognize. A monster."

"You're not a monster," Lochlan said the moment I'd finished. My lips trembled when he reached up to cup my cheeks. "Even now, in the face of so much adversity, your light shines through. You've remained steadfast and true to your beliefs, refusing to let others change you."

A tear slid down my cheek and he gently brushed it away. "I don't see a monster, McKenna. I see a strong woman who protects those she loves. I see determination and willpower to fix things that have been broken for far too long. I see hope. So much hope that everyone around you sees it too. You're making them *believe*. You're making them choose you because you're worth choosing. You're everything, McKenna. My world. My kingdom's salvation. You'll save us all just by being you. Of that, I have no doubt."

I clung to his words, desperate for them to be true. "But what if I can't? What if I fail to break the curse in time?"

"You won't fail," Lochlan said, lightly stroking my cheeks. "Fate brought us together. The rest will work itself out in due time."

I stared at his resolute expression, allowing his emotions to wash over me. To cleanse my mind of doubt. I grabbed onto his unwavering belief and held on tight.

"Thank you," I finally replied with a watery smile. "For comforting me. For letting me get that off my chest."

His expression softened, and he returned the smile. The sight was enough to make my heart flutter. "Anytime. I'm always willing to help you get things off your chest. Even clothing."

My smile froze. When his left dimple made an appearance, I sputtered out a surprised laugh. "That was terrible."

He shrugged. "Never said I was good at everything."

"Well, your jokes might need work, but you're plenty good at other things."

His grin turned devious. "Like what?"

"Uh . . ." Against my wishes, my thoughts went haywire, conjuring naughty images.

Ah crap.

Just like that, Lochlan's gaze heated. He swooped down and captured my lips in a kiss that took my breath away.

CHAPTER 13

LOCHLAN

I was drunk on her.

So intoxicated that it was getting harder to think. To do anything but hole myself up in that cabin drenched in our scent and make love to her. She couldn't possibly know how difficult the mate bond frenzy was for me. How challenging it was for me to speak coherently, let alone act like a gentleman.

She wasn't complaining though, which only made me crave her more. As she stood on tiptoe in the snow, sliding her fingers into my hair to pull me closer, I lost the battle.

Tossing the need to hunt aside, I backed her up against a tree and deepened our kiss. When she whimpered at the feel of my tongue on hers, a thrill went through me. Every time. Every single time she made one of those little sounds of pleasure, I combusted with male pride. Not that I needed a bigger ego when it came to her. She held nothing back, letting me clearly see and hear how much I affected her, and it drove me crazy with desire.

Even in my inebriated state, I remained alert to threats. Aware more than ever how precarious our position was. Our relationship was a ticking time bomb. At any moment, it could explode in our faces. I didn't know how much my brothers knew, only that they were now aware of our soulmate bond. They'd let me take her away out of respect for the bond, but that didn't mean much. They could still seek to tear us apart. To sever the bond out of a misplaced sense of worry for me.

Kade would do his best to keep them away though. He understood. Probably the only one who did. I just needed a few days—a week tops—to soothe this incessant itch beneath my skin to devour my mate. Then we could focus our efforts on breaking the curse and stopping this impending war.

She whimpered again and my attention snapped back to her, on satiating my raging hunger. My fangs began to descend but I quickly willed them away, knowing it was too soon to feed on her. Hence my reason for hunting. I'd already taken too much earlier, desperate in my need to reclaim her. With Kade's blood still thick in her veins, her cells were already rapidly replenishing what she'd lost, but I wasn't going to take any chances.

Not with her. Never with her.

Which was why I had to convince her somehow that becoming a vampire wasn't the solution. It was too risky, the transition too unpredictable. Even if I were the one to turn her, she could still reject my blood. Still die. I'd never recover from that.

Suddenly desperate to be inside her, to feel that soul-deep connection only we could share, I unbuttoned my jeans. The moment I reached to undo hers, she snaked a hand inside my pants and gripped my cock through my boxer briefs. I immediately swelled beneath her touch, groaning into her mouth at the sensation. When those greedy little fingers pried back the waistband of my briefs and allowed the hardened length to spring free, my brain fogged, overcome by the frenzy.

With a flick of my wrist, I had her jeans undone. Another flick and they were down past her thighs, along with her underwear. She gripped me again before I could penetrate her, this time skin-to-skin.

It was the first time she'd done so, and I didn't even think to flinch. How fast she'd learned how to control her Syphon magic was incredible. Only a few short days of practice and she had no problem protecting my skin from hers.

As she boldly slid her hand along the shaft, I nearly came undone. "McKenna," I groaned, catching myself against the tree when she ran her thumb over the swollen head.

So soft, she inwardly whispered, probably not realizing that I could hear.

My breath came in ragged pants as she continued to stroke me, driving me wild with need. Unable to restrain myself a moment longer, I slid my fingers between her legs, gratified at how wet she already was. She gasped at the contact, gripping me even harder. I loosed another groan and cupped her backside, wholly succumbing to the need.

Sliding my cock between her thighs, I found her entrance and thrust in deep. She threw back her head and released a throaty moan, shifting her hands to grip my shirt front. I lifted her a few inches off the ground to more thoroughly penetrate her, pleased when her lips parted in a cry of pleasure.

More, she breathed through our bond. *More, more, more.*

Her need barrelled through me, stealing the last of my sanity. I captured her parted lips again in a passionate kiss and moved inside her. Slowly, then faster. Our breaths quickened and our pleasure built at a rapid pace. When she came a few minutes later, hot and fast, I swallowed her scream. She orgasmed over my cock, wringing my own ecstacy from me. One more thrust and I jerked inside her, coming hard.

While our frantic breathing and thundering heartbeats slowed, I stayed inside her. Continued to hold her close, occasionally kissing her damp brow. Only when I heard the faint snap of a twig a mile or so away did I regretfully pull out of her.

Rebuttoning my jeans, I waited a moment for her to do the same before saying through our bond, *Time to hunt. Stay close to me.*

She blinked at me dazedly, muttering, *Oh, okay.* I smirked and kissed her forehead again before taking off. I started out at human speed, making sure she could keep up, then increased the pace. Soon, we were racing through the woods, hunting our prey as a pair. Pride and contentment swelled in my chest, and I found myself smiling. Laughing as we skimmed over the snow together.

I didn't know I could feel this alive, this *happy.* That the world could look and smell so vibrant, so rich with promise. I'd barely been living before her. And now, thanks to this exquisite creature by my side, I couldn't get enough.

Her love was a gift, one I didn't deserve. Just like I hadn't deserved her forgiveness earlier. But I would do everything in my power to make her as happy as I felt. To cherish and protect her. Not just her body, but her heart and spirit. She deserved everything I could give her, and I'd happily spend an eternity doing just that.

When I heard the rapid pulse of our intended prey, I slowed, gesturing at McKenna to do the same. I usually struck fast and hard, not bothering with stealth. Not having a need to. But with my mate here, I had this ridiculous notion to impress her, one I couldn't shake. I wanted her to see how capable I was of providing for her. Even if it was the predator in me speaking, I followed my instincts, hunkering down behind a felled tree.

When she joined me, I pointed at a spot several yards off. *Deer. One o'clock.*

She squinted, then nodded, but I heard her whispered words, *Poor Bambi.*

I almost laughed. Nearly did when she caught my smirk and

poked my bicep.

I'll make it quick, I assured her, then threw her a questioning look. *Unless you want the honors?*

Her eyes widened in horror. *No. No, I'm good. You go right ahead.*

My shoulders silently shook and she glared daggers at me. Unable to help myself, I captured the back of her head and pressed my mouth to hers. Kissed her thoroughly, drawing a slight gasp from her, before rising to my feet and lightly hopping over the tree.

My self-satisfied smirk remained in place as I stalked toward the deer, making sure my scent was downwind. Hunting had always been a necessity to me, not something I found pleasure in. But I reveled in it today, thrilled to share this experience with McKenna. She stayed behind the tree while I inched forward, dividing my attention between her, our surroundings, and my prey.

Only when I was within striking distance did I focus solely on the doe, watching as her head whipped up, ears flicking back and forth. Even though I hadn't made a sound, the animal could detect when a predator was near. Air puffed from her nostrils as she tried to catch my scent, but by the time she did, I was already moving.

Blindingly fast.

Barely stirring the snow, I sped toward her and leapt, tackling her to the ground. She bleated in fright and struggled for a split second, then it was over. Her lifeless body slumped to the snow, her neck bent at a slightly odd angle.

I quickly rose with her in my arms. Hoisting her over my shoulder, I began the trek back to McKenna, a smile stretched across my face. Then froze. Panic surged through me and I dropped the animal.

MCKENNA, I bellowed through our bond, rushing forward.

When I reached the fallen tree, she was nowhere to be found. Darkness edged my vision as the beast inside of me threatened to emerge. I tried to calm myself, to focus, but my fear was too great. Charging in the direction of her tracks, I desperately searched for her heartbeat. When I heard *two* hearts beating, a furious roar tore from me and my claws shot out.

I burst into a small clearing not far away and there she was. She whirled toward me in alarm. It didn't dawn on me that she was alarmed by *my* presence. My only thought was on discovering who was with her. On destroying the being who would *dare* take her from me.

When I saw a flash of silver bolt into the trees, I pursued, only for McKenna to surge toward me with her hands raised.

"No, stop!" she said, blocking my way. "It's just a fox. Please don't kill her."

I only stopped when she tried to push me back, her desperation coming through loud and clear. Grasping her shoulders, I searched for injuries, thoroughly checking every inch of her. My voice was gruff, deeper than usual as I said, "Are you okay? What happened? Why are you over here?"

"I'm fine. I'm fine, Lochlan," she replied in soothing tones, placing her hands on my chest. "I just . . . I felt something and had this irresistible urge to find it. Then I spotted the fox. I don't know. It was like I was drawn to her. I can't explain it."

I zeroed in on the treeline where the creature had disappeared, a growl rumbling in my chest. *Mine*, I inwardly snarled, pulling McKenna into my arms. The instinct to stake my claim came hot and swift, completely catching me off guard. Although unexpected, I couldn't ignore or stop it. "*Mine*," I said again, this time out loud, curling my lip back to reveal my fangs.

McKenna shifted in my arms to see my face. "What's wrong? What did I do?"

"Nothing," I quickly reassured her, but the tension in my body didn't ease. It wouldn't, not until we were far away from this place where prying eyes couldn't see us. Couldn't see *her*. Scooping her into my arms, I moved swiftly toward the safety of the cabin.

"I can walk," she protested, squirming in my arms to be let down. "Besides, you forgot the deer."

"I'll get it later," I muttered, tightening my hold on her.

She blew out an exasperated sigh. "Lochlan, put me down. I'm not in any danger out here."

I ignored her at first, but when she sent me an image of her slamming the bedroom door in my face—and locking it—I threw her a mildly annoyed look. "I thought someone had taken you."

"Well, I'm right here, safe and sound," she sassily quipped, kicking her feet in the air. "We're the only humans—err, you know what I mean—for miles around."

I grumbled under my breath, but deep down, I knew she was right. I'd overreacted, not that I was going to tell *her* that.

"You just did," she sang, clearly enjoying herself at my expense.

Scowling, I set her down on her feet before sending an image of my own—of me repeatedly smacking her backside. Her *naked* backside.

She stiffened, her eyes rounding to the size of dinner plates. I briefly wondered if I'd gone too far, but not for long. Her face suddenly flushed a rosy hue and she cleared her throat, looking everywhere but at me. I expected to feel her embarrassment next, so was doubly shocked when desire—followed by the cloying scent of her arousal—hit me.

My pants tightened in response and I found myself chuckling, once again amazed at how perfect she was for me. Without touching her, I placed my mouth near her ear and purred, "Would you like that, mate?"

She swayed toward me but kept her hands fisted at her sides. "No," she said, yet her thoughts betrayed her with a resounding *Yes*.

I chuckled again and she shivered, turning her head toward mine. I allowed our noses to brush, but when she stood on tiptoe to kiss me, I pulled away with a wicked grin.

Now it was her turn to scowl. My grin only broadened as I said through our bond, *Dominant alpha male, remember? Challenge me and I can't help but respond.*

Her scowl deepened. *Let's see how you respond to this*, she said, flipping her hair back as she swiveled on her heel and stomped off.

I gave her a ten second head start, brazenly watching her hips sashay back and forth as she stormed from the clearing. Then charged. The moment I did, she squealed and took off running. Excitement pounded through me and I gave chase, smiling when her laughter danced on the breeze. She only made it a few yards before I was on her, grabbing her waist to twirl her around.

The world stopped as she threw her head back and laughed. Sounding more carefree, more happy than I'd ever heard her. I openly watched her merriment, feeling my heart painfully expand at the sight. But it was a good pain for once. A pain I was only just getting to know. To crave.

I slowed, waiting for her eyes to find mine before whispering, "I love you."

Her answering smile, so blindingly bright, could have fueled a thousand suns. This time, when she rose on tiptoe to capture my lips, I met her halfway, kissing her mouth with enough force to bruise. She didn't complain. She never did. She grabbed my face to return the kiss with equal force, and my heart burst with unimaginable happiness.

This was my mate. The completion of my soul. The joy of my life. And I would thank fate every day for giving her to me.

CHAPTER 14

KENNA

She appeared out of the swirling mist, her startling pale blue eyes fixed on me.

A jolt of recognition shivered through me. Of familiarity.

Her head cocked to the side, and she looked at me as if to say, Come.

I felt no hesitation, no fear. Only rightness as I rose to honor her request.

"Wait for me," I whispered to her, unconcerned when the mist swallowed her form.

Somehow, I knew exactly where to find her.

I was aware of my actions, of slipping free of Lochlan's slumbering embrace to silently tiptoe from the bedroom. Of dawning a coat and boots over my pajamas before exiting the front door.

I was surprised when he didn't wake. Exhaustion from our time apart must have claimed him, along with a food coma from all the venison and deer blood he'd consumed today. One taste of the blood and I'd refused to drink more. It really was revolting stuff. He'd clearly needed it though, if the amount he'd quickly ingested was anything to go by.

The rest of our evening had been spent curled up on the living room couch, listening to a fire cheerfully crackling in the fireplace. We'd rested in each other's arms for hours, content to simply be together.

Since our time outside, we hadn't been intimate again, mainly due to how tired we were. But the need was still there, an ever-present ember warming my insides. We'd fallen asleep early, fully clothed. But, despite Lochlan's arms tightly caging me in, I'd managed to slip free without him noticing.

It was better this way. He wouldn't understand my need to leave in the middle of the night. He'd freaked out earlier today when I'd barely left his sight. If I told him where I was going now, he'd probably refuse to let me. Or attempt to scare her off again. I couldn't let him do either.

I *had* to see her. Had to know why she was calling me. Why I felt connected to her somehow.

The moment I stepped from the porch, snow lightly fell on my head and shoulders. Fog blanketed the night, limiting my view.

"Mist," I breathed. Just like in my dream—or whatever it had been. I followed the path we'd taken earlier, careful to tread quietly. Only when I could no longer see the cabin did I start to relax. To focus on finding her instead of worrying over Lochlan. I wouldn't be gone long. His concerns were valid. Danger could be anywhere, even up here where it felt so safe.

Not for a second did I think *she* was dangerous though. I just knew, the moment our eyes had met, that she meant me no harm. I wasn't afraid to seek her out in the woods, just like I hadn't been with Lochlan.

As the fog and light snowfall obscured my vision, I continued at a sedate pace, somehow knowing that I wouldn't have to go far. Sure enough, I felt her about a mile from the cabin. While Lochlan's presence made me shiver with awareness, hers had a calming effect. Like a blanket wrapped around my shoulders by a doting parent.

"Hello?" I called into the surrounding mists, pausing when I caught a whiff of her scent. A mixture of warm fur and coconut. "I got your message. I came alone. There's no need to be afraid."

The light padding of paws on snow broke the night's stillness. The mist directly in front of me stirred. I saw her eyes first, their pale blue brilliant enough to see even at night. Then her silver and white face. She flicked her large black-tipped ears, as though listening for threats, then took another step.

The fog slowly gave up the rest of her. First her snowy white neck ruff and socks, then her sleek silver body, all the way to her white-tipped tail.

So beautiful, I thought to myself, never having seen a silver fox before.

I'm not afraid, a cultured female voice suddenly spoke in my mind. *And thank you. I rather like this animal form.*

Startled, I stumbled back a step, nearly losing my balance and tumbling into the snow. "W-wait," I stuttered at the fox when I'd recovered enough to speak. "Was that *you?*"

Or am I losing my freaking mind?

You are perfectly sane, Kenna, the voice spoke again. *And yes, it's me.*

My mouth fell open. "You know my name?"

Somehow, that was more shocking than a fox *mind-speaking* to me.

I know many things. That you're a Syphon witch. That you're eighteen human years of age. That you're mated to a vampire prince. I know because I've been observing you. Not for long. Only for the past month or so. I lost track of you a little over a week ago, but you're back and newly mated. Congratulations.

"I . . . thanks?"

What the crap was *happening?*

I apologize, the fox said, actually *sounding* apologetic. *Where are my manners? I haven't properly introduced myself.* She bent one of her forelegs and bowed, saying, *My chosen name here on earth is Silver. I am a celestial spirit embodied in animal form. A sliver of my essence resides in you, and I have come so that my spirit self can be whole again.*

No. Freaking. Way.

Did that mean . . . ?

"Are you my *familiar?*"

At the word, she gave me an odd look—if foxes even had facial expressions. *That is what your kind call my kind, yes. I am much more than your familiar, though.*

"Oh, sorry. I didn't mean to offend you. I'm just new to this spirit and witch stuff." Even as I said the words, I internally squealed. I had a familiar!

It's perfectly okay, Kenna. I know you had no ill intentions. We will both learn over time to better understand each other.

I nodded. "Story of my life the last couple of months. I didn't know supernaturals existed before then. I've had a lot of growing pains."

She made a strange yipping sound, almost like a fox's version of a laugh. *From what I've seen, you're adjusting beautifully. But I will gladly share my knowledge with you in exchange for your acceptance and protection.*

My eyes rounded. "I thought it was the other way around. That familiars—err, spirits—accepted and protected witches."

It goes both ways, actually. But I have already made my intentions known to accept and protect you by revealing myself to you today. For you to do the same, you simply have to touch me, showing through physical contact that you wish me no harm.

"Oh." I bit my lip, willing my fingers not to fidget. "Aren't you afraid of what my touch will do to you? I mean, I've recently learned to control my abilities, but I'm . . . I'm still a Syphon."

Oh, my darling, Silver compassionately said. For whatever reason, it made a lump form in my throat. *Do not be afraid of who you are. I have given those powers to you. They are the best part of me, the part I'm most proud of. They are rare among my kind. Even rarer in this world. They are powers worth coveting, not fearing. It wasn't easy for me to give them up, but I so desperately wanted to experience life on earth. The price was harsh but worth it. I am now reunited with the part I've been missing. And I have you as well, which I'm most excited about. I believe I chose well in gifting you a piece of my spirit.*

Wow. I was speechless. And crying. Yup. Those were tears.

She was like me. Well, *used* to be. In a different life. And she wasn't the least bit scared of my abilities. She *understood.* There were no words to describe how amazing that felt. Releasing a tremulous laugh, I wiped my wet cheeks and moved to kneel before her.

She was small, the top of her head no taller than my knee, but her presence felt so much bigger. Like I was feeling the *spirit* part of her. Sniffling, I lifted my hand toward her and said, "With this touch, I promise to accept and protect you."

Not knowing what else to say, I focused on my fingers, on shielding my magic from hurting her. I didn't know how my touch would affect her, only that she was a supernatural being. It would devastate me to harm her, even unintentionally. When my fingers brushed against her wet nose, then the soft length of her muzzle, she leaned into my touch. Before I knew it, I was running my hand over her head and scratching behind her ears.

She emitted a soft purring sound like a cat, her tail thumping against the snow as she rubbed against my hand. A grin split my face and any traces of hesitation vanished. When I leaned forward to better reach her, the purring stopped. She stiffened and said, *Your mate is approaching.*

I froze, my eyes widening as they met hers. *Please don't leave,* I spoke telepathically, hoping she could hear. *I'll talk to him.*

He's very protective, she immediately replied. *He'll see me as a threat.*

I won't let him hurt you, I said, letting her see through my eyes the truth of my words. When she flicked a nervous glance behind me, I gave her a reassuring pat and stood to face Lochlan.

He appeared out of the mist like a malevolent shadow, his tall dark form and blood red eyes the stuff of nightmares. Anyone else would cower, would run screaming for their lives at the sight of him. But I knew better.

I stepped toward him, saying in soothing tones, "Lochlan, hear me out."

"Step away from the creature," he rumbled, his voice too beastly for my liking.

"She isn't a threat to me. I need you to—"

"McKenna, *now*," he growled, striding toward me.

"No!" I roared back, catching him by surprise. He stopped in his tracks to blink at me. "Just stay where you are. Don't come any closer."

He curled his clawed hands into fists, but actually listened. Probably not for long though, judging by the overwhelming emotions flooding our bond. "Explain," he tightly said, and I hurriedly did just that. When he heard the word *familiar*, his lip curled back in a silent snarl.

Your completed mate bond is still too new, Silver said from behind me. *A male's need to claim and possess his mate will drive him to shun everyone else. Until that instinct is satiated, he will be jealous of anyone who gets too close to you. And in your alpha mate's case, violence is inevitable. I should come back later, when he's calmed down enough to think more rationally.*

"No," I immediately replied with a shake of my head. "I want you here. Stay."

Lochlan's growl of rage shook the ground. "Did she just *mind-speak* with you?"

"Yes. It's how she communicates with me. I was given a piece of her spirit at birth, so we have a bond similar to—"

"*No,*" Lochlan thundered, his eyes flashing murderously. "You are *mine*. Not hers. Not *anyone* else's."

Stunned at how irrationally possessive he was being, just like Silver had predicted, I didn't react in time. I blinked and he was in front of me, wrapping his fingers around my bicep.

"We're leaving, Kenna, and you're *not* coming back," he said in a dangerously low growl, tugging on my arm. His hold didn't hurt, but I balked at the domineering move, digging my heels into the snow.

"Stop telling me what I can and cannot do!" I snapped at him. "Just because I'm your mate doesn't mean you can *control* me."

Something about the words sank into his thick skull. He dropped my arm with a hiss. Turning, he jerked his hands through his hair and paced in a tight circle, clearly wrestling with himself. I stayed silent yet held my ground, hoping he'd come to his senses. After a long moment, he heaved a deep sigh and said through our bond, *I'm sorry, McKenna. Please forgive me.*

My heart immediately softened and I went to him. With his back still facing me, I slid my arms around his waist and pressed my cheek between his shoulder blades, whispering, "Of course I forgive you.

I'm sorry I left without telling you."

"I don't blame you for sneaking out," he replied, twisting around to face me. His hand came up to feather across my cheek. "I'm not handling my territorial instincts very well."

I bit my lip to keep from smiling, from sarcastically agreeing with him.

He fixed me with a look of chagrin. "Go ahead and say it. I already know you're thinking it."

Huffing a laugh, I rose up and lightly kissed his cheek. *I love you. Even when you're bossy.*

A rumble vibrated his chest, more a purr than a growl. He pulled me against him, resting his chin on the top of my head. And no doubt eyeing Silver behind me. "So how is this going to work?"

With those words came a flood of relief. I grinned and hugged him fiercely.

Tell him I will remain close by, but I won't enter your dwelling until he fully accepts me, Silver said.

I peeked over my shoulder at her with a frown. "But I don't want you to be left out in the cold."

She made that same high-pitched yip sound again. *I've lived outside in the elements ever since I took this form. I'll be fine.*

Lochlan tensed while I communicated with Silver, but to his credit, he didn't speak or even growl. Still not happy with leaving her outside, I offered her the only thing I could think of. "We have venison. Lots of it. Can I at least feed you?"

She bobbed her head. *That would be most appreciated. Thank you.*

Smiling once again, I relayed her words to Lochlan and he nodded his consent. *I won't harm her or run her off. You have my word*, he said through our bond, and I counted that as a win, even though he hadn't yet spoken directly to her.

She followed us to the cabin, keeping a healthy distance. Every few steps, I'd glance back at her, worried that she'd melt into the mist and I'd never see her again. But she didn't run away. And when I hurried into the cabin to fetch some meat, she was still there, waiting for my return.

After a few parting words, I let Lochlan usher me inside. Let him lead me upstairs to the bathroom where he proceeded to remove my clothing. I didn't question or stop him, already knowing through our bond what he wanted. What he needed. As he slid the last of the clothing from my body, I remained perfectly still, allowing him to take in my naked form.

His gaze heated and he made quick work of removing his own clothes. When he revealed his hard erection, desire swept through me. Still, I didn't move, letting him lead. Watched as he started the shower and tugged back the curtain to step inside.

Come, mate, he said through our bond, and I shivered at the soft command, readily obeying.

Stepping under the warm spray, I looked up at him, waiting for him to make the next move. He searched my face for several moments, along with my emotions and thoughts. Then picked up a chunk of my wet hair and wound it around his hand. He urged me forward with a light tug on my hair, until my piqued nipples brushed against his chest.

You are mine, his voice rumbled inside my mind. He released my hair to grasp the nape of my neck.

Yes, I agreed, my lashes fluttering shut when he lowered his head, his lips a breath away from mine.

"Say it," he breathed aloud, allowing his bottom lip to graze mine. I shuddered with need, but remained perfectly still.

"I am yours," I whispered, earning another brush of his lips. I gasped as he suddenly whirled me around. One of his hands encircled my throat. The other slid over my stomach to press me against his erection.

"Again," he lightly growled in my ear, nipping at the lobe. "Say it again."

"I'm yours," I breathlessly repeated, struggling to keep my trembling hands at my sides.

He rewarded me by slipping his fingers between my legs. When they found my center, I threw my head back and moaned.

Again, he purred through our bond, stroking me deeply with his wet fingers. I whimpered, barely able to stand as pleasure barreled through me. He cruelly paused, demanding once more, *Again*.

"I'm yours," I desperately choked out, silently begging him to continue.

Instead, he lifted one of my legs. I didn't understand at first what he was doing, but when his swollen head pressed against my entrance from behind, my eyes flew wide. We'd never done it this way before, and I had a moment of panic. But when he slowly pushed inside, every inch of me trembled with want. At the sensations the new angle gave me, I cried out, squeezing my eyes shut.

After a few slow thrusts, he released my thigh. Only to slip his fingers between my legs again. The combined pleasure from both locations was too much. I clawed at the shower tiles, a scream building in my throat.

"Please," I gasped, not even sure what I was begging for. Without pausing, he tilted my head to the side. His lips found my jaw, kissing a wet path down the length of my neck.

"Bite me," I panted, arching against him.

He blew out a trembling breath, thrusting more deeply inside me.

"Bite me," I said again, reaching back to grasp his hair. To guide his mouth toward the right spot. "Please, Lochlan."

He didn't break the rhythm, didn't stop pleasuring me as he lightly kissed my neck and said, "I don't want you to become addicted to my venom."

My hold on his hair tightened, and I pressed his mouth more firmly against my skin. "Too late. I'm already addicted to you."

His pleased growl vibrated through my insides.

"Now, Lochlan, *now*," I pleaded, already struggling to hold off my building orgasm.

In one swift move, he sank his fangs into my neck. The pain barely touched me, my current ecstasy too great. But nothing was greater than his venom, than the euphoria that poured through my bloodstream and lifted me to the highest peak. We groaned at the same time, basking in the pleasure our bodies gave each other.

His hand slid down to stroke my breasts and I was officially gone. Wholly possessed. Completely undone by him. In a world where only he existed. My body was his. Solely his. To do with as he pleased. He knew exactly how to wring the utmost pleasure from me. To make me feel more than I ever thought possible.

I'm yours, I gasped through our bond, repeating the words again and again until we shattered together.

CHAPTER 15

KENNA

"So, how old are you?"

I cringed the second the words were out, not knowing if the question was offensive or not.

As a fox, only eighteen human years, Silver replied without hesitation, and I relaxed again, dangling my legs over the dock's edge. *But as a spirit, I am what you'd call ancient. I can't remember the exact number anymore, but it's been over five thousand years since I've been fashioned into existence.*

I knew I was gawking like a serious creeper, but my mind was having trouble digesting her words. She didn't seem to mind though, wrapping her fluffy silver and white tail around her body as she sat on the snow-encrusted dock beside me.

It was our second day of getting to know each other, and Lochlan had generously given us some space, choosing to take a walk while we chatted by the frozen lake. He wasn't far, but the distance gave the illusion of privacy, which seemed to put Silver more at ease.

He hadn't verbally expressed his acceptance of her, but there'd been no resistance when I'd asked to spend the afternoon with her. All the sex must have helped calm his raging territorial instincts. The second I'd woken this morning, he'd slipped his hand inside my pants. Then, after preparing a delicious venison sausage breakfast, he'd taken me right there on the kitchen table. And yet again, just as we were heading outside, he'd pulled me into the downstair's hall bathroom.

Yeah. We had it bad.

At this rate, I was going to orgasm on every surface of the cabin. Not that I was complaining. I couldn't get enough of him and his touch. If my body didn't need time to recuperate, I'd happily spend all day in bed having sex with him.

Feeling my face—and other parts of my body—flush at my wayward thoughts, I quickly focused on Silver again, blurting, "Are you an angel or demon in spirit form?" Freaking fates, I shouldn't be allowed to ask questions. At least I hadn't asked her if she was good or evil.

I am what you'd call a Seraphim, or Seraph, for short, Silver again replied without pause. *As a celestial being, I have six wings, the most of any angel. A Seraph's duty is to protect God's throne and to deliver earthly messages. In all my years though, I was never chosen to deliver a message. Hence why I decided to shed my wings for this earthly animal form.*

I was gawking again. But I couldn't help it. My familiar was *so cool.*

"Can you ever become an angel again?" I hedged, suddenly nervous of the answer.

Yes. If my animal form perishes, my spirit will return to heaven, retaking the form of a Seraphim. But the part of me that now belongs to you cannot be recovered. In whatever form I take, my spirit will never be whole again.

Seeing the tear that slipped down my cheek, Silver stirred from her spot to rub against my arm.

Do not grieve for me, my darling. It was my choice to sacrifice a piece of myself for a chance at this life. I have no regrets.

I soaked up her comfort, even as I fought back more tears. "How long can you live in this form? As a fox, I mean."

Since I'm still a celestial being in spirit, I cannot die of old age. I can be killed though, just like everything else on this earthly plane.

I breathed a little easier, relieved that she wasn't subjected to a fox's short lifespan. Even though I'd just met her, my heart ached at the thought of losing her. We had a bond. Not a soulmate one, but I still felt a deep connection to her. Almost like the mother-daughter relationship I'd never had.

We companionably stared across the iced-over lake, watching as the sun slowly drifted below the treeline. The sky darkened, but I had no trouble seeing, my temporary vampire abilities still holding strong. I opened my mouth to ask if she'd like more venison for dinner, but as I did, she suddenly growled.

Kenna, she said, her tone clearly worried. *Get to your mate. Now. There's someone—*

Before she could finish, I caught the sound of approaching footsteps. They were moving *fast*. Inhumanly fast. I was up on my feet in a flash. So was Silver. We whirled at the same time, but her reaction to the oncoming threat was faster. As the dark figure blurred toward us, she charged with a speed that took me by surprise. Leaping into the air, she sank her teeth into their forearm and held on tight.

All I heard was a pained hiss. Then nothing as a force knocked me clean off my feet. I flew back, back, back, striking the ice *hard*. My head whipped back and I momentarily blacked out from the vicious blow. When I came to seconds later, the world spun nauseatingly and I nearly threw up my venison breakfast. Before I could orient myself, hands grasped my coat and yanked me to my feet.

"So we meet again," a voice hissed, a voice I'd know anywhere. One that often kept me up at night as I replayed the horrific moment he'd savagely ripped into my neck.

I blinked the spots from my vision and, sure enough, there he was. The rogue who'd nearly drained me. Except now, he had a patch over his left eye, making him look like a vampire pirate.

Catching my stare, his expression filled with hatred. "You wanna see what that blasted crow did? *Here.* Look your fill." He whipped the patch off, revealing an empty eye socket. I cringed back but he grabbed a chunk of my hair and yanked me closer, snarling in my face, "You're to blame for this. You and that blood of yours. It's a good thing my orders have changed. I no longer have to bring you in. If I want to drain you of all that precious blood, I can go right ahead. I'll be smarter this time about your skin though. Maybe kill you first, then drain you."

Fear gripped me. So strong that I couldn't move. Couldn't call for help. Couldn't do anything but tremble, horror stricken as he twisted my head to the side. But when he exposed my neck, eyeing the spot where Lochlan had claimed me, something shifted. Something powerful. A fierce instinct that shoved the fear aside and drove me to attack. To defend my soulmate's mark at all costs.

With a savage yell, I kneed my captor in the groin as hard as I could. It freaking hurt, even with my enhanced strength, but the blow stunned him enough that he let go of my hair. I did the worst thing I could think of then. I willed my claws to appear and swiftly jabbed my thumb into his eye.

The good one. The only one he had left.

As blood spurted from the socket, he bellowed in agony, knocking me to the ice with a vicious swing. Despite the blood pouring from his eye, he came at me like a tornado. I tried to roll out of the way, but his fist was already inches from my face. At this speed, the hit would probably cave my skull in.

There was nothing, absolutely nothing I could do. Could only watch as my mortality finally caught up to me.

His knuckles were a breath away from my nose. A split second from pulverizing my face. Then he was gone. Streaking across the lake's surface. Caught in the grip of a dark figure wreathed in shadows.

I felt the impact as the rogue slammed into the ice. Felt the ice tremble beneath me as it cracked under the violent force. I shivered as the shadowed figure—my *mate*—yanked the rogue up by his throat, his feet dangling above the ice.

"I've been waiting for this moment," Lochlan said, his voice nothing but a terrifying, beastly growl. "You bit my mate. You marked her with your scent. Now you will pay with your life."

"Mate?" the rogue wheezed, fruitlessly prying at Lochlan's hands. "I didn't . . . I didn't know."

"Doesn't matter. Soon, you will be dead. But not before you suffer first, just as you made *her* suffer."

I slowly rose to my feet in a trancelike state, unable to look away from what I knew was coming. I wouldn't stop it. Not this time. Not when I felt the fury coming from Lochlan. Red hot and boiling over, there was nothing that could stop him from seeking revenge. From destroying the creature who had dared touch his mate.

And destroy he did. Destroyed and tortured. Cruelly. Viciously. Tearing into the rogue without mercy.

He went for the throat first, savagely biting into his neck. A frantic gurgle rose from the rogue's mouth as Lochlan turned his head and spat out a chunk of bloodied flesh. I placed a hand over my mouth to keep from screaming. From begging him to stop.

I'd seen him kill before, but not like *this*. So deathly calm. So concretely sure in his movements, as if he'd practiced ahead of time what he wanted to do.

But I kept silent, watching as he shredded the rogue's skin with brutally efficient strokes. As he slowly broke each of his fingers, then ripped them from their sockets. I thought the wet screams would never end. Thought Lochlan would tear and rip until pieces of vampire littered the lake's surface. But with a bellowing roar that shook the ice, he swiftly decapitated the rogue and ended the torture.

He stared down at the bloodied remains for several moments, then fished a lighter from his pocket and set the body ablaze.

Movement in my peripheral caught my eye and I turned to see a dark form by the dock take off into the woods. I panicked for a second, searching for Silver, but found her not far from where I'd left her. She was favoring her right foreleg, but otherwise appeared unharmed.

When I turned back to Lochlan, he was inches from me. This close, I could see the blood glistening on his face and staining his clothes. But as our eyes met, there was no sign of the calculating monster. Only him. My soulmate. My home. And when he lifted a hand toward me, one that had mutilated a body mere seconds ago, I didn't shy away. Didn't cringe back in fear. I held still as he gingerly touched the back of my head, his fingers coming away wet with fresh blood.

He made a distressed sound deep in his throat, then carefully pulled me into his arms. He held me like I could shatter at any moment. Like I was something infinitely precious to him. I'd never felt more warm. More safe. But he ended the embrace all too soon, murmuring, "We should get off the lake before the ice cracks further."

I mutely nodded, too emotional to speak. I shuffled toward land, somehow still able to stand on my own two feet. When we reached the dock, though, Lochlan took one look at Silver and said, "You are welcome inside our dwelling, wherever that may be." Just like that, my legs gave out.

Lochlan caught me as I fell, as I broke down in heaving sobs. He carried me to the cabin, quietly explaining between hiccups that we needed to leave. That our little haven was no longer safe. I cried harder, even while knowing that it was only a place. Lochlan, Silver, and I were walking away in one piece. As long as I had them, it didn't matter where we went.

Still, I grieved the loss. Mourned having to say goodbye to a place so full of memories. Lochlan allowed me to cry, offering his silent comfort while I packed up my few belongings and headed out the door. As we walked down the hill toward the car, I glanced back at the cabin one last time, certain I would never see it again.

We arrived at the lakehouse still covered in blood.

Silver was curled up on the backseat, using a paw to wash her face clean. She insisted the injury to her right foreleg was minor, but I still felt guilty. She wouldn't have been hurt at all if it wasn't for me. Those rogues had been out for *my* blood. By allowing her into my life, I'd compromised her safety.

A hand slid over the middle console and captured my fingers before they could pinch my thigh. "You're not to blame for any of this," Lochlan said, shutting the Volvo's engine off.

He's right, Kenna, Silver agreed, lowering her paw. *You are a victim of your circumstances. I'm fully aware of that and do not hold you responsible for what happened.*

I sniffed back tears, grateful for their support. Having them *both* listening to my inner monologue would take some getting used to, though. Before I could respond to either of them, the front door of the lakehouse opened and three dark figures emerged.

Lochlan bristled, tightening his hold on my hand. I instantly recognized who they were, so was confused by his reaction.

Until Silver explained, *You've only been mated for a few short days. Even friends and family will seem threatening to him until the bond settles.*

What should I do? I said to her, hoping Lochlan couldn't hear. When he didn't respond, I focused solely on speaking to my familiar.

Keep your distance from other males, especially unmated ones. Your mate will feel the need to challenge them if they touch or even look at you too long.

Well, crap.

The moment I opened my door, I knew things were going to get ugly if I didn't do something quick. Kade trotted down the front stairs, hollering, "Done already? That was fast. I thought Lochie boy would have more stamina than that." When he was still several feet from the car, Lochlan shot from the driver's seat to block him.

Silver called to me as I scrambled from the car, but I was already bent on stopping Lochlan from hurting his friend. Before I could come between them, Kade backed up with raised hands.

"Whoa, calm down, buddy. I got the message loud and clear. She's all yours." He flicked a glance at me and that was all it took. As Lochlan lunged at his friend, I put on a burst of speed and barrelled into him from behind. The moment my arms encircled his waist, he ground to a halt.

"What happened?" Everett said, descending the steps at a more cautious pace. "Why are you covered in blood?"

A violent tremor shook Lochlan's body, but with my arms still around him, he held still while his brother approached.

"Two rogues found us," I explained, realizing Lochlan couldn't.

Three, he said through our bond.

I blinked up at his profile in surprise. "Three?"

One went after me too. Probably as a distraction so I wouldn't get to you in time.

"But you did," I whispered, pushing comforting thoughts toward him. *You did get to me in time.*

Lochlan reached behind him and tugged me against his chest. I squeaked as his hold abruptly tightened. "Stop looking at her, drothen," he growled.

Kade burst out laughing. "You've got it *bad*, Lochie." Despite Kade's general lack of concern, telling Lochlan about the bond I now shared with his best friend would have to wait. For a long time, if his current possessiveness was anything to go by.

"Did you kill them all?" Troy interjected, leaning against the porch railing with his arms crossed over his chest. As usual, a baseball cap shadowed his eyes, hiding his expression.

"One got away," Lochlan responded, his voice still growly. "Which was why we came back early. Our location was exposed."

"This isn't about your stamina then," Kade egged, and it was my turn to throw him a warning glare. Except I should have known better. Should have tried harder to stop him somehow. But he opened his mouth again before I could do anything. "So how many times did the Lochness Monster come out to play?"

At his wink, I knew he hadn't meant Lochlan's anger. My face immediately burst into flames. I willed the ground to open up and swallow me whole when Kade snickered, clearly not afraid of Lochlan's reaction. Everett rolled his eyes and muttered something about immature innuendos, while Troy kept surprisingly silent. Then again, *insulting* innuendos were more his thing.

"My stamina is just fine," Lochlan smoothly responded, shocking the crap out of me. "But make any jokes about my mate and *yours* might not be. That goes for all of you." Kade made a choking noise, but quickly sobered when I threw him another death glare.

"Jokes aside, we have a lot to discuss," Everett said, gesturing at the house. "I doubt rogues will try to attack with all four of us here. We'll stay for tonight."

Before any of us could move, Troy straightened with a low hiss. "Someone else is here." His gaze shot toward the car and he tensed as if ready to attack.

I ripped free of Lochlan's hold, yelling, "She's with *me*. Don't hurt her." Ignoring the warning Lochlan barked through our bond, I took up a post in front of the car and stared the vampires down. "Promise you won't hurt her or I'm leaving. *Promise.*"

"I promise," Kade instantly replied, his curiosity pinging through our fledgling bond.

Everett took longer to respond, but with a nod from Lochlan, he too uttered the words.

It was Troy who didn't seem inclined to promise me anything, stubbornly refusing to say a word for several tense moments. But when Everett gave him a sharp look, he blew out a disgruntled sigh and agreed.

Only after I heard Silver say, *It's okay, Kenna,* did I slowly open the door. When she hopped out, four pairs of eyes zeroed in on her. Fates, it felt like I'd just thrown her to a pack of salivating bloodhounds. Readying myself in case she needed protection, I nervously waited for their reactions.

No doubt sensing the supernatural in her, Everett sniffed at the air, then frowned. "What is she?"

"A spirit in animal form. But she's also my familiar," I honestly replied. Hopefully vampires didn't have a vendetta against them too because of their ties with witches.

"Don't worry, little Kenna, she's safe with me," Kade said, then added with a smirk, "I've always wanted a pet."

Silver sneezed, shaking her head as if mildly annoyed at his flippant words. And, just like that, the ice was broken. Just like that, all six of us lowered our guards enough to enter the house peaceably.

But I doubted this would be the last standoff. And I doubted we would all get along in the foreseeable future. We were still on edge for various reasons, and that was sure to cause a few problems.

Especially now that we were all under the same roof.

CHAPTER 16

KENNA

Dinner didn't go well.

Every time one of his brothers or Kade looked at me too long, Lochlan got all growly. When the conversation became too tense for me to handle, I excused myself to retire early.

Lochlan rose to follow, but I quickly said through our bond, *Stay. I'll be perfectly safe upstairs. You four still have a lot to discuss, but it'll be easier for you if I'm not here.*

I knew they wanted to go over the rogue problem and our unexpected soulmate bond in more detail, something they wouldn't do while I was there. I also knew Lochlan didn't want me to leave his side. His protective instincts flared up, along with a stab of guilt. But I didn't give him a chance to protest, sweeping from the room with Silver in tow. When we reached the third floor where his bedroom was, I leaned against the hallway wall with a weary sigh.

Give him time, Silver gently urged, rubbing against my leg. *Mate bonds are hardest on males. Considering there are three other dominant males in close proximity to you, he's doing pretty well.*

I couldn't hold back a soft snort. Mate bonds, dominant males, and talking animals. How had this become my life?

"I think I'll just wait for Lochlan in his room," I told her. "Would you like to join me?"

Oh, no thank you, she replied with a small shake of her head. *Foxes are solitary creatures, and I'm still getting used to so much company. I will find a quiet place for myself. Enjoy your evening, Kenna.*

I watched her go, surprised in a good way by her independence and ability to adapt. She made this having-a-familiar thing super easy. At least she didn't sit on my shoulder twenty-four-seven like Headmistress Mayweather's crow. I shuddered, suddenly realizing that the bird had *literally* been telling Clarice everything I said and did while he'd been spying on me.

Although, having Silver as my spy could be useful. I wondered if she would mind. I still had a lot to learn about her kind, which I was looking forward to.

Pushing off the wall, I headed into Lochlan's bedroom and shut the door. We'd both showered earlier to wash the blood from our skin, so I decided to change into pajamas and snoop around his room for a bit. Grabbing one of his t-shirts from a dresser drawer, I shed everything else but my red lace underwear. Like a drug addict, I greedily inhaled his faint scent on the material, even though he was right downstairs.

I couldn't get enough of him. My body was already pining for his presence after only a few minutes apart. I had it bad. *Really* bad.

To distract myself, I began a self-tour of his personal space. I hadn't paid much attention the first time. My focus had been on more pressing matters. But I took the time now, wandering over to his bookshelves. They were packed with classical fiction, along with historical nonfiction. I shouldn't have been surprised, but I felt a smile tug at my lips all the same.

There was something missing though. I tapped my chin, not quite able to put my finger on it. But as my gaze lifted to the topmost shelf, I grinned.

Journals!

Not as many as he kept at the castle, but there were a few. Standing on tiptoe, I snatched them up and dove onto the king-sized bed. Before my itching fingers could crack them open though, my conscience got the better of me. Hesitating, I bit my lip and quickly blurted through our bond, *I'm going through your journals.*

There. I'd asked for permission first.

As I flopped onto my back and opened one, I felt his warm presence inside my mind. Instead of answering with words, he sent me an image. One of me bent over his knee. He was spanking me. I barked a laugh. When traces of his humor lit up the bond, I settled more comfortably against the mattress and began reading.

He found me a couple hours later, propped against the headboard and surrounded by pillows. Still reading.

I briefly glanced up at him, then back to the pages. "I didn't know werewolves often live together like an actual wolf pack. Or that they help raise each other's children like one big happy family. Or that it's super hard to conceive vampire babies. Or that witch elders are elected by power, not age. These journals should be called Supernatural Creatures For Dummies."

While I rambled, he closed the door and crossed the room, pausing at the foot of the bed. When I continued to flip through the pages, all but ignoring him, amusement flickered through our bond.

"McKenna."

"Huh?" Flip.

"I'm becoming jealous of a book."

"What? Oh, sorry. Almost done."

Flip. Flip.

I yelped as fingers suddenly gripped my bare ankle, dragging me to the bed's center. They let go, only to pluck the journal from my hands and toss it on the mattress. "Hey," I protested, then promptly forgot everything when Lochlan crawled onto the bed to hover above me.

"I was feeling left out," he murmured, wrapping a strand of my hair around his index finger.

"Needy much?" I teased, even as I shivered at the contact.

"Of you? Always," he breathed, lowering his head to kiss my neck. I arched into his touch and let my eyes flutter shut. "I'm sorry about earlier," he whispered against my skin, slowly kissing the length of my throat. "I'm having a hard time . . . controlling myself."

"I'm sorry too," I said, turning my head to give him better access. "I know how important control is for you."

"You can help me," he said between kisses, pausing to nuzzle "his spot" where he liked to bite me.

When I felt the light scrape of his fangs, goosebumps erupted over my flesh. "How?" I gasped, struggling to hold still.

"By letting me have my way with you. Right here. Right now." He gently nipped my collarbone, drawing another gasp from me.

As his words finally sank in, my eyes flew wide and I abruptly sat up. "Are you crazy?" I whisper-yelled. "Kade and your brothers will hear us."

"Let them," Lochlan purred, adjusting his position to nibble at my right earlobe. Freaking fates, the man *seriously* knew how to use his mouth. "We're newly mated. They're expecting us to be intimate. And often."

I squeaked in protest. "I still don't want them to hear when it *happens.*"

He pulled back, only to fix me with a cunning look filled with challenge. "Then don't let them hear."

Oh, he didn't.

He *didn't.*

But he did. There was no denying what he wanted me to do.

"Lochlan," I warned, scooting back on the bed. But when he grasped my thighs and slowly pulled me toward him, I knew he'd won. Knew I wouldn't resist as he gently laid me flat on the bed. Knew I'd give him control to have his way with me. Even if keeping silent was impossible. Even if Kade and his brothers overheard.

When he lifted the hem of my shirt and pressed a lingering kiss to my stomach, I knew I was screwed.

So. Freaking. Screwed.

Sure enough, as his tongue traced a lazy circle around my belly button, a whimper nearly escaped me. I pressed my lips together and swallowed the noise, tangling my fingers into the sheets. His wicked chuckle vibrated through my stomach, lighting a fire in my core. I squeezed my thighs shut, only for him to tsk and pry them back open.

My way, remember? his voice rumbled in my mind as he slid farther down to settle his body between my legs.

Yes, I agreed, my pulse thudding like crazy.

He hummed, clearly pleased with my answer, then did something unexpected. Something he'd never done before. Something I'd never felt, never even *knew* I could feel. Something that made me come apart at the seams.

Pulling my red lacy underwear to the side, he lowered his head between my thighs and licked. *Licked* up my center.

Holy. Freaking. Fates.

Every nerve ending charged awake. I bit my tongue to muffle a scream, hard enough to draw blood. Lochlan licked me again and my entire body bucked under the force of my pleasure.

I've wanted to taste you like this for so long, he murmured through our bond, slowly swirling his tongue around my sensitive peak. My back bowed and I sank my lengthening claws into the sheets to keep from floating away. *You taste exquisite, like the finest wine.*

I couldn't have replied, even if I'd wanted to. He was so thoroughly wrecking me, driving me to the highest ecstasy. I could barely stand it. Could barely function in any sense of the word as his tongue found a rhythm. As it ran over my sensitive peak again and again until I was a mess of raw nerves. Until I could no longer keep in a breathless gasp. Trying to hold it together, I clung to the sheets so tightly that they tore under my claws.

Lochlan chuckled again, the vibration enough to wring another small sound of pleasure from me. *I'm impressed*, he purred, lightly digging his claws into my thighs to keep me from squirming. *I thought you'd be screaming by now.*

My growl ended in a pathetic whimper. Still, I managed to say, *I'll get you back for this.*

Looking forward to it, he replied with devilish amusement, flicking my peak with the tip of his tongue.

I released a muffled cry, unable to suppress it. Unable to concentrate on anything but the bundle of nerves at my apex and his wicked, wicked tongue. He continued to work me into a mindless frenzy, until I was begging him to let me come. But he drew out my pleasure. Drew it out until I thought I would die. Then, with one final swirling lick, he let me climax. So hard that I nearly blacked out.

Despite the intensity of the orgasm, I didn't utter a sound.

But when I felt his approval, his *pride* that I'd won the challenge, I huffed a weak laugh.

I squirmed on the kitchen stool as Kade threw me another look. A *knowing* look. One that was going to get him in trouble if he didn't

stop.

Lochlan was sitting on the stool next to me while I ate my bacon and scrambled egg breakfast, turned sideways as he engaged in conversation with Everett and Troy. No one besides me and Silver were actually eating food. Everyone else was sipping blood from coffee cups, which should have grossed me out but didn't.

Silver had taken her bacon strips to an isolated corner of the house and Kade was standing across the newly-repaired kitchen island from me. When he chanced another peek at me over the rim of his cup, I couldn't take it any longer.

What? I mouthed at him, making sure he felt my annoyance through our bond.

He flicked a glance at Lochlan, who'd so far been chill this morning compared to last evening, before whispering, "Did you hear anything *unusual* last night?"

The eggs on my fork plopped soundlessly onto my plate as I gaped at him. I felt his amusement, but quickly schooled my expression into neutrality before whispering back, "No. Did you?"

"Nope," he replied, ending the word with a *pop*. "I heard your heart beating a mile a minute, which concerned me at first. But when I felt your excitement, I knew there was nothing to worry about." At my horrified look, he hid a smirk behind his coffee cup.

"You're such a child," I threw at him, stabbing my eggs hard enough to crack the plate.

As Kade snickered like said child, Lochlan swiveled toward me. He took in my broken plate and beet-red face before fixing Kade with a severe look. "What happened?"

"Nothing," I quickly spoke up, my blush deepening when both his brothers stopped talking to eye me. "Just Kade making jokes again."

Lochlan's expression suddenly turned murderous. "Jokes about *you?*"

Ah crap. I'd stepped into that one.

"Ah, c'mon, Loch. Lighten up a little," Kade said before I could do damage control. "You know how I feel about sex. There's no need to hide what you're doing. It's a beautiful thing and I only want to express my happiness for you both."

Okay. I officially needed to disappear now. And maybe never show my face to anyone ever again.

Surprisingly, Troy saved me from further embarrassment by saying, "We should get on the road. Father's been going ballistic ever since you all left. He wants us back as soon as possible." Not that he spoke the words for *my* sake, I realized, as he narrowed his eyes at me while sauntering from the kitchen.

But it was enough to defuse the tension.

Everett excused himself, and Lochlan rose to collect the cups. As I went to dump my broken plate in the trash, I heard Lochlan mutter to Kade, "We need to talk about boundaries."

Seemingly unfazed, Kade tossed me a wink before turning to help with the dishes. Deciding to give them a moment, I went in pursuit of Silver and found her curled up on a cushioned window seat in the foyer. The moment I sat down next to her, she rubbed her head against my thigh in greeting. Smiling, I sank my fingers into her thick fur.

Your mate's drothen is . . . exuberant, Silver remarked, having just found out about Lochlan and Kade's bond.

I snorted. "That's one word for him. I'm guessing you overheard what he said in the kitchen?"

Yes. His words are impulsive, but I can sense their genuineness. He cares deeply for you and your mate. I'm having a harder time reading the two brothers, though, especially the younger one. His feelings are ... clouded.

Chewing my lip in thought, I switched to mind-speak. *Will you keep an eye on him for me? I'm still not sure about him either.*

Of course. But not the older one?

Everett and I ... we've come to an understanding.

At least, I *hoped* so.

He and Troy descended the stairs moments later, both in dark-washed jeans and thin sweaters that outlined their defined pecs and muscular arms. Troy almost looked lean compared to his eldest brother, but not many could compete with Everett's rock-solid build.

As much as their striking facial features and rich coloring resembled Lochlan's, my heart didn't skip a beat at the sight of them. Sure, they were stupidly good-looking, but I much preferred black as charcoal eyes and artfully messy hair. Plus, neither of them had a sexily adorable dimple or thorny-vine arm tattoos.

Should I be jealous? a voice in my head purred, right before I spotted Lochlan leaning against the foyer wall. He'd clearly caught me watching his brothers, but didn't seem all that worried, surprisingly.

When I rolled my eyes in reply, his amusement trickled through our bond.

"We should take two cars this time," Everett said upon reaching the foyer. "I'll leave the Volvo here and ride with Troy. The rest of you can take Kade's car."

"How do we know they'll return to Sanctum Isle with us?" Troy stiffly replied, obviously not happy with the arrangement.

"Loch made a promise to me through a pactum," Everett began.

"We'll return," I interrupted. "You have my word. I want the curse broken just as much as you do."

Troy's upper lip curled, the only outward sign of his agitation that I'd spoken. Without a word, he tugged his hat low over his eyes and headed out the door.

When Everett joined him, Lochlan glanced at Kade with a frown. "What happened to my Lexus? I thought you drove it here."

Kade rubbed the back of his neck. "Yeah, about that. I kind of drove it into a gas station—like, inside the actual store—so it's in the shop."

At Lochlan's exasperated look, I burst out laughing, the kind that quickly produced tears. Despite how crazy the last few days had been, we were all here in one piece. And soon, we would meet up with Isla and Noah again, the rest of my found family.

I was relieved and nervous and excited for what was to come. But mostly, I was grateful. Grateful that two vampires had followed me to school one day and were now a fixture in my life. A *permanent* one.

One I was never going to give up.

CHAPTER 17

KENNA

The trip to Sanctum Isle was nothing like the first time.

For one, I wasn't sandwiched in a car filled with unbearable tension and hostility. For another, we reached the bridge in under an hour, and I spent the next hour asking questions about everything I saw. Both Lochlan and Kade humored me, regaling me with stories of how and when the vampire island had been founded.

Despite everything, I was actually *enjoying* the trip. It helped that, this time, I mostly knew what to expect at the end of it. Although, I had no idea how King Ambrose was going to react to our leaving the castle so abruptly. Or our soulmate bond, for that matter.

He can't know, Lochlan suddenly said inside my head, having listened to my thoughts. *Not until I'm certain he'll accept you.*

But won't he be able to tell that you claimed me? I replied back, nervously fiddling with my hands.

Yes. He shifted in the front passenger's seat to glance back at me. *But I'll make him think that it was simply for your protection.*

I blinked. Oh. That could work.

Maybe.

If the mate bond frenzy didn't give us away.

That's what I'm afraid of, Lochlan admitted, turning to face forward again.

"Okay, guys, it's way too quiet in here," Kade spoke up from the driver's seat, throwing Lochlan a suspicious look. "Are you all communicating telepathically without me? Because that's not fair. How am I supposed to know if you're talking smack about me? I think we need to set some ground rules—except for the fox, since she can't actually speak. How about—"

He suddenly slammed on the brakes, trying to avoid Troy's car ahead as it went airborne. When my seat belt painfully cut into my sternum, I made a grab for Silver beside me. The Mustang swerved off the road, nearly plowing into a tree.

I could hear Troy's car flipping. Over and over and over. Tumbling, rolling. Glass breaking. Metal shrieking. I glanced back just as a tire shot toward us. Lochlan lunged into the back seat, shielding me with his body while the windows imploded.

"Kade, get us out of here," he bellowed as glass shards rained down on our heads.

Kade swore sharply. "Loch, we've got company!"

Something slammed into the car and I screamed. The world was suddenly tilting, tilting, tilting. The last of the windows shattered as the car thudded onto its hood, sliding several feet down an embankment.

My teeth clacked together, biting into my tongue. Blood filled my mouth. My arms were still around Silver and Lochlan's around me, but the second the car settled, he burst into action.

"Everybody out," he ordered, unbuckling my seat belt. When it didn't immediately cooperate, he yanked the whole thing out of the seat. I fell with a gasp, but he caught me, lowering my body to the glass-strewn hood. "Kade, I need eyes."

"On it," Kade grunted, ripping off his own seat belt. Before his body could fall, he blurred from the car through the shattered front windshield.

Just as quickly, Lochlan kicked out the back door and gathered me into his arms. I gripped Silver tightly as he blurred us from the wreckage. We didn't get far before several figures dressed head-to-toe in black blocked our way. At first, I thought they were SCA operatives, but when one came at us blindingly fast, dread filled my gut.

Rogues.

Lochlan hissed, whirling to set me on my feet. "Don't let any of them reach her," he barked before turning to face the attacking rogue. I nearly leapt out of my skin when Kade suddenly appeared beside me, squaring off with the rogues on the other side.

"Stay in the circle, Kenna," he said, ignoring the blood dripping into his eyes. He'd been injured the worst in the car wreck. Several gashes marred his face, and pieces of glass were still embedded in his jacket. But there wasn't time to worry about that right now.

Behind me, Lochlan let out a roar. The rogue crashed into him, and they grappled for a few short moments. The fight ended in a blood-curdling scream as Lochlan tore the rogue's tinted goggles and mask off. The vampire's face immediately blistered, smoke rising from his red skin. Then completely burst into flames. He fell to his knees, howling in agony as his entire head burned to ash in seconds. When it was gone, the rest of his body toppled into the snow.

There was a moment of stunned silence. Then chaos as the rogues surrounding us all charged at once.

Lochlan and Kade became whirlwinds of teeth and claws, protecting me as best they could from the attack. But there were so *many* of them. More than I'd ever seen at one time before. They came from all directions, unmindful of the deadly sun, all their focus on getting to me. My heart thudded with fear, with desperation as I searched for a way to help.

Siphon me, Silver said, so suddenly that I flinched, almost

153

forgetting that I was holding her. *At my core, I am made of magic. Take what you need to wipe these foul beasts from the earth.*

My eyes widened. *But won't I turn into a fox like you?*

No. My animal form isn't supernatural. You will only take on my magical essence.

But I-I don't want to hurt you.

There's no time for fear or hesitation, Kenna, she said, her voice laced with authority. *This is a time for* strength. *Now siphon me before it's too late.*

So I did.

While the chaos reigned around us, I dug my fingers into her fur and let my Syphon abilities surge forth. Warmth immediately infused my palms. Red fire engulfed my hands soon after. Foreign magic shot through me, except that it didn't feel foreign at all. More like an extension of what I already possessed. It felt good. *Right.* Like two pieces being forged together. Two pieces that were meant to be one.

More, Silver demanded. *Take more.*

Gritting my teeth, I did as instructed. I took and took until her body shuddered beneath my touch. "I can't," I gasped, wrestling my abilities under control again. "I can't take any—"

A force suddenly rammed into me, and I went flying through the air. With a cry, I hit the ground, losing my grip on Silver as I rolled several feet. Lochlan immediately bellowed in fury, his panic flaring through our bond. I glanced up to see a rogue bearing down on me.

There was no time. No time for anything but to defend myself.

Lifting my hand, I called on my magic. It surged through me, bursting from my fingertips in a shower of undulating red. Just like when I'd magically shoved Jordan and Mei, he tumbled backward. As I scrambled to my feet, a surge of inhuman strength joined the magic warming my insides. This time, I knew what it was. Knew that Lochlan had sacrificed some of his strength for me.

There was no time to demand he take it back, to worry that he'd given me too much. Before I could rejoin him and Kade, another rogue grabbed me from behind. They shoved me toward a tree, intending to bash my head against it. I whipped around, fast enough that I blurred. Every movement was an instinct, a desperate cry of survival.

Breaking their hold, I pushed them back and prepared to run. To seek the safety of my soulmate's protection like I always did. But my instincts wouldn't allow me to. They raged at me to finish what I'd started, to protect my mate from the dangers surrounding us.

So I listened.

I raised my hand toward the rogue who'd grabbed me. Magic readily sprang to my fingertips as if eager to be used. But instead of letting it surge from me, I held it in my hand. Molded it to my will. Used it to grip at the air as if gripping a neck. The second I did, the rogue stopped in his tracks. I squeezed my fingers into a fist and he made a desperate choking noise, reaching up to grab his throat.

Calmly, *too* calmly, I slowly twisted my hand. His head followed the motion, turning sideways at a sharp angle.

I blinked, realizing what this meant.

Kill him, my instincts roared. I started to tremble, terrified of what I wanted to do. Power thrummed in my veins. I somehow knew that, with a flick of my wrist, I could end this being's life. Not just snap his neck, but completely remove his head from his body. All without touching him. I could kill him so easily. I *wanted* to.

But I didn't.

Another instinct beckoned to me and I grabbed onto it like a lifeline. Instead of tearing the rogue in two, I slashed my arm through the air. His whole body whipped sideways and slammed into a tree. As he went limp, I released my hold on him and he crumpled to the snow.

When a sharp *whoosh* announced the presence of more vampires, I whirled, magic crackling at my fingertips. Seeing that it was Everett and Troy, I focused elsewhere, only to find that I was once again protected from all sides. Silver was nowhere to be found, but I didn't let myself panic, choosing to believe she'd found someplace to hide.

Letting the magic die on my fingertips, I turned to Lochlan.

And found him already staring at me.

He was frozen in place, lips half-parted in shock. He took me in as if seeing me for the first time. I stared back, suddenly unsure of my actions.

Had the sight of me using my magic scared him?

Before I could doubt myself any further, he strode toward me. His steps were sure. Purposeful. Nothing could sway him from his path. A rogue got too close and his hand shot out, gripping their neck. Without pausing, without taking his eyes off mine, he snapped their neck and dropped the body.

A thrill shivered up my spine from witnessing such strength. From having that powerful gaze solely focused on me. When he reached me, there was no hesitation. No thought of the ongoing battle or who was watching. He simply swept me into his arms and captured my mouth in a breath-stealing kiss. My feet left the ground as he hungrily pressed me to him, stealing the last of my air.

Overwhelmed by his sudden display of passion, I let the sounds of fighting dim. Let my doubts go, let *everything* go, so that I could fully return his kiss. Time slowed to a crawl, the world around us vanishing while Lochlan kissed me as if possessed. His hands slid up my spine. Tangled in my hair. Tugged my head back so that he could deepen the kiss.

My heart thundered as I desperately tried to keep from drowning. From being utterly consumed by the moment.

It was insane what we were doing. Completely illogical under the circumstances.

But it was freaking glorious.

I could feel every last one of his emotions. His burgeoning pride. His powerful desire. All directed toward me. But his love eclipsed them all. Radiant and bright like the sun, shining down to wholly envelop me in its warmth.

All too soon, he pulled away, heaving in breath after breath. But he didn't let go, ignoring the chaos around us a moment more to say through our bond, *You are magnificent. I should have seen it before. How beautiful your magic is. How powerful it makes you.*

Before I could respond, a rogue broke through the circle and streaked toward us. I threw up a hand to stop them in their tracks and Lochlan did the rest, swiftly snapping their neck.

He turned back to me, heat simmering in his gaze. *Keep that up and I'm going to take you against that tree over there. Right in the middle of this bloody battlefield.*

Shocked by how deadly *serious* he was, I choked out, "Don't you dare. Your *brothers* are here."

His expression turned wicked, and for a split second, I panicked. Panicked, because I would totally let him. Excess magic and strength still thrummed through my veins, making me feel invincible. Reckless. Combined with the way my mate was looking at me, I was also horny as hell.

Despite the danger still surrounding us, a chuckle rumbled in his chest. I could only stare, never having seen him like this before. Not when my life was in jeopardy. It was like a switch had been flipped the moment he'd witnessed me single-handedly take down a vampire. The Lochness Monster was nowhere to be found. In his place was someone I didn't recognize. Someone I desperately wanted to stick around.

This new side of him gave me a heady sense of confidence that I could be useful. That I wasn't simply meant to be protected but to protect others in return. That he *wanted* me to. And that meant more to me than I realized, making me fall in love with him all the more.

Not long after, the last of the rogues were chased off. The second they were out of sight, Troy stormed over. I bristled when he got in Lochlan's face and snapped, "What was *that*? When have you ever stopped in the middle of a fight to suck face with a witch?"

Lochlan bared his teeth in a silent snarl. "Back off, Troy. You're too close."

"Too close to what? Your *mate*?" He spat the word as if it tasted sour.

"Cool it, Troy. He's newly mated," Everett said, coming up behind his irate brother. "We can't expect him to behave rationally during the frenzy period."

Troy rounded on him with a growl. "And when did *you* of all people become Team Syphon? How are you okay with this?"

"Why does it bother you so much? You never cared before. You were totally fine with Loch having sex with her only a few days ago."

"That was before I knew they were *soulmates*. Why am I the only one who realizes how screwed up that is?"

"Take it down a notch," Everett bit out. "We made a brotherly pact to protect each other. That includes our mates, if we ever find them. Any harm to them would harm us."

"But she's a witch. A *Syphon*," Troy hissed, jabbing a finger in my direction. "Being bonded to her is poison."

"Soulmate bonds are rare and sacred, no matter how diverse the pairing is. It's not my place to question fate's decision."

"Well *someone* has to," Troy roared, stunning us all with his ferocity.

It was Everett who recovered first, who said in a matter-of-fact tone, "We don't have time for this right now. The rogues are clearly getting desperate if they're willing to risk broad daylight. Who knows when they'll attack next. Both cars are destroyed, but the castle is only a mile away. I say we make a run for it before they can regroup."

"We'll take him with us," Lochlan said, jerking his chin at the rogue I'd knocked unconscious. "It's about time we properly question these bastards."

"I want to question him first," Troy said, sounding a lot less angry. Still, I shivered when he added, "I have some tension that needs working off."

Everett snorted, their earlier conversation all but forgotten as he replied, "Deal. So long as you save a piece for me."

Troy chuckled, bumping shoulders with his brother good-naturedly before taking off through the woods.

While Everett and Kade secured the rogue prisoner and collected a few belongings from the wrecked vehicles, I stayed where I was, still trying to process all that had been said.

"Troy'll come around," Lochlan murmured beside me, acknowledging Silver's presence when she slipped into view, unscathed. "He always does. I'll make sure of it."

I sure hoped so. Because if he didn't, there wasn't a doubt in my mind that Troy would tell King Ambrose—and anyone else who'd listen—that Lochlan and I were soulmates.

No matter how steep the price.

CHAPTER 18

KENNA

We arrived at the castle in a swirl of wind and snow and chaos.

The moment we entered through the massive front doors, Lochlan set me down, having refused to let me run on my own. We'd covered the mile in under a minute, determined to avoid another attack. I too set Silver on her feet, then immediately wanted to pick her up again as several pairs of feet scrambled around us.

"Close the doors," King Ambrose bellowed at his guards, shadows following in his wake as he stormed into the grand entryway. Troy trailed him at a more sedate pace, watching his father bark orders and call more guards to the entrance. I'd never seen the king this furious. With a growl, he gestured at a pair of guards to take the rogue from Kade and throw him in a cell.

The second he spotted Lochlan though, the anger vanished. He stopped in his tracks, words dying on his lips as he took in his son. I didn't know what reaction to expect from him, but tears certainly weren't it.

Was the powerful and formidable five-hundred-year-old vampire king *crying*?

While the doors slammed shut with an echoing thud, he strode toward Lochlan and enveloped him in a bone-crushing hug. "You're safe. Thank God," he murmured against his son's neck, emotion thick in his voice.

At the unexpectedly touching reunion, my own eyes started to burn with unshed tears.

After a moment, he reached for his eldest son, including Everett in the tight embrace.

I realized something then. Something that softened my heart toward the vampire king. He was a father who cared deeply for his sons. I hadn't seen it until now, the loving familial bond between them all. They might squabble on occasion, but the D'angelos really were a tight-knit family. I couldn't help but compare their family dynamic with my own. Couldn't help but feel the pain of what I'd lost.

As though reacting to my pain, Lochlan pulled back from the embrace to glance at me with concern. Quickly brushing a stray tear from my cheek, I subtly shook my head at him. *Your father*, I said through our bond. His mouth tightened, but he nodded and turned to Kade.

With a single glance, Kade was at my side, placing a comforting hand on my back. Reminding me of what I'd found. Of the *family* I had here. I bit my trembling lip as more tears threatened to fall.

"Troy told me the SCA were responsible for you being taken," the king said, holding his son at arm's length to give him a once over.

Lochlan shook his head. "We don't need to worry about them anymore. They won't be back."

His father raised a skeptical brow. "Are you sure?"

"I'm sure. We should be focused on finding out who tipped them off and containing the growing rogue problem. They're becoming more organized in their attacks."

The king nodded, squeezing Lochlan's shoulders before letting go. He chose that moment to direct his attention to me. I instinctively stiffened as his deep burgundy eyes swept me from head to toe. "You honored our deal. You didn't try to escape." He lifted a brow as if surprised.

Gulping, I managed to stutter, "O-of course I didn't try to escape. I meant what I said about wanting to help break the curse." Then added before I could lose my nerve, "I hope you honored our deal too in regards to Noah Andrews."

His penetrating gaze became impossible to bear. Just when I was about to look away, he chuckled. "I actually started to miss you while you were away, Miss Belmont. I look forward to engaging in more conversation with you. But first"—he shot a calculating look to where Silver quietly stood beside me—"I'd like to know why a witch's *familiar* is in my home."

My protective instincts flared up and I slid in front of her, breaking his stare. "She's mine. Wherever I go, she goes."

His gaze lifted to mine once again. "Well, well, aren't you full of surprises? I've heard that familiars hardly ever seek out their witch counterparts. You've been gifted with a rare bond."

I peeked at Troy still loitering behind him, worried that he'd spill the beans about *another* rare bond. But I was surprised by his rather sullen expression, like the reunion hadn't gone the way he'd hoped.

Before I could respond to the king, I caught sight of something small and bright streaking toward us. Toward *me*. Both Lochlan and Kade shouted a warning, but it was too late.

The thing struck me square in the chest and I let out a pained *ooph*, staggering back under the force. Wiry arms wrapped around me before I could fall, squeezing so tightly that all the air left my body in a whoosh.

"I'm sorry I tried to attack you, Kenna. I've got it under control now. I promise never to bite you, no matter how much I want to taste that delicious-smelling blood of yours," the thing gushed against my chest. The thing that sounded a lot like—

"Isla, *stop*. You're hurting Kenna," Kade's voice cracked through the air. "Let her go."

I stopped breathing—not that I had a choice with her strong little arms squeezing me half to death—and glanced down at the blonde head beneath my chin. Before I could fully realize that it was my human-best-friend-turned-vampire hugging the crap out of me, she quickly pulled back. Almost as if she'd been forced to. Her spine snapped straight, arms falling rigidly to her sides like a marionette doll.

I'd barely sucked in much-needed air when another pair of arms came around me from behind, strong yet gentle as they tugged me farther away from my friend. Recognizing them as Lochlan's, I let him pull me a safe distance away, feeling his protective instincts flare up.

I only had a moment to take in her pink-tipped hair, stormy blue eyes set in a heart-shaped face, and fine porcelain skin, before Kade planted himself between us. Through the gap between his arm and side, I saw Isla's hands ball into fists as she glared up at the vampire who'd saved her life.

"Is this far enough away, *master?*" she said, bitterness coating each syllable.

My jaw dropped. What the crap was *that* about?

The sire bond must have kicked in, Lochlan replied inside my head.

Sire bond? My eyes widened as Kade's entire body stiffened, a mixture of hurt and frustration clouding our bond.

Kade made Isla into a vampire with his blood. He now has the ability to influence her actions through what we call the sire bond. It's the only way a vampire can control another vampire, similar to how thrall works. But it's frowned upon to use the ability, unless absolutely necessary.

My eyes widened further. *So he can* control *her?*

Lochlan shifted on his feet, clearly uncomfortable with the word. *Yes, but Kade's a good guy. He won't abuse his sire abilities.*

Say that to Isla, I muttered, cringing when she abruptly swiveled on her heel and stormed away, her pretty pink skirt swishing angrily against her thighs.

Before I could attempt something reckless, like go after her, I heard the king say, "Your friend has quite the mouth on her. She's been inquiring about you nonstop since you left, insisting I keep her updated."

I glanced over to find him watching me. Lochlan's arms tensed, but he didn't let me go. So I did what he couldn't, stepping away to create some distance between us. King Ambrose tracked the move without comment. "That's what I love about her," I said, hoping the words would divert his attention.

Sure enough, his eyebrows inched upward. "Even though she tried to attack you? Even though she's now a vampire?"

"Of course," I instantly replied. "She's still the same person, even if her appearance and appetite have changed."

He stared a moment more, then slowly smiled, nodding as if I'd passed a test. "Come. I'm sure you'd all like to rest after the ordeal you just went through, but first, I have a deal to uphold."

While we followed the king, I took in the castle's many priceless gold, marble, and jeweled artifacts—not a speck of silver to be found. Nothing had changed while we'd been away, but everything felt different. Maybe because *we* had changed, just like Isla had. The same, yet different.

Instead of heading for the throne room, the king led us underground down a flight of steep, winding stone stairs. I shivered as the air chilled, as the passage grew darker and darker the deeper we went. The wall sconces looked ancient, their dim lighting barely enough to see by. My heart suddenly tripped in panic.

Just as quickly, a hand came to rest between my shoulder blades. *What's wrong?*

My night vision is gone, I told Lochlan, struggling to see through the gloom so I wouldn't trip and break my neck.

You must have exchanged your vampire abilities for witch powers when you siphoned your familiar.

Crap. Well that explained why the thought of drinking blood suddenly sounded disgusting.

When he shifted his hand to my shoulder, a silent reassurance that he wouldn't let me fall, I pushed my gratefulness toward him. Remembering how Jordan had conjured a magical orb to see by, I lifted my hand and willed light to spring from it.

After several failed attempts, I dropped my arm with a frustrated huff. My magic only responded to life and death situations, apparently.

"As you all know, someone betrayed us the night of the ball," King Ambrose suddenly spoke ahead of us, his voice echoing dully off the stones. "I've interrogated the guards and staff, but haven't found any leads. Since we don't know who that someone is, we should be on our guard at all times. They could still be freely roaming these halls, preparing for their next attack. It could come from anywhere. Or anyone."

A thin thread of light greeted us when we finally reached solid ground, weakly penetrating the darkness from a narrow window high above. Air puffed from my mouth, a visual sign of how cold it was down here. Not that I needed it. Even with my coat still on, I could feel the chill sinking into my skin, a sensation I'd barely felt since becoming a temporary vampire.

"The dungeon is usually reserved for newly-turned Feltore who can't control their bloodlust. When their recklessness threatens to expose us to the human population, we contain them in these specially-made cells for as long as it takes," the king continued, pausing at a locked reinforced door guarded by two vampires. "But as the permanency of the curse presses down on us all, a few bloodthirsty younglings are the least of our concerns."

He reached out to touch the door, but at the last second, his fingers curled into a fist and he dropped his arm. Turning, he resumed walking down a corridor lined with similar rooms, all empty.

Except for the last one.

I swallowed, suddenly nervous to discover what lay on the other side. The king stopped before the locked door, fixing me with a stern look. "He can't know about what happened here. I won't have witches aware that our walls were breached so easily. That not all inside are loyal to the crown. Promise me your silence and I will open this door."

The breath froze in my lungs.

"Noah?" I weakly whispered. "You kept Noah down here this entire time?"

He studied me curiously. "No further harm has come to the warlock and he's received food daily. He's lucky to still be alive, considering you left the island without permission."

"I get that, but . . ." I made a frustrated sound, completely forgetting who I was talking to. "He's not a *vampire*. It's freezing down here, for one thing. And did anyone bother to tend his injuries? I . . . I need to see him. I need to make sure he's okay."

Overwhelmed with guilt and worry, I did something stupid then. I rushed toward the door without thinking. As I reached for the handle, King Ambrose firmly gripped my arm, halting my progress.

The second he touched me, Lochlan's territorial instincts went haywire. In the blink of an eye, he severed his father's hold with a ferocious growl and hauled me against him possessively.

Holy. Freaking. Crap.

Except for a growling Lochlan, everyone else went deathly quiet. All eyes went to the king, waiting for his reaction. He seemed shocked by his son's behavior, keenly watching the animalistic way Lochlan held me to him. At the same time, he didn't seem shocked at all. Which terrified me the most.

Lochlan, you need to let me go, I said as calmly as I could.

But when he snarled, *Never*, and only pulled me closer, I knew talking sense into him right now was futile.

I shot a helpless look at Kade, but his expression mirrored my own.

Expecting the king to be furious, I was stunned when he smoothly said, "From the moment you brought her before me, I knew you had feelings for her, my son. Your public vow at the ball revealed how deep they went. And now, I can scent your recent claim on her."

"For her protection," Lochlan gruffly replied.

"Perhaps," his father said, sliding his hands into his pockets. "But I fear your attachment will end with a broken heart, and that I cannot abide." His expression suddenly darkened, and the look was so fierce that I couldn't help but tremble. "Needless to say, witches do not belong in the vampire world. Kenna will only be with us for a short while, whether the curse breaks or not. When her time here is over and she returns to her world, I need to know that my son will be left unscathed."

He directed the last bit at me, and I quaked under his powerful gaze. I was wrong about him. Oh so terribly wrong. He didn't just love his sons. He loved them *fiercely*, enough to destroy anything that caused them harm.

I could see it in his eyes. The warning to tread carefully. Without a doubt, he wouldn't hesitate to end me if I hurt Lochlan. Not just physical hurt, but hurt of any kind.

I lowered my gaze in submission, keeping my mouth firmly shut. There was nothing I could say anyway. He clearly didn't accept me. Not as his son's lover, and most *definitely* not as his soulmate. I was still an outsider, one who was already wearing out her short welcome. And if I wasn't careful, my time here could end in my death.

Hours later, my nerves were completely shot.

A thumb brushed over my cheek, there and gone again in a blink.

I'm sorry about earlier, Lochlan said through our bond as we traversed the hallways together in silence. *I thought my father would be more reasonable. I should have said something. I should have—*

No, I quickly interrupted, sniffing back a sudden bout of tears. *I'm glad you didn't. He wasn't ready to hear it anyway.*

Still, he threatened you. His words in my head were a growl. *No matter what happens, I won't let him touch you, McKenna. If he refuses to accept you, then we'll simply create our own world to live in.*

Stunned by his words, I stopped in the middle of the hallway to look up at him. *You would leave your family?*

Not all of them, he said with a shrug. *Kade would come with us.*

Crap. Why did he have to be so . . . so freaking *wonderful*? A tear escaped my control and slid down my cheek.

Lochlan stared at the tear like it personally offended him. Stared some more, then swiftly brushed it away.

You shouldn't do that, I said, stepping back. *Someone will see.*

He clenched his jaw, but didn't bridge the gap between us or pursue the matter. I could feel his unrest though. The tension thrumming through his body. I knew how he felt. I felt it too. The need to be close, to further strengthen our bond. To explore him in every way possible, allowing him to do the same to me.

He closed his eyes and groaned. *I can smell your arousal, McKenna.*

Fates!

Why did it always turn me on when he said that?

I clasped my hands behind my back, desperate to keep them to myself. But when his eyes opened and he fixed me with a hungry— no, *starving*—look, my resolve weakened.

"There you two are," a voice suddenly interrupted, almost startling a yelp out of me.

As Kade strode toward us, I did my best not to look guilty.

Or horny.

No such luck.

The second he came within range, Kade lifted his nose and inhaled loudly. Sputtering out a laugh, he said, "Smells like I came to find you just in time."

I gave him a withering look, expecting Lochlan to growl at him. When he didn't utter a sound, both Kade and I glanced over to find him stiff as a board, his eyes once again glued shut.

Kade immediately sobered, slowing to approach his friend more cautiously. "Okay, buddy, let me help you walk it off. That's it. Get the blood flowing to other parts of your body."

Heat crept up my neck at his bold observation. Sure, he'd saved us from blowing our cover, but did he have to be so *candid?*

Steering Lochlan down the hall as if he were drunk, Kade briefly

169

glanced back at me to say, "How's your warlock friend?"

I followed at a safe distance, struggling to cool my overheated skin. "He'll survive. Finding him a room in the servant's quarters was a good idea, especially since they're all human. But he's in pretty bad shape. I know King Ambrose didn't want Noah to portal out of his cell, but I can't believe his wrists were bound the entire time. He was barely able to feed himself."

I was still mad about it. But mostly sad.

When I'd entered his cell hours earlier, he'd seemed but a husk of his former self. Defeated. Broken. His stare had been vacant, and I'd worried that he didn't even recognize me.

"Is Silver still with him?" Kade inquired, throwing me a sympathetic look.

"Yes. They're comfortable around each other, which I think he really needs right now. It's going to be hard for him not being able to leave this place. Even harder when he finds out about . . ."

"You didn't tell him?"

I swallowed past the lump in my throat. "I don't know how to. He's going to be so crushed."

"At least she's alive," Kade gently said, yet I could feel his guilt.

"Yes, and I'm so grateful, Kade," I rushed to say, wanting to comfort him. "Please know that."

"I do," he replied with a small smile, then slowed as we neared our destination.

When a rush of nerves battered at my stomach, Lochlan finally turned to face me.

Are you sure you want to do this? he tightly said, still not completely in control of himself. I could tell he wanted me to change my mind, but I was resolute in my decision. I needed to be the one to do this.

So I nodded, showing him more confidence than I felt. *I'll call for you right away if anything happens.*

Protectiveness flashed through our bond, but he jerked his head in a sharp nod anyway.

Searching his face a moment more, I steeled my spine and turned to knock on the door.

"We'll be right outside the entire time, little Kenna," Kade quietly said as a rustling noise came from inside the room.

I tried to smile, but failed, too nervous about what awaited me on the other side of the door. But when it finally opened, revealing the person within, my nerves fell away. Tears sprang to my eyes at the sight of her. Emotion clogged my throat as I managed to whisper to my best friend, "Oh, Isla. I missed you so much."

CHAPTER 19

KENNA

Except for the hungry way she eyed my neck on occasion, it was like nothing had changed between us.

We hugged and cried, then hugged some more. After reassuring me that she'd just fed and her bloodlust was under control, Isla had dragged me to her bed. Even before we'd settled on the plush white comforter, she was talking a mile a minute, asking me question after question.

"Hold on," I said with a laugh, my heart overflowing with relief and joy that she was still her old bubbly self, despite the new set of fangs. "Before I tell you anything, just know that the guys are right outside the door listening."

Her smile dimmed, then disappeared completely. With a toss of her pink-tipped hair, she said, "I don't care if Kade hears what I have to say. He's a dick and deserves to know it. Do you know what he did before he left to find you? He told me to stay. And do you know what I did? I stayed. Like a frickin' *dog*."

"Oh, Isla," I whispered.

"I'm sorry, Kenna. I know he's your friend, and I know he saved my life or whatever, but . . . but this stupid *sire* bond changes everything. He can take away my *free will*. He can put me in a cage and throw away the key. I've been thralled and kidnapped and drained by vampires. Now *this*?"

At her lost expression, my heart sank and I drew her into another hug. I ached for her situation, but I also ached for Kade's. Knowing him, he was only trying to keep her safe.

She suddenly laughed and pulled away to grab my hand. "How are you doing this anyway? The last time you touched a supernatural, crazy things happened."

Understanding her need to change the sore subject, I responded with a weak laugh of my own. "Yeah, um, I have a few things to tell you. But before I do . . ." I gripped her fingers and inhaled a fortifying breath before plunging forward. "Your brother is here."

There. I'd said it. I'd ripped the bandaid off and—

"*Noah* is here?" she hollered, springing to her feet.

Just like that, the door flew open with a *bang* and Lochlan charged in. I was safely caged between his arms and halfway across the room in two seconds flat. Ignoring Kade as he quietly shut the door and leaned against it, Isla gaped at us with her jaw halfway unhinged.

Sorry, I mouthed at her, which only made her eyes comically bug out.

Owlishly blinking several times, she finally cleared her throat and muttered, "So the intensity between you two has gone up a notch, I see."

Waiting for Kade to make a wisecrack remark, I was shocked when he stayed silent. In fact, he wasn't even looking at us, choosing to blankly stare at a spot on the far wall. I tuned into his emotions and immediately felt his sadness and regret. It took everything in me not to go to him, to comfort him as he so often comforted me. But doing so could hurt Isla, so I forced myself to refocus on her instead.

"Just a little bit, which is something I need to talk to you about. But . . ."

"But Noah," she finished for me. "How in the world did he get *here*, of all places?"

I sighed. "It's a long story, but I want to tell you everything before you see him. He's . . . not in a good place right now. Mentally, I mean."

She sank onto the bed again, her brow creased with worry. "He's going to flip when he finds out what happened to me." She sat in silence for a moment before her chin began to wobble. "How am I supposed to face my dad like this? What if he . . . what if he *hates* me? How can I ever go home? I can't even go out in the *sun*."

When she heaved a sob and covered her face with her hands, Kade took a step toward her. He immediately halted, looking torn over what to do.

I shifted in Lochlan's arms to give him a pleading look. *I'm safe with her. She needs me right now.*

His hold tightened, then slowly fell away as he released me. *We'll give you space and time to talk. We're not scheduled to speak with my father until this evening anyway. But the second she looks at you funny—*

I'll call you, I rushed to say, standing on tiptoe to kiss his cheek. The second I did, I jerked back, an apology springing to my lips.

Don't you dare say you're sorry, his voice rumbled in my mind. Our eyes met and held. Only for a moment, but so many words were spoken in that single blip of time. So many promises. So many hopes and dreams. Our eyes continued to communicate as he backed out of the room, as he nudged Kade into following him and quietly shut the door.

Blowing out a pent-up breath, I turned to my grieving friend, determined to ease her suffering in any way I could.

By the time night came around, exhaustion pulled at every square inch of me.

Isla and I had talked for hours, sharing the many experiences we'd had during our time apart. We cried together. Laughed together. And when I'd told her about my soulmate bond with Lochlan, we'd unapologetically swooned together.

But not before she'd crowed, "I knew it!"

Even after I'd insisted she couldn't have possibly known, she wouldn't take back the words. I'd then spent the next several minutes trying and failing to dodge her probing questions about our sex life. In the end, she knew way too much and was one giddy-looking girl because of it.

I'd stayed with her while she transitioned into her vampire form, watching her pale skin become the darkest of blacks. When the transformation was complete, I'd barely recognized her. But when she showed me her black claws and said, "Aren't these bad boys the coolest?" I knew she was still my Isla.

Promising to visit her before the night was over, I'd then headed to a meeting. Apparently a *secret* one, held in a soundproofed room attached to the king's private office. Only the king, his sons, Kade, and I had attended. Noah hadn't been invited, as the king didn't want Headmistress Mayweather to know about it.

More and more, I wondered if the new council he'd put together was a sham, only meant to appease Clarice so she'd hand me over to him without a fuss. That or including her had been part of their pactum agreement. Either way, he was most definitely the one in control. He'd grilled us for hours, wanting to know about everything that had happened since the night of the masquerade ball.

The entire time, I'd struggled to keep my composure, terrified that one of Lochlan's brothers would blurt about our soulmate bond and doom us both. But they hadn't, even going so far as to gloss over the details of the time Lochlan and I had spent at the cabin—almost as if they'd rehearsed their stories ahead of time.

By the time the meeting—more like *interrogation*—was over, I desperately needed sleep. Especially since there was another more official meeting scheduled for the next morning. Still, I checked on Noah and Silver, then Isla, making sure they had what they needed before heading to my old room.

The room I hadn't even slept in.

The room King Ambrose insisted was safe for me to stay in.

Alone.

Not that I expected him to be okay with me sleeping in Lochlan's room, but still. Whoever had laced their drinks with silver could still be in the castle. Who knew when and where they'd strike next. And maybe, instead of calling the SCA to infiltrate the castle again, they'd ally with the rogues.

I knew the king wasn't shortsighted when it came to safety, but letting me sleep in a room by myself seemed like a recipe for disaster.

"I'm not letting you stay here unprotected," Lochlan suddenly said, breaking into my thoughts. "I'll stand guard from the hallway. And I want you to drink a vial of my blood every day."

"Why?"

"I don't want anyone thralling you."

Remembering the rogue at the gas station who'd nearly thralled me into draining a human, I nodded without argument. After thoroughly scanning every inch of my bedroom for potential threats, Lochlan turned to me, relaxing his rigid posture. He too looked exhausted and I hated the thought of him standing watch all night without sleep.

The king hadn't stopped him from walking me back to my room, but I had no doubt he was keeping a close eye on us. He might have even ordered his guards to spy on our activities for him. I couldn't exactly ask Lochlan to stay in my room with me.

Lochlan's expression softened as my concern for him traveled through our bond. "I'll be fine, McKenna. Your safety is worth losing sleep over."

"But what about *your* safety?" I said, stepping toward him. When his eyes hungrily tracked the movement, I forced myself to stop. "You were the one who was taken."

"My father has upped the castle's security since then. I won't let anyone get the drop on me so easily next time." When I still looked doubtful, he slowly approached me. I held still, barely daring to breathe as he lifted a hand to my hair, curling a thick mass around his finger. "Don't worry, love. I won't let anyone take me away from you. Ever again."

CHAPTER 20

LOCHLAN

I replayed my promise to McKenna long into the night.

I meant the words with every fiber of my being, but I'd made a promise to her before. To never leave her alone, ever again. And I'd had to break that promise.

I prided myself on my control, on my ability to assess the dangerous world around me and come out on top. Ever since my time with Edith—the conniving Syphon who'd taken me as her blood slave—I'd learned how to curb my baser instincts so that I'd never be caught unaware again. To always be watching for the next attack. To never let my guard down. To question everyone and trust no one.

Then I'd met her. My soulmate. And everything I'd taught myself started to unravel.

I'd lost control, over and over. I'd succumbed to rage. To lust. And everything in between. I'd made mistakes. Stupid ones. Terrible ones. I'd made vows and pactums and promises, ones that I now feared I might have to break. Because my safety was no longer my priority. *Hers* was. And I'd foolishly lose control, make mistakes, and break every vow I'd ever sworn if it meant keeping her safe.

But I needed to purge the mate bond frenzy from my system somehow. It was clouding my judgment, making me say and do things that could put her in jeopardy. As much as I hated losing control, I hated putting her in danger even more.

If only we'd been given more time to cement our completed

bond. Seeing my mate surrounded by so many males was the worst kind of torture. My instincts demanded that I rip the heads off anyone too close to her—or possessively claim her in front of them all. Being unable to do either, to not even *touch* her, was tearing jagged holes in my sanity.

Something had to give soon or I was going to snap.

It was around midnight when I finally felt her drift into a restless sleep. Around two in the morning, the first image struck. I straightened from my position against the wall outside her room, caught off guard by the vibrant image inside my head. When another followed, then another and another, it hit me that I was seeing her dream.

Or rather, her nightmare.

I was through the door even before she choked out a terrified scream. At the sound of my abrupt entrance, she startled awake and shot up in bed. Seeing me, she slapped a hand over her mouth to stifle a sob. I immediately went to her, unable to ignore her pain. As the bed's mattress dipped under my weight, she tried to wave me away. To assure me she was all right.

But I had seen her nightmare. And she was anything but all right.

She stiffened when I propped myself against the headboard beside her. The second I pulled her against me, though, she melted. Every inch of me flooded with contentment to have her where she belonged.

"It was only a nightmare," I told her, listening to her thundering pulse gradually slow.

She sniffled, tightly gripping my shirt front. "It . . . it was so real."

"I saw."

Surprise flitted through our bond.

"You saw my dream?"

"Yes. Subconsciously, you must have shared it with me."

She was silent for a moment, then, "It could really happen though. If I don't break the curse in time, you'll all be vulnerable. You, Kade, Isla . . . My parents. All the people I love. Exposed to humans. Unable to hide their true forms." Her voice lowered to a faint whisper. "You could all be taken from me."

I immediately regretted my earlier promise, realizing it had brought on her nightmare. It was her greatest fear to have everything she loved taken from her. To be left all alone. I brought my hand up to gently run my fingers through her thick hair.

"I have nightmares too," I said in hushed tones. "Of some unknown threat stealing you away, right from under my nose. And no matter how hard I look, I can never find you again."

She made a sympathetic sound before pressing a kiss to my chest. To my heart.

The comforting gesture made it hard to breathe. To say the words I needed her to hear next. But I managed, because I couldn't keep this a secret. She deserved to know. To understand the sacrifice I was willing to make. No—*had* to make.

The words were strained but unwavering, resolute in every way as I said, "I'd rather the curse become permanent than lose you trying to break it."

CHAPTER 21

KENNA

"The interrogation was a bust. I'm telling you, most of these rogues are following blind. They have no idea who's calling the shots, only that they want in on this crazy pipe dream. We should be discussing ways to actively stop them, not waiting for their next ambush. Not hiding, like we're *afraid* of a bunch of traitors."

Everett's impassioned speech filled the soundproofed room, further adding to the tension saturating the air.

The morning meeting was in full swing, but this time, Noah Andrews and Clarice Mayweather had been summoned to attend. Despite his rather subdued expression, I hadn't missed the hate-filled glare Noah had sent the headmistress upon her arrival. She'd barely glanced at him, but I knew the feeling was mutual.

I still hadn't told him about Isla, but before the meeting started, I'd quickly informed him that Clarice was secretly an elder. His face had flushed red with anger, giving me hope that there was still fight left in him. He may have lost his right to a coven when he'd helped me escape Thornecrest Academy, but I was determined to help him keep his magic from being bound.

All he had to do was follow me around and report back to Clarice on the curse-breaking progress. Then he'd be free to go. After everything he'd been through, he deserved a fulfilling life outside of the academy that had become his prison. I would make sure he got that chance. It was the least I could do after all his help—and after he'd befriended me when no one else would.

"I agree that the rogue situation needs to be addressed, but let's stay on topic," King Ambrose replied to Everett's outburst, gesturing for him to sit back down. "The month is nearly halfway over, leaving us with only a month and a half until the hundred years are up. We need to discuss our theories on how best to break this curse."

Everett swiftly glanced at me and Lochlan before resuming his seat, but made no further comment.

"What have you tried in the past?" Clarice spoke up, earning another glare from Noah. Nautilus, her crow familiar, was perched on her shoulder as usual, all but a feathery extension of her body. I'd opted to leave Silver out of the meeting, wary of Clarice's reaction to her.

"Mostly blood sacrifices," Troy responded in a bored drawl, acting much more like himself this morning. He kicked his feet onto the heavy mahogany table, earning a disapproving frown from his father.

Clarice's eyes widened behind her gold half-rimmed glasses. "In what way are these sacrifices conducted?"

The king cleared his throat in warning, but Troy plowed ahead anyway, raising his fingers to tick off the list. "Let's see. We slit the first Syphon's throat, letting her blood spill out onto a sacrificial altar. The second chose to attack us before we could sacrifice her, which ended in her swift death. The third was bitten and drained by a high council member, killing them both. We experimented more with the fourth, keeping her alive for several months as we tried different rituals. Unfortunately, she died of hypothermia. The fifth was killed by rogues, and the sixth is not-so-helpfully sitting across from me right now."

All the blood drained from my face.

"*Troy*," Lochlan thundered beside me, slamming his fist on the table. I jumped as the massive piece of wood split in two with a loud *crack*. Kade grabbed his arm, keeping him firmly in his seat with a sharp headshake.

King Ambrose looked between his sons, then sighed heavily, slumping back in his chair.

"And you thought these barbaric *methods* would work?" the headmistress seethed, clearly upset. Even Nautilus looked ruffled, shaking out his feathers with a short caw.

"Most of the ideas came from my council," the king said, as if that made the violent murders okay. "They thought the prophecy was alluding to a sacrifice of blood. Not just from the Syphon, but from us as well. We've all spilled blood for this curse. Blood is what vampires know. What we value most. The mixing of it, the consuming of it, even the spilling of it holds meaning to us. It's how we are made. It's how we thrive. Many of the vows and bonds we forge require blood sacrifices, so why shouldn't this curse?"

"I think you're interpreting the prophecy all wrong," Clarice curtly replied, tapping her nails on the armrests of her chair. "A sacrifice must be made, yes, but a choice must be given as well. Did you ask these girls if you could take their blood? Did you give them a choice at all? I can already tell by your expressions that you haven't. Your narrowmindedness in the matter has led to the deaths of several innocent witches and nothing more."

The silence that followed was deafening.

Despite her accusatory words, Clarice seemed unruffled by the looks being thrown her way, most of them hostile. She and King Ambrose stared at each other for a long moment, heat building between them both, before he finally said, "I think we've had enough for today. Ponder on what has been said and prepare to offer solutions the next time we meet. You are all dismissed."

"Noah, a word?" the headmistress said as we all rose to our feet. I glanced at him, worried that he was still too upset to speak with her. Although his face still sported cuts and bruises from Everett and Troy's rough treatment, he gave me a small reassuring smile before moving to join her. As Clarice led them to a corner and activated a sound-blocking spell, I nervously chewed on my lip.

Are you okay? Lochlan's concerned voice filled my head.

No, I honestly replied without looking at him, afraid his father would figure out we were mind-speaking. *Those poor girls . . .*

I suppressed a shiver. Under different circumstances, I could have been one of them. Split open like a prized pig. I *still* could.

I'm sorry you had to hear that, was his only reply.

I released my lip as we filed from the room. *Do you think the prophecy is referring to a blood sacrifice?*

No. Maybe at one time, but not anymore. I think the meaning is deeper than that. More metaphorical, less literal.

I chewed on that instead of my lip while waiting for Noah to emerge, wondering what kind of metaphorical sacrifice could free an entire race from a curse. By the time Noah joined us, my brain hurt from the multitude of possibilities.

"What did she say?" I asked him, assuming Clarice had already left by way of a portal.

He shot a distrustful glance at both Lochlan and Kade, but when I gave him an encouraging look, he said, "Nothing much. Just wanted to remind me of my duties here and the consequences should I fail to uphold them."

I grimaced. "Did she say anything about the elders and their decision to bind your magic or not?"

His expression darkened. Like *really* darkened. I could have sworn lightning flashed in his stormy blue eyes. "No. Knowing her, she'll dangle that over my head until she gets what she wants from me. She's an elder, after all. It's what they do."

"I'm so sorry, Noah. I'm sorry about everything."

He shook his head. "It's not your fault. You didn't do any of this." I winced as he shot another glance at Kade and Lochlan. We both knew his beef wasn't really with them, but he carried a lot of surplus anger for vampires as a whole at the moment. Which was going to make this next part suck big time.

Deciding to show him instead of trying to explain, I started walking. The guys followed me without comment, and soon Silver joined us. Noah's face seemed to brighten a little when he saw her, and the sight made me smile. As we neared our destination, I couldn't help but feel both nervous *and* excited.

For the first time ever, I was going to unite the people I cared about most in the world. My found family. They were all here. Together in one place. And, despite the many hardships ahead of us, that was worth celebrating.

When I knocked on her door, my stomach was doing backflips. But when the moment of truth finally arrived, I wasn't prepared in the least for the outpouring of emotions that hit me.

Noah froze, his mouth parted in shock as he beheld his little sister. The sister he had thought was dead. Isla's eyes were round, almost frightened as she took in her brother's reaction.

"Isla?" he whispered in disbelief, staring at her like she was a ghost, the same way I had. For a second, I thought he'd keel over from the shock of seeing her. But instead, he came alive. No—burst *awake*. Breathing her name again, he swept her into a tight embrace.

She released a sob. Then a laugh. Her arms wrapped around his neck as he picked her clean off the floor.

Tears streamed down my face as I witnessed their heartfelt reunion. Lochlan's fingers feathered down my spine and I leaned into his touch, too overcome with emotion to worry about spying eyes. He pulled me back against him, dipping his head to breathe me in.

You're amazing, he said through our bond, and I couldn't help but laugh. But rejoice in this moment filled with so much love.

It didn't matter that I'd ducked and rolled in record time. I still felt the hot sizzle of magic against my bare skin as it blasted past.

I popped up on my feet a second later to find Lochlan inches away, silently seething as he stared Noah down. Noah and I groaned at the same time, drawing a frown from Lochlan.

"You said so yourself," I told him, trying to take his attention off my trainer. "Magic makes me stronger. More powerful. I need to learn defense as well as offense in case we're attacked again."

"This is how witches learn how to use their magic," Noah added from his spot across the matts, exasperation coating each word. "I won't let her get badly injured."

"Badly injured?" Lochlan hissed, lifting my arm to show off the nasty burn on my bicep.

"Give her a little of your blood afterward and she'll be good as new," Noah replied with more than a little snark. A devilish twinkle entered his eye, and before I could stop him, he added, "I still can't believe you passed me up for this guy, K-Bug. I didn't think you'd go for the possessive alphahole type."

Lochlan lunged at him, so fast that I couldn't intervene in time. But, with a flick of his wrist and a few muttered words, Noah had him frozen in place. From his spot against the wall, Kade straightened, looking two seconds away from charging at the warlock himself.

"Ugh, everybody *stop* attacking each other," I groaned, rolling my eyes to the ceiling high above. "I'm trying to practice here."

This wasn't the first time in the past two days that Noah had put a freezing spell on Lochlan. The moment he'd been reunited with his sister, Noah had gotten his old mojo back, irreverent snark and all. Even after discovering that Isla was now a vampire, all he could see was his living, breathing little sister.

When both Clarice and King Ambrose had given us approval to train in an unused wing on the sixth floor, Noah's confidence and snarkiness had grown to epic levels of stupidity. Isla had warned me about his trouble-maker ways, but I hadn't realized just how reckless he could be.

Once he'd figured out that Lochlan and I were a thing—a *secret* thing—he'd made it his mission to get under Lochlan's skin. True to his nature, Lochlan exploded every time, seeing the provoking jabs as a threat. Especially when Noah was stupid enough to flirt with me.

Every day that passed—every second that Lochlan and I were forced to keep our distance—was getting harder. Except for the occasional lingering touch, we hadn't been intimate in over three days. I could see how it affected him. Feel his pent-up need and frustration. Being stuck in meetings while I trained with a man he barely knew or trusted wasn't helping matters. And seeing me spar with Noah, and sometimes get hurt, was stretching him to his breaking point.

Sure enough, the second the spell wore off, Lochlan's claws shot out and he loosed a growl. At the promise of violence in the sound, I slid up behind him, resting my hand on his trembling arm.

Do you want me to stop training? I asked through our bond,

187

hoping the connection would help soothe him.

No, he immediately growled, then made an effort to soften his next words. *It gives me peace of mind knowing that you can defend yourself. And I want you to feel confident in your abilities. But that warlock . . .*

I pressed my lips together so I wouldn't do something stupid, like smile. *He's provoking you on purpose because you make it super easy.* When I felt his annoyance, I quickly added, *I don't think Isla told him about our soulmate bond. He just thinks you're being overprotective and doesn't understand how hard this is for you.*

He likes you. The muscles bunched in Lochlan's arm as he formed a fist.

He's a womanizer, I said, trying not to roll my eyes again. *He likes a lot of girls.*

"Can someone explain to me what's going on here?" Noah suddenly said, his brow furrowing as he looked between us in confusion. "Is this like a 'calm the beast' ritual I'm unaware of? Granted, I don't have personal experience dating vampires, but—"

"Okay, time for a break," Kade called, jogging toward Lochlan before he could lunge at Noah again. Stepping between them, he peered at me over Lochlan's shoulder with an almost desperate look. "Maybe you should work on your offense, little Kenna. Over there. Like *way* over there."

Wisely taking his advice, I hightailed it to the far corner where Silver was basking in a patch of sunlight. The only one not here was Isla, who couldn't bear the room's brightness at this hour. Silver flicked her tail in greeting as I approached. *Done with practice already?*

No, I replied, crouching to sit cross-legged beside her. *Things just got too heated again between the guys.*

Ah. Your mate is jealous of the warlock's attention on you.

It was on the tip of my tongue to deny it, but there was one thing I'd learned about my wise familiar in the short time I'd known her: she was usually right.

What can I do? I asked her, wiping a trail of sweat from my brow.

He needs reassurance that you only have eyes for him. Unfortunately, in his case, words aren't enough. As a dominant alpha newly mated, he needs . . .

Heat rose to my cheeks as she let the sentence hang.

Sex, I finished for her, feeling my face heat even more, along with other body parts. *He needs sex.*

She lifted her head to blink at me, but didn't reply. She didn't need to. Biting back another frustrated groan, I swiftly peeked at the source of our conversation. Finding his eyes already on me, my body lit up like a freaking sparkler.

You can use that restless energy to fuel your abilities, Silver said, and I reluctantly focused on her again.

How?

Channel it into your magic, as magic is but a form of energy itself. The mixing of the two might allow you to have better control and conjure spells more readily.

Kind of like a caffeine boost?

She stood up and stretched before primly facing me, elegantly curling her tail around her body. *The comparison is suitable, though I've never had caffeine.*

Oh, right. Stuck in a fox body.

"That's kind of sad," I murmured, propping my chin on my fist.

Is it? she responded with a tilt of her head. *Can you really be sad about missing out on something you know nothing of?*

I contemplated the question for a moment, then said, "Isn't that the reason you came to earth?"

She blinked, as if caught off guard by the words. *You're absolutely right, Kenna. That's exactly why I came to earth.* She made a short yipping sound, like she was surprised to have learned something new.

The words had surprised me as well. For as long as I could remember, I'd carried an unknown sadness within me. I just hadn't realized until now that I'd been pining for something. Something that would complete my soul. That would bring unimaginable joy into my life.

Even before I knew he existed, I had missed him. I'd missed my soulmate.

CHAPTER 22

KENNA

I sighed as the shower's scalding hot water beat down on my sore muscles.

Both Noah and Silver had continued to train me in offense and defense magic for hours, until I'd nearly collapsed from exhaustion. But I'd made progress, and I was excited to show Lochlan my new skills. He wasn't going to be happy about the added injuries I'd received from Noah's Cosmic magic though. He hadn't seen them yet, because I'd kicked him out of the training wing.

For his own good, of course. And mine.

It was too distracting being in the same room as him. Too painful. Even after working my sexual frustration into the offensive magic Silver was teaching me, I still burned for him. It was getting worse, the incessant ache in my core that only he could ease. No amount of training, sore muscles, or exhaustion would make it go away. There was only one way to get rid of it, but having sex with him wasn't an option.

Sighing again, this time with all the frustration I felt, I tipped my head back to scrub the shampoo from my hair.

What are you doing, solemae? his voice suddenly filled my head. At the silken quality of it, so smooth that the words practically slid through me like water, my knees weakened.

Instead of replying, I sent him an image. Of me naked in the shower. The second I did, I regretted it. Teasing him would only worsen the pain, for *both* of us.

A growl immediately rumbled through my mind. A *hungry* one.

Crap, crap, crap. I *really* shouldn't have done that.

Before I could apologize though, he was speaking again. Words that made my breath hitch.

Come to me.

What? But . . .

Trust me, love.

Your father . . .

Is in a dinner meeting with disgruntled council members who aren't happy that he's been keeping you from them. He won't be out for a while.

Fates above, I was out of excuses. Not that I needed any. Or remembered why I was trying to make them. Wringing out my dripping hair, I turned off the shower and reached for a towel.

Where are you? I finally replied, noticing that my hands were trembling.

Come to me, was all he said, then sent me an image of the hallway outside my room.

I bit my lip and hurriedly got dressed in a cropped t-shirt and yoga pants. Not even bothering with shoes, I crept to the bedroom door and peered out. No guards. No servants. Not a single soul in sight. Everyone must be focused on the king's dinner meeting.

My stomach fluttered with nervous excitement as I stepped into the hall and quietly shut the door. *Where next?* I asked Lochlan, and immediately received an image of the stairwell. I followed his silent directions, tiptoeing to the third floor, then down a deserted hallway I'd never been to before. At the far end of the hall, he sent me an image of a set of gold, ornate doors. Reaching out, I grasped a cold door handle and nudged one of the doors open.

Inside, the air was warm, but slightly stale and musty. I slipped through the door and paused, adjusting my sight to the dim lighting. When I could see better, my eyes widened. There were books everywhere, lined on golden bookshelves that rose to the high ceiling. Gold ladders climbed equally as high, stopping midway at a narrow balcony that circled the white marble room. The only light in the room came from a white marble fireplace inlaid with gold. The flames smoldered softly, barely making a sound.

"Hello?" I dared to whisper, but didn't receive a reply.

A chill suddenly swept through me and I shivered, backing up toward the door. When it clicked shut, I whirled around to find a dark figure there. At the sight of an intense pair of glowing red eyes, a startled squeak left me. But as the shadows shifted, revealing a dearly familiar face, all the need I'd been feeling for him spilled out in a rush.

As I whimpered his name, he came to me in a swirl of amber, sandalwood, and musk. He stopped mere inches away, making me hate those cursed inches more than anything in the world.

"I can't keep my distance any longer," he whispered huskily, slowly raising his hand toward my face. "I need to touch you. Kiss you. Make love to you. My body hurts from wanting yours so badly."

I trembled from the effort of holding still, ready to combust the second his skin touched mine. When his thumb feathered across my cheek, I released a short cry. He was moving before the sound could finish leaving my lips, capturing my face to seal his mouth over mine.

Too long. Too freaking long since I'd felt this.

My body reacted instinctively to his, returning the kiss as desperately as he gave it. I rose on tiptoe to encircle his neck with my arms, pressing our bodies together. His kisses were intoxicatingly full. Drugging. Drawing little sounds of pleasure from me. He continued to swallow them. To make sure no one could hear. Protecting us, even as he showered me with his undivided attention.

When I sought out his tongue with mine, aching to deepen the kiss even more, he shuddered against me. Greedily accepting my offer, he met my tongue with firm, languid strokes. A jolt of heat shot to my core and I was suddenly being lifted into the air. At the feel of his hands on my backside, I snaked my legs around his waist. As he moved again, easing me back against a bookshelf, I clung to him tightly.

When he slowly ground himself against me, I moaned into his mouth, loving the feel of his erection pressed to my core. He did it again and again, continuing to stroke me with his tongue. Until all I knew was utter bliss. But as my pleasure built, as he showed no signs of stopping, I struggled to clear the fog from my brain. Struggled to regain use of my thoughts enough to say, *It's my turn.*

CHAPTER 23

LOCHLAN

I could have died. I could have died when she said those words.

It's my turn.

The second she uttered them, I knew what they meant. Knew what she wanted to do. I wasn't prepared. Wasn't ready. At the same time, I'd never wanted anything more in my entire life.

She was asking for control. Demanding my submission.

And *gods*, I wanted to. I wanted to submit to this achingly gentle yet stunningly powerful woman. For the first time in my life, I wanted to give up control. Give it up, so that I could give it to her. So I did, even as I trembled with residual fear. Even as a wave of nervous energy slammed into me.

Allowing her body to slide down mine, I let go of her. Let go, and watched as she took the lead like the alpha female she was. I knew she was inexperienced, that I'd claimed all her firsts, but she didn't need my help with this. Didn't need me to do a single thing other than give her what she wanted. I didn't deny her. Didn't want to. My breath came faster and faster as she lifted the hem of my shirt and tugged it over my head.

While the material soundlessly fell to the floor, she laid her hands on me. Hands that could so easily render me useless. Could bring me to my knees within seconds. I stayed perfectly still, *trusting* her, as they swept over my chest and down my torso, exploring every inch of my skin. I stayed still as her mouth joined in, kissing and licking a tortuous path to my navel.

The air left me when she began unbuttoning my pants, tugging the remainder of my clothing to my ankles. Leaving me exposed and vulnerable in a way I never had before. For the first time in my life, I actually wanted this. To feel completely vulnerable and at the mercy of another. Without a shred of doubt or hesitation, I wanted her to take me. To have her way with me.

To *love* me, as no one else had. As only *she* had.

My erection was hard and throbbing, involuntarily twitching under her unwavering gaze. As she lowered herself to her knees before me and gripped the shaft, pleasure shot through me. With a single touch, she nearly drove me to my knees. My eyes threatened to close, but I forced them open, wanting to see. Wanting to fully experience this moment with her.

When she at last leaned forward and took my swollen head into her mouth, my legs buckled. I caught myself on the bookshelf, scattering books. Gouging my claws into the wood to keep from falling. A groan rolled up my throat, but I swallowed the sound, not willing to give us up. To give *this* up.

This gift. This moment of being reborn. Of watching my past be wiped clean by my present and future. I continued to watch, refusing to miss even a second. Even when she took me fully into her mouth. Even when ecstasy burst through me in pulsating waves. I didn't take my eyes off her.

She was my soulmate. The love of my life.

And now more than ever. My salvation.

CHAPTER 24

KENNA

From our spot in front of the library's fireplace, we companionably watched the flickering flames. Neither of us had spoken for several minutes. There was no need.

Something had shifted between us during that last intimate act. An act I'd been nervous to perform on him, but instantly loved the second I'd taken him into my mouth. The taste and feel of him on my tongue—and his emotionally raw reaction to it—was an experience unlike any I'd ever had before.

And, somehow, I just knew he felt the same. Despite his past experiences, this was a first for him as well.

That knowledge made me feel closer to him than ever. Made our bond that much stronger. Instead of our souls embracing each other, they felt forged together. Encased in a protective layer of granite.

From his position behind me on the velvet sofa, Lochlan brushed my hair aside to lightly kiss my neck. Cradled between his legs, I snuggled back against him with a contented sigh. He continued to kiss and nuzzle my neck, pausing at "his spot" to graze the sensitive skin with his fangs.

I sucked in a quiet gasp, arching my neck for him in invitation. When he did it again, desire for his bite, his *venom*, shuddered through me. *You haven't bitten me in several days*, I breathlessly said through our bond, need coating each word.

His hand possessively encircled the base of my throat. *My father will know if I do. And you were becoming addicted to my venom.*

A small sound of disappointment escaped me. *Can vampires bite without leaving behind their scent and venom?*

Yes, but my desire to claim you is still too strong. Besides, biting you without venom would be extremely painful.

When I hummed as if considering it anyway, he rumbled my name in warning. I thrust out my bottom lip, but dropped the subject.

For now.

Tracing a finger up the visible veins in his forearm, I said, *How much time do we have left?*

How much time until we had to pretend we weren't madly in love with each other.

We should leave soon, just to be safe. But I'm the only one who ever visits this library. No one will intentionally seek out our secret hideaway.

Our secret hideaway.

A smile crept onto my face. *I like it here. It's cozy. Could use some curtains though.*

His nose brushed the shell of my ear, drawing a shiver from me. *Curtains?*

I have a thing for them. Every window should have curtains. Oh! I abruptly twisted around to face him, grinning like a crazy person. *I learned something new today. Wanna see?*

He blinked at me in surprise. Then his features relaxed as he gave me an adoring smile, complete with a sexy dimple. Fates, I was one freaking lucky girl. *Show me*, he said, settling back more comfortably against the couch cushions.

Biting my lip, I raised my hand and concentrated on my energy, just like Silver had taught me. It took me several long seconds— probably because having Lochlan this close was *seriously* distracting—

but a flaming red ball eventually sprung from my fingertips to hover in the air.

I can create my own light now! I internally squealed with excitement, looking to Lochlan for his reaction.

With the magical orb hovering inches from his face, his red eyes were almost iridescent. He studied my newfound skill for several moments, then reached up to lightly touch it. A zap of pain traveled through our bond as he made contact, and I quickly snuffed it out, an apology springing to my lips.

Don't be sorry, he said before I could. Despite the pain, a small smile curved his lips. *I've told you once and I'll tell you again. You're amazing, McKenna. Don't stop becoming who you were meant to be.*

My throat tightened with emotion, and I whispered, "And who am I supposed to be, exactly?"

Lovingly caressing my cheek, he whispered back, "Whoever you *want* to be."

Despite the impending curse looming over our heads. Despite the tension and unrest with the old council and new. And despite the continued threat that rogues still posed to us all, Christmas day dawned bright and beautiful.

Isla was the first to arrive, barging into my room without knocking. "Merry Christmas," she sang, bouncing over to my bed like an overeager kid. Avoiding a thin stream of sunshine filtering through the curtains, she flopped onto the mattress while I sat up with a groan.

"Did you train last night with Noah again?" she said, frowning at the massive purple bruise on my left shoulder that my tank top failed to hide.

I rotated the shoulder with a wince, my voice still thick with sleep as I mumbled, "You should see the bruises I gave *him*."

She rolled her eyes, making it clear how she felt about our rather obsessive training regimen. But she also knew why I did it. Knew how awful it felt to be helpless against someone stronger.

In less than two weeks, my magic skills had improved tenfold. With only me as his student, Noah had focused all of his attention on whipping me into shape. I could now defend myself against his attacks, even do some damage of my own, thanks to the use of Silver's magic and her patient tutelage.

The next skill I wanted to master was portaling. Even Noah was cautious about that one though, worried that I'd accidentally portal myself outside. But after two weeks with no rogue attacks, and no sign of a traitor in the castle, everyone was less on their guard. There was even hope that the rogues had given up trying to stop me from breaking the curse. Not that I'd had any luck decoding the prophecy, to the chagrin of—well—everyone.

"Just don't let Loch see that bruise," a new voice said from the open doorway. "You know how he gets, and I'm tired of breaking up his spats with Noah."

I smiled at Kade in greeting, which faltered when Isla abruptly stood, muttering something about needing to feed. She managed to edge around Kade without touching him, then scurried to her room down the hall. At his crestfallen expression, I urged my sore body out of bed and went to him. He readily accepted my hug, avoiding my bruise as he wrapped his arms around me in return.

"You haven't tried talking to her yet?" I said, my voice slightly muffled against his chest.

"I've tried," he replied with a heavy sigh. "She doesn't want to listen."

"Do you want me to speak with her?"

He propped his chin on the top of my head. "No. This is my mess, little Kenna. You have enough on your plate."

I hummed my understanding, even as I said, "Just say the word and I'll go to bat for you. I hate how miserable you've been. Both of you, actually."

"Thanks, Kenna," he murmured, kissing my hair. "I'll be okay."

"Not if you don't get your hands off my mate in the next two seconds," a deep voice rumbled from just outside the door.

Instead of releasing me, Kade smirked against my hair like a wicked fiend and said, "But we haven't finished our morning cuddle yet. Patience. You'll get your turn soon."

In the next instant, I was alone, left gaping in the doorway as Kade was snatched from me. The two friends were a blur, tussling in the hall like teenage boys. Well, ones with inhuman speed and strength. The mock fight only lasted seconds, but it was enough to wring a laugh from Kade. They stopped in front of my door, arms slung around each other's shoulders. Lochlan had a good-natured smile on his face despite his earlier words.

"Merry Christmas, old friend," he said, reaching up to roughly tousle Kade's caramel-colored waves.

"Merry Christmas, you possessive alphahole," Kade replied with another laugh, ducking when Lochlan swung at him.

I took in the playful scene with a big smile of my own, happy that we'd finally come back to this place. That Lochlan no longer saw Kade as a threat. That we could freely joke and laugh together like a family. It had taken two weeks. Two weeks of glares, growling, and repeatedly sneaking off to our secret hideaway, but he was finally calming down.

Well, around his drothen anyway.

Which was a relief, since Kade had temporarily moved into the bedroom next to mine. To give Lochlan a break from guarding my door at night, he'd said. I couldn't help but wonder if he'd also done it to be close to Isla, though.

With nothing to do all day but work on controlling her bloodlust, she was growing restless. On more than one occasion, Kade had caught her trying to sneak out at night. Each time he forbade her from leaving the castle's safety was another nail in the coffin of their relationship. It saddened me to see their friendship reduced to ash. To see how the rift affected them both and not be able to fix it.

I cleared my suddenly tight throat, refocusing on the guys to find them staring at me. "What?" I said, feeling heat fill my cheeks.

"This is a worry-free day, so tell that brain of yours to stop overthinking and enjoy today's festivities," Kade said with a mock-stern look.

"And no training," Lochlan added, his stern expression completely serious as he took in my fresh bruise.

To divert his attention from my new injury, I said, "Vampires celebrate Christmas?"

"Of course we do," Kade replied, clearly offended by the question.

"Not all of us do, just like not all humans do," Lochlan corrected. "But most vampires on Sanctum Isle celebrate the holiday. We have traditions, just like humans."

This piqued my curiosity. "What kind of traditions?"

"Gift giving. Overindulgence in blood and sex," Everett answered, coming up behind his brother to give him a friendly slap on the back.

Lochlan rolled his eyes, but Kade actually laughed, adding before anyone could stop him, "Orgies are very common on Christmas day. Nothing says togetherness like a good—"

He let out a loud *ooph* as Lochlan jabbed an elbow into his stomach. I should be used to this by now. Talk of blood and sex and multiple partners. King Ambrose currently had fourteen human *wives*, after all. They were often seen parading around the castle in next to nothing, and the king wasn't shy about touching them in public.

Still, I blushed fiercely. Probably always would, even though Lochlan and I had sex as often as possible. Not as much as we wanted to, but with the king in meetings with his discontented council more and more often, we managed to sneak off nearly once a day now. Which had helped calm the mate bond frenzy quite a bit.

Desperately looking to change the subject before other parts of my body could warm, I turned and padded across my room to pull something out from beneath the bed. "Well, I'm glad gift-giving is a thing here, because I got all of you a little something."

Surprise flitted across Lochlan and Everett's faces. The only one not surprised was Kade, who'd set up an online account for me so I could shop. He was also my delivery guy, since UPS wasn't exactly dropping packages off here. I thought for sure Lochlan would have figured out what I was up to, but he'd been rather elusive in the evenings himself this past week.

As I handed him the first present, I spotted Isla and Troy loitering in the hallway, no doubt drawn to the noise. Despite not connecting with Troy like I had with Everett over the past couple weeks, I still welcomed his presence. It was Christmas, after all, and he was family, even if we didn't exactly get along. My attention was drawn back to Lochlan as he carefully unwrapped his present. Kade practically hummed with energy beside him, looking like he wanted to tear open the wrapping paper for him.

When Lochlan finally opened the white box containing his

present, I too struggled to hold still. I watched his face, then tuned into his emotions as he lifted a blue sweater from the bed of tissue paper. His expression and emotions remained blank for so long that I began to fidget. Finally, he looked up at me. Looked and looked, like he didn't know what to say. Eventually, he said, "This was your idea?"

"Kade helped," I replied, refusing to glance his way when I felt his emotions dance along our bond.

Lochlan pursed his lips and focused on the sweater again. More like what was embroidered *on* the sweater.

A big, green Loch Ness Monster. The original version.

"I didn't think you had one of those, but I can always return it if you do . . ." I casually said, and the comment put Kade over the edge. He doubled over in a fit of laughter, repeatedly slapping his thigh.

I somehow managed to keep a straight face, saying through our bond so only he could hear, *I got you something else too for later. If you wear the sweater all day today, then you'll get the second half of your present tonight."* I quickly flashed him an image of me in skimpy silk lingerie. *Red* lingerie.

His expression immediately heated, and I bit my lip to keep from grinning wickedly. *You naughty little thing,* he quietly purred, yet instantly tugged the ugly Christmas sweater over his head.

Kade laughed even harder, and I finally joined in, drawing a smile from both Lochlan and Everett. I gave out presents to Kade and Everett next, unapologetically smirking when Everett unwrapped a tall thermos with #likeaboss monogrammed on the side. Kade spoiled his present by sniffing the box first, but the delight that instantly sparked in his eyes made me smile.

"A triple-decker? With *strawberries?*" he gushed, revealing the cheesecake I'd made last night—with the generous help of the kitchen staff.

Somehow, he swept me into a bear hug without dropping it, carrying on like I'd gifted him the moon. Although, knowing him, he probably thought the moon was made out of cheesecake.

Isla received a pink fuzzy pajama set that had QUEEN sequined across the shirt front. Because that's what she was and she needed to know it. Troy got a new baseball hat. He, more than anyone, seemed shocked that I'd given him something.

When we met up with Noah and Silver at breakfast, I finished doling out the presents. A protective vest for him—since I was going to continue kicking his butt during our training sessions—and a soft bed for Silver. Although she still liked to sleep alone at night, she could at least have a comfortable spot to call her own now.

The only one I hadn't gotten a gift for was King Ambrose. I mean, what was I supposed to give a five-hundred-year-old vampire? A silly gag gift about being old as dirt? He still intimidated me, and the last thing I wanted to do was offend him. He continued to watch me and Lochlan like a hawk, and I feared his eyes saw far more than he let on.

It wasn't often that he joined us for breakfast, choosing instead to dine with his wives in his private suite. But he did today. The second he saw the smattering of gifts across the table, he stopped in his tracks. "What's all this?" Spotting Lochlan's ugly sweater, he did a double take.

"McKenna gave us Christmas presents," Lochlan replied, closely watching his father's reaction. I couldn't sense if he was worried so didn't know if I should be.

The king's attention landed on me. I tried not to squirm while he studied me for several long moments. Finally, he dipped his chin, giving me that *look* again, like I'd passed some sort of test. "That was very generous of you, Kenna."

Tilting my head in acknowledgement, I gave him a small smile. Hopefully he wouldn't ask where *his* present was or things were going to get awkward.

The rest of the day was filled with present-opening and relaxation, laughter and mostly-friendly banter. At one point, all fourteen of the king's wives joined us, and it wasn't as uncomfortable as I thought it would be. He kept his hands to himself for the most part, and they didn't fawn over him too dramatically.

Troy and Everett helped themselves to the female staff on more than one occasion though, drinking straight from their necks. The sight reminded me of Kade's joke about Christmas orgies. Sure enough, they both excused themselves early for the evening, towing a few females with them. The king chuckled and left with his wives shortly after.

Before my embarrassment could hit me too hard, Lochlan leaned over and whispered, "I have a present for you as well."

Still thinking about orgies, I nearly swallowed my tongue.

He must have caught the tail end of my thoughts, because his brows hiked upward.

"What is she thinking?" Kade interrupted our exchange with a mischievous tilt to his lips, like he somehow *knew*.

My eyes flew wide. *Don't you dare tell him*, I silently pleaded to a still surprised-looking Lochlan.

Only if you tell me why you're thinking about orgies, he responded, a slight smirk replacing his surprise.

What? Panic bubbled in my chest. *I wasn't thinking about them. Not like that anyway.*

Like what then?

Gah! He was totally toying with me now. I was so getting him back for this.

Like, I wasn't thinking about participating in one. I was just curious. Argh, that came out wrong.

Curious if I've participated in one?

Every inch of me froze.

Before my imagination could go crazy, he leaned even closer and whispered in my ear, "Because I haven't. I don't like to share."

With that, he stood, his smirk way too telling for my liking. He made a show of pulling me to my feet and slowly sliding his hand up the back of my sweater dress. "McKenna and I have somewhere else to be," was his only reply to Kade's question. When Kade guffawed, I narrowed my eyes at Lochlan.

You're enjoying this way too much.

He tilted his head to the side. *No, if I were enjoying this too much, I'd say something like:* "And before you ask, Kade, no, you can't join us."

Kade choked. Then inhaled a deep breath and roared with laughter, nearly falling off his armchair. Both Noah and Isla looked startled by the outburst, clearly confused by the exchange. I had no idea what Silver thought about it all.

Flabbergasted at Lochlan's behavior, all that came out was a squeak when I opened my mouth to scold him. His wicked grin was anything but repentant. Then he did the unthinkable. Without a lick of warning, he tossed me over his shoulder like a sack of potatoes and strode from the room.

Another shocked squeak left me, but the sound was lost to the cacophony that was Kade. The last thing I saw before Lochlan turned the corner was Kade's feet in the air as he rolled on the floor.

CHAPTER 25

KENNA

"Someone will *see*," I hissed at Lochlan, struggling to be let down. I yelped when he rewarded my struggles with a firm smack to my butt.

"The staff were let off for the evening. Christmas tradition. Even the guards get the evening to themselves. And my father and brothers are doing exactly what you think they're doing. No one will be walking these halls for several hours."

Holy crap, Christmas orgies were really a thing.

"Stop thinking about orgies or I'm going to get distracted," Lochlan commanded, his voice a husky rumble. Feeling spiteful after the show he'd just put on for our friends, I sent him several naughty images. His hand on my backside spasmed, then slid downward to hike up the short hem of my dress. I gasped when his fingers came dangerously close to brushing my inner thigh. "Is that what you fantasize about? Having sex with multiple partners at once?"

Even though it was my fault for sending him the images, I still blushed from head to toe at his words. "No, that was simply payback. I have no desire to be with anyone but you."

He released a low hum of approval, and I couldn't help but smile. Seeing him in such high spirits—and feeling his unwavering confidence as he boldly carried me down the halls—filled me with happiness. If only it could always be like this. If only we didn't have to hide our relationship. Still, I cherished this moment with him. I didn't think anything could top it.

That was, until he showed me my *present*.

"Close your eyes," he said the moment we hit the sixth floor. "Close them," he repeated when I didn't immediately cooperate. Wrinkling my nose at his uncanny perception skills, I did as instructed.

When he opened a door, it took everything in me not to peek. I wiggled to be let down again, and this time, he listened.

"Can I—?" I began the second my ankle boots hit the floor, but he was already replying back with a, "Not yet."

He guided me forward with light touches, then his hands fell away completely. "Okay," he said from behind me, a sudden tremor in his voice. "You can look now."

Nothing could have prepared me. Nothing in the whole world. The sight that greeted my eyes was . . .

"Oh, Lochlan," I whispered, placing a trembling hand over my lips.

He didn't respond, simply taking in my reaction as I slowly turned. As my gaze gobbled up every inch of the large, circular space. We were in one of the castle turrets. Everywhere I looked, there were red roses. Some in vases, arranged on every available surface. Others scattered across the floor, along with hundreds of rose petals. Tucked among them were flickering candles. Dozens and dozens of them, all lit. And the windows . . . they were covered in rich fabric. *Curtains*.

But there was something else in the room too. Something that made me want to sob.

"Is all of this—" I began, my voice shaking like crazy. "—for me?"

"It is," he quietly said. "I'd give you everything you've lost. Everything you've had to give up over the years. I'd give you the world if I could, but this will have to do. For now."

Tears rolled down my cheeks and I welcomed the release. *Needed* it. I was going to explode otherwise. There were too many emotions. Too many feelings balled up within me. I whirled and launched myself at Lochlan. He caught me with a surprised laugh, pulling me close as I wrapped my arms around his neck and hugged him *hard*.

"Thank you," I whispered against his neck. "Thank you, thank you."

His joy hummed through our bond, mingling with mine.

He held me for a long time, soaking up my happiness as I soaked up his. Then he murmured, "I'd better be the only nude model who poses for you in here. Kade isn't allowed, no matter how hard he begs."

I threw my head back and laughed. He waited a moment, letting my laughter bounce off the canvases and easels. The light table and standing desk. The endless pads of drawing paper and cups brimming with pencils, paints, and brushes. Then he leaned forward and captured my lips in a toe-curling kiss, swallowing the sound.

My bare feet soundlessly scurried along the marble floors. Practically skipping as I eagerly approached our secret hideaway. The halls echoed their emptiness, emptier than they'd ever been before. I hadn't spotted a single servant or guard since leaving my bedroom, now clothed in oversized sleepwear.

With red silk lingerie hidden underneath.

Knowing we would have the entire third floor all to ourselves tonight sent tingles of anticipation erupting across my skin. I'd been very careful not to be loud the many times we'd been intimate in the library, but maybe just for tonight, I wouldn't have to worry about making a little noise. Or a lot, since I was pretty sure Lochlan planned to give me multiple orgasms before the evening was over.

I was feet away. Feet away from our hideaway. From *him*.

When, out of nowhere, something struck my temple.

Swiftly.

Violently.

In an instant, everything went dark.

CHAPTER 26

LOCHLAN

I knew something was wrong the minute she didn't show up on time.

Five minutes passed. Ten.

Then I was out the door, scouring the halls for her.

McKenna? I said through our bond, hoping Isla or Kade had caused her delay. Maybe she'd seen a guard on the way here and had scurried back to her room. When I didn't get a reply, my steps became more urgent. *McKenna, answer me.*

Silence.

Dreadful, awful silence.

A terrible pit grew in my stomach.

Something was wrong. My very bones *ached* with wrongness.

When I caught a fresh whiff of her wintery mint scent, yet she was nowhere to be seen, I burst into a run.

Wrong, wrong, wrong.

She should be here. She should *be* here.

Soon, I was barging into her bedroom, searching every nook and cranny. The noise alerted Kade, whose eyes widened the second he saw my face.

"What happened? Where's Kenna?"

"I thought you could tell *me* that," I said, my voice like gravel in my throat. "Something's wrong. She didn't show."

We exchanged a look, one that grew more desperate with each passing second.

"We need to alert the others. *Now*," Kade said, and he joined me as I stormed out the door again.

While he barged into Isla's room without knocking, I flew up the stairwell to the fifth floor where my father and brother's rooms were. I barrelled into Everett's room first, ordering him to get dressed. He was already up out of bed, tugging on pants without question as I made for Troy's room across the hall. Feminine squeals of surprise greeted me when I opened the door to find my brother butt naked with three serving girls.

Barely glancing at the females, I ordered him to get dressed too and was out the door again in a flash. Heading for the east wing, I blew past the many rooms in my father's suite and burst into the main sleeping chamber. At any other time, I wouldn't have dared invade his personal space. We'd been taught at an early age that this room was strictly forbidden. That entering it would have consequences.

But I didn't bloody care right now.

He must have heard me coming, because he was already out of bed, yanking on pants when I arrived. All fourteen of his wives were in the room with him, most of them naked. They gasped and shrieked at my abrupt arrival, scrambling to cover themselves. With a growl, my father planted himself between me and them, shielding their nakedness from view. When he realized who the intruder was, his alertness switched to one of concern. "Loch? What—?"

"My mate is missing. I'm going after her."

Shock was the last thing I saw. Shock at my admission.

But I didn't care. I didn't care if he knew anymore, and I didn't care what he thought. I never should have hid our bond from him in the first place. If I hadn't, she would still be here right now. She would be safely in my arms, having no need to meet up with me in secret. She would never have been alone, left unprotected, even for a second.

This was all my fault. If I never found her again, I had no one to blame but myself.

Listening to my gut, I swiftly descended the stairs to the main floor, following the faint trail of her scent. When I found the front doors wide open, panic gripped my throat. I charged into the night, not waiting for the others. Not caring if this was a trap. Anyone who got in my way was as good as dead.

I continued to follow her scent. To call out through our bond. Trying to keep a level head. Refusing to let my rage and desperation consume me. She was out here. I knew it in my soul. Snatched from beneath my very nose. My worst fear, my *nightmare*, was becoming reality. And I had to stop it. Had to get her back before she was lost to me forever.

At least she was still alive. I would know if she wasn't. The death of a soulmate was said to be the most painful thing a soul could endure. Many didn't survive the excruciating agony of losing their other half. Most became a shell of their former selves, all but ceasing to exist.

And what would the point be of living with half a soul anyway?

When her scent trail led me straight to the island's edge, to the jagged cliffs and the churning ocean below, I lost control. Lost control as the trail went cold, leaving me helpless and terrified out of my mind. I threw my head back and roared my fury and pain, falling to my knees on the rugged shoreline. Shadows whipped from me, so forcefully that the ground shuddered and cracked.

The others found me tearing up and down the coast where I'd last scented her, half mad with desperation. Kade was the only one foolishly brave enough to approach me. I nearly took his head off when he barred my way, when he grabbed my shoulders to stop me.

He shouted my name but I didn't hear him. He yanked me into a fierce hug but I didn't feel it.

I only heard silence where her voice should be. Only felt the keen absence of her presence.

I was lost. Lost without her.

Nothing made sense.

Nothing mattered.

It was Silver who brought me back to myself. Who rubbed against my legs until I finally glanced down. Finally saw that I wasn't the only one in pain. I took one look at the grief in her pale blue eyes and bent to her level. When she threw herself into my arms, I held her to me without hesitation. Comforting her as she comforted me.

"She isn't lost," I croaked, burying my face in the fox's fur. "She isn't lost to any of us. I swear on my life, I'll find her. Even if I have to burn the world down first."

CHAPTER 27

KENNA

My head felt split wide open, like an overripe melon.

Nausea swirled in my gut, and I desperately tried not to throw up. After several attempts, I managed to peel my eyes open. Several more until I could see clearly. The second I could, panic sent my heart into overdrive.

I was on a bed—one I didn't recognize. And directly above the bed, attached to the ceiling, was a freaking *mirror*.

Ignoring the pounding pain in my skull, I surged off the bed. Or tried to. Metal bit into both my wrists, sending me sprawling back onto the mattress. With horror, I noted the shackles secured to the concrete wall on either side of the bed, keeping me in place. I yanked on my bindings with growing desperation, but they were ironclad.

Before I could call out to Lochlan through our bond, a door from across the room creaked open. I froze as a dark figure filled the doorframe. Definitely a vampire. And male. His red eyes were fixed on me as he entered the room and swiftly shut the door. Not immediately recognizing him, I opened my mouth to scream.

He was at my side in a flash, so quickly that I choked on the scream.

"Remember me?" he said, setting a bowl and washcloth on a shiny mirrored nightstand beside the bed. "We never got to finish our fun."

At his voice, terror gripped my throat.

"B-Bones," I stuttered, leaning as far away from him as my restraints would allow.

"Aaaww, she remembers my name. I feel so special," the rogue who'd almost made me drink from a human crooned, perching on the mattress's edge. "Since you broke my neck, I suppose we're familiar enough with each other to be on a first name basis. Right, *Kenna?*"

I shivered at the bite in his words, pulling back even more when he picked up the washcloth and reached for my face. "D-don't touch me."

"Now now, I'm not here to hurt you. For the moment, anyway. You took quite the blow and need a little cleaning up, is all. I'd much rather *lick* the blood off, of course, but I'm guessing you'd love to use your witchy powers on me again."

As the washcloth touched the side of my face, I stilled. Bones took that as a sign of my submission. He scooted closer to better clean my blood-encrusted skin. The second he did, I lunged for his arm. The shackles snapped taut, robbing me from touching his skin. He jumped back with a hiss, knocking the bowl of water over.

While the ceramic crashed against the floorboards, I willed magic to my fingertips. A red fiery ball shot through the air, slamming into Bones' face. With a howl, he stumbled backward, batting at his sizzling skin. I threw another magical orb at him, gratified when it struck him square in the chest. His shirt immediately burst into flames and he screamed in agony, clawing at the material.

The door banged open and another vampire stormed into the room—this one female. I launched a fiery ball in her direction too, but she ducked at the last second and it smashed into the wall. "*Enough!*" she roared, coming at me like a freight train. Fat chance of that happening.

Before she could reach me, I managed to unleash one more blast of magic, scorching part of her burgundy trench coat. As payback, she pounded a fist into my jaw, rendering me unconscious once again.

The blow to my jaw must have destroyed a few brain cells. I struggled to regain consciousness, slipping into darkness again and again. No matter how hard I tried, I couldn't stay awake. Which made contacting Lochlan impossible. Which made *escaping* impossible.

When I finally came to for more than a few seconds, I heard fierce whispering. *Angry* whispering. ". . . needs blood . . . too hard . . . brain damage," I managed to catch, before the pounding in my head drowned out the rest.

As I started drifting off again, a hand slid beneath my head. I felt myself being lifted. Felt something cold pressed to my lips. A cup, maybe.

"Drink," a male voice said. Bones. When liquid—warm and coppery—trickled into my mouth and down my throat, I gagged. *Blood.* He was feeding me blood. When I tried to spit it out, his grip on my head tightened. Blinding pain shot through my skull and I nearly passed out again. "Drink it, you stupid girl," he hissed, giving me a little shake.

The motion sent shards of ice through my brain. I lost my weak grip on reality and plunged into the waiting darkness.

When I awoke next, the throbbing in my head and jaw had dulled.

Enough that I pried my eyes open in record time. I was still on the same bed, chained to the wall, but I was alone this time.

Instead of struggling to break free right away, I closed my eyes and pretended to still be asleep. Pretended so that I could finally, *finally* make a connection.

Lochlan? I called, pushing all the urgency I felt into the word.

His answer was immediate. Loud. Demanding. Frantic with worry. *McKenna, are you all right? Where are you? Tell me who has you.*

I don't . . . I don't know where I am. A room covered in garish gold with a mirror above the bed. I'm chained to the wall and can't get free. Rogues have me.

This far away, I couldn't feel his fear. But it coated each of his words as he said, *Okay. Okay, love, we'll talk this through. Tell me everything that's happened since you last saw me. Every detail matters. Sounds, smells, names, conversations. Anything you can think of, I need to know.*

So I did. I told him everything, including the fact that I knew my captors. The female was Dani, the rogue who'd led the gas station attack and managed to escape before we could question her. I didn't leave a single thing out, even the part about Bones feeding me blood.

Probably to heal your injuries when they realized how severe they were, Lochlan's voice growled in my mind. *I'm going to kill them. Slowly and painfully.* When I sent him images of their faces, he didn't recognize them. Nor the room I was chained in. *Just keep talking to me, McKenna. Let me know you're okay. I'm going to find you.*

An immediate response filled my thoughts, but I quickly snuffed it out. He didn't need anything else to worry about while he looked for me. He didn't need to know that I was going to try my hardest to get free on my own. That I wasn't going to sit here like a helpless damsel. I *couldn't*. Magic still thrummed in my veins and I was going to use it.

I opened my eyes again, double-checking that I was still alone before closely studying my restraints. Noah and I hadn't practiced moving and bending objects that much in the last two weeks, focusing more on conjuring orbs and perfecting my aim. But I slowly sat up in bed anyway. Silently raised a hand toward my left wrist shackle and willed my magic to *bend* the metal.

After several moments, the shackle trembled, then creaked. A crack formed. Frantic hope threatened to break my concentration. I kept at it, trying to be as quiet as possible, doggedly determined to free myself. Sweat slid down my face, the effort depleting my energy. But, with a *snap*, the shackle suddenly broke in two.

Yes, yes, yes!

I doubled my efforts into breaking the other shackle. In under a minute, that one cracked in half too. As my restraints fell away, every instinct screamed at me to run. But I didn't, calming my racing heartbeat before soundlessly slipping off the bed. The door across the room beckoned to me, but I ignored it, choosing instead to focus inward.

To channel the remaining magic within me into creating a portal.

I knew how to do it. Knew the importance of focusing on a clear destination. But I'd never entered one by myself before. Didn't know what would happen to me if I did it wrong. Conjuring and entering portals could be dangerous if not done right. You could end up in the middle of the ocean, or even lose a limb. A few witches had even died, lost to the swirling ether.

Despite the risks, I lifted my arms and pushed magic toward the room's empty center. Adrenaline gushed through me at the sight of an ever-growing red circle. The edges flamed bright, but I knew they wouldn't hurt me. My arms trembled with fatigue the bigger the circle became, but I was seconds away. Seconds away from completing the circle. From stepping through and getting out of this hellhole.

But at the last second, something blurred toward me. So fast that I couldn't step through in time. I was inches. Inches from escape. When one of my captors yanked me back. I lashed out, roaring my fury and frustration, only to feel a sharp prick in my neck. A prick that swiftly deadened my limbs and mind. As oblivion sucked me under, I cried out to my soulmate.

Cried out, because it was the only thing left I could do.

My captors quickly learned from their mistakes. They kept me sedated. Kept me unconscious until the last of my magic drained away. But more importantly, until the vampire blood in my system had been flushed out.

When it was gone, when I was all but helpless, they let me wake.

At least a day had passed. Probably more.

My mouth was desert dry and hunger pains lined my empty stomach. Another headache pulsed at my temples, this one due to dehydration.

I was on the bed again, with one marked difference. My wrists weren't shackled. Immediately bursting into action, I scrambled off the bed and reached for my magic.

Gone. Depleted. Like an empty gas tank.

Before panic could overtake me, I hurried to the door. Paused to listen. Then carefully grasped the handle. I had no plan. Only an incessant chant in my head to *escape, escape, escape.* Holding my breath, I turned the handle. Only, it wouldn't turn. Locked. Of course it was.

The panic started creeping in. I yanked on the handle with all my strength, no longer keeping silent. When it wouldn't budge, I willed magic to my fingertips. Still nothing. My heart sped up. My breath came in gasps. I backed away from the door, frantically searching for another way out. A window high above the bed caught my eye and I raced over. But even standing on the bed wouldn't let me reach it. I jumped for the thin ledge, but it was too high.

Panicking in earnest now, I tore across the room, upending tables and chairs, lamps and vases. They noisily clattered and crashed to the floor, but I paid no heed. Jerking open a closet door, I recoiled at the sight that greeted me. Dozens and dozens of racey negligee and transparent nightgowns. Plus a few strappy leather pieces that couldn't be called clothing. There wasn't enough of it to cover anything important.

Where the crap *was* I?

I was shoving aside the material, hoping to find a hidden trapdoor inside, when I heard the bedroom door creak open. Whirling, I lunged for a ceramic shard on the floor and picked it up, brandishing it before me like a weapon. Every muscle in my body was stretched taut as I waited for Bones to enter. I couldn't best a vampire's strength and speed, but I had enough adrenaline pumping through me to do some damage. Maybe enough to incapacitate him for a few seconds so I could dash through the door and figure out where I was.

But it wasn't Bones who entered.

Not even Dani.

It was Troy.

CHAPTER 28

KENNA

My first thought was that I'd been rescued.

Nothing else made sense.

He must have seen the relief on my face, the *hope*.

But when I said, "Where's Lochlan?" his expression changed. A wicked light entered his gaze and he blurred toward me. It happened so fast, so unexpectedly that I didn't use my makeshift weapon on him. Didn't even *think* to.

Before I could fully grasp what was happening, he was inches away, looking deeply into my eyes. "Forget Loch. Forget he exists," Troy purred, his words sliding through me like thick tar.

My heart stopped.

As I felt a tug, a *pull* to obey his command, fear crashed into me. I struggled against the words, desperately trying to look away, but I was ensnared in his thrall like a helpless rabbit.

"P-please," I whimpered, squeezing the ceramic shard. My skin split wide open. Blood gushed over my fingers. Troy's nostrils flared as he scented the blood, but he didn't let it distract him.

"*Forget* him," he said again with more bite, more power.

And I had no choice. A soundless scream filled my head, my mind, my *soul* as the one I loved slipped from me. I couldn't call out to him. Couldn't even remember how. I forgot his name. Who he was. Until all that remained was a confusing blank spot. A dark, empty pit.

It took me a moment to realize that I was sobbing. My face was damp with tears, and I didn't know why. Why did it feel like my heart had just broken into a billion fragmented pieces? Why did it feel like there was a crater-sized hole in my chest? Why did it feel like all the oxygen had left the room? Like a thousand-pound weight was pressing down on me? Like I was suddenly, devastatingly alone?

Troy saw the moment when all hope left my eyes. He stepped back with a self-satisfied smirk, ignoring the way I still squeezed the shard. Ignoring the blood dripping and pooling on the floor. He took in the mess I'd made of the room with a soft tsking sound. "I'm assuming my pleasure den isn't to your liking?"

Blinking was hard. Painful. But the words jogged some sense into me. Reminding me of where I was. Of who had taken me.

"You . . ." I croaked, then swallowed and tried again. "You're one of them?"

He gave me a distasteful look, like I'd insulted him. "If you mean a Feltore, then no. I'll never be one of them."

"N-no. I mean . . . I mean a rogue." When he continued to stare at me like I was daft, I suddenly knew. The realization hit me like a vicious slap to the face, but I barely felt it. Barely felt anything except the cold, vast emptiness where my shriveled-up soul was. Calmly, calmer than anyone had a right to be, I whispered, "You're the rogue's leader."

Troy slowly grinned and mockingly sketched a bow before me. "Give the lady a prize. You finally figured it out. You're the first one too, which is kind of sad, really. I thought my brothers—especially Everett—would have figured it was me by now. No Feltore could have planned something like this and pulled it off successfully. They aren't smart enough."

"Kade is."

He looked at me sharply and I gulped, not knowing why I'd said that. My memories of Kade were disjointed. Huge chunks were missing, which made me want to cry again. But I knew that he was my friend, and defending him felt like the right thing to do.

"Kade is nothing more than a lap dog," Troy replied with a sneer. "The only vampires who truly matter are Venturi. I'm looking forward to finally putting him in his place once the curse becomes permanent."

It was like he'd snatched the floor out from beneath me. I staggered back, barely feeling the pain as glass crunched beneath my bare feet. "Why? Why are you doing this?"

"Isn't it obvious? Venturi were made to rule the world. We're superior to every other species, including the lesser Feltore. Yet we've been forced to hide who we are from much weaker beings. Beings that should be our servants, not our captors or killers. My father refuses to see this, so I've taken matters into my own hands. Once the curse is permanent and the entire world turns on us, I know he'll see things my way. Venturi deserve to be in power. Everyone else will be made to fall in line."

Fates above, Troy had a *major* god complex. One that was going to destroy the world.

The back of my legs struck the bed, but I refused to sit. Doing so seemed like a weakness, and Troy was already acting like a predator looking for any excuse to attack. "And what will you do with me?" I dared to ask, already knowing that I wouldn't like the answer. Still, he hadn't killed me yet, so that was something.

"At first, I didn't really care what happened to you," he said, slowly stepping toward me. "I played with you a bit out of curiosity, even told a few rogues where to find you. They failed to acquire you, of course, which I'm blaming on their watered-down Feltore genetics. It didn't bother me all that much though. As long as you were kept busy, you couldn't try to break the curse. But when my brother showed more than a little interest in you, I needed to know why."

"Everett?" I questioned, confused by his words.

Ignoring my question, he said, "I closely watched you two together, and soon realized I'd misjudged your naivety. Your sweet innocence was a cover for your cruel cunning. I would know. I've seen it before. I thought a few rolls in the sack would get you out of his system, so I didn't intervene right away. But when it was clear he'd become *attached*, I sought to drive you apart by any means necessary."

"Th-the traitor in the castle," I stammered, leaning away from him when he got too close. "The drinks laced with silver. That was you."

He shrugged. "It was easy enough. Who would suspect me when I'd been drugged as well? And the SCA were all too willing to accept a tip on your whereabouts."

I frowned as my memory of that time went glitchy again. The SCA hadn't taken me. They'd taken someone else. But *who?*

"When we returned to Sanctum Isle," Troy continued, "I knew the truth of your attachment to my brother. I didn't simply want to get you out of the way anymore. I wanted you dead. But after a few more failed attempts by my rogues, I decided to bide my time. Wait until everyone's guards were down. Since you two screwed like horny rabbits almost every night, I figured out your routine. It was easy to convince one of the royal guards to kidnap you. The promise of global domination is hard to resist. It's every vampire's wet dream."

He smiled at that, running his tongue down a lengthening fang.

I shuddered at the sight, but refused to look away. To show him any sign of fear or submission. He continued to crowd in close, close enough that I felt the heat from his body penetrate my clothing. But I wouldn't sit. Wouldn't give in to his intimidation tactics. "And what do you plan to do with me now?" I asked, gripping the shard even harder.

At the small movement, he glanced down in the thin space between us and tsked again. "Your weapon won't harm me. Nothing you do can."

I clenched my teeth. "I may have exhausted my magic supply, but I can still kill you."

And I wanted to. I suddenly wanted to with every fiber of my being.

Troy chuckled softly, not an ounce of fear in his eyes. "You could try. I'd like you to, actually. I have a thing for feisty women. Bending them to my will is a huge turn on."

"You're sick," I hissed with all the disgust I felt for him.

His lips twitched with devilish amusement. "Oh, that's nothing, fiery one. Haven't you figured it out yet? I'm the one who ordered your parents to be drained of all their precious human blood."

Every inch of me froze in horror. It was like he'd stabbed the shard into my chest, then viciously twisted. When he continued to smile, to *gloat* without a single stitch of remorse, rage gushed through me. Hot and fast.

I blindly lashed out at him. He grunted as the jagged shard sank into his stomach. A second later, he was moving. He had me on the bed, both arms pinned above my head, before I could finish gasping. My long-sleeved top protected his skin from mine.

"You bastard!" I screamed, fighting against his superior strength with all my might. He simply laughed. *Laughed.* And settled his weight on top of me, rendering my struggles futile.

"I find you quite irresistible right now, fiery one," he crooned. "I like you best this way. Underneath me. Completely helpless."

"Don't touch me," I bit out, wincing when the shard still in his stomach dug into mine.

"Ah, but I could so easily change your mind," he continued to croon, in a way that utterly terrified me. "With a few simple words, I'd have you *begging* me to ravish you."

I froze again, completely horrified when I realized the truth of his words. If he decided to thrall me, my resistance would fade away. He could do whatever he wanted and I wouldn't put up a fight.

"Please don't," I whispered, trembling with fear despite myself. "Anything but that."

He cocked a brow. Too late, I realized the mistake of my words. "Anything?"

"N-no. I meant—"

"No take-backs," he said, grinning like a fiend. He suddenly pushed off of me, barely flinching as he grasped the shard in his stomach and yanked it out. The wound gushed blood for a moment, then trickled to a stop. Carelessly dropping the bloody shard onto the floor, he added, "I'll send someone in to clean up this mess and tend to your injury. But in the meantime, I want you to change. Your clothing is filthy."

I glanced down at my top now smeared in his blood and tried not to grimace. "Change into what? I don't have any—"

"Into one of the garments from the closet, of course. Any of them will do," he said, his smile nothing short of evil.

My heart started beating a mile a minute. "No way. Most of them are *see*-through. I might as well not wear anything."

"You can go nude too. Up to you," he replied flippantly, backing toward the door. "But if you're not naked or wearing one of those garments when I return, I'll be undressing you myself."

The door clicked shut behind him with finality. Leaving me to fret over his awful words. Words that promised retribution should I fail to obey them.

My fingers shook, so hard that I dropped the dress.

Cursing under my breath, I picked it up again. Looked at it for several moments. Then tossed it into a corner of the closet.

Over the last hour, I'd tried on several "dresses," but had steered clear of the leather straps. Shiny leather pieces that barely covered the naughty bits were no doubt a kink of Troys. He probably enjoyed taking them off, then whipping his partner with them. At the disturbing thought, my palms dampened with sweat.

Bones had already returned to clean up the room, but I'd refused to let him come anywhere near me. I'd disinfected and wrapped my self-inflicted wound myself, which he seemed all too happy to let me do. While he cleaned, I'd shut myself in the walk-in closet, trying and failing to find a suitable outfit to wear. Every time I glanced at my reflection in the mirror behind the door, I'd quickly torn the clothing off and shucked it in a corner.

I had two choices: wear a sheer dress that revealed my nipples, or give in to Troy's kinky leather fantasy. I wouldn't even consider the third option: going nude.

But as the hour wrapped up and Bones left the bedroom, I knew the choice would be taken from me if I didn't decide soon. So, inhaling a deep breath, I squeezed my eyes shut and reached for a random dress. Without even looking, I slipped the filmy material over my head and opened the closet.

If I didn't look, I wouldn't know how bad it was. Right?

The second I stepped from the closet, the bedroom door opened. I almost dove into the closet again, mortified to have anyone see me like this. But I didn't, choosing instead to quietly face whoever was entering the room. Hiding wouldn't help me. It would look weak. Cowardly. And I couldn't afford that right now.

As Troy appeared, it took everything in me not to cross my arms. To hide the breasts I knew he could clearly see. Somehow, I kept my arms at my sides, though they trembled uncontrollably when his gaze slid down my body. The lower half of my body was covered a bit more, but not by much. I quaked as his eyes scoured every inch of me. Mocking me. *Humiliating* me.

He made me endure this torture for a solid minute. Then another. Before finally resting his gaze on mine. "I prefer my females a little more curvy, but I can see the allure. Most males would jump at the chance to bed you, even if your breasts and hips are harder to grab onto."

Shame and abject embarrassment heated my face. I savagely bit my tongue so I wouldn't cry. So I wouldn't scream at him for doing this to me.

Despite how wretched I felt, I lifted my chin, unwilling to let him see me squirm.

A slow grin crept across his face. "There's that fire again. You're a tough one, I'll give you that." His grin suddenly disappeared. "It won't last though. I will break you to nothing as she broke him. I will warp your mind so completely that you will no longer think for yourself. You will be mine. Mine to control. Mine to destroy. And before this is over, you will *beg* me to kill you."

CHAPTER 29

McKenna. McKenna, answer me.

There was that persistent voice in my head again. The one that got louder with each passing day. The one that wasn't real. That couldn't be. My master had told me again and again and again that the voice was a lie. That I should never speak to it. That I'd be punished if I did. That the longer I ignored it, the faster it would fade away. Until it disappeared completely.

But it hadn't faded, not even a little. And, secretly, I didn't *want* it to disappear.

So I continued to silently listen to the voice.

My master couldn't stop me from doing that. From absorbing it like a dry desert parched for water. From drawing comfort from it.

I felt more than just comfort, though. *Far* more. I didn't feel afraid when I heard that voice. I didn't feel alone, or lost, or desperate, or weak. I felt . . . important. Cherished. The opposite of what my master made me feel.

McKenna, please. I need to hear your voice. I need to know you're okay. Give me a sign. Anything. I can't stand not knowing what's happening to you. It's killing me. I feel so lost and helpless.

I touched my suddenly damp pillow, then my cheek. I was crying again. I only dared cry when *he* spoke to me. I cried and ached for him to hold me. It was like my body knew him, even if my brain didn't. His words hit me extra hard this time. He was feeling exactly how I felt: lost and helpless.

When I was left alone with my thoughts, or when my master came to keep me company, I felt dead inside. Like something inside of me had broken.

I was a shadow. A weak reflection of myself.

And sad. So unbearably sad.

But when I heard his voice—whoever *he* was—something in me brightened. Even smiled, albeit weakly. His voice gave me hope, whatever that meant. Hope that I'd survive this somehow, whatever this was. I didn't care if the voice wasn't real. That it was all in my head. That I was going insane. None of that mattered, because I *needed* the voice.

Without it, I feared that I'd wither away into nothing.

Time started to lose meaning.

A part of me was certain that I'd only been in this room for a couple of weeks. But another part was just as certain that I'd been here my entire life. That it had always been me and my master. Nothing and no one else.

And then I'd catch glimpses of memory, of names and faces of people that I loved. Some of the images confused me. Some made me cry. But I clung to them anyway, like I'd drown if I didn't.

On the really bad days, they were the only thing keeping me afloat. When my master would spend hours smothering me with hateful, mocking words, I focused on the memories. When he wouldn't feed me for days and days, when he left me alone in my room without a single light to see by, I focused on the names and faces. The ones that made me feel something besides emptiness.

I knew my master was cruel, but he was all I had. All I could see with my own eyes. All I could touch. Except that he never let me touch him. He said my skin was toxic. *Poison.* That no one would ever want to touch me.

I was starting to believe him.

I couldn't remember the last time I'd been touched. Maybe I never had. Still, I ached to be tenderly embraced, to be physically loved. But not by my master. I shuddered at the very thought of it. He was handsome, even devilishly charming at times, but his gaze on me was unsettling. If he ever did decide to touch me, I doubted it would be out of love, or even desire.

I viciously pinched my thigh, a habit I couldn't seem to break, and turned my thoughts toward someone else. Someone forbidden. Someone that I was commanded to fear, yet was even more afraid to lose. He didn't have a face, at least in my mind, but I imagined it was devastatingly beautiful. It had to be. His voice sure was. What would it be like if *he* touched me? Just the thought of it sent shivers up my spine. Pleasant ones.

Something stirred in my chest the longer I thought about him. Something warm. Something foreign yet achingly familiar. It flared up every time I thought about him for too long, warning me. Warning me that he was thinking about me too. That he was about to speak.

Sure enough, his voice slid through me like honey, awakening parts of me I thought were dead. *McKenna, I know you're there. I can feel you. Please speak to me, love.*

My breath caught.

Love. Did he love me? But how? I'd never even spoken to him before.

Somehow, I must have slipped. Must have accidentally spoken my thoughts to him. Because his next words were, *McKenna? Thank*

God. I didn't know what to think when you wouldn't respond. Please don't go silent on me again. I can't do this without you. Are you all right?

You . . . love me? Shocked that I'd spoken the words, that I'd even been *able* to, I slapped a hand over my mouth. Master was going to be *so* mad at me.

Of course I love you, came his immediate response. *I love you more than my own life. More than anyone and anything I've ever known. And I'll continue to love you until the earth and stars and sun are nothing but dust. I'll love you always, solemae.*

I felt a smile form on my lips. Unlike my master's words, these words sounded nothing but genuine. I wasn't afraid of them being weaponized against me. Allowing that last word to marinate in my mind for a moment, I finally managed to say, *Solemae?*

Yes, love. You're my soulmate. Always will be, no matter how far apart we are. No matter how much time passes. I won't let anyone take that away from us.

My breathing sped up. Soulmate, soulmate, soulmate. He said we were *soulmates.*

But . . .

But Master . . . The words hurt to say, like trying to shove my head through a barbed wire fence. It always hurt when I tried to disobey my master. It was my punishment. He *hated* disobedience.

But . . . but I had to. I had to know *more.*

Master said . . . I was . . . his.

Panic filled me when the voice remained silent for several moments. Had I angered him too somehow? Was he going to tell on me for being disobedient?

I'm . . . I'm s-sorry, I quickly said, doing my best to ignore the pain. *I shouldn't have—*

Who's your master, McKenna? the voice interrupted, in a tone I'd never heard before. Calm. *Too* calm. Like the deceptive eye of a storm, before all hell broke loose.

I don't . . . I paused to catch my breath, to press a hand over my roiling stomach. What I was doing was wrong. Then why did it feel so *right?* Summoning the last of my strength, I said, *Don't . . . know . . . his name.*

It's okay, love. We'll figure this out. Can you show me an image? When I paused in confusion, he added, *Think really hard about what he looks like, then share that image with me through our bond.*

Our bond. Was that what this was? A connection of some kind? One that made me feel only good things. Not bad, like with my master.

I suddenly knew in my gut that my master didn't want me to feel good. *Ever.* That he only wanted me to feel misery and desolation for the rest of my days, until I'd rather die than feel anything a second longer.

And that knowledge, that *certainty*, gave me the fortitude to do the worst thing possible.

To utterly betray my master by giving up his identity.

CHAPTER 30

LOCHLAN

My roar shook the club's narrow hallway. The dingy lights overhead swayed and flickered under the force. I whirled and punched a hole clean through the concrete wall.

I'd never felt such betrayal. Such *anger*. In my entire life.

A human couple came around the corner, then immediately backtracked at the sight of me. I wasn't in my true form, but I might as well be. Nothing about me right now said "human." More like "raging homicidal maniac."

And I didn't care. Didn't care if they called the cops. Didn't even care if the SCA showed up.

I only cared about one thing right now. One *person*. A person with a soul so pure that God had no doubt spent extra time creating it. And that beautiful soul was being tortured. Was being twisted and torn in ways I couldn't fathom.

Fear couldn't describe what I was feeling. Not even terror.

There were no words for the emotions assaulting me from all sides. For the frantic thoughts slicing through me like serrated knives.

Something urgently butted at my legs and I looked down at a worried Silver. The familiar and I had bonded over the last couple of weeks, growing closer as our fear over McKenna's safety grew. She relied on me for any new updates, and I relied on her to keep me grounded. We'd spent every waking and sleeping hour together, scouring the earth for any trace of her.

It had been *Troy's* idea that we split up. That he, Everett, Kade, and I should go different directions and cover more ground. Even Isla and Noah were out looking for her.

It had been his idea. *Troy's* idea.

And now I knew why.

"I know who has her," I told the silver fox, already whipping out my phone to call Kade. He picked up on the first ring, demanding to know if I'd found anything. None of us had slept much since McKenna had disappeared, and we were all at our breaking point. I could hear the desperation in my drothen's voice, made stronger with each passing day.

For two weeks, we hadn't smelled, heard, or seen any sign of her. Despite how she'd been abducted, we knew the SCA hadn't been involved. The only other scent I'd picked up before her trail went cold had been from a vampire. A guard who'd been loyal to the royal family for nearly five decades, to be exact. Needless to say, we hadn't found any trace of him either.

After learning from McKenna that rogues had her, we'd targeted every single den, nest, and hideout in the area we could think of. Hoping against hope that she hadn't been transported farther away. I'd interrogated dozens of vampires to no avail. Threats hadn't helped, and Silver had to stop me more than once from killing the obstinate ones.

My powerful telepathic connection with McKenna had been our only hope, but she hadn't spoken in weeks. I knew she was there, though, and her silence had nearly driven me insane with worry.

"It's Troy," I answered Kade, nearly choking on my brother's name. The betrayal bludgeoned me again, almost driving me to my knees. Silver rubbed against my legs, offering me comfort the only way she could. Not giving Kade a chance to respond, I added, "We need to track his phone. Find out where he's keeping her before she has to endure even one more bloody *second* with him."

"I'm on it," Kade said, absorbing the shocking news with a calmness I couldn't duplicate. "I'll find his phone records, GPS locations, and anything else that could lead us to her. But Loch? Promise me you're under control. Promise me you won't seek revenge. Not yet. Not until she's safe."

I could already feel my control slipping. Feel the beast rearing up, demanding I release it. So I crouched, silently pleading Silver for her help. She let me dig my trembling fingers into her fur, let me use her warm, steady presence to ground myself. It might not be enough, though. Only my soulmate could truly calm my inner monster.

"I promise," I told him, knowing it would be the hardest thing I've ever had to do.

CHAPTER 31

KENNA

It was a good day.

I couldn't remember ever having a good day before.

Even the sheer white dress I'd been forced to wear today couldn't dampen my mood. I hated the white ones the most. They didn't hide a single thing. I might as well be naked. But I knew the punishment for complaining about the dresses: my master would strip me bare. He'd only done it once. After that, I'd made sure to never complain again.

Sitting in front of the room's vanity mirror, I picked up a brush and slowly drew it through my thick chestnut hair. Hair that had grown dull and lifeless. Nearly as lifeless as my silver-gray eyes. But today, both had a slight shine to them. Or maybe I was just seeing things differently.

All thanks to *him*. The voice in my head that insisted we were soulmates. That we shared a bond. That he *loved* me.

He'd checked in several times last night to make sure I was okay, and I'd responded every single time. It still hurt to disobey my master's will, but it was getting easier. My resolve had hardened, making some of my strength return. I didn't feel so helpless anymore. So lost and alone.

Even though I hadn't heard from him for a few hours, I could still *feel* him. And that was enough. Enough to give me hope. To make my day a little more bearable.

It was almost dinner time now. I could tell by how dark the room was. My master only allowed me to turn the lights on when he was in the room, which was usually just as the sun went down. I was pretty sure he wanted me to cower at his nightly transformation, but his appearance wasn't what terrified me. His actions did.

He often brought human females into my room, making me watch while he fed on them. Sometimes the feeding led to sex, and he made me watch that too. Made me watch while he ravaged them on my bed, often ordering them to do unspeakable things. To him and themselves. Things I couldn't unsee, no matter how hard I tried.

I'd started sleeping on the floor weeks ago.

A part of me hoped he would be alone tonight. At least he was fully clothed then. But when it was just us two, his presence was the hardest to endure. All of his attention was on me, and he took pleasure in making me squirm. In breaking me down bit by bit until I felt like the lowest of creatures. Like an insignificant bug beneath his shoe.

I was still waiting for the day when he'd squish me and this would all be over.

Feeling the fear and anxiety return while I waited for him to arrive, I set down the brush and folded my hands into my lap. Only a minute passed before I was reaching for my thigh, pinching it as hard as I could. I winced from the pain, an all-too-familiar ache that I gratefully welcomed. Despite the mess of tender bruises on my upper legs, I didn't stop. I pinched and pinched until tears welled in my eyes.

Somehow, the pain helped me to control the negative emotions. I knew it was wrong, that I was only abusing myself, but I didn't know what else to do. I had no one to talk to. To vent or cry to. Maybe I wouldn't need this destructive habit if I did.

My thoughts strayed to *him* again, and I immediately relaxed the fierce grip on my skin. What if I tried talking to him? Not just wait for him to speak, but actually initiate a conversation?

When my heart fluttered at the thought, I blinked in surprise.

I suddenly wanted to speak to him more than I'd wanted anything in my entire life. The strong desire eclipsed any fear I had of being caught. I glanced at my reflection in the mirror, startled to find an actual smile on my face. I stared at the foreign sight for a few moments, then closed my eyes, still smiling as I prepared to initiate contact with him for the first time.

The bedroom door flew open with a loud *bang*.

I jumped to my feet, terrified when my master stormed inside.

"WHAT DID YOU *DO?*" he thundered, so loud that my heart nearly gave out.

"I-I—" I weakly stuttered, tripping over the chair as he came at me.

"Answer me!" he roared, getting in my personal space.

When I became tongue-tied, overwhelmed with fear at the anger in his blazing red eyes, he grabbed a chunk of my hair. I yelped as pain zinged through my scalp, as he wrenched my head back at an awkward angle.

"You can't have him," he hissed, his sharp fangs inches from my exposed throat. "If I can't sever your disgusting bond with him, then I have no other choice. He'll forgive me someday, when your toxic filth no longer pollutes his body. He'll understand that this had to be done. That I was only trying to protect him. Protect *us*. Just like we promised. No witch will ever have power over us. *Ever* again. I'll make sure of it."

Before I could put up a fight, he had me on the bed, helplessly pinned beneath him. I frantically bucked and writhed, but I was no match for his strength. Still, he hadn't secured both my hands. Only one of them. Instinct barrelled through me and I suddenly knew what to do. Knew that I needed to touch him. So I did, grabbing his arm before he could stop me.

Almost immediately, he bellowed in agony, shocking the crap out of me. I felt heat rush through my palm and almost pulled back, not understanding what was happening. When he sagged on top of me, nearly crushing me with his weight, I struggled to breathe, to hold on. Whatever I was doing was working. Only a few seconds more and—

"STOP," he barked. My response was instantaneous. I let go of his arm like I'd been burned. Internally, I railed at my body for being so weak. For giving in to his command so easily. But I was powerless. Powerless to resist him when he spoke like that.

He didn't move for several long moments, continuing to crush me as he recovered from whatever I'd done to him. When he did move, it was to pin me with a glare. The hatred spewing from his eyes practically singed my irises. I tried to look away, but he had me ensnared.

I'd lost.

And now, he would punish me.

"Listen carefully," he said, pushing so much authority into his voice that I stopped breathing. "You will not struggle. You will not scream. You will not use your magic against me. You will lay here like the powerless witch that you are. You will obey me, because I am your master. Is that understood?"

A tear slipped from my control, dampening the pillow beneath me. "Yes," I whispered.

"Yes, what?"

"Yes, my master." My lips began to tremble.

"Good," he said, and his wicked grin was the last thing I saw. The last thing before he yanked my head back and plunged his fangs into my neck.

CHAPTER 32

LOCHLAN

When I felt her warmth flicker erratically, I stumbled against the wall. Gasping for breath, I pressed a hand to my chest. To the spot where her soul warmed mine.

"Loch, what's wrong?" I heard Kade say, as if from a great distance.

Like a flame about to die, her presence within me sputtered weakly. It dimmed. Cooled.

I doubled over in agony.

Hands gripped my shoulders, keeping me upright as my legs threatened to collapse. "Loch! What's happening?" Everett this time.

"She . . . she's . . ." I struggled to finish the sentence. To keep breathing so I wouldn't pass out. ". . . dying."

The second I said the words, I wanted to rip out my own tongue. She couldn't be dying. There had to be another explanation for this cold, barren emptiness filling me up inside. This vast hopelessness that was threatening to swallow me whole.

I called out to her through our bond, a bond that suddenly felt thin, like a fraying thread about to snap. Fear chilled me to the bone. I called out to her again and again, but there was no response.

"Help me," I croaked, unable to bear my weight a moment longer. Two strong pairs of arms came around me from both sides, shouldering my weight between them. They all but carried me the final few steps to the building.

The building where I knew my soulmate was.

We'd expected a drove of rogues to attack us the moment we arrived, but the dwelling felt . . . empty.

I couldn't detect a single heartbeat. Not even McKenna's.

We'd found the modern glass and concrete dwelling not far inland, but far enough that the ocean couldn't be heard. Pine trees surrounded the gated property for miles and nothing else. We probably never would have found her on our own.

The second we forced our way inside, Silver shot through the house like a bullet. I wanted nothing more than to dash after her, but I could still barely stand. Everett and Kade stayed with me, while Isla and her brother took off to search the house's upper floors.

"Follow Silver," I said to the males on either side of me. "Hurry."

Within seconds, we were descending a flight of steps to a basement where we found Silver pacing anxiously in front of a reinforced door. A surge of desperation gave me enough strength to stumble forward on my own and turn the handle. It easily gave way, and the door swung inward with a faint creak.

My gaze skipped over the garishly gold room with its many mirrors, the decor exactly as she'd described it, and went straight to the massive bed. A part of me had hoped to find this room empty. To discover she'd been transported to a new location. At least then, the deafening silence would make sense. At least then, I could believe she was still okay.

But the room wasn't empty.

There was a small female form on the bed. Frail-looking and still. So very still. As I drew closer, one shuffling step at a time, I took in every detail of the form. She was swathed in white, the fabric so sheer that I could see the thin outline of her body. *Too* thin. Her hands casually rested below her breasts, as if she were simply taking a nap. Her thick mane of hair was fanned across the sheets, like a dark golden halo.

Her eyes were closed. Her beautiful face serene. Her lips . . . pale. Too pale. Her neck . . . flawless. No marks. Even her dress was unblemished. Not a single drop of red marred the white surface.

She looked so peaceful. And I dared to hope. Dared to believe she was simply sleeping. Simply waiting for me to arrive, like a knight in shining armor.

But when I looked at her chest. *Really* looked.

It wasn't moving.

And her heart . . .

My knees cracked against the floor. Even as the last of my strength faded, I continued to move toward her. To crawl. To drag my body to where she lay. Every inch of me shook as I grabbed onto the bed to pull myself up.

The bed that smelled like *him*.

My brother.

Other scents hit me too, strong enough that I almost vomited.

Sex. The bed smelled like sex.

Crippling pain racked my body, but I reached for her anyway. Oh-so-carefully, I slid my arms beneath her slight frame and lifted her. Cradled her close, freeing her from that foul bed. Sinking to the floor, I slumped against the wall with her in my arms. Her cheek rested against my chest, as if she were listening to my heart beat.

My eyes burned at the sight. I began to slowly rock. Back and forth. Back and forth. "You're safe," I whispered, but the sound was hollow. Empty. "You can open your eyes now, love. Open those gorgeous silver eyes for me."

When she remained limp in my arms, I reached a hand up. Paused. Then slowly curled a strand of her hair around my finger.

She didn't respond.

There was one thing left. One last shred of hope. One final test I clung to with all my might.

I touched her cheek.

It was cold.

Not a speck of warmth.

And her power . . .

It didn't flare up to meet me.

Her skin was lifeless. No longer lethal.

No longer anything.

And that was when I lost all hope. When darkness rose up to claim me.

Shadows burst from my skin. A strangled cry tore from my throat. I pressed my cheek against hers, trying to share my warmth. I pushed what little strength I had left through our bond, giving her everything I had. But the bond . . .

It was gone.

"NO!"

I threw my head back and roared. Screamed. Sobbed until I could no longer breathe. Shadows continued to whip around me, around *us*, sheltering us from the world. From everyone and everything as my heart, my *soul*, splintered into a million jagged pieces.

My claws raked at my clothing, at my chest, tearing through material and skin. They gouged in deep, aiming for my still-beating heart. Prepared to make it stop. Without her, I didn't want to live. Without her, I *couldn't* live.

She was my light, and the light had gone out. I could no longer survive in a world of darkness.

Hands grabbed at me. Tried to stop me from tearing out my own heart. I fought and lost, too weak to fend them off. A small warm body pressed against my hip, but I didn't have the will to push it away. A whine, a mournful howl faintly reached my ears.

Reminding me that I wasn't alone.

Kade's face swam before me and I tightened my hold on McKenna, terrified that he would snatch her away. His mouth was moving, but I struggled to hear. Didn't *want* to hear. Nothing he said would fix this. I'd lost my soulmate, the one thing I feared to lose most in the world. Nothing would be okay ever again.

" . . . was drained," my drothen's voice said, finally penetrating the darkness and shadows. "She can be *turned*, Loch. Don't give up hope yet."

I blankly stared at him. His words held no meaning for me. Tears stained his cheeks, but I had no comfort to offer him. A tiny paw came to rest on my arm, but I barely glanced down.

Someone else crouched before me. Everett. He too looked crestfallen. Behind him, I caught a glimpse of Isla, crying and clinging to her brother. Everyone here mourned my loss. Mourned *theirs*. McKenna's light hadn't just touched my life. Her tragic death would be felt by many. The whole world, in fact.

"Loch. Please answer me," Kade spoke again, with more force this time.

"If she's turned, the prophecy will be undone. She'll no longer be a Syphon," Everett said. My ears pricked at that. At the tiny sliver of hope they offered.

Claws dug into my arm. Silver's. She pawed at me urgently, nudging me repeatedly with her nose. Telling me to listen. To respond.

"I don't care," I finally said, the words like gravel in my throat. "I don't care about the prophecy. Or the curse. Without her, I have nothing left to lose."

Everett stared at me for a long moment, his jaw working as he contemplated the ramifications of my words. Finally, he nodded sharply. "Then do it, brother. Bring your mate back."

That was all it took. All it took to rekindle my hope. To make me move. To begin the process of turning McKenna into a vampire. It was simple, in theory. With all the blood removed from her body, she needed a vampire's blood to restart her organs before they shut down completely. The healing properties of vampire blood would restore the dying tissue and force the heart to beat once again.

But the mortal body was weak.

Sometimes, the shock of the system repairing itself was too great. Sometimes, the body simply didn't want to live again.

But McKenna had so much to live for. I had to hope she still remembered that. That Troy hadn't broken her completely. That she *wanted* to come back. For me. For everyone else who loved her. For herself.

Not wasting another precious second, I bit into my wrist and brought the rising blood to her lips. "Come on, baby, you can do this," I said to her in soothing tones, forcing the blood past her lips. "We're all here for you."

Kade gently grasped her jaw to pry her mouth open, and I didn't stop him. Didn't stop Everett from massaging McKenna's throat to coax the blood down.

Sometimes, the mortal body responded after a few swallows. Sometimes, it took more than that. *Much* more. We continued to coax blood down her throat for what felt like hours. I bit into my wrist again and again, not letting the wound close. Not letting myself spiral into doubt and despair, even as her body refused to respond.

"Has a Syphon ever been turned before?" Everett dared to ask what we were all thinking.

When no one responded, Noah said, "Not that we know of."

"What if . . ." Everett began, but I cut him off, hissing, "Don't say it. This has to work."

Everyone lapsed into silence again as I continued to pour more and more blood down McKenna's throat. My body trembled with fatigue, but I wouldn't stop. Wouldn't stop until she was breathing again.

Silver suddenly pawed at my arm again. I threw her a questioning glance, blinking in surprise when she started biting at her front leg. So hard that blood soon saturated the silver and white fur. When I stared at her in confusion, she yipped and jumped onto McKenna's lap. Blood soaked through her dress where the fox landed, and a growl pushed at my throat. Silver growled back, baring her pointy little fangs at me.

Stunned at her ferocity when she was usually so calm, I let her limp up my mate's torso and chest. When she brought her injured leg to rest on McKenna's throat, I knew what she wanted me to do.

"It could make things worse," I said, resistant to the idea. Mortals could only be turned with vampire blood. Mixing in blood from other species could ruin everything.

The fox growled at me again, then inched her paw even closer to McKenna's mouth.

I looked to Kade and Everett for help, but they both appeared as uncertain as I felt. Finally, I fixed my attention on Silver again, saying with all the force I could muster, "Are you sure?"

She simply stared back, her gaze strong and unwavering. Certain.

Gritting my teeth, I shoved aside my growing fear and reached for her paw. Soon, her blood was dripping into McKenna's mouth too. We all waited, barely daring to breathe. Listening for any change. Any sound. The flutter of a newly-beating heart. The twitch of a finger. Anything.

But it was the bond that warned me first. The bond that faintly hummed, then warmed, whispering to me that my soulmate was coming back to life.

CHAPTER 33

KENNA

I awoke with a startled cry.

Awoke to my heart thudding. My blood racing. And my body tingling with heightened awareness. Every inch of me burned with energy and *life*.

The fog I'd been in for weeks evaporated like smoke. Memories poured in. *Real* memories.

Names. Faces. People I loved.

Lochlan.

I felt a featherlight touch on my cheek. The fine hairs on my skin stood on end, as if gravitating toward that touch. As if *knowing* that touch.

Soulmate, my body seemed to sigh.

Wait. I wasn't trying to protect his skin from mine. How was he touching me without getting hurt?

My eyes shot open.

The first thing I saw was his devastatingly beautiful face in vampire form. He was smiling down at me, with so much love that tears sprang to my eyes.

"Hello, beautiful," he said in a strained whisper, touching my cheek again with no ill side effects. "Welcome back."

Not quite believing this was real, I reached up to touch him in return. My fingers froze inches from his face. Fingers that were black as midnight and tipped in claws. My heart thudded even harder.

"You're okay, love." Lochlan continued to speak in soothing tones, capturing my fingers with his. "Your body is adjusting well to the shock. It'll just take your mind a moment to catch up."

I opened my mouth, and immediately felt the fangs there. Swallowing my surprise, I nearly choked at the thickness in my throat. The dry burn. The *thirst*.

When had I become a temporary vampire again?

Images slashed through my mind. Ones I'd sooner forget. Of my master—of *Troy*—thralling me into submission. Of him biting my neck. Of him drinking. And drinking. And drinking. Until I could no longer hold open my eyes. Until my will to live slipped from my grasp. And I fell, fell, fell into nothing.

With a gasp, I shot upright, wildly searching for him. For the devil who made me forget *everything*. Everything that made me who I was. I blinked, belatedly realizing I could see clearly, even though it was night. I was in the backseat of a car, nestled between Lochlan's legs.

"Where—?" I began, but my spasming throat cut off the rest.

"We're in my car. I didn't want you to be in that filthy room a second longer. You're safe now. He can't harm you anymore." Despite how soft the words were, I heard the hard edge to Lochlan's voice, the slight tremor.

I focused on the other faces in the car. Kade, Everett, and Silver. Hovering just outside the open doors were Isla and Noah. The desire to cry grew stronger.

"Welcome to the vamp club, little Kenna," Kade said with a watery smile. My throat closed even more. "Red eyes look good on you."

Unable to speak, I glanced in the rearview mirror. Sure enough, red glowing eyes stared back at me. I touched my face, the skin as black as my fingers. My breathing grew labored.

"Did . . ." I croaked. "Did I die?"

At the pained looks everyone gave me, my bottom lip began to tremble.

"The . . . the curse. My Syphon powers . . ."

"We can worry about all that later," Lochlan replied, his voice once again gentle. "The only thing that matters now is that you're alive. That you're here with us, safe and sound."

I glanced in the mirror again, studying my face a moment more before it finally hit me.

I wasn't just a temporary vampire. I was a *real* one. A permanent one.

Holy freaking fates.

You are breathtaking, love, Lochlan hummed through our bond. *Strong. Whole. And irrevocably mine for the rest of eternity.*

Which meant . . .

I was now immortal.

I suddenly lost it.

Flat out sobbed, trembling like a leaf as I let myself break down. Let myself cry like I hadn't been able to in weeks. Lochlan cradled me close, pressing my wet cheek to his beating heart. But it wasn't close enough. I'd been deprived of him. Deprived of everything for too long. I'd had nothing and no one, and now I had *everything*. Everything I held dear. They were all here.

My family.

It was all too much to take in at once. Too much, yet not enough.

I needed more. More of them. More of him. *Especially* him. I shifted in his lap so that my arms could wrap around his neck. So that my legs could straddle his hips. I pressed myself as closely as I could, deeply breathing in his scent.

The second I did, saliva rushed into my mouth. A powerful instinct, a powerful *need* kicked in and my limbs locked around him like steel clamps.

When Lochlan grunted, Kade barked a laugh. "Looks like the baby vamp is hungry."

"Not helping, Kade," Lochlan wheezed as my arms—my super *strong* arms—all but strangled him.

"Here. She can have my thermos. It's almost full," Everett said.

"McKenna," Lochlan said in soft tones, like one would to a wild animal. He lightly circled his hand around the nape of my neck, gently coaxing me to release my fierce hold on him. "You need to feed. Let me—"

"Mine," I hissed against his neck, punctuating the word with a firm nip. I had everything I needed *right* here. He froze, every muscle in his body tense. But when I nipped him again, he shuddered violently.

Both Kade and Everett muttered curses.

"Everybody out," Lochlan said in a guttural voice.

"Yeah, we got that," Kade replied with a strained laugh. I felt more than saw their mass exodus. Doors slammed and we were suddenly alone.

The moment we were, Lochlan tightened his grip on my neck. I hissed again and prepared to give him another warning nip, but he held my head just out of reach.

"I'll let you do this, mate," he said, his voice an octave lower, "but you will stop when I tell you to stop. Understood?"

I lunged for him again, but he proved in that moment who was stronger, keeping me at bay. "Understood," I growled, flashing my fangs at him. We stared each other down, fighting for dominance, but a rogue tear chose that moment to betray me.

He tracked the tear, then searched my face. No doubt my mind and emotions as well. I knew what he would find.

Desperation.

To convince myself that this was real. That *he* was real. That I was in fact free. Both in body and mind. That I was no longer helpless and lost. That I wouldn't be controlled again.

I didn't just need his blood. I needed *him*. His body and soul. His comfort and protection.

I needed him to wipe away all the bad memories and replace them with something good. Something that would erase the sights and sounds and smells that had haunted my every waking and sleeping moment.

I needed to claim him. And he needed to let me.

He must have seen all that. Must have felt it. Maybe even heard it. Because his hold gentled, and he guided my mouth toward his neck. Submitting to me.

At his willingness to give up control, pure, unadulterated excitement gushed through me. My gums burned as my fangs dropped to their full length, aching to pierce his skin. I trembled with need a moment more, nuzzling the throbbing vein in his neck.

Then struck.

As my fangs sank through his flesh, he jerked against me with a breathless groan. Euphoria immediately spiked through our bond, assuring me the bite brought him pleasure, not pain. When I took my first pull and his blood filled my mouth, we both trembled. His other hand cupped my backside and squeezed, the action pressing me against his swelling shaft.

"Not too fast, love," Lochlan hummed when I greedily swallowed. "You'll get drunk and lose control."

I whimpered against his skin, already feeling halfway unhinged.

I didn't want to hurt him, but he tasted so freaking *good*. And if he didn't stop rubbing me against his erection, I was going to do other things besides drink his blood.

He released a low chuckle, clearly having listened to my thoughts. "You can do whatever you want, McKenna. You're in control."

My body went haywire at that, burning up with need and desire. I took another long pull from his neck and he cursed softly.

"On second thought, maybe I shouldn't have—"

He groaned, loud and long, as I ground myself against him. I did it again and again, ravenous in my need to have him. *All* of him. More blood slid down my throat like melted chocolate, and I sank my fangs in even deeper.

"Bloody hell, Kenna," he grunted, his hand spasming on my neck. But he didn't haul me back. Didn't stop me from taking another long pull. His breathing suddenly sped up, and he choked out, "Your venom, love. It's too much."

He shook all over, so high on ecstasy that I feared his heart would give out.

But I couldn't stop. Couldn't stop the greedy, insatiable instincts that had taken over.

My fingers went rogue and began unbuttoning his pants. Unable to retract my claws, they scraped against his skin, dragging another breathless moan from him. Soon, he was helping me, tugging my white dress up my thighs. When his erection sprang free, he guided me on top of him. I paused mid-swallow to fully savor the feel of him stretching me. Filling me. I had ached for this. Ached for so long.

A sob pushed at my throat. A cry of bone-crushing relief.

I'm here, solemae, he whispered through our bond. *I'm here.*

I clung to his words. Letting myself believe them. We were together again. I was free. Not without scars or sacrifice, but I had survived. *We* had survived. And moments like this would mend the many breaks. Would make us stronger than we were before.

When I'd fully taken him inside my body, I rose and fell on top of him. Slow at first, then with increasing desperation. He tried to slow my frantic pace, grasping my hips to pull me down. Seating me deeper than I'd ever been before. My walls clenched around him and we both moaned this time, lost in each other. In the joy our reunion brought. I thought I would burst, overwhelmed by the physical and emotional sensations coursing through me.

My soul felt at one with his, and they basked in each other's glow as we did.

Our hearts thundered in sync as our pleasure grew. As our desire and desperation collided. As we clung to each other, needing this moment more than we knew. Not simply for the pleasure, but for the relief. For the comfort and wholeness it brought.

The buildup came swiftly, our pent-up energy from weeks apart finally finding release. We climaxed together in a rush, feeling all that the other felt.

Keeping him inside me, even as the aftershocks wore off, I continued to feed from him. My pulls were languid now as I reveled in the taste of him, rolling the blood around on my tongue before swallowing. His head had fallen against the seat, his fingers lightly stroking my back while I drank.

With effort, he finally managed to say, "We need Kade." When I stiffened in surprise, he added, "I can't stop you. I lost the strength to a long time ago." He laughed quietly at the alarm he no doubt felt through our bond. "What can I say? I'm already addicted to your bite."

Well, then. If that wasn't a confidence booster, I didn't know what was.

Don't call Kade yet, I warned Lochlan. *You still have your dick inside me.*

His entire body shook with laughter this time. *Good call. He would love being a part of this moment way too much.* I whimpered when he pulled out, but he was right. We shouldn't stoke Kade's fantasies. He was already swimming in them.

When he arrived, my territorial instincts kicked in. I growled, needing to protect what was mine. He only chuckled and gripped my jaw. With a little pressure, my mouth sprang open.

As my fangs finally slid from Lochlan's neck, they messily dripped blood down his shirt front. I winced in apology, but he only reached up and gently wiped the blood off my lips and chin. I glanced at the bite mark on his neck—*my* bite mark—but the twin puncture wounds were already sealing shut.

When I leaned forward to lick the blood off his skin, Kade threw himself into the driver's seat, grumbling, "I seriously need to get laid after this."

I laughed, for the first time in weeks.

We were an hour from the castle when the air grew uncomfortably warm. I full-body shivered, so hard that everyone in the car noticed.

"What?" I said, when all three guys looked at me with concern.

"You're cold?" Kade said, briefly glancing at my barely-there dress. Yeah, I needed a change of clothing *pronto.*

"No. Hot, actually." Still, I began rubbing my arms. "Did you turn the heat up?"

He shook his head, exchanging a look with Lochlan in the rearview mirror.

When I met Lochlan's gaze, he was studying me closely. After a moment, he touched my forehead. His fingers came away damp with sweat. "You're burning up," he quietly said, yet I could feel a spike of alarm through our bond.

I shrugged, trying to put him at ease. "Maybe I'm coming down with something. I haven't gotten much sleep lately."

His brow creased. "Vampires don't get sick."

My eyes widened in surprise. "Ever?"

"Ever."

I shrugged again, but with a little less confidence this time. "Maybe my body is still adjusting to all the changes. I'll just sleep it off."

The guys continued to exchange glances. Even Silver keenly watched me. But I was suddenly too exhausted to care. Curling up against Lochlan, I shut my eyes, determined to sleep it off and put their worries to rest.

But the heat and chills only got worse. Soon, I was shaking uncontrollably, my dress sticking to my sweaty skin. Heat swept through me in waves. My blood felt like it was boiling, like molten lava.

When I could no longer suppress a cry of pain, Lochlan barked at Kade to step on the gas. The engine roared as we shot down the winding road. Lochlan dragged me into his lap, holding me securely while the car jerked and fishtailed. Silver yipped, her claws scrabbling for traction on the seat. When I tried to grab her, my arms wouldn't cooperate. Not even my eyelids would lift. They were like leaden weights, trapping me in darkness.

I burned and burned and burned, growing hotter with each passing second. Until I was deaf to the world. Deaf to my screams. I was only able to feel pain, greater than anything I'd ever felt before. It raged through my body, destroying me. Breaking me down. Sapping my strength. Leaving me to helplessly writhe in Lochlan's arms, unable to answer his frantic calls through our bond.

At one point, I thought I heard Silver's voice in my head, her words calm and soothing as she said, *Hold on, Kenna. It'll be over soon.* But I was too delirious to pay attention.

The agony was endless. Scorching my insides to cinders. Everything hurt. My eyes, my teeth, my fingernails. It felt like my skin was melting, my hair curling up in smoke.

Fear pounded through me. Fear that my body was rejecting the new changes. Fear that I would soon be nothing more than a pile of ash.

My body suddenly seized, robbing me of breath. I violently shook. My fangs sank into my bottom lip, drawing blood. I trembled for what felt like hours, unable to stop. When I finally did, my body went limp. Sucked dry of all energy. The pain raged on, but I didn't even have the strength to whimper.

A jostling motion made me aware that I was being lifted. Out of the car and up a flight of steps.

"MOVE!" I dimly heard Lochlan bellow as he carried my lifeless body into the castle.

I could feel his fear and desperation, but there was nothing I could do to comfort him. Nothing I could do but hold on. Hold on and try to survive. Another second. Another minute. So that I wouldn't go where he couldn't follow. So that he wouldn't lose me forever.

Time crawled, then sped up. Then crawled again. I was disorientated, forgetting up from down. Forgetting how to breathe. To think.

Suddenly, I was swimming. Surrounded by water. Submerged.

My skin cooled for a blissful second. One blissful second.

Then I was raging out of control. Screaming. Roaring. Emerging from the water in a fiery gale. My eyes shot open, just in time to see my skin burst into flames.

CHAPTER 34

KENNA

Warmth surrounded me.

It was just the right temperature. Perfect, even. So perfect that I languidly stretched like a cat.

A deep chuckle interrupted my stretch. "Careful, love."

When arms wrapped around my middle from behind, pressing me against a hard body, my eyes popped open. As a room came into focus, I panicked for a split second, thinking I was back in Troy's lair of torture and debauchery. The panic quickly vanished when I recognized where I was, then flared up again when I caught sight of my fingers.

They were back to normal.

Had I only imagined that I'd been turned into a vampire? Had the last two nightmarish weeks been just that—a nightmare?

But why was I in Lochlan's bedroom? In his *bed*? In the middle of the day?

King Ambrose could come in at any moment and find us.

I tried to scramble out of bed, but Lochlan's hands froze me in place. One shifted to cup my breast while the other slid between my legs.

Holy fate babies.

My eyes blissfully fluttered shut as he once again dragged me against him possessively.

"How are you feeling?" his voice pleasantly rumbled near my

ear, making me shiver.

Swallowing with difficulty, I managed to croak, "Good."

More than good. Freaking *awesome*, actually. Not just because Lochlan's hands were awakening my body in the best way possible, but because I felt rested. *Truly* rested, for the first time in what felt like forever. I also couldn't feel a single cut, bruise, or ache anywhere. I felt . . .

Reborn.

"What happened?" I said, humming softly when his fingers began to move, to slowly pleasure me.

"You don't remember?"

"No," I replied, too distracted by what he was doing to remember my last name.

His fingers stilled and I whimpered in disappointment. "You burst into flames. Like a bloody *phoenix*."

My eyes popped back open. "What?"

He rolled me onto my back, propping himself on an elbow to look down at me. "I thought you were dying. For *good* this time. Your skin was so hot that I could barely touch you. And when fire consumed every inch of you, I was blown across the room. There's still a body-sized indent in my bathroom tiles. You've been unconscious for nearly a day and a half now."

My brain struggled to remember, but there were only bits and pieces of memory. Images that were too crazy to be real. I really blew him across the room?

I suddenly gasped. "Did we have sex in a car? Did I . . . did I *bite* you?"

Surprise colored his expression, then he slowly grinned.

Fates! All the memories were real then. Which meant . . .

"So I'm a vampire now? A Feltore, like Isla?"

He shook his head. "We're not sure. You've been transitioning forms day and night like a vampire, but your skin is . . . it's lethal again."

Shocked, I glanced to where one of his hands still rested on my stomach. My *clothed* stomach. Not the sheer white dress, but a comfortable pair of pajamas. I looked back up at him in alarm. "Did I hurt you?"

His expression softened. "I'm fine, McKenna. When your Syphon magic returned, I felt nothing but relief. I don't know what it means or what it makes you, but I frankly don't care. I only care that you're somehow still alive. That I didn't lose you again."

At the pain I felt through our bond, I touched his cheek, consciously putting up a barrier between our skin to protect him. "I'm sorry," I whispered, lightly running my fingers through his short stubble.

He leaned into the touch, briefly closing his eyes with a sigh. "You have nothing to be sorry about."

"I'm sorry for all the pain you went through. And I'm . . . I'm sorry about your brother."

He stiffened, his jaw beneath my fingertips hardening to granite. Images flashed through my mind. Violent ones. Ones he probably hadn't intended for me to see. After a moment, the anger in his eyes faded, but the rigidness in his body remained. "Did he . . ." When his voice cracked, he cleared his throat and tried again. "Did he touch you?"

Another image flashed through my mind. Of the massive golden bed he'd found me on. I instantly knew what he was asking, and my heart fiercely ached for him. For the fear he must have felt, must *still* be feeling, not knowing what happened to me.

"No," I quietly reassured him, and immediately felt relief crash through our bond. He squeezed his eyes shut and heaved a sigh, clenching my shirt hem with a trembling fist.

"His scent was everywhere," he roughly said. "I thought for sure he must have forced himself on you."

Swallowing the lump in my throat, I admitted, "He did have sex in the room, but not with me."

More anger flashed through the bond. "He made you *watch?*"

I shivered at his fierce growl, uncertain if I wanted to calm him or join him. "Many times."

He surged from the bed, shoving both hands through his hair as he paced. "I'm going to *kill* him."

I knew he meant the words. What shocked me was that I knew I wouldn't stop him if he tried. I *wanted* him to, unlike the time he'd almost killed Everett.

"Don't feel bad for wanting Troy dead, McKenna. What he did was unforgivable."

He stopped pacing when I quietly said, "I don't. For the first time, I don't feel bad at all. I just . . . I feel bad for *you*. He never would have done this if you'd been given a vampire soulmate. Or even a human one. Because of me, you lost a brother."

He was on the mattress again in an instant, tugging me into his lap. "The only one to blame is Troy and his insecurities, not you. I only wish I had paid more attention to the warning signs. Ever since Edith left him for dead, he's been on a power trip, preying on those he considers beneath him. Humans are property to him. Witches are like exotic playthings. Even Feltore have become lesser to him over time.

"Power is his armor, worn so that he'll never be seen as weak again. The sad part is that he's become the very thing he fears most: a monster who takes pleasure in exploiting others. He would have done this even if our soulmate bond didn't exist. He wants to watch the world burn, and you were standing in the way of that. So don't feel bad for me, McKenna. I lost my brother a long time ago, even if I didn't realize it until now."

Sighing, I rested my head on his shoulder, still offering him comfort despite his words. He may be riding on a cloud of anger right now, but losing his brother—no matter how twisted he was—had to hurt.

After a beat of silence, I whispered, "You saved me in there while I was trapped under his thrall. Without the reassuring sound of your voice, I would have begged him to kill me." Pain squeezed my chest. His pain. I laced my fingers through his. "Thank you for finding me. For freeing me from that terrible prison."

He heaved a sigh, lifting our joined hands to kiss my fingers. "I will always find you, McKenna. Always. Not even death can keep you from me."

A knock at the door interrupted our moment, followed by Kade's voice. "We can hear you in there. Stop hogging our whatever-she-is mystery girl and get your butt out here."

Lochlan snorted softly. "I can make them all go away if you want. Just say the word."

"No," I murmured, lightly kissing his neck before I scooted off his lap. "I want to see them." Even if I ended up sobbing like a baby the second I did.

The first to greet me was Kade. He took one look at my face and swept me into a bone-crushing hug. I hugged him back just as fiercely, so hard that air whooshed from his lungs. "Yep. You're definitely still part vampire," he grunted with a surprised laugh. "Whatever you are, I'm just glad you're alive, little Kenna. I was going out of my mind with worry."

At the emotion in his voice, my throat closed. We held each other a moment more, drawing comfort from the close contact, before he kissed my hair and set me back on my feet.

Isla was in front of me the next second, her face already a mess of tears. "Oh, girl," was all she whispered before drawing me into a tight hug. So much was said in those two words. So much understanding. We'd both been victims of Troy. Whether directly or indirectly, we'd both suffered and died at his hands.

I squeezed her in return, feeling the beginning of tears form. When it was Noah's turn to hug me, Lochlan didn't protest. I couldn't even detect a hint of jealousy.

Everett caught me off guard the most though, reaching for me without hesitation. Startled at his firm embrace, I didn't react at first. But when he whispered "I'm sorry" against my hair, tears slid down my cheeks. I accepted the embrace as well as his apology, wrapping my arms around him.

Silver was the last to approach me. I'd barely knelt to her level before she was in my arms, her body a wriggling mass of excitement as she whined and yipped in greeting. *I knew you'd pull through*, she said through our bond, rubbing her cheek against my shoulder.

How? I replied, burying my face in her fur.

Because, during your darkest moments, you were surrounded by those who love you. That kind of love can carry you through just about anything.

My chin wobbled and I let myself cry some more. She was right. She was absolutely right. I was surrounded by love, and that love gave me all the strength I needed to survive.

Do you know what happened to me? I asked her. *Why I regained my Syphon powers?*

I gave you some of my blood while your mate was trying to turn you, she explained, so calmly that I pulled back to gape at her. *Your body had a delayed reaction to it, but you eventually went through the transformation process of becoming what you now are.*

My eyes widened further. "You know what I am?"

At that, everyone around us reacted. Lochlan, Kade, and Everett crouched in front of me, demanding answers. Noah and Isla started whispering to each other, arguing about what I could be. Ignoring them all, I focused on my familiar, waiting with bated breath.

I do, she finally answered, twitching her black-tipped ears. *You're a hybrid.* When I stared at her blankly, she went on. *Half vampire, half witch. Created by the mixing of two different blood sources. Under normal circumstances, the transition wouldn't have been possible. But with the help of the powerful bonds you possess between me and your mate, the two incompatible blood sources merged, forming an entirely new entity.*

My jaw dropped. "Incompatible? So you're saying that without the bonds, I would have gone up in smoke?"

Kenna, she said with an almost hurt expression. *I wouldn't have allowed that to happen. I knew you could handle it.*

I gnawed on my lip in thought. *So am I immortal then?*

As immortal as a hybrid can get, she replied, which put me at ease. Mostly.

I still had so many questions, but Lochlan's worry and impatience were pumping strongly through our bond. I turned to him and quickly explained out loud what she'd told me. He went still. *Too* still. Then pinned Silver with an almost angry look. Whoops. He must not have known how risky the blood mixing had been.

"So what does this mean?" Isla said. "Can she still break the curse if she's half Syphon?"

"She's still our best bet. Our only bet," Everett responded.

"But she's cursed now too, right?" Noah this time. "How can she save the vampire race if she's now one of them?"

"Enough," Lochlan firmly said, watching me closely. Probably feeling my growing worry through our bond. "We still have two weeks. Nothing has to be resolved today. McKenna deserves a day of rest."

Everyone nodded, throwing me apologetic glances.

"I agree," a new voice said, one that brought us all swiftly to our feet. "Miss Belmont has earned herself a reprieve after the hell she's been through."

As the vampire king approached, Lochlan planted himself squarely in front of me. The rest crowded in close, shielding me as well. My heart swelled at their selflessness, and I struggled not to cry again. But I didn't want them to fight this battle for me. Whatever the king had to say—whatever he *felt* about me—I would face head on with my chin raised.

The second I stepped out from behind Lochlan, he stiffened but didn't stop me. When I pushed my gratefulness toward him, he responded by grasping my hand and sliding his fingers through mine. Right in front of the king. His father tracked the deliberate move without comment, stopping only a few feet away from us.

Despite how nervous I felt, I managed to hold still as he took me in from head to toe. After several long moments, he murmured, "Words cannot express how deeply sorry I am for my youngest son's actions. We were all blinded to how lost he's become."

Shocked at his genuine remorse, I didn't react when he stepped forward and grasped Lochlan's hand. The hand that still held mine.

"But one good thing has come from this tragedy," he continued, lifting our joined hands. "My second son has found his soulmate, and that is something worth celebrating." I suppressed a gasp as he folded both of our hands in his, willingly touching my skin.

"What are you saying, Father?" Lochlan said, tightening his grip on my hand. When hope feathered through our bond, I dared to hope as well.

"I'm saying, my dear son, that I already knew. What else besides a soulmate bond could have brought you back to yourself? What else could have made you smile again? Could have made you this happy? And that is all I've ever wanted for my sons. Your happiness."

"Then why . . ." Lochlan began, his voice cracking. "Then why the threats? Why make McKenna feel so unwelcome?"

The king chuckled. "If fate ever gifts you children of your own someday, you will understand why I had to test the integrity of your mate and the strength of your bond." His gaze rested on me again, and there was a warmness in his expression I'd never seen before. "I had to make certain you were worthy of my son. I hope you can understand."

Even as I felt Lochlan's frustration through our bond, I nodded. Because I *did* understand. And I respected the king even more for his decision.

He smiled at me. A smile without secrets or hidden intents. One with true kindness and maybe even a little affection. "Good," he said, squeezing our hands before letting them go. "Because the perfect way to welcome you home is with a bonding ceremony. Preparations are already in progress, so come. Your dress fitting awaits."

As Lochlan went poker straight beside me, I frowned in confusion. "Bonding ceremony?"

"Every bond is celebrated in the supernatural world, but soulmate bonds even moreso," King Ambrose explained, his excitement over the topic clear. "They are so rare that it's tradition to hold a public ceremony for the couple once they've consummated their bond."

I nearly swallowed my tongue at the word consummated. He knew then. He knew we'd had sex.

Wait a second. Was this ceremony like a *wedding?*

Okay, I was kind of freaking out now.

"Can McKenna and I have a moment?" Lochlan abruptly said, and his father's smile faltered.

"Of course," he smoothly replied, despite the flicker of confusion in his eyes. "Come find me when you're finished. I need your opinion on a few last-minute details."

When Lochlan simply gave him a curt nod, he left with a troubled frown. The moment he was out of earshot, Everett rounded on him. "You're not thinking about denying him the ceremony, are you? You know how devastated he is over Troy's betrayal. This is his way of dealing with it all."

A muscle jumped in Lochlan's jaw. "I know, but he didn't even ask. We just got back and McKenna is still recovering. Besides, I didn't want to do it this way."

Do what this way? I asked him through our bond, drawing his attention down to me.

He considered me a moment before admitting, *I don't want our traditions sprung on you like this. I want you to feel comfortable with them, not blindsided. As for the bonding ceremony, I was going to present it to you first in the customary way.*

"What's the customary way?" I whispered, suddenly lightheaded with nervous anticipation.

"To offer a gift," he said, his voice and expression softening.

"What kind of gift?"

"One that expresses just how committed I am to the bond," he replied, letting go of my hand to twist the gold and ruby ring off his left pinky finger. "One that holds both intrinsic and sentimental value."

When he picked up my hand again, my *left* one, Isla slapped both hands over her mouth, muffling an excited squeal.

My eyes were round, my heart frantically pounding as he slowly slid the ring onto my ring finger. Watching me closely, he said, "By gifting you my royal family ring, I'm expressing my intentions to keep you by my side. To permanently invite you into my home and family. Should you accept it, that is," he added, pausing midway up my finger, a question in the dark depths of his eyes.

I bit my suddenly trembling lip, barely able to see past the tears blocking my vision. My voice shook with all the emotion I felt as I whispered, "Yes. With all my heart, yes. I accept your gift."

His smile was radiant, brighter than any diamond. I laughed as he swept me into his arms, twirling me round and round. When he captured my mouth in a heated kiss, cheers, whistles, and clapping filled the hall. I smiled against his mouth, feeling him do the same.

He might not have wanted to do it this way, but sharing this moment with the people we loved couldn't have been more perfect.

CHAPTER 35

KENNA

Nerves were eating me alive as the final touches were made to my ceremonial dress. But at least I had my best friend to keep me company.

"Relax," Isla said from where she lounged on my bed, trying and failing not to wrinkle her own dress. "You're stiffer than a pubescent boy peeping through a girl's bedroom window."

The human servant fixing the hem of my dress made a choking noise, and my face burst into flames. Isla started to cackle, making me roll my eyes and mutter, "I can't believe you just said that."

"You're welcome," she unapologetically sang, adjusting her plunging top before her nipples could show. The strapless black silk number was simple and elegant, hugging her generous curves. Already in vampire form for the evening, she looked fiercely sexy. Her expression suddenly grew thoughtful. "Did he . . . did Troy make you . . . do anything?"

I blinked, caught off guard by the question. I'd made it clear earlier in the evening that I was open to talking about what happened to me, but this particular question seemed . . . personal. As if by asking, she could face what he did to her as well.

Eventually, I replied, "He made me forget everything and everyone I ever loved, until I was nothing more than his dutiful slave. I was lonelier than I'd ever been before. So lonely that I wanted to die."

When tears welled in her eyes, I struggled to contain my own. "I'm so sorry, Kenna. He's going to pay for what he did to us. I won't let him get away with it."

I smiled weakly at her, but didn't comment. Vengeance simmered in her eyes, and I didn't think encouraging it was a good idea. Troy was dangerous, plain and simple. I didn't want him to hurt her again. So I shifted the conversation to a safer subject—more or less. "How have things been with Kade while I was gone?"

Her face pinched, but at least the vengeance had disappeared. "About the same. We speak when necessary. Our conversations are civil. Mostly. Since I've gotten better at controlling my bloodlust, he's given me more space. He even allowed me to go out looking for you, as long as I was with Noah and paid close attention to the sun." She sighed wistfully, adding, "I miss that the most. Feeling the sun on my skin. You're so lucky it doesn't burn you."

We'd figured that out shortly after I'd woken up. Either because of my bond with Lochlan or the fact that I was still half Syphon, the sun didn't harm me. But I was most definitely still a vampire. My thirst for blood was strong, stronger than when I'd been a temporary vampire.

Controlling my bloodlust was easier for me than for Isla, though. I could be in a room with humans as long as I'd recently fed. Isla, on the other hand, still had trouble controlling herself, even after a month of being a vampire. She often carried around a thermos of blood so she wouldn't be tempted to snack on the staff.

Besides the bloodlust, the curse continued to force me into my vampire form at night. I stared at my reflection in the full-length mirror, still getting used to my new look. I didn't mind it, but I could see how being stuck this way without the ability to change back would make life challenging.

With only two weeks left until the curse became permanent, I was determined to break it more than ever. It touched the lives of everyone I cared about in some way or another.

Instead of gently prodding Isla to give Kade another chance, I steered the conversation in a new direction. "Do you think you'll ever go back to school?"

She sat up, swinging her legs over the side of the bed. "I don't know. Are there schools for vampires? Because I'm pretty sure most humans will notice my aversion to sunlight. Plus, I won't be able to hide my claws and fangs if the curse becomes permanent."

I noted the slight bitterness in her voice and couldn't help but feel guilty. All her normal teenage dreams had been dashed the moment she'd become my friend. Mine had as well, but I wasn't ready to give up hope yet. There was still time to fix this. Isla and I could still pursue our dreams—our *human* dreams—even if a few adjustments had to be made.

That was life, whether we lived one lifetime or several. Nothing stayed the same for long. Change was inevitable. We didn't have to be vampires to know that.

"It's time," Isla suddenly squealed, springing off the bed. Even though my heightened senses allowed me to easily track fast movement, I still jumped at the abrupt action. Isla chortled. "Are you sure you're ready for this? Your heart has been racing for hours."

"Of course," I immediately replied, fiddling with Lochlan's ring on my finger.

Her expression softened. "It's okay if you're not, Kenna. A lot has happened in a very short amount of time. If you don't want to do this right now, I'm sure Loch will understand. You're only eighteen, after all, which is a little young to be getting married."

My jaw dropped and I sputtered, "Isla Andrews, this is *not* a wedding."

She bent over with laughter before I could say more, so I stuck my tongue out at her. "Well, *whatever* this thing is," she said when she could breathe again, "I'm sure Lochie boy wouldn't mind *consummating* it later."

"You're impossible," I groused, feeling my cheeks heat again. Still, a smile curved my lips as I looked at her reflection in the mirror. "I'm really happy you're here, Isla. I love you like a sister and just wanted you to know that."

"Oh, girl," she whispered, her lashes fluttering as tears glistened in her eyes once more. "I completely feel the same. And I'm sorry if I ever sound ungrateful to be here. I'm lucky to still be alive. It's just . . ."

"You miss how things were," I finished sympathetically.

She sniffle-laughed. "Which is crazy, since I was bored out of my mind living in Rosewood. But I miss going to school, and seeing my friends, and . . . and my dad. I said some pretty awful things to him before I was kidnapped. I really need to apologize."

Despite a muffled protest from the seamstress, I turned to hug Isla. "You'll have those things again. I'll make certain of it," I promised her, determined to make it so. "And your dad loves you. I'm sure he's already forgiven you."

She sniffed again. "You're seriously the bestest friend a girl could ever ask for. But, Kenna?"

"Hmm?"

"Your blood still smells frickin' *amazing*, so we'd better . . ."

"Oh," I said, quickly pulling away. "Yeah. Sorry."

We stared at each other for an awkward moment, then busted out laughing. We were clutching our sides, doing our best not to ruin our makeup, when a knock came at the door.

Still giggling, I smoothed the front of my dress and answered it. Kade was the first to see me. As usual, I blushed at his reaction, which was just shy of indecent. His mouth formed a silent *Wow* as he looked me up and down several times, taking in my wavy updo, sparkling gold jewelry, and figure-hugging red dress.

It too was silk, but was fashioned into a halter top with a neckline that plunged to my navel. My back was completely bare, showing off the twin dimples low on my hips. The front hemline was short, skimming the tops of my thighs, but the back fell in waves to the floor, forming a billowing train.

Before he could say anything to deepen my blush, his gaze caught on Isla behind me. At the sight of her, his nostrils flared, as if scenting the air. As if scenting *her*. I couldn't see her reaction to his attention, but I suddenly felt desire flood my bond with Kade.

Desire for her.

Ah crap. How long had *that* been going on?

Pretending I hadn't felt anything, I glanced past him to where Noah, Everett, and Silver stood. When I smiled at them in greeting, Kade's attention snapped back to me and he grinned as if nothing had happened. As if he hadn't just been *drooling* over my best friend.

"So how does this work again?" I asked him when I noticed the red string in his hand.

"Simple," he said, reaching for my right hand to tie the end around my pinky finger. "Go find Loch. If you're drawn directly to him, you're publicly proving that your soulmate bond is complete."

"And the string? What does it mean, exactly?"

"The red string of fate symbolizes your unbreakable bond. You were destined for one another, and no matter how far apart you are, you will always find each other again."

I blinked back sudden tears. "That's beautiful."

"Tug on the string," he said, letting go of my hand.

I did, and immediately felt a tug in return.

Knowing it was Lochlan, I grinned like an idiot.

"No cheating now," Kade warned, waving at me to drop the string again. "You have to find him through your bond without aid from the string."

I nodded, taking a deep breath before closing my eyes. *Hello*, I called into the void where I knew my soulmate was.

Hi, he called in return, and my grin widened even more. *Looking for me?*

Yes. Where are you?

Oh, that would be too easy, love, he purred in my mind. *I want you to feel for me.*

I wrinkled my nose. *What?*

Use your mind to cast out your senses. Through the bond, you will be able to see, hear, smell, taste, even touch me. With your senses, you can locate where I am.

But . . . but how is that possible? Why haven't we tried it before?

Like when I was kidnapped for two weeks. It would have been handy to know about this little trick then.

I hadn't meant to share that last part with him, but he must have heard it anyway. *We couldn't do it before*, he replied, his voice heavy with remorse. *I tried, McKenna. With everything I had. But I only just discovered it was possible. Our bond must have strengthened further when you claimed me. And now, when I cast my senses toward you, I can actually feel where you are.*

Can you see me?

I didn't spy on you while you were dressing, if that's what you're asking.

I snorted, internally rolling my eyes at him. *Are you sure I can do this?*

I know you can. Come find me, solemae.

With that, his voice faded into silence.

Freaking fates, I was so going to get him back for this!

"Anything wrong?" Kade said, breaking my concentration.

Squeezing my eyes shut even tighter, I grumbled, "Remind me to kick Lochlan's butt when the ceremony is over."

Ignoring his bark of laughter, I refocused on the soulmate bond. On the numbskull who dared throw me a curveball at a time like this. When I heard Lochlan chuckle, I sent him an image of me scowling.

Focus, McKenna, he said. *Focus on my voice. On hearing it clearly. Not just in your mind, but as if I'm right beside you. Think about my scent. My taste. Seek them out. When you find them, you'll be able to see and touch me.*

So I did. I focused on him with all my might. On his voice's sexy rumble, on the intoxicating scent of his skin and blood, on the taste of him on my tongue. My senses were swimming in him, *drowning*, until I felt a tug. Not on the string, but on the bond. Without hesitation, I followed the tug, shooting past walls and floors as my senses carried me to him.

I was suddenly surrounded by his scent. His *warmth*. As if he were in the hallway beside me.

I can feel you, his voice whispered through my mind. *Open your eyes, McKenna. Open your eyes.*

I paused, knowing he didn't mean literally. Somehow, he wanted me to open them inside my *head*. Like a window. So I could see him. Really see him.

Continuing to use my senses, I reached for him in the dark. My fingers blindly swept the pitch black before me, determined to feel him. To *touch* him. When they suddenly brushed against warm skin,

I gasped and jerked my eyes open. Not my physical ones, but my mental ones.

And there he was, grinning at me so wide that his left dimple appeared.

It wasn't like looking through a window at him after all. I was there, right in front of him. Not just seeing him, but the room beyond him as well. It was so real. *He* was so real, like I could reach out and touch him.

Hello, love, he quietly said, then did just that. Reached out and touched me. His fingers feathered across my cheek, and it felt so real that I shivered. But he didn't stop there. No, he let his fingers trail down my neck, then lower. And lower. Causing my breath to falter.

When they paused between my breasts, he said in a wickedly amused voice, *What are you wearing?*

His gaze jumped back up to mine when I abruptly danced away from his touch. *Nope*, I teased, flashing him a grin. *That would be too easy.*

At his mock frown, I laughed and broke the connection. I immediately snapped back to myself. To my *real* self. I opened my eyes to find that I was still laughing. Everyone was staring at me like I'd lost my senses, but I was too giddy to be embarrassed.

I'd freaking seen and *touched* my soulmate through my mind!

"Do you know where he is?" Everett asked dubiously.

Even his doubt couldn't faze me. In fact, I couldn't help but gloat a little. "I approve of the ceremony decorations. Those ice sculptures are a nice touch." At his stunned expression, I laughed again and swept down the hall, calling over my shoulder, "What are you all waiting for? We have a ceremony to attend."

CHAPTER 36

KENNA

The ballroom looked nothing like the last time I'd seen it.

Everywhere I looked, there were twinkling lights. They danced in the air like little stars, thousands and thousands of them.

The only other light in the vast space was an intricate golden floor candelabra in the room's center. In front of it stood Lochlan. The flickering candlelight accentuated his dark form, making him look even more strikingly handsome than usual. He saw me before I saw him, and his eyes were already glowing with desire as he took in every inch of me.

Ensnared by his powerful gaze, everything else ceased to exist for a moment. I held still at the top of the stairs as his eyes softly caressed the curves of my body. When they glittered with approval, a shy smile pulled at my lips.

Found you, I eventually said through our bond, taking the time to admire him in return. He wore a deep red collared shirt beneath his black suit, open at the neck. The ceremony wasn't as formal as the masquerade ball had been, which put me more at ease.

You did, Lochlan replied back with a pleased grin, winding the red string around his hand. As it stretched taut between us, he gave it a gentle tug. *Now get down here so I can touch you. For real this time.*

My eyes widened and I suddenly realized we had an audience. A big one. Not as large as last time, but there were still a couple dozen vampires milling on the edges of the room.

My father's council, Lochlan explained before I could panic too much. *It's customary for them to witness bonding ceremonies.*

Descending the stairs, I watched them closely through my lowered lashes. I recognized some of them from the ball, even if we hadn't actually spoken. I wondered how many, if not all of them, had encouraged the king to sacrifice the previous Syphons. With my heightened hearing, I caught their whispers. Apparently, they hadn't expected to see me in vampire form this evening. To find me *cursed,* just like them.

Can they be trusted? I hedged.

Most have been loyal to my father for centuries and have never given us a reason not to trust them, but I'm not taking any chances. You'll be at my side the entire evening. If you need to go pee, I'm going with you.

A laugh slipped free before I could stop it. Ignoring the surprised looks the council threw my way, I continued to follow the gentle tug on the string. When I neared, Lochlan held out his hand toward me and I took it without hesitation. There were fewer gasps this time as our skin touched, fewer murmurs when he slid an arm around my waist to pull me close.

I was still nervous about their reactions though. Still worried that there'd be a riot like last time. Emotions that Lochlan didn't seem to share. He felt . . . calm. Content. Happy, even. Like the cares of the world couldn't touch him right now.

Ducking his head, he whispered in my ear, "You look good enough to eat, solemae. In fact, I plan to do just that later this evening."

My face flamed at the implication, at the *promise.* "Behave," I softly hissed in return, peeking at our guests to see if they'd overheard. "I expected Kade to be the naughty one tonight, not you."

He quietly chuckled. "Oh, I plan on being nothing but naughty tonight, love, so don't hold your breath." Gently nipping my earlobe, he straightened to unapologetically smirk at my dumbfounded expression.

More and more, he was catching me by surprise, this mate of mine. This man who was still a mystery in many ways.

A thrill of excitement suddenly shivered up my spine. Despite the uncertain future we still faced, I couldn't wait to know him better. To peel away every single fascinating layer that made up Lochlan D'angelo.

Responding to my excitement, his eyes darkened and he trailed his knuckles up the bare length of my back. "Keep that up and I'll be tempted to misbehave right *now*, in front of everyone," he whispered huskily, causing my stomach to flutter erratically.

Before I could respond, a throat cleared. When King Ambrose appeared in front of us, my nervous energy from earlier returned. It was still too new. Too weird that he was okay with us being together. On top of that, he was acting like some marriage officiant, even though I knew this wasn't a wedding ceremony.

As Kade, Everett, Noah, Isla, and Silver joined the council, the king said in an official voice, "Friends and family, we are here today to set aside our worries over the impending curse so that we may celebrate Prince Lochlan's bonding to his mate, McKenna Belmont. As you have all just witnessed, they are able to mentally communicate, which means their bond has been consummated. Soulmate bonds are rare and precious, and we rejoice in their union.

"But, during these trying times, this bond may seem threatening to some," he continued. Lochlan tightened his hold on me when a few council members grumbled their agreement.

"Which is why I invited you all here today. To bear witness to my words, so that you may go out and spread them to the rest of my kingdom. Let it be known that I, Ambrose Marceau D'Angelo, king of the vampires, sanction this bond. McKenna has proven herself to be a worthy mate for my son, both in strength and loyalty. She will make a fine wife to him someday and, if fate allows it, mother to his sons."

Lochlan's amusement trickled through our bond as my face reddened.

"They will now complete the claiming ritual, to which you will all bear witness and see for yourselves the genuineness of their bond."

My heart began to thunder as the king stepped back, leaving only me and Lochlan at the room's center. I'd been told about this moment. Prepared for what I'd have to do. But I suddenly couldn't breathe.

Focus on me, McKenna, Lochlan said in soothing tones, reaching up to lightly grasp my chin. *We don't have to hide our relationship anymore. Whether they accept our bond or not is up to them, but they need to see with their own eyes that you are mine and I am yours.*

Despite my trembling limbs, I nodded. This was the vampire way. It was now *my* way, even if I was silently freaking out.

Lochlan ran his thumb over my chin, giving me a moment to calm myself. Then said for everyone to hear, "McKenna Joy Belmont, I claim you today in front of these witnesses. Not just as my soulmate, but as my lover, my partner, and my equal in every way. I claim you as my own, so that no other may do so. So that you belong to me and none other."

My heart swelled. Not at the words themselves, but at the genuineness behind them. At the love and care he so obviously felt. At the clear pride that I was his. When he smiled at me softly, I practically melted into a puddle of goo.

Still gripping my chin, he tilted my head to the side and feathered his lips over my jaw. As they slowly trailed down my neck, I stilled, preparing for the pain. "Now that you're a true vampire, you might find this to be a bit more pleasurable," he whispered against my skin. "Brace yourself, love."

And then he bit me. Bit me *hard.*

And I . . .

I exploded in ecstasy.

He caught me as my knees buckled, intimately fitting our bodies together. With each passing second, my pleasure grew, until I could no longer suppress a moan. My eyes rolled back and I forgot about everyone else in the room, clinging to his suit jacket as he took a long pull from my neck.

Lochlan had been right. *So* right.

Being bitten really was a vampire's greatest desire.

Bliss thrummed through my body, awakening every nerve ending and tightening my core with need. As if reacting to my need, his shaft noticeably hardened where it was pressed between my legs. *Lochlan,* I groaned through our bond, barely able to stop myself from rubbing against him. *If this goes on for much longer, I'm going to orgasm in front of everyone.*

The last thing I expected him to do was cup my backside and press me more firmly against his erection. When I gasped out loud, he simply chuckled and replied, *It's not unheard of for the mated couple to orgasm during the claiming ritual. Some get caught up in the moment, regardless of the audience.*

Freaking fates, he did *not* just say that.

Nope. That wasn't going to be me. I wasn't a public orgasm kind of gal.

But when he chuckled again and chose that moment to pump

his venom into me, I actually considered it. Actually considered climaxing in front of all these people, I was *that* turned on.

Somehow, I avoided rubbing against him though. Avoided epic embarrassment by keeping the moment PG-13 instead of R.

But Lochlan didn't make it easy. He continued to tease me, keeping our bodies flush together, his hand still brazenly caressing my backside. So when it came my turn to claim him, thoughts of revenge danced in my mind.

After repeating the pledge, I bit him greedily. Possessively. Gratified when he responded with a guttural groan, I followed my instincts and let my venom bleed into him. He jerked against me and bit out a curse, digging his claws into my hips.

I could feel how euphoric he was, both through our bond and his pants. He couldn't get much harder, and even the tiniest amount of friction made him tremble. I smiled wickedly against his neck, teasing him as he teased me. He growled a soft warning, but I simply licked his skin in reply.

By the time the claiming ritual was over, our desire soaked the air. Lochlan looked two seconds away from tossing me over his shoulder and finishing what we'd started in the privacy of his room, but a smattering of applause—plus a loud whistle from Kade—dispelled the moment. Instruments began to play, the quartet from the ball having sneaked in at some point. Human servers scurried about with golden goblets of blood, winding in and out of vampires who eyed *them* more than the drinks.

In no time, the celebration was in full swing. Several council members tentatively approached, their curiosity over me plain. But as they conversed with Lochlan, clearly knowing him well, the animosity I'd felt from them at the ball was nowhere to be found. In its place, there was a guarded respect. A hope that hadn't been there before. Some even spoke to me, introducing themselves by name.

Despite knowing how they'd treated the past Syphons, I allowed hope to build in me as well. If century-old vampires set in their ways could soften their hearts toward a vampire witch with a lethal touch, then maybe miracles really could happen.

Maybe, just maybe, we could beat this curse after all.

We were dancing, the spirits in the room high, when *she* arrived.

The pungent scent of her magic had several heads turning toward the stairs. Lochlan tensed, pulling me to a stop. Hissing filled the air and the music died. My gaze rose to the top of the stairs where she stood, and I found her already staring at me.

She looked stunned.

And livid.

I'd never seen her so angry before. Dark purple magic crackled at her fingertips as her eyes swept me from head to toe.

"What is the meaning of this?" Headmistress Mayweather said, her voice cracking through the air like thunder. When Nautilus loudly cawed from his perch on her shoulder, I heard a low growl from Silver. Seconds later, she planted her little body between my legs in a protective stance.

Demon, she hissed through our bond. The crow's beady eyes latched onto the fox as if she were a tasty snack.

At the sight of her, Clarice grew even more irate. "Is this your familiar? And you're still bonded to her, even as a vampire? That's *blasphemy*. The elders won't stand for this."

Before I could respond, the crowd parted and King Ambrose swept forward. "Clarice," he said appeasingly, with a slight edge to his voice. "Our council meeting is not scheduled until tomorrow. You are breaking our agreement by coming here uninvited this evening."

"Breaking our agreement?" she said incredulously, and slowly descended the stairs, unmindful of the many powerful vampires below. "You *lied* to me. You said there were no new developments and Kenna was fine. She was the last Syphon witch who could break the curse. Our last hope for peace without bloodshed. And now she's a *vampire*. I should have known you'd screw this up, just like you did with all the previous Syphons."

"Clarice," Noah interjected. She paused halfway down the stairs as he stepped forward. "Kenna still has her Syphon powers. I can prove it to you."

When he reached for my hand, clearly intending to share his magic with me, Clarice slashed her arm through the air. "Stop," she ordered.

Noah reeled back with a muffled curse. The scent of his blood thickened the air, and I watched in horror as a long red line darkened his white shirtfront. Both Isla and I gasped and moved toward him, only for Clarice to stop us in our tracks with a freezing spell. I could still see everything, even hear twin growls from Lochlan and Kade, but couldn't move a muscle.

I could only listen as Clarice said to Noah in a booming voice, "You've failed your elders for the last time, Noah Andrews. Because of your inability to follow orders and protect your own from harm, I, Clarice Mayweather, respected Darken elder, bind your magic."

She tossed something into the air. Two objects, round and silver. Purple magic shot from her fingertips to engulf the objects, then flew forward to latch onto Noah's wrists. As if they burned him, he threw his head back and roared. It was over as quickly as it began. When the magic faded, he dropped to his knees with a defeated groan. Lifting both arms, he stared at his wrists. Identical silver bracelets encircled each one.

"You dare come here and attack one of my guests in my own home?" the king seethed, clearly out of patience with her.

"This is witch business," Clarice firmly replied, not giving an inch. "Besides, the deal was for Noah to be my emissary while he remained here. Since he failed to communicate what has been happening with Kenna, I can no longer trust him to fulfill his duties.

"Furthermore, his entire family is a disgrace to all witches. His mother defied her superiors by hiding Kenna from us, then contacted the SCA for help instead of her own kind. His father failed to control his unruly family and still works with the SCA against our wishes. Even the sister couldn't keep out of trouble and is now a vampire. I and the entire witch community wash our hands of them. Do with Noah Andrews as you will."

"Regardless of your jurisdiction in the witch world," King Ambrose said, "this is my island. *My* castle. You will leave now and await my summoning, whenever that may be."

Her dark gaze narrowed dangerously. "That wasn't our agreement, *Ambrose*. I have every right to be a part of the decision-making as you do. Too much is at stake, for both our peoples. Which is why I've come here tonight, regardless of your lies. One of our Oracle elders has received a vision, and upon seeing Kenna, I can now understand why. The premonition is this:

"In thirteen days' time, an event shall occur.
The fanged ones will emerge, to claim what is theirs.
Exposed they will be, for all to see.
The streets will run red, as many fall dead.
Sides will be chosen, in this battle for power.
The fate of all will be decided, in this darkest hour."

The second she finished, the room erupted into chaos. Several of the council shouted, each trying to be heard over the other.

"Enough!" the king bellowed, and uneasy silence descended. Even in my still frozen state, I could see how shaken everyone was. Including the king. Despite the vampire's continued animosity toward witches, there was no ignoring a witch's prophetic words.

"This is no doubt referring to the rogues," Ambrose calmly said. "They must think Kenna is dead and have no reason to believe the curse will be broken. They must think that a preemptive strike on humans will force our hand. That we'll have no choice but to join them."

"And will you?" Clarice bluntly asked. "Will you join the rogue's cause? Your *son's?*"

Oh crap. She did *not* just say that. How did she even know about Troy's betrayal?

The king was silent for several moments, his expression chiseled from stone. Shadows flickered around his taut form, the only sign that her words had struck deep.

"Kenna is still half Syphon," he finally replied, his voice eerily quiet. "She can still stop this from happening."

"Can she?" the headmistress said, staring at me dubiously—and with no small amount of pity. "Because where I'm standing, she looks as cursed as the rest of you. Still," she continued, ignoring the hisses directed her way, "witches look after their own, even ones with tainted blood. I would like to take Kenna back with me now, instead of in thirteen days' time. It's the least you can do after what you've done to her. I'm sure your wayward son would be more than happy to kill her again should he find her still alive. I will keep her safe from the upcoming bloodshed."

Lochlan growled and tightened his arms around me. "You won't be taking her *anywhere*, Darken."

"Oh, really?" she coolly replied. "Well, your father and I have a pactum agreement that says otherwise. Whether or not Kenna is able to break the curse, she is to be returned to her coven. She was never yours to keep permanently."

My arms twitched in shock, the only movement I could manage. Lochlan turned to his father, hurt and disbelief thick in his voice. "You agreed to give McKenna *back?* How could you?"

The king's eyes filled with remorse. "Not in a thousand lifetimes did I ever think you'd fall in love with a Syphon. Not after what you endured. But I was wrong. So wrong about everything. She has brought you unimaginable joy and happiness, and for that, I must break the pactum."

The startled gasps that followed were deafening. Lochlan's devastation through our bond was louder. Managing to unfreeze my hands, I placed them over his, offering him what little comfort I could.

"You can't," he whispered hoarsely. "The cost is too great."

King Ambrose simply smiled, love for his son radiating through his eyes. "No price is too high for my children's happiness."

Clarice harrumphed, drawing my attention back to her. Expecting to see anger in her gaze, I was shocked to find vindication instead. She was glad. *Glad* that the king had broken their pactum. Still, her voice was laced with offense as she said, "So you refuse to honor our deal? You refuse to give Kenna back to me in thirteen days' time as agreed upon?"

He lifted his chin, looking every inch the proud king that he was. "That is correct. Kenna is no longer mine to give. She belongs to my son, and I'd rather face death than take her from him."

The second he finished uttering the words, pain contorted his face. When he doubled over in silent agony, Everett rushed forward, catching him before he could fall.

At the sight of their weakened king, several of the council surged toward Clarice. With a sweep of her hand, she blasted them back. As curses and growls ripped through the air, I caught the barest flicker of fear in her eyes. She wasn't invulnerable after all, then. I could even see sweat beading her brow, as if wielding so much magic had taken a toll.

She must have realized this as well, must have seen how precarious her position was, because she suddenly fixed me with a pleading look. "There's no need for you to remain here any longer, Kenna. The vampire kingdom will fall, but we can be far away when it does. Come with me now where it's safe. I promise the witch community will treat you and your familiar with fairness."

I stared at her outstretched hand for a moment, stared while worry trickled through our bond. Worry that I'd fall for her flowery promises. When I reassuringly squeezed Lochlan's hand, he still held me tighter. Still doubted, if only a little bit, that I would stay.

And that doubt thawed the last of the freezing spell. Made me say more vehemently than I intended, "Why would I want safety if it costs me my family? I made a deal, Clarice. Even if I can no longer save the vampires from their curse, I won't break my promise."

Her shock—and disgust—was palpable. She quickly cleared her expression, but I already knew how she felt about my loyalty to the people around me. Dropping her hand, she said, "I'll be back. Maybe when the world sees vampires for who they really are, you'll realize how foolish it is to remain here. Decide which side you're on, Kenna, and do it quickly. You can't choose both."

With that, a purple portal swirled into existence behind her. She stepped through, leaving us all to deal with the destruction in her wake.

CHAPTER 37

KENNA

Everyone burst into action the second she left.

Isla raced toward her brother, Kade a step behind her.

Lochlan joined Everett in supporting his father, who was now trembling like a leaf and muttering incoherently. Most of his council gathered around, silently watching their broken leader. It was clear they'd never seen him like this, and their mixed expressions raised the hair on my arms. I couldn't forget that, at their core, vampires were predators. Would they see the king's weakness as a sign that he was no longer fit to lead them?

"How long will the effects of the broken pactum last?" I spoke up, hoping to divert their attention.

"It depends on the strength of his fears. It could be weeks before he realizes they're nothing more than a waking nightmare. Even then, they will leave a lasting scar, which is why pactums aren't to be entered lightly," Lochlan somberly replied, peering at his father's blank expression. After a moment, he fixed a determined gaze on Everett. "Take Father back to his chambers. Make sure only our most trusted guards stand watch over him."

Everett nodded without hesitation, once again taking on the full weight of the king. "And what will you do?"

"Begin preparations for battle," Lochlan said. As he turned toward his father's council, I shivered at the dangerous glint in his eye. "We have thirteen days. I won't rest until I'm certain we're ready, and neither will any of you. It's our responsibility to stop Troy and his misguided followers from wreaking havoc on the world. We will seek out allies, but not before everyone here swears via a pactum not to spread news of the king's weakness. Can everyone agree to that?"

Nods and murmurs of assent rippled through the Venturi, many lowering their heads under the force of Lochlan's powerful gaze. Pride warmed my chest. Pride for my mate, for his willingness to step up and lead when all seemed hopeless.

As I watched him converse with the council like a prince—no, like a *king*—I made a vow of my own. That I wouldn't rest either, even for a second, until I'd saved us all from this wretched curse.

"Can I see?" I said, lowering myself next to Noah where he sat dejectedly on the bottom stair.

Hours later, we were still in the ballroom. Lochlan, Everett, and Kade had been in a meeting with the council ever since Clarice left. Tensions were high, and I'd opted to stand on the sidelines after receiving a few cold looks.

Clarice's speech had shaken the council's tentative hope in me. They too doubted my ability to break the curse. They too thought I was cursed with no way to save myself, let alone an entire kingdom.

But I wasn't going to let their doubt stop me from trying. We'd sacrificed so much. Every single one of us. That couldn't have all been for nothing.

Noah didn't glance up when I joined him, but he lifted an arm, letting me see one of the silver bracelets that bound his magic. From her persistent spot between my legs, Silver sniffed at the bracelet, then sneezed in disdain.

Magic was never intended to block or bind other magic, she said with a twitch of her black whiskers. *It is the cruelest torture for a magic user.*

"Can it be removed?" I asked her, but it was Noah who muttered, "Only by the witch or warlock who put it there."

I frowned, feeling my dislike for Headmistress Mayweather increase tenfold. When I reached out to touch the bracelet, Silver yipped a warning, but it was too late. The second my skin made contact with the silver, blistering heat engulfed my fingers. I yanked them back with a startled hiss.

Lochlan and Kade rushed over, no doubt responding to my pain through our bond. Lochlan's wild gaze scoured every last inch of me before settling on my smoking fingertips. When he crouched to gently grasp my hand, I struggled to push past the pain, to protect his skin from mine. Within seconds, the pain started to fade, and the angry blisters disappeared.

Lochlan's eyes lifted to search my face. "What happened?"

I grimaced at my error. "Um, I stupidly forgot that I'm a real vampire now and sorta touched some silver."

Kade clicked his tongue in sympathy. "I did that once. You learn fast."

"No kidding," I huffed, still feeling the phantom pain. Lochlan slowly swept his thumb over the newly healed skin, replacing the pain with tingling warmth. I grasped his fingers, recalling the many times he'd been hurt by silver. I couldn't imagine the crippling pain before, but I could now.

"It's late. You should get some sleep," he said, tucking a wayward curl behind my ear.

I shook my head. "I'm not leaving this spot until Noah's magic is unbound."

When my words fully sank in, a deep frown pulled at his mouth. "McKenna . . ."

"I have to," I quickly cut him off. "I'm the only one who can bypass the spell. At least, I think I can. I won't let him suffer like this, knowing that I could do something about it."

"K-Bug," Noah groaned. "Don't—"

I cut him off too, then Kade and Silver, throwing Isla a warning look for good measure as she returned from her bathroom break. "What good am I if I can't help my friends and family when they need it? This is the one thing I *know* I can do. Even if I fail to break the curse—"

"You won't," Lochlan quietly said.

I inhaled a fortifying breath. "Even if I do, I won't hide while the world goes to war. I will do whatever I can to protect you all, starting with unbinding Noah's magic."

Pride mingled with Lochlan's fear as he studied me thoughtfully. "So brave," he whispered, then reluctantly let go of my hand and stood. "I won't stop you from trying, but once I feel your pain, I might lose control."

"I got your back, buddy," Kade said, dropping an arm over his drothen's shoulders. "I'll keep the Lochness Monster in check."

"Me too," Everett said, finally joining us.

I flicked a nervous glance at the council hovering nearby, their curiosity obvious. Fates, no pressure or anything. It felt like I was being tested all over again. And if I failed, their hope in me would die. For good this time.

I *couldn't* fail. No matter what. No matter how freaking painful this was going to be.

"Okay, then," I said, turning back to Noah. "Let's get started."

CHAPTER 38

LOCHLAN

The second she screamed, I lost it.

I roared my fury when Kade and Everett dragged me back before I could reach her. She shook and sobbed, refusing to let go of those blasted silver bracelets. Her pain was endless. The scent of her burning flesh permeated the air, driving me into a wild frenzy.

I cursed Kade and Everett, threatening to end them. To torture them slowly before ripping them limb from limb. They doggedly held on, even while my shadows pounded into them. They jacked my arms behind my back to keep me from tearing into their flesh.

All the while, my mate remained steadfast in her goal. She didn't look at me once. Didn't stray from her need to help her friend. In my frantic state of mind, I wanted nothing more than to yank the warlock's arms from their sockets. Problem solved. No more bound magic, and McKenna would no longer be in pain.

But Kade and Everett wouldn't let me reach him. Wouldn't allow me to protect my mate from harm. And the need, the need to *protect* her, was shredding my sanity.

It felt like hours. *Hours.* Before the screams faded and McKenna slumped forward. Noah caught her. As he did, both silver bracelets fell from his wrists. They clanked against the marble stairs and rolled across the floor like harmless jewelry.

When I surged forward this time, they finally let me go. I was at her side in an instant, gathering her into my arms. Infinitely careful not to touch her smoldering hands. She was barely conscious. Still riddled with pain. I struggled to breathe. To wrestle myself under control again.

The second I could speak, I said to Everett in a low growl, "See the council out. I'll be tending to my mate. No one is to disturb us."

Before he could respond, I was halfway up the stairs with McKenna securely in my arms. I stormed down hallway after hallway, still trembling with fury. We were nearly to my room when she whispered, "I did it. I freed him."

When she weakly laughed, I dropped my gaze to her face. To the slight smile there. An actual smile, despite the utter agony she'd just endured.

My heart cracked wide open at the sight. At the pure relief and joy she felt for saving her friend.

How could I ever possibly deserve this selfless woman?

When I pushed all the love I felt for her through our bond, her smile widened. "I'm far luckier than I have any right to be," I responded hoarsely. "My body. My heart. My soul. They are eternally yours, solemae."

I felt the warmth of her love for me in return and almost wept. Almost fell to my knees as she touched my cheek with her freshly healed fingers and said, "We're going to be free too, Lochlan. Together, we'll free them all."

Twelve days.

Twelve days of preparation came and went.

Twelve days of trying to break the curse and failing.

On the thirteenth day . . .

We readied for war.

CHAPTER 39

KENNA

Everything was prepared.

Weapons and transportation.

Check.

Rendezvous point.

Check.

Rogue's location.

Check.

Allies gathered.

Check.

Determination to win.

Check.

We were all set to stop Troy and his goons from wreaking havoc on the human populace. All set to face whatever future that fate had in store for us.

But, despite our readiness, I couldn't decide what to *wear*.

I mean, if this *was* the beginning of the apocalypse, I wanted to be properly dressed for it. Problem was, I didn't know what an end-of-the-world outfit looked like.

Grumbling under my breath, I tossed yet another shirt on the bed's discard pile and reached for another. When it was halfway over my head, I heard the soft click of a door opening.

"Need any help?" an amused voice said.

With a frustrated sigh, I yanked the shirt off and threw it on the discard pile. Only in my underwear now, I flung myself at the bed, landing on my back with a groan. "This is so stupid. It's just clothing, for fate's sake. But, for whatever reason, picking the right outfit feels . . . important."

When I opened my eyes, Lochlan was hovering above me. His amusement was gone, replaced with a searching look. I knew he was gauging my mood internally as well, sifting through my emotions and thoughts. I didn't try to hide them from him, because I was suddenly desperate for him to make sense of it all. To tell me why I was acting so . . . crazy.

"You're not crazy," he said, reaching for my hand to pull me up. When I was on my feet, he lightly gripped my chin, tilting my face up toward his. "You're nervous and scared. We all are."

"You?" I raised my brow skeptically. "You've been nothing but a pillar of strength for the past two weeks. You've been keeping us all from falling apart, what with your father still unwell and an opinionated council to manage. If you're nervous, you're awfully good at hiding it."

His lips twitched into the barest of smiles. "I've been strong because I've had to be. But I'm still nervous about the outcome of this battle. I'm still scared about what tomorrow will bring."

My throat closed. I quickly dropped my gaze before he could see the tears forming. But he already knew. Fates, I couldn't hide anything from him.

"Stop," he quietly said, raising his other hand to cradle my face.

I bit my trembling lip. "But I didn't—"

"*We* didn't," he corrected, stroking my cheek. "This burden was never just yours to bear. It never should have been your burden in the first place."

He wiped away a fallen tear, and I struggled not to cry in earnest.

I'd been doing that a lot the past few days. Holding back tears. Trying to stay strong and hopeful as time ran out. But now that the deadline was hours away, I wanted nothing more than to sob and sob and sob. Until my guilt and grief were crushed beneath a wall of numbness.

I hadn't broken the curse.

Despite hours and hours and hours of trying to make sense of the prophecy, of refusing to eat and sleep until I found a solution, nothing had worked.

For all my abilities, I'd failed the most important task of all.

I'd failed to save the people I loved.

I let Lochlan hear my thoughts, let him feel how utterly wretched, how utterly *sorry* I was. His lips thinned, but he didn't stop my self-flagellation. As if he knew his efforts would be in vain anyway. Instead, he lowered his head and kissed me. Softly. Tenderly. So sweetly that a shuddering sob finally broke free. He kissed me again, saying without words how he felt about me, despite my failure.

Do you trust me? he said through our bond, sliding his fingers into my hair.

Always, I immediately replied, gripping his waist with trembling hands.

Then let me take the pain away. Let me have this moment to comfort you.

I uttered a weak protest, a sound that was instantly swallowed by another kiss. *They need you out there. They need your leadership. The rogues could strike at any moment.*

You need me more, he stubbornly persisted, tipping my head back to kiss me more thoroughly. My toes curled. *Besides, they have Everett. I'm only asking for a moment, love. One moment to touch you. To kiss you. To replace your pain with pleasure.* "Please, McKenna," he whispered against my lips. "Just one moment."

Fates alive, how could I say no to that? How could I say no when this could be our last intimate moment together? Anything could happen in the dark hours ahead. We could both die, for all I knew.

And so I found myself giving in. Found myself whispering back, "Just one moment." Because I did need it. Desperately so. I needed to be close to him, as close as humanly possible. I needed to breathe him in, soak up the warmth of his skin, and bask in his essence. I needed to meld my body against his, flesh-to-flesh, until we became one entity. One heart. One soul. Until I felt complete.

Until I felt certain we would both survive the night. Until I had the strength to face whatever tomorrow brang.

And so, regardless of who might hear us, we made love. Exploring each other's bodies as if for the first time. As if for the *last* time. Clothes were hastily shoved aside. Sheets tangled around our bodies as we fell onto the bed in a mess of limbs, holding each other tighter than we ever had before.

He claimed me swiftly. Passionately. Drawing a shuddering gasp from me. I rode the high of his bite and venom, all while he thrust inside me. Before either of us could climax, though, I reversed our positions. Straddling his hips, I sank on top of him. Then claimed him in return. Reveling in the pleasure it gave him.

Our moment was beautiful yet sad. Euphoric yet heartbreaking. We thoroughly loved each other, as much as two soulmates could. Pouring all of our hopes and fears into that single moment of fleeting time.

And prayed that it would be enough. That our love would carry us through.

Whatever the outcome ahead, I could endure anything.

As long as my soulmate was there to face it with me.

"Now that's both kickbutt *and* sexy," were the first words out of Kade's mouth when he saw my outfit.

For once, I didn't blush at his blunt observation. Because that's exactly how I felt in the clothing I'd finally chosen, and I was going to freaking own it. The cropped top and leather pants molded perfectly to my body like a second skin. Thigh-high boots and a leather jacket completed the outfit.

Smirking, I sketched a quick bow, then gave a little twirl for good measure. He whistled in encouragement. When Lochlan came up beside me and threw him a dark scowl, Kade simply chuckled. Except for my red vampire eyes, I was covered head-to-toe in black. An intentional move, one we'd all made to help us blend into the night.

Earlier in the day, we'd received a call from our allies that a suspiciously large group of Feltore was amassing on the outskirts of Rosewood. There could only be one explanation for that: the rogues were about to reveal themselves. And instead of choosing a heavily populated area for the big reveal, Troy had targeted my hometown.

Even though most of the residents were safely tucked inside their homes for the evening, we'd prepared for the worst. Our goal to stop the rogues without being seen by humans was probably impossible.

"Still no sign of Clarice?" I asked Kade, whose job had been to keep a lookout for the headmistress over the past two weeks.

"Nothing. Not even a hint of her magic," he assured. With the deadline practically upon us, everyone assumed she'd hunkered down behind the school's wards and left me to my fate.

Well, everyone except me.

I'd seen the way she looked at me in the ballroom before she left.

She wasn't finished with me yet. Whatever her endgame was, I was a part of it.

But before I could start worrying about her again, movement on the stairs drew our attention. "Kenna," Everett said as he reached the landing. "Tess wants to speak with you before we head out."

My stomach swooped with nerves. When I nodded and headed for the stairs, Lochlan moved to follow.

I should go alone, I said to him through our bond, turning to place my hand on his chest.

I was the one who'd called her, after all. Who'd presented a deal the SCA couldn't refuse: the vampire kingdom's permanent cooperation in return for their aid. And she'd cared enough. Cared enough to listen, to propose the deal to her superiors on my behalf. The least I could do was face her on my own. Show her that I held no ill will. That I trusted her enough to go alone.

But she hadn't seen my true vampire form yet. I'd warned her ahead of time, knowing that springing it on her wouldn't be the best move. She hadn't said much. Hadn't reacted with anger or disappointment. But I had no idea how she felt, or what she would do at the sight of me. Still, I needed this moment with my ex-guardian.

Lochlan must have felt that through our bond, because he simply nodded and pressed a lingering kiss to my forehead. "I won't be far," he said, stepping back with only the slightest hesitation.

I smiled at him, making sure he felt my gratitude. Considering how she'd tried to separate us not too long ago, his willingness to let me see Tess alone was commendable.

I found her with my heightened sense of smell, nodding at Isla, Noah, Silver, and several council members on my way out the front door. The group of SCA who'd arrived earlier in the evening had opted to remain outside or in their vehicles. The lakehouse was packed with powerful Venturi, so I could understand why, but the intentional segregation still put us all on edge.

We were allies now. A deal had been struck. We both wanted to take down the rogues before they exposed themselves to humans, but I knew the SCA was having a hard time differentiating us from them. We all looked the same, even if we didn't want the same thing. They were afraid of being double-crossed.

But so were we.

In a matter of hours, a new day would be upon us. *The* day. If the sun rose and we were still in our vampire forms, that meant the curse had become permanent. Vampires everywhere would be exposed, whether they wanted to be or not. In the panic that followed, the SCA could very well turn their back on us. Could take up arms against us and destroy us all.

Out of everyone, we had the most to lose. But we couldn't afford to be cautious right now. Clarice had made it clear she wasn't interested in lending her aid. Our options were limited, and we needed all the help we could get. I'd even called Reid, the werewolf quarterback from Rosewood High I'd befriended. He'd been shocked to hear from me. To learn about all that had happened in the two short months I'd been away. Even more shocked when I'd asked for his help.

"If vampires are exposed, so will werewolves," I'd told him, the only useful thing I'd learned from Headmistress Mayweather. All supernaturals would be at risk after today, even the neutral ones who wanted no part in this. Who simply wanted to live normal lives—or as normal as they could.

He'd promised to discuss it with his pack, but I hadn't heard back from him since yesterday, even when I'd texted that the battle would take place in Rosewood. There was nothing I could do about that right now, though. All I could do was focus on the hurdle before me, on closing the front door and facing the SCA operatives on the front lawn of Lochlan's property.

Several noticeably stiffened at the sight of me, which was an odd feeling. To be objectively seen as a predator. A monster. When, less than half a year ago, I was one of them. A human in every way, except for the dormant magic locked inside of me. So much had changed. My world had turned upside down more times than I could count, and it still was. Still spinning out of control, a pinwheel of chaos that took and gave, took and gave.

But as I laid eyes on the woman who'd raised me, as memories of my childhood and the last several months circled through my head, I couldn't help but stand a little taller. Everything I'd been through had prepared me for this moment. Had made me stronger and more confident, so that I could face my past with an unwavering gaze. So that I could descend the stairs with sure steps, knowing that I was a better person for all I'd endured.

And I couldn't regret any of it. Even the painful moments. Because those moments had allowed me to see just how utterly blessed I was.

Here. Now. On the cusp of war.

I was blessed to be alive. To have found friends and family who cared. To have been given a love that was soul deep, fulfilling me in ways I couldn't have even imagined.

Yes. So much had changed. And when I stopped in front of the woman who'd been my only family and connection for years, I knew that I'd already forgiven her. For everything. Because I had so much to look forward to in my future, even if I was labeled a monster for the rest of my days.

I'd found love. That was all I'd ever wanted, and all I'd ever need.

Tess openly gawked at me. I let her, waiting patiently while she took in my red eyes and midnight skin. I knew that other parts of me had changed as well. My movements were more graceful. Faster. Even when I didn't intend them to be. I could hear her mortal heart racing. Smell her intoxicating blood. Sense her nervousness.

But she wasn't afraid. She didn't fear the sight of me.

And that fact alone sent relief coursing through me. Made me give her a small smile and say, "Thank you for coming."

She blinked several times, as if trying to fit my familiar voice to my foreign body. Clearing her throat, she replied, "Of course. It's the SCA's job to de-escalate supernatural situations before they get out of hand."

My smile wavered. "Oh. Well, thank you for helping. We appreciate it."

As we lapsed into an awkward silence, I fidgeted with Lochlan's ring. When I caught her staring, I dropped my hand.

"Is that . . . is that his?" she hesitantly asked, glancing at the ring again.

"It is," I replied, unable to suppress a grin.

At the sight, her eyes widened.

"But we're not married," I hurriedly added, feeling heat creep up my neck.

When her face relaxed, I had the sudden urge to laugh. Good thing she hadn't witnessed our bonding ceremony. She would have fainted from shock.

"But you're together still. You and . . . and Prince Lochlan," she said, clearly already knowing the answer.

"Yes," I replied without the slightest bit of hesitation. "We'll always be together. Forever."

Her breath hitched, then she quickly nodded and looked away.

Not knowing what else to say, or if there even was more to say, I murmured, "I should get back. It was . . . good talking to you, Tess."

As I moved to leave, she gave me an almost desperate look and blurted, "Are you happy?"

Caught off guard by the question, it was my turn to gawk. She'd never asked me that before. Not once. If she had, things might have turned out differently for us. Bitterness threatened to well up, but when I saw tears glistening in her eyes—tears for *me*—my expression softened. "I am. So very happy."

She swallowed, swiftly brushing a tear from her cheek. "I'm glad. I'm really glad to hear that." Blinking the last of her tears away, she added, "I'll do everything in my power to protect you, Kenna. Whatever tomorrow brings, I want you to know that."

At the words, my composure finally slipped. A tear escaped my control. Even in the darkness surrounding us, she saw it. Saw and didn't frown in disappointment. Didn't scold me to stop. Instead, she did the last thing I expected her to do.

She stepped forward and drew me into a hug. A tight one. A fierce one.

Recovering from my shock, I returned the hug, holding her equally tight.

And let fifteen years worth of unshed tears start to flow.

CHAPTER 40

KENNA

"You should go see him," I told Isla as we watched the new arrivals through the window. One in particular stood out, with his large frame and shock of blond hair gleaming in the moonlight. He'd just turned from speaking to Tess so he could focus on the equally blond, broad-shouldered man approaching him.

At the sight of his son, Sheriff Andrews' face lit up, brighter than the full moon overhead. I could hear the relief and joy in his voice when he said Noah's name and strode forward to embrace him.

Isla made a small distressed sound, covering her mouth as she witnessed their reunion. Her eyes were round, equally filled with hope and fear. "I can't," she whispered, slowly backing away. She darted her gaze around the room, as if looking for a way to escape. When she spotted Kade leaning against a wall nearby, openly watching her, she ducked her head and quickly muttered, "I need to feed."

As she took off for the kitchen, I sighed, wishing she would let me help her.

"She'll face him eventually," Kade said, joining me at the window. Despite the optimism in his voice, I could feel his resignation through our bond. I doubted the emotion had anything to do with her dad, though.

"How do you know?" I asked, blinking up at him.

He shrugged, his jaw working as he took in the scene outside. "Her need to resolve things will force her into action soon enough.

We just need to be patient."

I bumped his arm with mine. "That's very observant of you, Dr. Carmichael." He smirked in reply, dropping an arm over my shoulders to tuck me against him. After a moment of companionable silence, I added, "I think you're right though. She just needs a little more time. Don't give up on her yet."

Surprise flickered through our bond. I didn't offer him more, but I didn't need to. He knew I wasn't referring to her dad. Eventually, he blew out a sigh and whispered, "I won't."

It was around three in the morning when the call came in.

The rogues were on the move. And *fast*. Heading straight for Rosewood's most densely populated neighborhood.

The minutes that followed were a blur, literally, as we dashed from the house and into our vehicles at vampire speed. We'd foolishly hoped this moment would never arrive. Stupidly believed that Troy would see common sense at the last second and call off the attack.

No such luck.

This was happening.

We were going to war.

By the time we arrived, the streets were already rife with chaos. Rogues were dragging people from their homes, cruelly laughing as they did. Terrified screams rent the air. Cries of pain as human after human fell prey to the insatiable vampires. They openly fed from their victims, tossing their limp bodies to the ground afterward.

The streets ran red with their blood.

It was complete pandemonium. The vampires were acting like savage beasts. Like mindless predators. Every human they spotted was a free-for-all snack. There was no order. Only carnage.

"Any sign of Troy?" Lochlan said from beside me, his body thrumming with tension.

"Not yet," Everett replied from the front passenger's seat.

"Remember the plan. We take him down together." Lochlan jerked on a pair of leather gloves, protecting his skin from the many silver weapons adorning his body. Everett and Kade did the same.

The second Kade slammed on the brakes, Everett was out the door. He threw himself into the fray without hesitation, cutting down a rogue in one fell swoop. When I reached for my door handle to join him, Lochlan grasped my arm and pulled me back. I looked up at him, at the most intense expression I'd ever seen on him.

"Stay by my side the entire time, McKenna," he said, his tone brooking no argument. "Promise me."

"I promise," I immediately replied, gasping when he took my mouth hard. Desperately. The kiss only lasted seconds, but it left a searing brand on my lips.

"Kade," he simply said, pulling back to draw a gun from its holster.

"I'll guard her with my life," his drothen replied, palming his samurai sword.

I glanced at Silver, making sure she was ready, and then we were moving. From the car behind us, Noah and Isla joined our group. Worry niggled at me. I knew Noah could take care of himself in a fight, but Isla was the least practiced in hand-to-hand combat. When Noah and Lochlan took the lead, Kade moved to shadow us both, which helped ease my worries some.

I readied my magic, letting the energy rush to my fingertips. Energy that both Silver and Noah had shared with me over the past few days. Being able to simultaneously use my Syphon powers *and* my vampire abilities definitely gave me an edge, one I was desperately going to need if the rogues realized who I was.

I could still break the curse, however unlikely. Still mess up their plans. Well, mess them up *more*. The Venturi council and SCA were trickling in, adding their strength to our numbers. As far as I could tell, the rogues still outnumbered us though. They were *everywhere*, streaking through the night like ferocious cockroaches.

"The moon is full," Noah reminded me over his shoulder as he whipped up a hand to stop a rogue in his tracks. "Draw on its energy. You'll get more punch." With a flick of his wrist, he cracked the vampire's neck.

Emboldened by his example, I zeroed in on a rogue breaking into a nearby house. He was grinning wickedly as he did, clearly toying with the scared inhabitants. Startled when I realized who it was, I shouted, "Bones!"

He whirled around, looking equally shocked at the sight of me.

Our group slowed as I paused to face off with him. Lochlan scented the air and immediately growled.

"Where's Dani? I have unfinished business with her too," I called, gratified when Bones looked ready to pee himself. He didn't answer, but he didn't need to. His eyes told us all we needed to know, flicking to a spot over my shoulder.

"Kade. Everett," Lochlan said in a guttural voice, never once taking his eyes off Bones.

"On it," Kade said. With a whoosh, he and Everett streaked after the female rogue who'd nearly caved my skull in.

"You're mine," Lochlan snarled at the male rogue who'd thralled and tortured me.

At his words, the stench of Bones' urine wafted in our direction. The last of his bravado fell away and he bolted.

"Let me," I quickly said before Lochlan could go after him. Lifting my arm, I stopped Bones in his tracks with my magic. "There. He's all yours."

"It's sexy when you do that," Lochlan rumbled in my ear, palming my backside as he brushed past me. I bit my lip, willing myself not to blush. We were in a battle, for fate's sake!

I didn't look away or even cringe when Lochlan strode up to the sadistic vampire and, with one swift stroke, decapitated him. I wasn't sorry. Vampires who preyed on others for fun needed to be dealt with. This was a mercy killing, really, since I knew Lochlan had wanted to do it slowly. Painfully.

Everett and Kade rejoined us soon after, the latter's sword now stained with blood. Once again, I didn't cringe at the sight, relieved that one less evil vampire would plague my dreams at night.

As Lochlan came up beside me, I caught the slightest hint of something. A scent on the breeze. One that would undoubtedly haunt me for the rest of my days. Every hair on my body stood on end and a growl tore from my throat.

Lochlan tensed, then he too growled. Everett and Kade did as well. As one, our senses led us straight to the source. To the vampire who'd betrayed us *all*.

"*Troy*," Everett barked, his voice cracking like a whip. "Show your face, you coward."

After a beat, the youngest D'angelo brother slowly emerged from the shadows. He sauntered around the side of a house to pause directly beneath a street lamp. The darkness of his form stood in stark contrast to the light surrounding him. As usual, he wore a hat over his jaw-length hair.

The hat I'd gifted him.

With my heightened senses, I could clearly see his expression. Cleary read the malice in his blood red eyes as he looked directly at me and purred, "Hello, fiery one. Welcome to the revolution."

Every inch of Lochlan bristled. When his rage ripped through my chest like a living breathing thing, I trembled under the force of it. "Don't you dare speak to her," he snarled. When Troy refused to acknowledge the warning, he pressed, "How could you do this to us? To your *family?*"

Troy finally looked at his brother. Righteous indignation burned in his gaze. "I did this *for* us, Loch. We've been cursed to walk in the shadows long enough. We're royal Venturi, *born* for greatness. But we continue to be disrespected. I'm freeing us, brother. Giving us the justice we deserve. Screw breaking the curse. Screw relying on a witch to save us. This is our chance to claim our rightful place in the universe. Join me and you'll see just how right I am."

Lochlan slowly shook his head. "No, Troy. You're not the hero here. You're blind to who you've become. The very thing you hate most. *Her.* The witch who stole your innocence. Who stole your pride and power. Your need for revenge has poisoned you. Made you do despicable things. You took and tortured my mate. You *drained* her. I will never forgive you for that."

Troy's nostrils flared, and a tiny crack formed in his righteous mask. He switched his attention to Everett. "And you? Do you feel the same about what I rightfully did to a Syphon? To save our brother from becoming *enslaved* once again?"

Despite the ongoing chaos around us, Everett calmly replied, "If you'd been paying attention instead of plotting behind our backs, you would have seen that we've accepted Kenna as one of our own. Even Father has. She's part of our family now."

Shock contorted Troy's features. His gaze shot to my hand. To the *ring* on my finger. His brother's ring. A gambit of emotions flooded his face. Hurt. Disbelief. Anger. *Rage.* He suddenly laughed. A short, cruel sound. Before fixing his gaze back on me.

"I should have defiled you in every way possible while I had the chance. I should have ripped out your heart so that you couldn't be turned." He flashed me a grin of pure evil. "In a few short hours, the curse will become permanent. We'll see what they think of you then. And when they cast you out, I'll be waiting, fiery one. Waiting to destroy you for good this time."

"Don't you touch her, you *murderer!*" Isla abruptly shrieked. She was moving at lightning speed before anyone could stop her.

"No!" Kade bellowed, taking off after her.

It all happened so quickly.

A second. A mere blip of time.

Isla was inches away from reaching Troy. Inches from certain death. His strength far surpassed hers. His cruelty even more. He'd probably let her get one good hit in, then rip her head off.

Kade must have thought the same thing, because he grabbed her in the nick of time. Swinging her around with one arm, he attempted to block Troy with the other.

Then Troy did the unthinkable.

Swiftly and savagely, he sank his claws into Kade's sword arm. With a sharp yank, he tore the arm clean off.

A scream exploded in my eardrums.

It was mine, I realized, so wretchedly loud that it nearly drowned out Kade's roar. But not his agony. As he fell to his knees, his pain became mine. I stumbled toward him, only for arms to hold me back. To tightly wrap around me, equally protecting and comforting me. I struggled against Lochlan, crying out to Kade. Isla's hands were slick with his blood as she tried to staunch the flow. Her eyes were wide with fear, but not for herself.

For him.

Without moving from his spot beneath the street lamp, Troy tossed the severed arm aside like trash. "That should knock you down a peg, *Feltore*," he drawled. "Maybe you'll stop interfering where you don't belong after this."

Kade's head bowed.

My worry and fear were suddenly replaced by an eerie calm. The emotion wasn't mine though.

It spilled out of Lochlan's mouth in the form of words. Words that sent a shiver down my spine as he quietly said, "Troy Josiah D'angelo, you are no longer under my protection. We may share the same DNA, but you are dead to me. I would love nothing more than to rip your cold, callous heart out, but you're not worth breaking royal protocol over. As acting regent, I arrest you for your crimes against our people and kingdom. You will be tried and punished for said crimes. You can come peaceably or not. The decision is yours."

Troy went deathly still. He stared at Lochlan for a long moment, then Everett. When he found his eldest brother equally resolute, a sneer pulled at his lips. "You're both making a huge mistake. But you'll see. When the morning breaks, you'll see how right I am. And when you do, *I* will be the one forgiving *you*."

I knew what he was going to do next. Apparently, so did Lochlan.

Before Troy could move a muscle, he raised his gun and shot his brother point blank. Troy reeled back, clutching his arm in shock. He shot him again. And again. When Lochlan aimed at him a fourth time, he took off at vampire speed.

Everett surged after him.

"Go," I said when Lochlan hesitated. "Don't let him escape."

He shot Noah a look.

"I'll watch over her," the warlock swiftly replied.

When he continued to hesitate, I growled through our bond, *Go!* He took off like a missile.

The second he vanished from sight, I ran toward Kade and flung myself by his side. His breathing was labored, but the blood had stopped spurting. Isla was now blankly staring at her hands, at the dark blood dripping from her fingers.

"My arm," Kade said through gritted teeth. "The wound is closing."

"W-what?" I stuttered, grabbing his good shoulder to steady him when he tried to move.

"My arm," he repeated, still struggling to rise. "I need to . . . reattach it."

My jaw dropped. "*What?*" I said again, like a freaking parrot.

"We should get off the street," Noah suggested, helping Kade to his feet. As they staggered toward a nearby house, Silver urgently nudged at me to follow.

"Isla, we have to go," I said, crawling toward my best friend. She was still staring at her hands, clearly in shock. I dragged her with me anyway, letting the council and SCA deal with the chaos behind us.

We'd only walked a few steps when Isla bent to pick something up. "Kade's arm," she whispered, clutching it to her chest.

A hysterical laugh pushed at my throat, a common reaction of mine in stressful situations. But as we ducked inside the house and I caught sight of Kade again, the urge to laugh faded. He was struggling to remove his jacket and shirt, and I hurried forward to help him.

"My sword," he puffed out, hissing when his shirt rubbed against the still-healing stump. "I need my sword."

"I'll get it," Noah said, and rushed out the door.

"What are you going to do?" I asked.

The second his shirt was removed, I caught sight of the grisly wound and nearly burst into tears. Clamping my lips together, I quickly looked away.

"I have to reopen the wound," Kade grunted, scooting back to prop himself against the foyer wall. "It's healing too fast."

Feeling faint, I plopped down in the space next to him. "How?"

"With silver."

The words didn't make sense to me at first. But when Noah came back in with Kade's sword—his *silver* sword—all the blood drained from my face. "Kade, no. That's—"

"Going to hurt?" he finished with a weak grin. "Oh, it's going to hurt like hell, little Kenna, but I need both my arms. I'm no good otherwise."

"Kade Carmichael, that's not true," I chastised, staring wide-eyed as Noah approached with the sword.

When Kade reached for it, Noah shook his head and knelt on his other side. "I'll do it. I've gotten quite good at stuff like this over the years."

"What, reattaching *arms?*" I squeaked.

Noah quirked a brow at me. "Witches are vicious when they train. I've dealt with all sorts of injuries."

Indeed, they were. He'd helped heal my broken wrist after a grueling training session at Thornecrest Academy.

He gestured at his sister still standing near the door. "I need the arm, Isla."

With her eyes locked on Kade's face, she haltingly approached. Kade watched her in return as she knelt and slowly relinquished his arm.

"I'll do this as quickly as I can," Noah said, juggling both the arm and sword. "Kenna, you might want to hold down his other arm."

My heart started to pound, but I did as instructed.

"Too bad we don't have alcohol," Kade weakly joked. "I could really use a distraction right about now."

"You can do this, big guy," Noah said, then pressed the flat of the silver blade to Kade's skin. It immediately sizzled and hissed. The sharp stench of burnt flesh permeated the air. Every muscle in Kade's body locked up and he bit back a groan.

When his raw pain filled our bond, tears blurred my vision. But I still caught the movement in my peripheral. Still saw the moment when Isla crawled forward. When she leaned into Kade and kissed him. Fully kissed him on the mouth.

He stiffened, but for a different reason this time. Surprise flooded our bond, nearly drowning out the pain. When she slid onto his lap and grabbed his face, desire surged up, hot and heavy.

I felt like an intruder, but couldn't look away from the intimate moment. Couldn't look away as Isla swept her tongue over his bottom lip. As he opened his mouth to greedily deepen the kiss. Her breath hitched, and his stomach muscles jumped in response. Hints of their arousal coiled into the air. As if restraining himself from dragging her closer, Kade clenched his good hand into a trembling fist.

Holy fate babies.

This was . . . unexpected. And kind of hot.

A throat cleared not long after, and Noah said louder than necessary, "All done. You can stop attacking my sister's face now."

It was Isla who pulled back first. Who slowly blinked, as if coming out of a trance, and breathlessly said, "I hope that was distracting enough."

Kade's chest heaved. He searched her face before replying, "Very much so."

Tension thickened the air between them, along with more arousal. When she abruptly tore her gaze away and jumped to her feet, I exchanged a quick glance with Silver. *What was that about?*

She cocked her head to the side. *Repressed feelings?*

I had to agree. It looked like my best friend didn't loathe Kade as much as she let on.

CHAPTER 41

KENNA

We remained in the abandoned house long enough for Kade to regain use of his reattached limb. At least an hour had passed, an hour of listening to the sounds of fighting beyond the walls. An hour of worrying that dawn was nearly upon us. That Lochlan hadn't returned yet.

I used our bond more than once to check on him, feeling for him with my senses instead of speaking so as not to distract him. When a shiver of awareness suddenly raced up my spine, I dashed to the door and yanked it open. Kade and Noah both yelled a warning, but I was already flying down the steps.

Lochlan paused at the sight of me, and I threw myself into his waiting arms with violent force. He caught me with little effort, burying his face in my neck. I whimpered in relief, locking my arms and legs around him. We held each other, ignoring the battle around us.

"Is Kade okay?" he said against my skin.

"Noah reattached his arm and Isla kissed him. Like *really* kissed him." Before he could respond, I asked the more pressing question. "Did you get Troy?"

"He put up a fight, but he's been subdued. Everett's guarding him. We'll bring him back with us to Sanctum Isle where he'll stand trial. I'm guessing the council will vote for his execution."

To my utter shock, I found myself blurting, "Making him rot for an eternity in a reinforced cell would be a more fitting punishment. Being powerless without the ability to control anyone would be a fate worse than death for him."

Lochlan pulled back to search my face, and probably my emotions as well. I unblinkingly held his gaze, wanting him to see and feel how sure I was about this decision. It wasn't just for me. It was for him as well. He may still want his brother dead, but maybe this would allow him to better heal. To gradually face the hurt Troy had inflicted without losing a piece of himself in the process.

"I agree with Kenna," Isla said, stepping toward us. "Troy should suffer. A swift death is too good for him."

"Well, I want him wiped from this planet for everything he's done," Noah said from behind her.

Lochlan didn't reply, and after a second, I knew why.

He'd spotted his drothen.

With me still wrapped around him, he strode forward and pulled Kade into a fierce embrace. Kade laughed, enveloping us both in a one-armed hug.

"Careful now," he said. "You'll get my hopes up about a threesome."

"Not happening," Lochlan growled, but there was no bite behind the words.

"The rogues are retreating," a new voice said as Lochlan set me on my feet. "There are a few dozen scared and confused humans wandering the streets though. We could use your special abilities to contain the situation."

I turned as several SCA operatives approached, Tess in the lead. Her arm was bleeding, but she was otherwise unscathed. I flicked a glance at her loaded crossbow, still nervous about how they'd react once vampires everywhere were stuck in their true forms. She noticed my look and lowered the weapon.

While Lochlan issued orders for the humans to be thralled, I surveyed our surroundings, belatedly realizing that we'd won. We'd *won*. With barely any casualties, considering how many rogues there'd been.

But that didn't mean this was over.

Once the curse became permanent, they could attack again out of desperation, like cornered wild animals with nowhere to go.

Tess must have been thinking the same thing, because she tentatively said, "So you haven't had any luck breaking the curse?"

Biting my lip, I shook my head. "I've tried. I've tried *so* hard. But the prophecy could mean many different things. We've made so many sacrifices that I've lost count of them all."

"And the choice given?"

I blinked, surprised that she knew the actual words. I shouldn't have been though. She'd sacrificed the last fifteen years of her life protecting me from this very prophecy. I shook my head again. "I—"

Before I could finish, the powerful scent of magic permeated the air. Vampires up and down the street hissed, searching for the source. Lochlan was at my side in an instant. His body rippled with tension as the scent grew stronger and stronger, until, with a brilliant display of color, several magical portals sprung into existence.

White, yellow, orange, blue, and green brightened the night.

But it was the dark purple portal that captured my attention. That made all the hair raise on my arms.

Headmistress Mayweather stepped from it, Nautilus on her shoulder, as always. Her pale pixie-cut hair was like a beacon in the pre-dawn gloom, but so was her outfit. Instead of the usual dark pantsuit, she wore a white, floor-length robe. They all did. All twelve of the witches and warlocks emerging from their portals.

A cold chill swept through me.

These must be the elders.

When their portals closed behind them, they silently gathered in the middle of the street like a freaky cult mob. There were two other familiars among them: a dog and a black cat. Upon seeing Silver beside me, the cat hissed. The fur on my familiar's back raised, but she didn't utter a sound.

The SCA and Venturi council loosely gathered around us, whispers of uncertainty flitting through the crowd.

"You're too late," Lochlan called, choosing to speak first. "We've already dealt with the rogue problem."

"That's not why we're here," Clarice replied, taking a step forward. "We've come to take back what is ours."

He growled, already knowing what she meant.

Me.

She wanted me.

"I already told you," Lochlan bit out. "Kenna isn't going anywhere."

"And I told *you* that she wasn't yours to keep," Clarice airily tossed back. "Despite her unfortunate vampire side, she is still a witch. A unique and *powerful* one. The elders have all agreed that she is to receive special training. And when she completes it, she will be given an opportunity every witch dreams of."

"And what's that?" I said, gulping when all twelve elders swung their attention my way.

Clarice's gaze softened, almost becoming motherly as she replied, "The choice to become one of the most powerful, respected witches in all the world, dear. We want you as our thirteenth elder."

Holy. Freaking. Crap.

To say I was shocked would be an understatement. My mouth

326

dried, rendering me speechless. But the people around me had no such problem. There was arguing and yelling, growling and hissing. It was clear that no one approved of this offering. The elders stood their ground, motionless as they calmly took in the anger and confusion.

Clarice continued to stare at me, a victorious smile curving her lips.

And it was that smile, that stupid gloating look, that made me blurt, "Was this your plan all along? To offer me an elder position right before the vampire kingdom falls?"

"Making you an elder was always the plan, but whether the vampire kingdom fell or not was up to you. Now that it's certain, we have chosen our side—to stand by as the vampires destroy each other and the human populace. Once they have caused enough damage, witches will rise from the world's ashes as saviors. As *gods*. The survivors will be so grateful for our assistance that they'll revere us. *Worship* us. We will remake this world into something better. A world where witches are free to publicly practice their magic without consequence.

"I know you want that, Kenna," she continued, her eyes bright with passion. With excitement. "You want to fit in. To feel connected and loved. And you *will*. I can give you all that and more. So much more. You will be adored. The world will tremble in awe at the mere sight of you. Come with us now and you will be treated like royalty. No one would dare harm or defy you once you're an elder."

"Kind of like how *I* defy you?" Noah loudly interrupted. "Like how my mother did, which got her *killed*?" He boldly stepped forward, hands clenched tightly at his sides. "You elders make me sick. Hiding behind your lofty positions and empty promises. All you do is control and manipulate and *take*. The world would cower in fear under your reign, afraid to be different. To think for themselves and speak their minds. You would steal their freedom and demand their allegiance."

He scoffed. "Choice? You're not giving Kenna a choice. If she doesn't agree, you'll kill her, plain and simple."

"You ignorant *fool*," Clarice snapped. "Your own mother could have become an elder if she hadn't blatantly rejected our offer. But that's not why I called for her execution. She chose to abuse her gifts, to defy our wisdom and leadership by hiding Kenna from us. She risked the safety of *all* witches. For *that* she was killed."

"It was you?" Noah whispered, stunned by her admission and betrayal. "*You* killed my mother?"

When she didn't deny it, he roared. A powerful explosion of magic rocketed from his hands, headed directly for her. It blasted her backward, knocking Nautilus clean off her shoulder. When the crow hit the asphalt with a meaty thwack, Clarice whirled around with a cry. He twitched, then stilled. As the light left his eyes, she released a whimper.

For several moments, she simply stared at her dead familiar. Then she turned. Slowly. Fury drove the grief from her face. Raising an arm, she pointed at Noah and said, "That was your *last* offense, Noah Andrews."

And then she slashed her hand through the air.

Noah immediately choked and clutched his throat. I gasped as the smell of his blood thickened the air. As it slid through his fingers and down his throat.

"Noah!" Sheriff Andrews bellowed, rushing toward his son.

Isla got to him first, catching him when his knees buckled. She lowered him to the ground, her gaze fixed on his injury. On his *blood*.

Oh no.

Before I could intervene, she tore her gaze away and bit into her wrist. "Drink," she whispered to her brother as he faded fast. Blood continued to rapidly pump from him, draining him of life. If the wound didn't close soon, he was going to bleed out. A fact that Isla seemed to realize as well. "*Drink!*" she screamed, shoving her wrist against his mouth. "You'll end up like me if you don't!"

She started crying. Sobbing. We helplessly stood by and watched the heartbreaking scene. When hot tears slid down my face, Lochlan wrapped his arms around me. I clung to him, silently begging Noah to accept the blood. When he did, when he parted his lips and allowed the blood to trickle inside, I shuddered in relief.

He was going to be okay. I just knew it.

His dad knelt beside him, but his gaze was on Isla. On the fierce way she fought to save her brother. On the skin and eyes and claws that made her look so different. Without a word, he slowly reached out and touched her cheek. When her head snapped up, he didn't flinch back in fear. Only stared at her with tears in his eyes.

"Oh, Daddy," she choked out. "I'm so sorry."

Over her fresh sobs, I heard him say, "No, sweetheart. *I'm* sorry." Then he drew her into his arms.

Something about the scene filled me with sudden clarity.

About everything.

Everything.

I knew what I had to do then. Knew what would free us all.

I turned to face Clarice once more. As I did, a wolf's mournful howl rose in the distance, followed by another. And another. The headmistress's eyes narrowed when I smiled at her.

"Have you made your decision?" Unease bled into her gaze. Unease at the way I was looking at her. She raised her chin a notch.

"I have."

"And?"

"And I'm going to make sure you never hurt my family again. But first, I'm going to break the curse."

As I'd predicted, alarm filtered through the elders, especially Clarice.

"You never truly wanted me to break the curse, did you?" I said to her, already knowing the answer. "The thought of the vampire kingdom falling was too appealing. Of leading witches into a new era. There's a glaring problem with that plan though. They won't follow you. No one will. Not after they know the truth about how corrupt elders are."

Feeling my confidence grow, I continued without pause. "But you did one thing right. You told me how to break the curse. It's simple, really. Simple, yet impossibly hard. Because a choice can't be given without sacrifice, and that's where we've all gone wrong. *Both* are needed. A sacrifice and a choice without any strings attached. Two things that, once put together, are the ultimate gift. A gift that no one has been willing to give.

"The selfish need to control, to *rob* others of choice has plagued mankind for thousands of years. But what if that's the point of this curse? What if the previous elders saw the disease infecting the world and decided to *do* something about it? To sacrifice their lives so that future generations would finally see things clearly? The prophecy isn't unclear. We've just been blind. All of us. By greed and vengeance and self-importance.

"Even my soulmate has been blind. His fear of losing me has stopped him from breaking the curse. I was never meant to break it on my own. Without his sacrifice to set me free, to give me a *choice*, I can't save anyone."

Devastation lined every inch of his face. "McKenna," he brokenly whispered. As his guilt and pain and fear flooded our bond,

I struggled not to cry.

I knew what I was asking of him. To do the hardest thing of all. The impossible thing.

To give up control.

To risk losing me.

But it was the only way. Without his sacrifice, the endless loop would go on and on. History would continue to repeat itself, and no one would truly learn from this curse.

"Give me the freedom to choose my own fate," I said, cupping his face in my hands. "Trust that I'll make the right decision for *me*, Lochlan."

He opened his mouth.

Clarice interrupted before he could say a word. "It's too late. The red dawn is rising. You can no longer save them from their fate."

Moans of dread rose around us. Sure enough, streaks of red adorned the sky, chasing the night away. Making way for the . . .

I whipped my panicked gaze toward Isla, shouting, "The *sun*. Isla, get out of here!"

She stared at me like a deer in headlights, completely frozen. As she did, her skin started to lighten. Her claws retracted and her red eyes became a dusky blue. I looked down at my own transformation and dared to hope. Dared to believe the curse had been broken.

Cries of joy swept through the crowd, then shouts of alarm.

"No," I whispered, my heart sinking as my skin bled black again. As claws shot from my fingertips.

My head jerked back up at Isla's cry of pain. Her exposed skin was smoking, turning to ash under the rising sun. I lunged for her, but Kade was already there, whisking her away in a blur.

More wolf howls reached us, this time closer. *Much* closer. Magic sprung to the fingertips of many elders.

"Kenna, this is your last chance," Clarice warned, taking another step toward me. "World war is inevitable now. You can either be on the winning or the losing side."

I held my ground, drawing strength from my mate and familiar on either side of me. "I will *never* choose to be an elder," I shot back. "The only way I'm coming with you is by force."

Her lips formed a determined line. "Then force it is."

Magic surged to my fingertips as I readied for her attack. But she did the impossible then. She freaking rose into the air. Higher and higher, until she cleared the rooftops. Her robes billowed about her legs as she levitated. Like a supervillain.

Holy crap. Could *I* do that?

When her Darken magic sliced toward us, I dove out of the way, shouting, "Run!"

Right at that moment, a giant black wolf-like creature loped onto the street. It saw the attack and launched into the air, snapping at Clarice's heels. *Reid.* Several more wolves—*werewolves*—bounded onto the asphalt and went straight for the elders.

I lost sight of them then, too busy trying to avoid Clarice's magic. She was clearly out for blood, not afraid to hurt me, now that I had healing abilities. I paused to throw some magic back at her, earning a stinging cut across my cheek for the effort. My hiss of pain was drowned out by Lochlan's furious bellow.

He shot his gun at her. The bullet would have hit her had she not whipped up a hand to stop it. With a flick of her wrist, she reversed its course to shoot it back at him. He ducked in the nick of time.

I sent another blast of magic toward the familiar cat who was attacking Silver. I whooped when the magic struck true, sending it tumbling across the street.

Lochlan suddenly streaked forward and launched into the air.

So high that he was able to snag the hem of Clarice's robe and pull. Down, down, down she went with an enraged scream. Lochlan rolled out of the way as they hit the ground. In that split second, she managed to utter a spell.

He froze in his tracks, unable to move a muscle.

My body flushed cold with fear. "Don't touch him!" I cried, hurrying toward him.

When she whipped up a hand, I stopped of my own volition. I stared at her with frightened eyes and she stared back, victory once again stamped across her face.

All around us, humans, witches, vampires, and werewolves fought. The street ran red with blood. Death permeated the air.

All seemed hopeless. All seemed lost. The curse was permanent and this fight was only the beginning. Soon, humans everywhere would notice the monsters living among them. Soon, the desperate struggle for power and control would touch every corner of this planet.

"What do you want?" I quietly asked the headmistress, letting the magic at my fingertips fizzle out.

She brushed dirt off her white robes, making me wait. Making me *squirm*. Punishing me for my disobedience. Finally, she said, "Simple. I want you to choose me. Once you do, we'll leave this place and never speak of the incident again. All will be forgiven."

McKenna, Lochlan pleaded through our bond, the only thing he could still do.

That one word broke me.

Give me the choice, I begged him back, unable to suppress my tears. *Make the sacrifice.*

Because I wouldn't stop hoping we could still fix things. I'd never stop, no matter how impossible things were.

When he remained silent, a strangled sob tore from my throat. I fell to my knees, utterly heartbroken.

There was nothing left for me to do. Nothing I *could* do except give in to the elders. And I would. To save my soulmate's life, I'd sacrifice everything.

Just as I prepared to say the words Clarice so desperately wanted to hear, I noticed something. A flicker of movement on Lochlan's hand. Which shouldn't be possible, since he was still very much frozen. But it happened again on his other hand, until both hands were . . .

The world stopped. Completely stopped. As it dawned on me what was happening.

His claws were receding. His skin was changing.

Holy. Freaking. Fates.

The curse was *breaking*.

CHAPTER 42

LOCHLAN

I let her go. Freed her. Gave her the ability to make her own choice.

Completely without consequence.

It was the single most gut-wrenching thing I'd ever have to do. Not that I didn't want her to have free will, but I'd been terrified for so long. Terrified that she wouldn't want any of this. Want *me*. That she'd choose something safer. Better. That I'd lose her forever.

So I'd held on. Held on so tight. Smothering her. Caging her. Stealing her freedom.

Doing to her what had been done to me.

I knew she loved me, but I'd still doubted that it was real. That she couldn't possibly choose me when she had so many other options.

And my doubt had doomed us all. She hadn't failed to break the curse.

I had.

But no more. Even if the curse could no longer be reversed, I was done being afraid. Done doubting her. She deserved everything I could give her, and I'd unwittingly held something back. Something precious.

So in that moment of utter vulnerability, I gave her the one thing I hadn't yet given her.

A sacrifice that only true love could give.

The gift of choice.

The moment I did, the curse began to lift.

I saw it from the corner of my eye. McKenna's skin lightened to its olive tone. Her claws shortened. She gasped, stammering, "H-how? How is this possible? You didn't . . . you didn't say anything."

I would have gone to her then. Would have smiled at her with all the love I felt. But I was still frozen, only able to move a few fingers. So I used our bond, pushing my love toward her. Saying words only she could hear. *Apparently, curses are similar to vows. They're forged with intention more than words.*

Her wonder and awe warmed our bond, then she laughed. The light and carefree sound was music to my soul. Then she said words I would never forget. They filled my heart to bursting, and I would cherish them for all of eternity. "Lochlan D'angelo, I choose you. Today, tomorrow, and the rest of my days. I will always choose you. Always and forever."

"You *foolish* girl," the Darken witch suddenly roared, rising into the air once more on a cloud of billowing purple magic. "You would choose *him* over *me*? Over the greatest honor a witch could ever receive? Ignorant, selfish child. You must be punished for your insolence. I will alter your memories until you once again see common sense. I must sever you from the thing that clouds your judgment."

I saw the moment McKenna's eyes widened with fear. Felt her panic. Heard her scream. But there was nothing I could do. Nothing. I could only stand perfectly still as a shrill whine reached my ears. As something sliced through the air and struck my back, piercing skin, muscle, and tissue.

I glanced down at the sword tip protruding from my chest. Kade's sword.

And then the searing pain hit.

CHAPTER 43

KENNA

When I felt his lifeforce flicker weakly and the warm bond between us dim, something in me roared to the surface. Something *dark*.

Seeing my soulmate on death's threshold blinded me with rage. A storm frothed within me. Building in volume. Wildly beating against my body. Demanding to be released.

I struggled to control it, but the more I did, the stronger it became. Until, with a powerful rush, it lifted me off the ground. The storm carried me higher and higher, raising me to Clarice's level. Her face was white with shock, with *fear* as she beheld me.

"It had to be done, Kenna," she said with false calm. "You don't belong with him. You belong with—"

Before she could say more, I screamed, unleashing the storm in a violent gale. It pulsed from me in punishing waves, aiming directly for *her*.

Protect, protect, protect, my instincts chanted. *Protect him. Protect my mate.*

No one would separate us again. *No one.*

Clarice raised her hands to ward off the attack. It harmlessly bounced off her invisible shield, crashing into a house below. I readied to defend myself in return when purple magic darkened her fingertips, but it wasn't directed at me. She was stretching her fingers toward Lochlan again, toward my *soulmate*, still intent on killing him.

With a furious roar, I let fiery red magic erupt from me like an atomic bomb. It struck her with so much force that she burst into flames. Fire engulfed her skin and robes. With a deafening scream, she fell out of the sky. Hurtling toward the ground like a blazing meteor. And when she struck . . .

There was nothing left of her but a trail of embers and ash.

I tried to rein in the darkness then. It was like a demoness from the deepest pits of hell. She was still hungry though. Still lusting for blood. She set her sights on the remaining elders and wickedly smiled.

Before she could unleash her power again, a featherlight touch on my cheek made her pause.

Come back to me, love, a voice whispered in my mind, so soft and soothing that some of the demoness's fire dimmed. *I'm safe. We're safe. It's over now.*

The fire dimmed some more.

When the phantom touch slid to my hand, gently tugging on my fingers, I glanced below me and saw him.

Mate, I breathed. A surge of worry for him smothered any remaining fire. The demoness sank into the shadows once again.

I descended quickly, nearly busting a kneecap on the asphalt in my haste to get to him. His lifeforce still flickered weakly, our bond a single sputtering flame. But he was breathing. Breathing and watching me intently as I rushed to his side. The sword still protruded from his chest, so close to his heart that an inch to the left—*one inch*—and he might already be gone.

He was lying on the ground, trembling as he slowly sat up. When he grabbed the sword with a gloved hand, attempting to remove it, I hurriedly stopped him.

"Let me," I said, waiting for him to let go.

And he did. He let go, trusting me to protect him. To *save* him.

His confidence in me warmed my insides, and I pushed every last bit of strength in my body into his. Preparing him for the inevitable pain to come.

"I love you," I whispered, slipping on one of his gloves so I could grip the sword's hilt.

I love you too, solemae, he said through our bond, in too much pain to speak. *Do it fast. It's the only way.*

My breath caught and I jerked my gaze to his. "But I'll hurt you."

Despite the agony he was in, his expression softened. *You've already saved me, love. I can endure a little pain.*

Tears coursed down my cheeks, but I nodded. He needed me. He needed me to be strong. To do the hard thing. So I held his steady gaze, whispering once more that I loved him, then ripped the sword out.

As he bellowed in agony, I dropped the sword and clutched him to me. I rocked him, whispering soft words of comfort. Eventually, his shaking and gasping breaths slowed. He wearily rested his head on my shoulder with a sigh.

I kept watch while he recovered. Protecting him as he so often protected me.

With the combined strength of the Venturi, SCA, and Reid's pack, the elders didn't last long. The sounds of battle soon dimmed. One by one, they retreated into their portals. Until finally, the last of them vanished in a swirl of magic.

I was gently brushing hair off Lochlan's forehead when he said, "You flew."

Surprised, I blinked several times before answering, "It was more like a hover, really."

When he didn't reply, I bit my lip. Unable to bear the silence a second more, I blurted, "Was my Kenna Demon super scary?"

Freaking fates, did I seriously just *name* my inner she-devil?

Lochlan smiled against my neck. Like *really* smiled, and replied, "It was sexy as hell, love."

EPILOGUE
4 Years Later

KENNA

Come to me, mate. I have a surprise for you.

Those were the only words he would give me.

To say I was nervous about meeting Lochlan was an understatement. Not because of the mysterious message, but because I had a surprise for him as well. One that currently had my stomach tied in freaking knots.

"Don't you dare throw up," I muttered to my unsettled stomach as I navigated the twisty road. My phone buzzed from the passenger's seat and I darted a quick glance at the text message.

Tell me all about the surprise the second you get a chance!

I smiled at Isla's enthusiasm before refocusing on the road. Another text immediately followed.

If the surprise is sex, I still want to know. All the deets!

I snort-laughed and shook my head. She was currently on a case and couldn't join us this weekend. Although I didn't see her nearly as often as I'd like, Isla and I still spoke almost every day. She'd decided to finish her highschool classes online, then jumped right into training to become a private investigator. It wasn't easy with her continued bloodlust struggles and sun aversion, but her dad had helped make her dream become a reality.

She wasn't the only one who'd followed their dreams. Ever since the elders had been cast out of the witch community, Noah's offenses had been wiped clean. He'd immediately signed up to become an

SCA field operative, which often allowed him to work alongside his father and sister. I was happy for them. Happy that they were healing. That they were reconnecting as a family.

I only wished Isla and Kade had explored what was between them. Because there was definitely something there. Something Isla still refused to acknowledge.

After the curse had been broken, they'd gone separate ways. It was an amicable parting, at least. They still crossed paths on occasion since she had an apartment in Rosewood and we often resided there too. They even conversed with each other during the holidays. I couldn't help but want more for them though. They were my best friends and deserved to find love.

Hey, they'd helped me and Lochlan get together. I only wanted to return the favor.

But I barely had time to sleep these days, let alone play matchmaker. After completing highschool at Rosewood High, my pursuit of art had kept me beyond busy. The college I attended was only half an hour from Rosewood, but between my commutes and finishing up my senior year, I was always on the move.

That and Lochlan demanded my full attention the second I arrived back home. Not that I was complaining. He showered me with love and affection, something I'd never grow tired of. I was hopelessly addicted to him in every way possible, and even the slightest time apart from him was torture.

Which was why I currently flew down the road a bit too recklessly. We hadn't seen each other in five days, the longest we'd been separated in over four years. Five days of mutual pining while I finished up my projects for the semester. Five days of flirty telepathic banter late into the evenings, which only fueled the flames of our absence.

Although the time apart was hard, we were both at peace about my decision to attend art school. At first, he'd wait for me just outside the school grounds, unwilling to let me be so far away from his protection. Even with Silver nearby at all times, he worried for my safety.

The rogue revolution might be over, but they were still out there. Still hiding in the shadows, even if they looked more human than monster now. But with Troy locked up in a high security SCA prison specially designed for supernaturals, there'd been no more attempts on my life. The SCA had done an excellent job containing that whole incident. Leaked footage of the battle had been minimal and supernaturals were once again the stuff of myths and legends.

As the years went by, Lochlan gave me more and more space to pursue my dreams. He had his own duties to attend to, what with the king having never fully recovered his strength. He and Everett had been helping him rule the vampire kingdom, dispelling any rumors about his health as quickly as they began. The work distracted him from obsessing over my safety too much. He never *completely* relaxed, but there was enough effort that I rewarded him any chance I could get. He especially loved it when I brought home new lingerie. Red, of course.

Are you going to tell him today? Silver said from her spot curled up in the backseat.

I glanced at my familiar in the rearview mirror, chewing on my lip before answering, "I doubt I'll be able to keep it from him. You know how active my thoughts are."

She made a short yipping sound, the fox version of a laugh. *Very true. It's how I found out, after all.*

My stomach gave another nauseating lurch and I tightened my grip on the wheel.

He's going to be thrilled, Kenna. You'll see.

Despite her calm reassurance, my palms began to sweat. I cracked open my window to let in the afternoon spring breeze and gulped in several mouthfuls of the salty sea air.

By the time I reached my destination, my hands were trembling. "I can do this. I can do this," I whispered over and over, inhaling one more time before exiting my car. It had been a gift from Kade when I'd started school again. I could have chosen a much more expensive vehicle, but I'd missed my old car, so a silver Honda it was.

The second the driver's door slammed shut, I felt eyes on me. I glanced up at the castle's front entrance and there he was.

My forever soulmate.

At the sight of him, my heart fluttered. After four and a half years, it still went crazy around him. Every single time. Probably always would, even after a thousand years.

I only managed one step before, with a *whoosh*, Lochlan was in front of me.

"I missed you, mate," he said, reaching up to capture my chin.

Sighing at his touch, I whispered, "I missed you more."

"Not possible," he purred, tilting my face up so he could thoroughly kiss me.

My nerves all but vanished as warm desire rushed through me. When I stood on tiptoe to snake my arms around his neck, he pressed me tightly against him. Our bodies instantly aligned in that perfect way. The way that sent both our hearts thundering and need coursing through our veins.

At my breathless moan, he nipped at my lips, making me gasp his name. He continued nipping a trail down my neck to "his spot," pausing to greedily inhale my scent.

Then he froze.

344

"You smell . . . different," he said against my skin.

My eyes shot open.

Oh crap.

Lochlan pulled back with a frown, giving me that searching look of his. The look that said he was also rifling through my thoughts and emotions. When I tried to make my mind go blank, he narrowed his eyes. "You're hiding something. What is it?"

"I'm just . . . curious about your surprise, is all," I deflected, inwardly cringing. That was *totally* lame. "What is it?"

But he knew me way too well—*freakishly* so—to fall for that trick. "Silver?" He shot a glance at the fox, only for her to slink away.

Traitor! I called after her. I was on my own for this.

His gaze slowly slid back to me. "You know what this means, don't you?" he said, lowering both hands to my hips.

"Don't," I pleaded and stepped back, only for him to pull me closer.

"You're giving me no choice," he quietly growled, his dark eyes lightening to a wine red.

"Please, Lochlan," I whimpered, squirming to escape.

But he attacked anyway.

Swiftly and without mercy.

I shrieked as his fingers dug into my sides, as he tickled me until I couldn't breathe. "Stop," I wheezed, even as I giggled like a lunatic.

"Not until you surrender," he replied, the pigheaded *brute.*

"I'll tell you, I'll tell you. Just *stop.*"

"I'm listening," he said, *still* tickling me.

"I'm . . ."

"Yes?" he goaded, attacking an especially sensitive spot.

"Argh, I'm pregnant!"

His fingers immediately stilled.

Struggling to catch my breath, I looked up at him. His face was unreadable, completely frozen. But his emotions. Fates, I couldn't even name them all.

I gave him a moment to process the shocking news, nervously twisting his gold and ruby ring around my finger. When he continued to blankly stare at me, I whispered, "Please say something."

His swallow was loud in the silence between us. Finally, he said, "How?"

I blinked. "Really? *How?* I'm assuming the traditional way. No protection plus *lots* of sex usually equals pregnancy, so—"

"But you're immortal," he interrupted, shaking his head as if to clear it. "It should be impossible for you to become pregnant."

I shrugged. "Silver said the same thing, but she's guessing it has something to do with my Syphon side. A loophole, so-to-speak."

"A loophole," he repeated, then laughed, sounding slightly unhinged. A second later, panic flared through our bond. "Did I hurt you? I'm so sorry, love. I shouldn't have—"

"I'm *fine*, Lochlan," I rushed to say, capturing one of his hands when he tried to pull away. I firmly placed it on my flat stomach. "All is well for both of us. I promise."

He froze again, staring with total fixation at his hand on my belly. I fell silent and watched him closely, trying to sort through his chaotic emotions. His fingers suddenly spasmed. "I felt something." He inhaled a ragged breath. "A heartbeat. I felt a heartbeat."

When he looked up at me with tears in his eyes, I heaved a sob.

"Oh, McKenna," he breathed, drawing me into his arms with infinite gentleness. "My brave solemae. What a miracle you are."

When I felt his love through our bond, his *joy*, I full-out ugly cried. I'd been so afraid that he'd freak out at the prospect of me being pregnant. That the impossibility of it would cause him to hate the idea. The risks were still unknown. I didn't know if the baby would be a Syphon or a vampire, or perhaps a hybrid of the two. I didn't know if the baby's skin could harm me, or if we were immune to each other.

I didn't know a thing. Only that I was somehow, against all odds, pregnant.

"We'll face this together," Lochlan murmured against my hair, no doubt listening to my thoughts. "Whatever happens, I'll be with you every step of the way."

I heaved a grateful sigh, pressing my cheek to his chest.

"Please don't tell me someone died," a familiar voice suddenly groaned.

My eyes popped open as Lochlan rumbled a warning growl in response to the newcomer. He whirled us around to face the "threat."

I was able to pull away a little, just enough to catch Kade's surprised expression. He looked between us before saying, "Can someone fill me in here? There's this weird tension in the air and I'm pretty sure I didn't cause it. Well, not intentionally. I suppose I could have—"

"I'm pregnant," I blurted, deciding it was best to get that out in the open, what with Lochlan's protective instincts suddenly going haywire.

Kade's mouth formed a large O. I almost laughed at how ridiculous he looked. Until he spluttered, "And who, pray tell, is the father?" I scowled at him instead.

"Kade," Lochlan growled, but the big vampire simply chuckled at his own stupid joke.

"I'm going to hug your mate now, Lochie," he said, amusement dancing in his voice. "No need to go all Lochness Monster over it."

Lochlan bristled at his drothen's approach, but didn't stop him from pulling me into a bear hug. "Careful," he snapped, and I could have sworn I felt Kade's eyes roll.

"He's going to be impossible to live with, you know," Kade playfully grumbled, resting his chin on my head. "The possessive alphahole will now have *two* females to protect."

I snorted. "What if it's a boy?"

"Then you'll have two infuriatingly possessive alphaholes to protect *you*."

A laugh burst from me at that.

Lochlan sighed, but didn't deny it. He knew it was true.

"Are you guys going to stay out here all day?" a new voice called, this one Everett's.

"Yes. If Loch keeps flashing his fangs at everyone," Kade hollered back.

I peeked at Lochlan and, sure enough, he was silently baring his teeth at his brother.

"What has his boxers in a twist now?" Everett said, which made Kade chuckle with wicked amusement. I sharply poked his side to silence him.

Surprisingly, it was Lochlan who said, "McKenna's pregnant."

Yet *another* male was reduced to stupefied shock.

Then, "By all the fates, how did *that* happen?"

Really?

Was a simple "Wow, congratulations!" too much to ask for?

"I'll tell you how," Kade began. "Loch's seed must be exceptionally—"

When I slapped my hand over his mouth to shut him up, he glanced down at me with a wink. Four years later and he was still just as incorrigible.

The second Kade relinquished his hold on me, Lochlan tucked

me against his side. I had a feeling it was going to be like this for quite some time. He'd just been given a new reason to protect, and I couldn't help but smile a little.

"What are you thinking?" he said as we headed for the castle.

My smile grew. "That our son or daughter will never feel unsafe. Not with you as their father."

His throat bobbed, and he blinked several times before saying, "I will protect him or her with my life. You have my solemn vow."

My smile wobbled. "I kind of love you, you know."

A slow grin spread across his face. "Kind of?"

"Kind of a lot."

"And how much is that, exactly?"

Enough to let you take off my clothes and have your way with me whenever you wish, I said through our bond, smirking when he threw his head back and laughed.

"All right, you two, get a room," Everett groused, falling in behind us as we entered the castle.

"Or not," Kade said. Of course he did.

Ignoring them both, I glanced around the foyer. "So what is this surprise of yours?"

"You'll see," was all Lochlan said, but he couldn't mask his excitement. Or nervousness.

I arched my brow, but didn't probe further. The guys talked companionably among themselves while we walked, and I was content to simply listen. I remembered the first time I'd walked these halls. How very different the mood was then. How Lochlan hadn't dared get too close to me.

He was now openly touching me without a moment's thought. We'd come so far in such a short time. We'd experienced loss and heartbreak countless times along the way. Yet we'd also experienced unfathomable peace and happiness. Joy beyond our wildest dreams.

If given the choice, I wouldn't change a single one of those experiences. I wanted to remember each and every one. To never forget. Because they had brought me here to this moment in time. One where my heart, body, and soul were filled to completion.

I couldn't foresee anything making me happier than I already was, but as Lochlan ushered me inside the throne room—as Kade, Silver, and Everett urged me forward with encouraging nods—I was happy to be wrong. Because there was something—*two* somethings, actually—I hadn't foreseen in the slightest.

They straightened at the sight of me, darting a quick look at the dais where King Ambrose lounged on his throne. He tilted his head at them, then at me, saying, "My son seems to have found something of yours, Kenna. Something he wishes to return to you."

When they refocused on me again, my heart started to pound. They looked exactly the same. Exactly like the old photo I still had of them. They hadn't aged a day, not since that fateful moment they'd been taken from me.

When my knees threatened to buckle, Lochlan lended me his strength. "Jack and Cynthia Belmont, this is McKenna, my wife. McKenna," he said, emotion thick in his voice, "it's about time I reintroduce you to your parents."

I couldn't breathe. Couldn't breathe as I stared at them and they stared at me. I'd thought this moment would never come. That too much had happened. That too much time had passed. That they wouldn't want me anymore.

But when tears filled my dad's eyes, and my mom opened her arms—opened them for *me*—I knew. I knew that love could conquer anything. The strongest storm. The longest separation. Even death itself.

And so, smiling so wide that it hurt, I stepped forward.
Without an ounce of hesitation.
Without a shred of doubt.
I stepped forward and embraced their waiting love.

ALSO BY BECKY MOYNIHAN

A TOUCH OF VAMPIRE SERIES
Shadow Touched
Curse Touched
Fate Touched
Sun Touched (spin-off standalone)

THE ELITE TRIALS TRILOGY
Reactive
Adaptive
Immersive

GENESIS CRYSTAL SAGA
Dawn till Dusk
Fall of Night
Stars till Sun

ACKNOWLEDGMENTS

My heart is so full after writing this trilogy. Loch and Kenna's love story touched me soul deep, and I hope readers feel the same way after reading it. This series was so fun to write, and I absolutely love how it's been received. This book won't be the last you'll see in this world! It may be the conclusion to Loch and Kenna's story, but readers have spoken and certain side characters need their HEAs too. I'm also excited to delve into the werewolf part of this world soon, so stay tuned for news on that!

I want to take a moment to mention a reader of mine who helped shape certain parts of Fate Touched. Mallory, I have loved our chats so much over the past few months! Thank you for gushing over these characters and giving me a certain Christmas scene idea. It was genius and I'm so glad I got to include it in the book!

There are also several more readers who have helped inspire me to keep writing with their excitement for this series. I can't thank you enough for reaching out and personally messaging me. Writing can be a very lonely process and I looooove being able to chat about my characters with you!!

To my ARC readers, I adore you. Your willingness to review my books in a timely manner means so much to me, and I absolutely love how excited you get when I drop a new ARC into your inboxes!

To my beta readers Melissa, Kate, and Morgan, thank you for your dedication and feedback!! Without you, I'd be a mess of doubt and uncertainty. No matter how many books I write, I still need validation that my stories don't suck, lol.

Lastly, I want to thank each and every person who's read this series. I am so grateful that you gave my books a chance. Your support and excitement are what I need to keep writing worlds you can get lost in. I'm super pumped for our next adventure together, wherever it may take us!

BECKY MOYNIHAN is a bestselling, award-winning author of YA/NA Fantasy & Science Fiction. Her debut series is *The Elite Trials*, a YA dystopian romance. Her newest series, *A Touch of Vampire*, is a steamy paranormal vampire romance. She's also co-written the *Genesis Crystal Saga*, an urban fantasy romance series. To stay up to date on new releases, sign up for her monthly newsletter: www.beckymoynihan.com.